A tremendous crash shrumble of collapsing wall
shrieked. Crocks fell fro
wooden floor crunched a
beneath the weight of the hill giant's heavy foot. Crosley
slapped his hands over two wailing mouths, but somewhere in the darkness a third child was sobbing and
screaming for her mother. A deafening bang erupted
from the trapdoor as the giant's club smashed it apart.
Pale rays of light streamed into the dusty hole.

The hill giant's churlish face appeared above the ladder. He had wiry black hair cropped short and ragged,
with a sloped forehead and vapid gray eyes.

"Hey, stupids!" The giant's breath filled the cellar
with an odor as foul as rotting swamp grass. "You pay
for hurting Pammy and Cece—all of you!"

NOVELS BY TROY DENNING

RETURN OF THE ARCHWIZARDS
The Summoning
The Siege
The Sorceror

THE AVATAR SERIES
Waterdeep
Crucible: the Trial of Cyric the Mad

LOST EMPIRES
Faces of Deception

THE TWILIGHT GIANTS
The Ogre's Pact
The Giant Among Us
The Titan of Twilight

THE CORMYR SAGA
Beyond the High Road
Death of the Dragon
(with Ed Greenwood)

THE GIANT AMONG US

THE TWILIGHT GIANTS

BOOK II

TROY DENNING

The Twilight Giants, Book II
THE GIANT AMONG US

Cover art by Duane O. Myers
First Printing: February 1995
This Edition First Printing: July 2005
Library of Congress Catalog Card Number: 2004116900

9 8 7 6 5 4 3 2 1

ISBN-10: 0-7869-3758-0
ISBN-13: 978-0-7869-3758-5
620-96707000-001-EN

U.S., CANADA,
ASIA, PACIFIC, & LATIN AMERICA
Wizards of the Coast, Inc.
P.O. Box 707
Renton, WA 98057-0707
+1-800-324-6496

EUROPEAN HEADQUARTERS
Hasbro UK Ltd
Caswell Way
Newport, Gwent NP9 0YH
GREAT BRITAIN
Please keep this address for your records

Visit our web site at **www.wizards.com**

To Don and Mary
With many thanks for the
time on the farm.

Acknowledgments

I would also like to thank the following people for their encouragement and support: all my friends in Coloma, WI, especially Don and Ruth and Sandy and Ralph, for their wonderful hospitality; my editor Rob, for his patience and kind words; my friend Bruce and my instructor Lloyd of the AKF Martial Arts Academy in Janesville, WI, for their thoughts on battling giants; Jim W. for his enthusiasm and priceless suggestions; and most especially, Andria, for reasons all my own.

Prologue

Crosley and his five young charges peered between the slats of the storm shutters, watching in silence as a pair of slavering dire wolves trotted down the alley. The beasts were as large as ponies, with matted fur and long red tongues wagging between their fangs. They moved along opposite sides of the narrow street, pawing at loose foundation stones and sniffing at windowsills.

Behind the beasts came their hill-giant handler. He was as tall as a house, with a stooped posture and a huge, barrel-shaped chest. He carried a knobby tree bole over his shoulder and wore a filthy tunic of untanned fur. When he tried to follow his wolves into the narrow alley, his hunched shoulders became lodged between the fieldstone walls. He merely grunted, then casually smashed his club into one dwelling's foundation. The structure crumbled, and the giant turned to smash the building on the other side of the lane.

"Hey, that's my house!" protested Thorley, the eldest of Crosley's charges. He was a freckled child of ten years, with red hair and flashing green eyes. The boy stretched his hand toward the storm shutter's latch. "Stop, you ugly—"

Crosley clasped a liver-spotted hand over the boy's mouth. "Be quiet, child!" he hissed, his old heart hammering with panic. "The giants are on a war march!"

"So they're going to kill us?" gasped a little blond girl. "Their dogs are going to smell us out, and then they're going to grind us up like pine grubs and put us in their porridge and eat us?"

This drew murmurs of alarm from the other children, and three of the youngest began to cry.

The old man released Thorley and took the little girl's

1

hand. She would be the key to keeping the other children calm, for her imagination was as contagious as a storyteller's. She could make other children see dragons in pine boughs and diamonds in raindrops.

"No, Dena, they're not going to do anything of the sort." Crosley forced a reassuring smile to his crinkled lips, then said, "We're not going to let them."

"What d'you mean we're not going to let them?" demanded Thorley. "How can a bunch of kids and a toothless old man stop a hill giant?"

"You'll see," Crosley answered. He took Thorley's hand, then led the way into the pantry of his small hut. The other children followed close behind. "We're going to outsmart them—just like Tavis Burdun outsmarted the stone giant to save Queen Brianna."

"How did he do that?" asked Thorley.

Crosley released the hands of Dena and Thorley. "You mean I haven't told you that story?" he asked. He pulled a string of tiny black peppers off a hook in the window, then looked at the children and winked. "Well, I suppose it's time I do."

Outside, the rumble of collapsing buildings was growing louder. The children paid the noise no attention and kept their gazes fixed on the old man. Crosley would have liked to send Thorley to the window to watch the dire wolves, but he did not dare. The boy's reports would no doubt be made with unnecessary frequency and urgency, alarming the other children. And if his charges were to survive, Crosley needed them calm and quiet.

The old man pulled his knife from its sheath, then began to slice the peppers and remove the seeds. "Do you know who Tavis Burdun is?"

The smallest boy shook his head, pouting.

"That's okay, Birk," the old man said. "Tavis Burdun is the best scout in the kingdom. He's a firbolg—"

"What's a firbolg?" Birk interrupted.

Crosley smiled patiently. Birk always asked questions. "Firbolgs are one of the giant-kin races—sort of cousins to true giants," the old man explained. His eyes were burning and watering, for the peppers he was slicing came from the Anauroch desert, and they were the hottest he had ever tasted. "Firbolgs are the most honest of the giant-kin. They can't lie, and they always obey the law. They're also the most handsome, because they look like us humans—though, of course, they're much taller."

"How tall?" demanded Birk.

"Most are about ten feet, but not Tavis Burdun," explained Crosley, gathering the pepper seeds in the palm of his hand. "You see, Tavis's mother died in childbirth, so a trapper brought him to an orphanage in Hartwick village—not far from the king's castle. There wasn't enough to feed a firbolg, so Tavis grew up to be a runt. He's only eight feet tall."

Crosley paused as if waiting for Birk to ask more questions, but he was really listening to the hill giant's approach. The crashing was so close now that he felt the floor tremble each time the giant's club smashed into a house. It wouldn't be long, the old man knew, before the dire wolves arrived and began sniffing around his little hut. He sprinkled the pepper seeds over the floor, then went to his root cellar and opened the trapdoor.

"Come along, children." He motioned his charges down the ladder. "We'll finish this story where it's quieter."

Thorley frowned. "In the cellar?" he demanded. "You're just trying to—"

"Yes, Thorley, I am," Crosley interrupted. He pushed the child toward the cellar, then resumed his story before the boy could object. "When Tavis was old enough, he joined the Border Patrol. He worked very hard, and he became the best scout to ever lead a company into the mountains. But one day the lady who ran the orphanage where he grew up died, and he had to go back to care for the children who still lived there. That's when he met the king's daughter and fell in love with her."

A window shutter clattered as something pressed against it, and Crosley heard sniffing on the other side. He climbed onto the ladder behind the last child, then pulled the trapdoor shut above him.

"And then what?" demanded Birk. "Tavis Burdun fell in love with the king's daughter, and then what?"

Crosley descended the ladder. He had to feel his way carefully, for he had not lit a candle and the cellar was as black as soot. "And then the ogres kidnapped her," he said, hardly daring to speak above a whisper. "Tavis found out about it and went to tell Brianna's father. But the king was afraid of starting a war and ordered his men not to go after his daughter."

"What a coward!" Thorley commented.

"But I'll bet Tavis loved the princess too much to let the ogres have her," surmised Dena. "He went after her anyway."

"Yes, that's right, with his good friends Basil and Avner, and also with the princess's bodyguard, Morten," Crosley said. "And do you know what Tavis found out on the way?"

"No," said Birk. "You haven't told us yet."

"Tavis found out that a long time ago, the king had asked the ogre shaman to help him win a war," Crosley said. "In return, he promised to give the ogres his first daughter. That's why he wouldn't send anyone to rescue Brianna after she was kidnapped."

"That doesn't make any sense," said Dena. "What would an ogre want with a human princess?"

The muffled crash of splintering wood reverberated through the trapdoor, followed by the heavy thumps of two dire wolves landing inside the hut. The animals' toenails began to clatter on the wood floor as they searched the premises.

The children abruptly fell silent, and two of them started to weep. Crosley crouched on the cellar's dirt floor and felt his way to the crying children, then pulled them close to smother their sobs against his breast.

First one, then two pained howls rang out from the hut above. The wolves began to tear around the room, growling, snapping at each other, and madly hurling themselves against the walls. The two children cradled against Crosley's chest wailed in fear, and Dena's imagination began to work again.

"They're trying to find us!" she cried. "They've smelled us, and now they're going to dig us up like rabbits!"

"They didn't smell us," Crosley said. "They can't smell anything with a snootful of hot pepper seeds. Be quiet, and we'll be fine."

The children obediently fell as quiet as the dead. They listened to the wolves scramble around for a few moments longer. Finally, the beasts hurled themselves out a window, and the hut fell silent again—save for the approaching rumble of the hill giant's club smashing into houses.

A small hand tugged at Crosley's sleeve. "Well?" asked Birk. "Why *did* the ogres want a princess?"

"I suppose we must finish the story," chuckled Crosley. "The ogres kidnapped Brianna because the Twilight Spirit wanted her."

"Who's the Twilight—"

"I'm coming to that," Crosley said. "The Twilight Spirit is the guardian spirit of giants, and nobody knows what he wanted with Brianna. Some say he wanted to marry her to the chief of a giant tribe, so a giant would become king of Hartsvale. Some say he loved her himself—but those are really just guesses."

"So, how did Tavis rescue her?" demanded Thorley.

"The ogres thought they'd be safe if they slept on a glacier," Crosley explained. "But Tavis and his companions sneaked through an ice cave and carried the princess off. The ogres chased them into the valley of the hill giants. Tavis tricked the ogres and giants into fighting each other so he and his friends could escape."

"Then they returned to Castle Hartwick and killed the king, and lived happily ever after!" suggested Dena.

"Not quite," the old man replied. "They returned to Castle Hartwick—but not to live happily ever after."

Crosley paused here. He no longer heard the hill giant smashing houses, and he regarded the silence as an ominous thing. The giant had not yet knocked his hut down, and the old man saw no good reason for the brute to leave it standing when he had demolished every other building on the lane.

"What *did* they do when they reached the castle?" asked Dena. "Is that when Tavis outsmarted the stone giant?"

"It is indeed," Crosley answered, with more patience than he felt. "You see, when they returned to the castle, Brianna told everyone what her father had done. The earls were so outraged that the king realized he could no longer rule Hartsvale, and he abdicated his throne. But there were two sentries from the Giant Guard with him, the stone giant Gavorial and the frost giant Hrodmar. They insisted on fulfilling the king's bargain and taking Brianna to the Twilight Spirit.

"But when Hrodmar leaned over to grab the princess, Tavis shot an arrow into his ear and killed him. Then the scout nocked another shaft and pointed it at Brianna's heart, and he swore he would kill his beloved before allowing her to be taken. Gavorial had no choice except to leave, for the giants had no wish to present a dead princess to the Twilight Spirit."

"And *then* Brianna became queen and married Tavis, and they lived happily ever after," Dena submitted.

"Then Brianna became queen," Crosley allowed. "But this is a true story, and no queen can marry a commoner—especially not a firbolg orphan. So Tavis has become her bodyguard, sworn to stand chastely at his beloved's side, and in his quiver he carries a golden arrow—"

A tremendous crash shook the cellar, followed by the rumble of collapsing walls. The children shrieked. Crocks fell from the shelves, and the hut's wooden floor crunched and cracked as it splintered beneath the weight of the hill giant's heavy foot. Crosley slapped his hands over two wailing mouths, but somewhere in the darkness a third child was sobbing and screaming for her mother. A deafening bang erupted from the trapdoor as the giant's club smashed it apart. Pale rays of light streamed into the dusty hole.

The hill giant's churlish face appeared above the ladder. He had wiry black hair cropped short and ragged, with a sloped forehead and vapid gray eyes.

"Hey, stupids!" The giant's breath filled the cellar with an odor as foul as rotting swamp grass. "You pay for hurting Pammy and Cece—all of you!"

Thorley grabbed a crock of pickled mallows and hurled it at their tormenter. The vessel shattered, spilling vinegar and sour buds all over the giant's chin. The brute wrinkled his nose, then pulled his head away and hefted his club.

"Leave us alone!" Thorley yelled. "Leave us alone, or Tavis Burdun'll come shoot an arrow into your ear!"

"Good!" The hill giant brought his club down. "Tavis Burdun don't scare nobody no more."

❖1❖
High Meadow

Tavis Burdun, personal scout and bodyguard to Brianna of Hartwick, slipped his bow off his shoulder and stole into the cold mountain fog. He entered the ruined village warily, creeping over the rubble as quietly as a wolf through the night, his senses straining for any sign of a lurking marauder. He discerned nothing: not a whisper of breath, not the odor of unwashed flesh, not even the gentle rumble of a single, stealthy step. There was only the stench of decay, the corpses lying half-buried beneath piles of stone and timber, the fly swarms filling the air with their mad, mad drone.

The scout had felt it before—the cold, sick ache sinking through his belly like a spoon through honey. But there was something different about High Meadow. He sensed it in the echo of his grinding teeth, the hair prickling at the nape of his neck, and the way his heart hammered inside his chest. This time, the giants were still here.

"Tavis, what's the delay?" Queen Brianna's question rang out from fifty paces down the trail, where she waited outside the village with her retinue and the royal guard. "Can we make our inspection?"

Before the scout could reply, a distant voice reverberated from somewhere deep in the village. "No, Milady! There are raiders about!" The words had a smooth, euphonious quality suggestive of a human nobleman. "You'd be wise to turn back while you can!"

"Who's that speaking? Identify yourself!" demanded Tavis. The scout yelled toward the mountainside so his words would echo over the village and make his location more difficult to pinpoint. "Are you one of Earl Cuthbert's knights?"

"Certainly not!" came the answer.

Before the fellow could say more, a series of thunderous footfalls pealed out of the fog. The stranger screamed an angry war cry. Tavis heard the distant crack of steel against bone, then a booming voice roared in pain. The ground bucked beneath the impact of a felled giant, and a deafening crash rumbled across the village.

As the roar died away, Brianna called, "I'll bring Selwyn and his men forward!"

"No, Milady!" Tavis yelled, still bouncing his voice off the mountainside. "And perhaps you should be quiet. From what the stranger said, there's more than one giant about. The survivors will be listening."

"What if they are?" the queen replied. "They're certainly not going to attack an entire company of my guard."

"Perhaps not, but why risk it?" the scout countered. "Take your guards and retreat to a safe place."

"Without you?" Brianna demanded. "I think not."

"I won't be far behind," Tavis called. "It wouldn't be right to abandon the stranger."

"Quite so. We'll wait here—in case you need help." The queen's tone left no doubt that she was issuing an order. "And keep yourself alive. Good bodyguards are hard to come by."

"My duty is to keep *you* alive," Tavis grumbled. "And that would be much easier if you'd do as I ask."

"Don't I always?" Brianna mocked. "Now hurry back. If you keep me waiting, I may lead the Company of the Winter Wolf into High Meadow myself."

The halfhearted warning was enough to send Tavis clattering down the rubble-filled street. Brianna was impatient enough to do exactly as she had threatened, and that was the last thing the scout wanted. In the thick fog, High Meadow seemed little more than a gray-shrouded tangle of smashed walls and splintered beams. Even the renowned Winter Wolves could not guarantee the queen's safety under such conditions.

As Tavis neared the center of the village, he saw a black, blurry cloud of crows hovering over what appeared to be a low mound of soft earth. He slowed his pace and cautiously stole forward, once again taking care to step quietly. The silhouette ahead grew more distinct. The scout saw two splayed feet the size of small sheep, and soon he could make out a flabby torso as large as a supply wagon.

This could not be the giant the stranger had just felled. A putrid odor of decay hung thickly about the corpse, and the crows had already reduced the body to a pallid mess of gore and bone. Only the heavy brow, drooping jaw, and gangling arms remained to suggest the carcass belonged to a hill giant.

Without a closer look, Tavis skirted the foul-smelling thing. He had long ago deduced the raiders' race from clues left behind at other sites: the tracks of dire wolf pets, cudgels made from broken trees, and bits of clothing made from untanned hide. The scout found the corpse's putrid scent more interesting than anything he was likely to discover on it. The body had been rotting for more than a month, and it was not like hill giants to linger at a massacre.

On the other side of the body, Tavis saw nothing but charred beams and more heaps of broken rocks, the shapes growing hazy with increasing distance. He found no sign of the stranger, or even of the giant the fellow had been battling. Save for the droning flies, High Meadow had fallen as quiet as stone.

The scout continued his search in silence. The razing of the village had left the ground so churned up that signs were difficult to read, but if anyone could find the man's trail, Tavis could. As Brianna's bodyguard, he was confined to Castle Hartwick much of the time, but the scout had not allowed his abilities to atrophy. He made a practice of delighting young pages and squires by showing them how to follow the sparrows from one perch to another, and once he had even won a wager for Brianna by tracking a trout for two miles up the Clearwhirl River.

The coppery aroma of fresh blood reached Tavis's nose. He turned into the breeze and followed the smell to an egg-shaped depression more than a pace long. A pool of dark, steaming liquid sat in the bottom, slowly seeping into the ground. Though he had little doubt that an enormous head had hit here, the hollow seemed quite large for the skull of a hill giant. The scout inspected the area with redoubled caution, for few things were more dangerous than a wounded giant.

It took only a moment to find the marauder's tracks, a series of oblong depressions with a string of blood puddles alongside. The footprints were spaced roughly every ten feet, the stride of a sprinting hill giant, which puzzled Tavis. The scout had heard no clattering or crashing, and he doubted any hill giant was graceful enough to run quietly across this rubble.

Tavis ignored the giant's trail and continued to circle the area. About fifteen paces from the crater, he came across a muddy courtyard with a shattered fountain in the center. The area was covered with a human's boot prints. The scout could see where the man had knelt beside the bubbling water to drink, and also where he had suddenly risen and turned.

Tavis worked his way around the edge of the courtyard until he saw a clump of fresh mud clinging to a rock's edge. He slipped over the rubble for a short distance. When he came across a muddy boot print streaked across a ridge-timber, he knew he had discovered the stranger's trail. The scout moved quickly over the debris, following sporadic smears of mud, until he came to another puddle of steaming blood. Here, the stranger's tracks turned toward the far end of the village, tracing the course taken by the bleeding giant.

Tavis began to suspect the stranger of being a rather reckless fellow. Few warriors had the courage to hunt wounded giants alone, and even fewer could hope to survive the attempt.

The scout continued cautiously onward. As the mud wore off the stranger's boots, the fellow's tracks grew increasingly difficult to follow. Soon, Tavis had no choice but to pursue the giant's bloody trail instead, trusting that the man would continue to pursue his quarry. Occasionally, he came across a tiny pellet of damp mud that confirmed his assumption, but eventually even these rare signs vanished.

The giant's trail led straight to the edge of town. Here, the rubble gave way to pastures lined by walls of stacked boulders, testimonials to a more peaceful time when giants would trade an honest day's labor for a dinner of three goats. The scout paused at the first wall, which acted as a boundary between the pastures and the village proper, and took the precaution of studying his back trail. The ruins were as calm as before, with nothing moving in the fog. Even the fly swarms appeared to hang motionless in the haze, their steady buzzing now so familiar that the drone seemed one with the silence.

Moving more cautiously than ever, Tavis followed the giant's blood trail along the base of the wall. The scout did not see so much as a scuff mark on the soft ground, and he began to think the stranger had changed his mind about pursuing a wounded giant.

Tavis came to the remains of the town gate, a simple oaken door hanging splintered and cockeyed from its leather hinges. Dozens of human footprints covered the ground here, all ringed by crusts of dried mud and therefore old as fossils—at least as far as Tavis was concerned. In the gateway itself stood a puddle of fresh blood, and in the soft ground beyond lay the sharp outline of a fresh giant track. He started through the gate to inspect the print more closely.

Behind Tavis, the fly swarms in the village abruptly raised the pitch of their drone. He spun around to behold a hulking, man-sized blur rushing out of the fog. The scout saw a pair of horns curving up from the silhouette's head, but the shape was so hazy that it was impossible to say whether the sharp points were part of a helmet or sprouted directly from the fellow's head. Although the figure's pumping legs were carrying him across the rubble at top speed, the man moved with such eerie silence that he seemed more apparition than human.

The stranger stopped a dozen paces away, bringing with him an arcane hush that spread over the ground like mist. Gray speckles appeared on his armor, creating a pattern of camouflage so perfect that Tavis nearly lost sight of him. The scout felt his mouth sag in wonder and promptly closed it, then raised his hand to greet the stranger. The warrior responded by cocking an arm to throw his warhammer.

"I come in peace!" the scout yelled.

"As do I." It was the same euphonious voice Tavis had heard earlier. "Now dive!"

The warrior hurled his weapon high into the air. With a loud whooping trill, the hammer tumbled past, a dozen feet above Tavis's head. In the same instant, the scout heard the hiss of a huge blade descending from on high. He threw himself toward the nearest rubble heap, barely clearing the top before the unseen instrument crashed down at his heels, spraying splintered timbers and loose stones in every direction. He hit the ground and rolled, spilling his quiver and scattering arrows all around him.

The stranger's warhammer struck home with a loud crack. A booming voice bellowed in pain, then the ground began to buck as the injured giant stumbled away. Tavis came to his knees in time to glimpse his savior's weapon sailing back toward its owner, then snatched one of his arrows off the ground. It was thicker than most, with red fletching, a stone tip, and runes carved along the shaft. The scout spun toward the gate, at the same time nocking the arrow in his great hickory bow, Bear Driller.

The giant had already vanished into the foggy pasture. Tavis found himself looking at a huge sword, lodged in the rubble pile over which he had leapt. The weapon was ten feet long, with a leather hilt and a double-edged blade as wide as a human body.

"Tavis?" Brianna's voice was barely audible across the length of High Meadow. "Report!"

"We're fine, Milady," Tavis yelled. He was glad she could not see him, for his cheeks were burning with embarrassment. The queen's personal scout should not allow a giant to surprise him. "We'll join you shortly."

The scout eased the tension on his bow and pivoted to find the stranger sitting hunched in the base of a shattered hut, barely discernible from the stones around him. The man was turned half toward the heart of the village, his horned helmet slowly twisting back and forth as though he expected a second giant to appear any moment.

Tavis followed the stranger's lead and crouched behind the remains of the hut. Although the scout could not sense the cause of the man's alarm, he had seen enough of the warrior's mettle to respect his judgment. He kept his arrow nocked and watched for the second giant.

An eddy appeared in the fog, about twenty feet above the stranger's head. The current resembled an inverted plume of steam, alternately billowing downward and upward, like smoke from the nostrils of a snorting dragon.

"Run, stranger!"

As the scout cried the warning, he drew Bear Driller's

mighty bowstring and loosed the thick arrow toward the eddy. The shaft hissed away into the fog, then ripped into something leathery. A gurgling cry rasped across the village. Red blood came spilling out of the sky and splashed into the rubble behind the stranger, spattering the man's armor with drops as large as his pauldrons. The astonished warrior sprang up and spun to face the giant.

The scout cursed the man's bravery. With the fellow standing so close, Tavis did not dare utter the command words that would activate his arrow's magic runes. "No!" he called. "Run!"

The stranger swung his hammer into the fog. The blow landed with a sonorous thump, and the giant grunted in pain. A huge silhouette limped out of the haze, stooping over to hold his knee with one hand.

Even hunched over, the marauder loomed over his foe like a mountain. He was easily half-again as large as a hill giant, with a wild mane of silvery hair, skin as white as snow, and a trickle of dark blood dripping from his arrow wound. With an air of hateful disdain, the great savage glared down at his attacker, and the stranger wisely froze to avoid triggering an assault.

Tavis no longer felt quite so foolish. The marauder was a fog giant, the sneakiest of all the true giant races. They had thick, puffy pads on the soles of their feet that enabled them to move in near silence. As their name implied, they took full advantage of their stealth by inhabiting foggy areas where their skin and hair coloring served as ideal camouflage.

The fog giant drew himself to his full height, his head vanishing into the hazy sky. Tavis screamed a mighty battle cry and started forward, hoping to draw the giant toward himself. The unknown warrior slammed his hammer into the marauder's leg. The massive knee buckled sideways.

An angry bellow pealed over the rubble, then a huge,

double-bladed axe arced down out of the haze and struck the stranger's enchanted armor with a sharp clang. The man did not disappear in a spray of blood, as Tavis had expected, but simply sailed into the fog. He crashed down some distance away, without even a groan to suggest he had survived.

The giant grunted, then stepped toward Tavis.

The scout yelled, "Basil is wise!"

A ray of shimmering blue lanced out of the giant's throat wound. The brute roared in astonishment and started to raise a hand to his neck, then the runearrow detonated. The marauder's head disappeared in a brilliant burst of sapphire light, leaving the body to teeter on its own. The corpse continued to stand for several moments, until the tension suddenly melted from its joints and it collapsed in a crashing heap.

When the rumbling died away, Tavis heard the distant clamor of clanging armor. The Company of the Winter Wolf was rushing through the fog at top speed, no doubt with Brianna in the lead. The scout did not bother yelling at the queen to turn back. She could not have heard him over all the racket.

Keeping one eye open for more giants, Tavis quickly gathered his spilled arrows, then went to look for the stranger's body. The scout found the warrior lying in the rubble of a small hut, next to a root cellar containing the mangled remains of several children and their guardian.

Tavis knelt at the stranger's side. The fog giant's axe had staved in the warrior's breastplate, splitting it apart and opening a horrible gash over the fellow's ribs. The scout reached up and flipped the visor open. Inside was a swarthy, handsome man with curly, dark hair and a cleft chin. His brown eyes were open and alert, focusing on Tavis's face. His broad mouth twisted into a weak smile.

"Basil is wise?" he groaned.

Tavis nearly leapt away, so astonished was he to hear

the man speak. "M-My runecaster's idea of a joke," he explained. The scout touched one of the red-fletched shafts in his quiver. "It's the command to activate these runearrows."

The stranger's bleary eyes widened in alarm. "By the Titan!" he cursed, trying to drag himself away. "I didn't mean—"

"Relax. The arrow has to be nocked before the command works." Tavis pushed the man back down. "How many more fog giants are skulking around this village?"

The warrior managed a condescending smile. "None, I suspect," he said. "I was hunting only two. You killed one, and I injured the other. I doubt he'll come back looking for trouble."

"Probably not," Tavis agreed, relieved to hear that Brianna would not be endangered. "But one can never be too careful. I'll post a guard as soon as the company arrives. In the meantime, I'd better have a look at your injuries."

The scout started to unbuckle the warrior's mangled breastplate.

"That's not necessary," the stranger said, raising a hand to stop Tavis. "Just help me up."

"Up?" the scout exclaimed. "If I do that, your insides will spill all over the ground. Take a look at yourself!"

The warrior obediently lowered his gaze. When he saw the rent in his armor and all the gore spilling out of his wound, his swarthy face grew as pale as the fog. "The armor will hold me together." Despite his brave words, the stranger's voice was quivering. "That's why I wear it."

With that, he grabbed the scout's shoulder and pulled himself to his unsteady feet. To Tavis's enormous relief, the stranger was right about his armor—nothing more than blood spilled from his ghastly wound. With an agonized groan, the fellow leaned over and retrieved his warhammer, then straightened his shoulders and started to lurch toward the pastures.

Tavis stepped to his side. "What are you doing?"

"Hunting down that giant I wounded, of course," the man replied. "I trust you'll be good enough to help."

"No! Absolutely not! The last thing I want is more fighting!" Tavis was thinking of Brianna and the Company of the Winter Wolf, which he could still hear approaching through the fog. "Besides, in your condition, you couldn't hunt a marmot. Come with me, and we'll have that wound looked after."

The scout caught the stranger by a shoulder pauldron and gently pulled him back.

"Unhand me!" the warrior ordered. The fellow grimaced, then stepped forward, clearly expecting the scout to obey his command. "That giant's about to escape."

"Good. Let him." Tavis retained his grip.

The stranger's feet slipped, and he would have fallen had the scout's grasp not been so secure. "How dare you!" the man blustered. He regained his balance and slowly turned around. "Do you know who I . . . ?"

The warrior found himself craning his neck to look into Tavis's eyes, and he let his sentence trail off. He looked the scout up and down, his mouth gaping open.

"No, I don't know who you are," Tavis replied. He raised his open hand in the traditional sign of friendship. "But I'm Tavis Burdun."

The man's astonished expression did not change, and he showed no sign of recognizing the scout's name. "You're a firbolg!" he sputtered.

The scout nodded, surprised it had taken the stranger so long to notice that obvious fact. As giant-kin, firbolgs were larger and more thick-boned than humans. Although Tavis was a runt by his race's standards—standing only eight feet to the normal ten or twelve—he was still big enough that his ancestry should have been obvious. "Does my race bother you, sir?"

The warrior shook his head. "Of course not. I was merely surprised that I hadn't noticed before." Remembering his manners, the stranger raised his hand in greeting, then cringed at the pain this caused him. "You may call me Arlien, my friend. Now, I really must go if I'm going to catch that giant."

He turned to leave, but Tavis caught him by the arm.

"What's so important about killing that giant?" the firbolg demanded. The Company of the Winter Wolf was now so close that Tavis could hear Selwyn's men calling through the fog as they struggled to maintain formation. "Is it worth the risk that you'll be the one who dies?"

Arlien rolled his eyes. "Don't be ridiculous, Tavis," he said. "*I* won't get killed."

"You're lucky you're not dead already." The firbolg pointed to the man's mangled armor. "And you still haven't answered my question. What's so important about killing that giant?"

The warrior regarded Tavis as though he were daft. "I should think that's obvious," he said. "The churl assaulted me!"

It was Tavis's turn to roll his eyes. "That's a reason?"

"It seems sufficient to me," Arlien retorted.

"Perhaps under different circumstances," the firbolg allowed. "But as it is, you can't go."

"I can't go?" Arlien fumed. "And just how do you propose to stop me?"

"I'm quite sure Tavis would find a way," said Brianna. "He's a most resourceful bodyguard."

The firbolg turned, then uttered a silent curse as he saw the queen quietly slipping out of the fog—well ahead of the soldiers assigned to protect her. She was extremely tall for a human, with a frame as sturdy as a man's and a height just a few inches shy of seven feet. From what Tavis gathered, most men did not consider her beautiful, but to him she was the picture of elegance. She had a striking face, with clear skin, a dimpled chin, and sparkling violet eyes. Her long tresses were as fine as spider silk and more yellow than gold, while she had a lithe figure with long, graceful limbs and gentle curves.

Brianna stepped to Tavis's side and began to look him over. "I heard your runearrow explode," she said. "Are you all right?"

"Thank you, milady. I'm well." The firbolg addressed her in his best formal tone. Although Brianna's attempts to conceal the romance between them were fast becoming a joke among her courtiers and earls, Tavis had learned enough about politics to know he should not flaunt their relationship before a foreigner. The scout reached over and gently turned Arlien so that Brianna could see the gaping wound in his side. "It's our new friend who needs your services."

Brianna's eyes widened at the sight of the injury, and she stepped to Arlien's side. "You shouldn't be standing," she said. "Lie down."

"That's not necessary, Lady," Arlien protested. "I'll be—"

"Dead, if you don't let me heal this," Brianna snapped. She scooped the warrior into her arms and lifted him off the ground, plate armor and all. "Clear a place for him, Tavis."

As the firbolg began tossing stones aside, he could not help smiling at the dumbfounded expression on Arlien's face. Lifting a fully armored warrior was ordinarily well beyond a human woman's capabilities, but Brianna could hardly be considered ordinary. She had inherited the extraordinary strength of her Hartwick ancestors, and could easily have matched any firbolg in a contest of might. Tavis had even seen her father defeat hill giants in such competitions, and some claimed that the first Hartwick king had bested storm giants.

All this was lost on Arlien, who finally recovered his wits and resumed his protests. "Put me down, Lady!"

"Very well, but you *will* let me heal you!" Brianna replied. "This wound is more serious than you realize."

A sheepish look came over Arlien's face as the queen returned him to the ground. "Dear lady, I thank you for your kind offer, but I assure you it isn't necessary," he said. "My armor will heal both my body and its rents within a few days' time, but you mustn't interfere. The enchantment will vanish."

Brianna's cheeks colored. "Enchanted, you say?" She bit her lip, then demanded, "Why didn't you tell me?"

Arlien's face darkened, but he managed to force a rather insincere smile. "I was trying," he said in a controlled voice. "However, in your kindly haste to look after my health, you neglected to give me the opportunity."

Brianna's smile turned to ice. "Well, I'm glad to see you survived." She removed a clean bandage from her shoulder satchel and passed it to the warrior. "I hope that a simple dressing will not affect your armor's magic. I really have very little desire to stare at your gruesome wounds."

"That *is* a relief, Milady." Arlien accepted the cloth, then turned away as he pressed it over the gash in his side. "I was beginning to think you rather enjoyed it."

Captain Selwyn arrived with the first soldiers of his scattered company, bringing the argument to a temporary halt. Tavis ordered the commander to have his men surround the area at a distance of fifty paces.

Brianna watched the Winter Wolves clang off to their posts, then fixed her coldest glare on Arlien. "By the way, what brings you to our kingdom? Cuthbert Fief is hardly the route most travelers choose to enter Hartsvale."

Arlien's eyes grew as hard as Brianna's. "My visit is not your concern, dear lady," he said. "But I will say this much: Your fief is in terrible peril. I'm sorry to report that standing before you is the sole survivor of a large caravan. A hundred of my fellows were massacred not far from here, by a tribe of more than two hundred frost giants."

"Frost giants!" Tavis exclaimed. "Are you sure?"

Arlien's only response was a condescending glance.

"Where did this happen?" Brianna demanded.

Arlien pointed toward the fog-shrouded pastures, which the scout knew from past visits lay beneath a craggy wall of ice-sheathed peaks. "On the other side of those mountains," he said. "Not three days ago."

"And what of the fog giants?" Tavis inquired. "Where did they come from?"

Arlien shrugged. "I suppose from the cold mists beneath the Endless Ice Sea, like all their kind," he said. "As to what they're doing here, I can't say. They were in the village when I arrived."

Brianna cocked her brow and looked to Tavis. "What are we to make of this?"

The scout narrowed his eyes. "No good," he replied. "Three different tribes of giants do not converge on the same fief by accident. I suggest we return to Cuthbert Castle and warn the earl to prepare for a siege."

Brianna nodded, then looked to the stranger. "You did us a great service," she said. "I invite you to share the safety of our company as we return to the castle."

Arlien inclined his head. "Thank you, good lady, but I ask only that you point me in the direction of Castle Hartwick," he replied. "I have business with your queen."

A crooked grin crept across Brianna's mouth. "Tavis, perhaps you should introduce me to your wounded friend."

"Very well," the firbolg replied, also grinning. He bowed to Brianna, then gestured to the newcomer. "Milady, may I present Arlien of . . . " The scout let his sentence trail off, leaving it to the warrior to finish.

"Arlien of Gilthwit," he said. "*Prince* Arlien of Gilthwit."

Tavis lifted his brow. He had heard rumors of a place called Gilthwit. It was supposed to lie somewhere on the icy plain between Hartsvale's northern border and the Endless Ice Sea. By all accounts, it was a frozen waste of a kingdom, so overrun by giants that humans had been reduced to mere savagery. Judging by Arlien, at least, the rumors were wrong.

If Brianna was impressed, she did not show it. "I've never met anyone from Gilthwit, *Prince* Arlien," she said. "In fact, I've always heard it was a legend, not a real place."

The prince gave her a warm smile. "Isn't it possible to be both, Lady . . . ?"

"Brianna of Hartwick," Tavis filled in. He bowed to the prince, then finished the introduction, "*Queen* of Hartsvale, of course."

Arlien's face turned as gray as ash. "Annam help me!" he gasped, looking Brianna over from head to toe—all seven feet of her. "You're the woman my father sent me to court?"

❖ 2 ❖
Cuthbert's Keep

The trapdoor opened with a sharp bang, despoiling the twilight refuge Tavis and Brianna had created for themselves atop Earl Cuthbert's keep. The pair stepped apart and turned toward the center of the roof, where they saw the horns of Arlien's helmet slowly rising through the portal.

Tavis grunted in aggravation. Arlien had already spent the entire journey from High Meadow assailing Brianna with stories of his father's lands. Now here he was again, chasing after the queen less than an hour after their arrival at Cuthbert Castle.

The scout took a deep breath, reminding himself not to be too harsh on the man. Arlien was a brave warrior and a decent enough fellow for royalty, and he had come a long way to court Brianna. Until the queen actually told him she was unavailable, it wasn't fair to blame the hapless prince for trying.

Swallowing his frustration, Tavis went to the center of the roof and kneeled beside the portal to help Arlien up. The prince's face had the pasty, ash-colored complexion of someone who had lost too much blood. He had covered his mangled armor with a red cloak, but even in the dusky light, Tavis could see a dark stain were the wound continued to seep.

"Shouldn't you be resting?" The scout could not quite keep the petulance out of his voice.

"How can I rest until your queen has accepted my apology?"

Brianna, who had retreated to the battlements that ringed the roof, turned to face Arlien. "But I *have* forgiven you, dear prince." Her voice was as cool as the dusk breeze. "Did I not say so this afternoon?"

"Please don't take me for a fool, Milady," the prince replied. "I know the difference between true absolution and a diplomatic courtesy."

Arlien allowed Tavis to clasp his wrist. The prince pushed off the ladder and together the pair hoisted his metal-cased bulk onto the roof. It was hardly customary for a warrior to wear a full suit of steel plate about the castle, but Arlien had explained that his armor would work its healing magic only while he was in it.

Once the prince had gained his feet, he looked directly at Queen Brianna. "I thought perhaps we could talk alone."

"We're as alone as we're likely to be," Brianna replied. "Feel free to say whatever you want in front of my body-guard."

Arlien glanced at the firbolg and shrugged. "As you wish," he said. "I certainly have nothing to hide from Tavis."

The prince took a large, flattish box of polished silver from inside his robe, then walked over to stand across from Brianna. Tavis followed close behind, positioning himself where he would see inside the silver case when it was opened. The scout doubted that Arlien intended any harm to the queen, but it was his duty to be cautious.

"As you can imagine, the journey from Gilthwit is a long and difficult one," Arlien began. He looked through the embrasure, to where the purple light of dusk was creeping across the craggy hills north of Cuthbert Castle. "I had to cross endless miles of frozen wastes, as forlorn and dangerous as the highest peaks among the Ice Spire Mountains. The plains were bitter cold, and full of dragons and giants—and many beasts even more ferocious and terrible."

"I know what the Icy Plains are like," Brianna interrupted.

"And so does my father," Arlien continued. "Yet, when news reached us that you had ascended Hartsvale's throne, he still asked me to make the perilous journey to your kingdom."

"Why?" Brianna demanded.

"For a thousand years, the giant tribes have let Hartsvale live in peace, but that has changed with your father's abdication—as you can see by the great number of marauders converging on this fief alone," the prince said. "Gilthwit, on the other hand, has always endured the enmity of the giants."

"And you have come to share your wisdom with Hartsvale."

"Both our kingdoms would benefit by an alliance," Arlien replied. "Gilthwit is a rich land that has endured in isolation too long. A trade route between our two countries, patrolled jointly by our armies, would greatly strengthen both kingdoms. Gilthwit would have a market for its jewels and rare metals, while the trade tariffs would swell Hartsvale's treasury. You would have the gold necessary to bolster your defenses against the giants, and a ready ally to fight at your side."

"What you propose has merit." Brianna's voice softened, and she laid a hand on the sill of the embrasure. "But if Gilthwit really exists, how come you're the first person I've met from there?"

"Because my people rarely leave Gilthwit," Arlien explained. "The kingdom is surrounded on all sides by frozen wastes as vast as they are deadly. I required a caravan of three hundred men and twice that many yaks to make the journey, and we lost two-thirds of our number even before the frost giants attacked us. Such treks are not undertaken lightly."

"And you want to open a trade route across such dangerous terrain?" Tavis scoffed.

"The route will never be a safe one," the prince admitted, continuing to look at Brianna. "But together, our two kingdoms can make it passable—and the rewards will repay our efforts tenfold."

"If the rewards are so great, why haven't you sent an envoy sooner?" Brianna asked.

The prince gave her a condescending smile. "At least *we* sent one, dear queen," he said. "I don't recall receiving any of Hartsvale's princes in my father's palace."

"Perhaps you will forgive us if you remember that we've always regarded Gilthwit as a legend," Brianna said.

"I must admit that Hartsvale seemed quite mythical to me, at least until I arrived in High Meadow," Arlien allowed. "Yet here we stand, two legends speaking to one another."

A neutral smile crossed Brianna's lips. "So we are," she said. "But you still haven't answered my question."

The prince inclined his head. "So I haven't," he said. "As I said earlier, Gilthwit has always been an enemy to giants. I doubt very much that King Camden, or any of your ancestors, would have traded peace with the giants for an alliance with us."

"And what makes you think I will?" Brianna demanded.

"Because *you* are not at peace with the giants."

"Hartsvale has always had marauders," the queen said. "The troubles in this fief don't mean we're at war."

"Come now, you don't believe that, and neither do I," the prince said. "You see, I know all about the circumstances surrounding your rise to power."

Brianna looked away, assuming a deliberately disinterested expression. "What circumstances would those be, Prince?"

Arlien smirked. "For one thing, your father agreed to sacrifice you to the giants' guardian idol—I believe they call him the Twilight Spirit—in exchange for supporting his throne. You forced him to abdicate by exposing the plot to his earls."

Tavis had to bite back an exclamation of surprise. Only a couple dozen earls should have known what the prince just stated. To ensure an orderly transition of power, Brianna had asked everyone present at her father's abdication to remain silent about the fact that it had been forced.

Showing no sign of surprise, Brianna calmly returned her gaze to the prince. "I've heard that rumor as well," she said. "But it hardly seems prudent to propose an alliance on the basis of gossip."

Arlien sighed, then pointed to the golden arrow Tavis always carried in a special pocket of his quiver. "If what I say is wrong, why does your bodyguard carry that arrow?"

"As a symbol of office, of course," Brianna responded.

"Really?" Arlien said. "I thought it was for you."

"That's a reasonable assumption," the queen allowed.

"If it's only an assumption, why is the shaft inscribed with magic to make your death painless and quick?" Arlien demanded.

The runes in question were hidden deep inside the scout's quiver, near the tip of the golden arrow, and only a handful of Brianna's advisors knew about them. Fearing her subjects would regard the magic as rather cowardly, the queen had agreed to have the sigils inscribed only because Tavis swore his aim would not be true unless he knew her death would be painless.

Tavis scowled and stepped even closer to the prince. "How do you know about the runes?" The scout's hand dropped to his sword as he made the demand. "You must have a spy in Castle Hartwick!"

When Arlien showed no interest in replying to the scout's accusation, Brianna came to Tavis's side and gently pulled the firbolg's hand away from his sword.

"Of course Gilthwit has a spy in my court," she said. All traces of her earlier suspicion had vanished from the queen's voice. "We shouldn't expect the king to send us one of his sons without knowing the situation in Hartsvale, should we?"

"It seemed only prudent," Arlien acknowledged. "Of course, such measures will no longer be necessary when we are allies."

In a carefully neutral voice, Brianna asked, "And this alliance is to be sealed by our marriage?"

The prince nodded.

"That seems drastic," Tavis commented. Brianna shot him a reproving look, but the scout could not restrain himself. "Why not a treaty?"

"Because blood is more binding than ink," Arlien replied. "Once we open the trade route, our kingdoms will be under many great pressures. To stand together, we must be a family."

"I'm sure Arlien and his father have considered this matter very carefully, Tavis," Brianna chided. She turned her gaze back to the prince. "I hope you'll allow me time to do the same."

The scout bit his cheek, afraid he would blurt out another objection. He could not believe Brianna would actually consider marrying a man she had met only that morning.

Arlien nodded. "Of course, Milady," he replied. "And I hope you'll do *me* the courtesy of accepting this, as a token of my sincere regrets for my unfortunate reaction this morning."

The prince opened the box he had been holding. Inside, resting on a bed of white velvet, lay a fabulous necklace of thumb-sized jewels. The gems were shaped like teardrops, and they scintillated with a pale blue light that seemed to arise from deep within their own hearts. They had settings of elegant simplicity, a bell of white gold encircled with a single scribe line, and they hung on a finely woven chain of red gold.

Brianna gasped and plucked the necklace from the box, laying it across her hand. She began to roll the jewels about, smiling in delight as rays of azure light danced over her palm.

"They're cold and warm at once!"

Arlien smiled. "We call them ice diamonds. Our miners dig them from the heart of the Endless Ice Sea itself," he reported. "It's said that as long as you wear these, you'll never cry."

Tavis was beginning to wish he had left Arlien in High Meadow. "It's healthy for humans to cry."

"Not for queens, Tavis." Brianna arched her eyebrows at the scout, as if to ask his forbearance, then held the necklace out to Arlien. "You are completely forgiven, dear prince. Won't you be kind enough to help me put this on?"

Arlien took the necklace. "Ice diamonds are but one of the many treasures Gilthwit has to offer," he said, undoing the clasp. "My caravan had samples of all our riches, but this was all I could save when the frost giants attacked."

"Whatever you lost, I'm happy you saved this."

Brianna lifted her silky hair and spun around, inviting Arlien to slip the necklace around her throat. Because the queen stood so much taller than he did, the prince had to raise his arms above his head. As he reached forward, he suddenly let out a deep groan and stumbled back in pain. A trickle of blood seeped from beneath his cloak and ran down his armored leg. Brianna turned around and took the necklace from the prince's hands, returning it to its silver case.

"Perhaps we'll put it on later." The queen took Arlien's arm and led him toward the trapdoor. "Now you should rest. We'll speak more of alliances as we ride back to my castle tomorrow."

Tavis moved to help, happy to be rid of the prince. As the trio approached the trapdoor, the scout heard urgent voices coming from the chamber below. By the time the three reached the opening, Earl Cuthbert's barrel-chested form was clambering up the ladder. He was a round-faced man of fifty, with a balding head, squinting eyes, and a pair of crossed shepherd's staves emblazoned on his leather jerkin.

The earl pulled himself onto the roof and gave the queen a perfunctory bow. "Have you seen them, Majesty?"

"Seen whom?" Brianna demanded, still supporting Prince Arlien's frail form.

"Giants!" the earl reported. "Serfs have been coming in from all corners of the fief, and some claim the brutes have already surrounded us!"

Without waiting for a reply, Cuthbert scurried to the battlements. Brianna followed close behind, with Arlien limping along at her side. Knowing that it was already too dark to see any giants lurking on the distant hills, Tavis stayed behind and peered into the chamber below to see whom the earl had been speaking with earlier.

The scout found his friends Avner and Basil standing at the base of the ladder, a large oval mirror resting on the floor between them.

"What have you there?" the scout asked.

Avner looked up and smiled proudly. He was a sandy-haired youth of sixteen, with the fuzz of his first beard clinging to his chin.

"You'll see soon enough." As nimble as a mountain goat, the boy scrambled up the ladder, then immediately swung around and stuck his arms back through the portal. "Go ahead and pass it up."

"It's heavy," Basil warned.

Without waiting for an invitation, the scout lay down next to the boy and stretched his own arms into the hole. Basil pushed the mirror up, then Tavis and Avner lifted the heavy thing through the portal. A pair of hinge pins mounted on the sides suggested it had come off some piece of precious furniture, such as Lady Cuthbert's dressing table. The looking glass's wooden frame

31

was thoroughly covered with the familiar carved lines of Basil's rune magic.

"I hope Cuthbert gave you permission to do this," Tavis groaned, guessing that such a mirror was worth about a year of his salary.

"The earl knows about it, anyway," Avner replied. "And when he sees what it can do, he won't mind."

The scout carefully laid the mirror aside, then peered down into the hole. He saw Basil climbing the ladder, moving much more carefully than the boy. It was a wise precaution, for the runecaster was a verbeeg, another of the races of giant-kin. He was even larger than Tavis, with gangling arms and bowed legs as thick as aspen boles. His distended belly and hairy, stooped shoulders gave him a gaunt, half-starved look, but anyone who had ever made the mistake of inviting him to a banquet knew that was not the case.

"Basil, what's all this about being surrounded by giants?" Tavis called.

"I can't say yet," the verbeeg replied, looking up. He had eyebrows as gray and coarse as the scrawny beard hanging from his chin. His thick lips gave him an affable—if somewhat sly—smile. "That's why I created the rune mirror. It'll be much more accurate than relying on the peasants. They're terrified, and you know how humans exaggerate when they're panicked."

The scout clasped his friend's wrist and pulled, helping him squeeze through the roof portal. Basil picked up the large mirror and balanced it on one hand as though it were a serving tray. He started toward Brianna and the others, the planks creaking and groaning beneath his great weight. Tavis took the precaution of staying a fair distance from the verbeeg. Although the keep roof was supposed to be strong enough to support an entire company of soldiers, the firbolg worried that the combined mass of two giant-kin would be enough to snap one of the weathered planks.

When Tavis reached the battlements, he stopped behind Brianna and peered over her head into the deepening twilight. He could still see the sentries on the outer curtain and the reflection of torchlit windows gleaming off the black waters of Lake Cuthbert, but very little else. If any giants were lurking on the dark lakeshore hills, the purple shroud of evening had already hidden them from sight. Even the distant mountains were hardly visible against the murky clouds beyond their summits.

"This is no use," said Arlien. "The light's too dim. We'll have to send out scouts."

"That would be both dangerous and unnecessary," said Basil.

Arlien turned to see who had contradicted him. His jaw clenched in rancor. "A verbeeg!"

"You don't seem very fond of giant-kin," Tavis observed.

The spite in Arlien's eyes did not fade. "In my land, verbeegs are not to be trusted."

"And in our land, people are judged on their merit—"

"Basil is no ordinary verbeeg, I assure you," Brianna interrupted. She stepped between Tavis and Arlien, then faced the runecaster himself. "What have you prepared for us, my friend?"

Casting a haughty smirk Arlien's direction, Basil took the mirror in both hands and turned the silvered glass toward the lakeshore hills. The reflection showed the rocky slopes as though the hour were noon instead of dusk. Tavis saw the stoop-shouldered figures of several hill giants scattered among the crooked scrub pines. The brutes sat on boulders or squatted atop rocky outcroppings, calmly watching the lakeshore below as a steady trickle of humans fled toward the castle bridge. Although it would have been a simple thing to toss a few boulders at the haggard serfs, the giants made no move to harass the refugees.

"Wasn't it fog giants you battled in High Meadow?" asked Avner. "Those look more like hill giants."

"They are," agreed Tavis. "No doubt the same ones that have been laying waste to Earl Cuthbert's hamlets."

"They're not ferocious enough." The earl stepped closer to Basil and squinted into the mirror. "If those were the giants who have been razing my villages, they'd be slaughtering my serfs, not allowing them safe passage."

Tavis shook his head. "Someone wants those people to reach us," he said. "The more crowded your castle, the more uncomfortable we'll be during the siege."

"Siege?" gasped the earl. "Here? Already?"

"I'm afraid so," Tavis said. "We know giants from at least three different tribes are converging on Cuthbert Fief—the hill giant marauders, the frost giants who ambushed Prince Arlien's caravan, and the fog giants in High Meadow. That can't be coincidence, nor can it be happenstance that the hill giants encircled the castle so quickly after our return."

"I've never seen giant tribes work together like that," Arlien objected. "They're too imperious. The chiefs would start a war over who gets to be leader."

"Not if they were taking their orders from a higher authority," Tavis countered.

"The Twilight Spirit?" Brianna asked.

Arlien furrowed his brow. "Who is this Twilight Spirit, and what does he want with the queen?" he asked. "My, ah, informant has told me little about him."

"That's because we don't know much," Brianna replied. If the prince's mention of his spy irritated her, she did not show it. "From what little Basil has learned, the Twilight Spirit is a ghost or phantom haunting someplace called the Twilight Vale. The giant chieftains rely on him for advice and counsel."

"And what does he want with you?" inquired the prince.

"I don't know," Brianna said. "And I'm not sure I

want to."

The queen was being less than forthright, but Tavis understood her reluctance to be entirely candid. Their best guess was that the Twilight Spirit wanted to use his magic to get a giant's son on her. Such a child would give the giants a claim to the throne of Hartsvale, which was an important trade center for all their tribes.

Tavis felt a guilty hollow forming in the pit of his stomach. "Milady, I've led you into a trap," the scout said. "I'm sorry."

"Don't be. It's not your fault." Despite her brave words, the queen could not keep the quaver out of her voice. "I'm the one who wanted to inspect the damage personally. You told me it would be dangerous."

"But a good leader goes where she is needed," Arlien said. "You were right not to shy away. It would have set a bad example for your subjects."

"Yes—um—well, at the moment we're all at risk." Earl Cuthbert's voice had a nervous edge to it. "And I fear my wife and daughters are not as courageous as our queen. The peasants' reports have already terrified them. What will they think when we start preparing the castle for a siege?"

"They'll think we are in grave danger, which we are," Brianna said sharply. "But I suggest you don't underestimate them, Earl. Women are made of sterner stuff than men realize. Tell them the truth and put them to work. They'll be fine, and you can see to the defense of your castle, which is what an earl should properly do at a time like this."

The earl's eyes flared at the rebuke, but he bowed to the queen. "Yes, of course, Majesty," he said. "It's been three hundred years since Cuthbert Castle was assaulted, so the shock of facing a siege so suddenly may have caught me off guard."

"How off guard?" Brianna demanded. "Cuthbert Castle does have an ample supply of stores, does it not?"

Cuthbert's face reddened. "The winter was a hard one, Milady," he muttered. "My serfs were starving—"

"How long?" Brianna demanded, cutting him off.

The earl looked out an embrasure. "We have ample water, of course," he said. "But food is another matter. There is enough to feed us and our soldiers for perhaps a month. But with all my serfs in the castle, the supply will last no longer than a week."

"One week." Brianna shook her head in disgust. "The winter wasn't that hard, Earl."

"I'm sorry, my queen," Cuthbert said. "But how was I to know? We didn't have this kind of trouble when Camden was king."

Brianna's face turned crimson, but she made no reply.

Tavis turned a thoughtful eye on Cuthbert's cringing face. Shortly after the giants had razed their third village, the earl had sent a frantic messenger begging the queen for a contingent of her best troops. She had complied immediately, yet now the man blamed her because his castle was about to be sieged. To the scout, such ingratitude spoke volumes about the fellow's character. The earl would bear watching in the days to come.

"Perhaps you should try to escape tonight, Your Majesty," suggested Cuthbert. "Before more giants arrive."

"Are you that much of a coward?" Tavis snapped. "Would you turn your own queen out to fight three tribes of giants?"

The color drained from the earl's face. He backed away from Tavis, as though he feared the firbolg would hurl him off his own keep. "That's n-not what I m-meant," he stammered. "But tonight's your best chance to escape. By tomorrow, we'll be s-surrounded."

"We're surrounded now," Tavis growled.

"Almost certainly," agreed Arlien. He pointed at the giants in Basil's mirror. "Otherwise, they wouldn't be sitting there. I'd say Tavis's grasp of the situation is absolute."

"Then we should shut the gate," suggested Avner.

"Don't say such things, boy!" Tavis scolded. "Don't even think them!"

"Why not?" the youth pressed. "The giants aren't bothering the serfs. It's Brianna they want."

Brianna laid a gentle hand on Avner's shoulder. "Your idea has merit, but if we lock the serfs out of the castle, the giants will turn Lake Cuthbert red with their blood."

The queen looked across the dark waters, staring at the mountains in the distance. Their summits marked the southern boundary of Cuthbert Fief, and, save for a single narrow pass, their steep flanks formed an impassable wall of stone and ice.

"Our only hope lies outside the fief, I fear," Brianna said, turning back to the others. "Tavis, you'll have to sneak over the mountains and fetch the rest of my army."

"But I'm your bodyguard!" the scout objected. "I can't leave without you."

"Well, you certainly can't leave with me," Brianna countered. "I'm not stealthy enough to sneak past all those giants. Besides, our only hope of saving Cuthbert Castle is speed, and you'll move faster alone."

"But if the giants storm the castle, you could be captured," the scout objected. "I wouldn't be here."

He didn't need to say why he needed to be present. They all knew what he was to do if the giants captured the queen.

"That's a chance we'll have to take." Brianna stared into the scout's eyes with a look of utter trust. "But you'll be back long before that comes to pass—and if I'm wrong, I have every confidence that you'll track me down and put your golden arrow to good use."

Tavis shook his head. "My place is at your side."

"Not right now." Brianna looked up at Basil. "Why don't you and the others see what's on the other side of the keep?"

The verbeeg frowned in confusion. "I'm sure we'll find

nothing but more—"

Avner grabbed the hem of the runecaster's cloak. "Come along, Basil. It won't hurt to check."

The youth pulled the verbeeg toward the far wall, with Cuthbert and Arlien following close behind.

Once the others were gone, Tavis said, "You know I can't leave your side, Brianna."

"Why not?" A mocking smile crossed the queen's lips. "Are you afraid to leave me alone with Arlien?"

Tavis knew better than to deny the charge. Like all firbolgs, he found it all but impossible to lie. The strain of uttering false words would cause his voice to crack, he would break out in a cold sweat, and his guilty conscious would not let him sleep for a week.

"My reluctance is due to more than Arlien," he said. His voice almost cracked. "If the giants capture you, tracking them down may not be as easy as you think. And I've never loosed an arrow against someone I love. My aim might not be true."

Brianna took his hand and squeezed it. "Your aim would be dead-on—I know," she said. "And you mustn't worry about Arlien. I have no feelings for him."

"Does that mean you won't marry him?"

"What difference would that make?" Brianna asked. "It's you I love."

"It would make a difference to me."

"Well, I'm certainly not making any wedding plans until I'm out of here." Brianna gave him playful smile.

Tavis would not let her dodge his question. "But you *would*, if you thought marrying him was best for Hartsvale."

Brianna's smile vanished, but she did not look away. "If that's what I thought, yes." The queen's voice grew stern, and she released his hand. "And Tavis, *you* must also do what I think is best for Hartsvale."

The scout closed his eyes and nodded. "I know," he said. "But it isn't easy, my queen. I'm only a firbolg."

◆3◆
The Library

Brianna held the lantern while Cuthbert fumbled with his tangled loop of keys. The queen and her plump earl stood before the iron-clad door to the keep's lowest subbasement, with the rest of their small party waiting behind them. The ceiling here was low, forcing the tall queen to stoop over the lamp. The fumes rising from its glass chimney were rancid and mordant, and she knew her hair would smell of burning lard when the time came to sleep. That was fine. As weary as she was, no odor in the land would keep her awake—her racing thoughts or sick heart, perhaps, but no mere odor.

"I hope this won't take much longer, Earl." Brianna glared down at Cuthbert's stubby fingers, which continued to fumble through his rat's nest of keys. "The idea is to catch the giants napping, and Tavis has a long swim ahead."

Cuthbert finally found the right key. He slipped it into the lock, then gave Brianna a reassuring smile. "I promise you, the time is well spent," he said. "Tavis will reach the shore in the Cold Hours, just as we planned."

The earl turned the key and led the way through the low doorway. Brianna ducked under the lintel and followed, with Tavis, Avner, and Basil close behind. Arlien was sleeping in his room—at least he was supposed to be. The good prince did not seem to realize that wounded men needed rest, for he had stayed up well past midnight to help prepare the castle's defenses. The queen certainly admired his stamina and devotion to duty, but his judgment was another matter. If he didn't get some rest soon, even his enchanted armor would not save him.

As Brianna's lamp cast its flickering light over the low room, Basil cried, "A library!"

The gloomy chamber seemed a jumbled contrast to Castle Hartwick's Royal Archives, where Basil kept two thousand volumes neatly ordered by title and content. Here, the books sat on the floor in knee-high stacks, spilled from open trunks, or lay agape on rough-hewn tables. In spite of the disarray, the spines of the tomes were in good condition, no pages were dog-eared, and open volumes were never piled atop each other.

Earl Cuthbert stopped a few steps inside the room. "I must ask you to follow my steps exactly," he said. "I don't allow the servants down here, so things are a bit cluttered. It wouldn't do to have you tripping over my books."

"Not at all," agreed Basil. "We wouldn't want to break a spine or rip a page."

As the earl started across the room, Brianna heard Tavis whisper to the verbeeg, "Keep your hands at your sides, my friend. I don't want you pawing Cuthbert's books."

"But there are so many volumes," the runecaster objected. "There must be titles we don't have in the Royal Archives."

Brianna paused, sensing the potential for catastrophe. Like most verbeegs, Basil had little respect for private property. He also had a pronounced fondness for books. The queen did not want a repeat of the first time she had lain eyes on him, when she had found him in Tavis's barn with a cache of stolen books lying at his feet.

"Basil, do as Tavis says." Brianna glanced over her shoulder to emphasize her command. The ceiling was so low that both giant-kin had to stoop over. "If you so much as open a cover without the earl's permission, I'll have you thrown into the lake."

Basil looked at the stone floor. "Yes, Milady."

"Is there a problem back there?" called Cuthbert. He was already halfway across the room.

"Nothing to worry about, Earl," Brianna replied. "We're coming now."

The queen caught up to Cuthbert and followed him on a zigzag course to an arched doorway on the other side of the room. As they passed through, she was amazed to discover that the earl's library spilled into this chamber as well, but the books here were of a strange sort. The volumes were as big as serving trays, bound by fine copper wire, and covered with thin slabs of granite. They had pages of black mica, but there did not seem to be any kind of writing on the ebony, at least not in the volumes that Brianna saw lying open.

From the back of the line, Basil gasped, "Biotite folios!"

Brianna looked back to see the verbeeg kneeling at a table, running his index finger down the glistening black page of a book. A column of glowing symbols appeared wherever he touched, changing from ruby red to emerald green and sapphire blue before the queen's eyes. The figures were as large as a human hand, with delicate loops and scrupulously curved arches.

The queen was about to utter a sharp reprimand when Cuthbert slipped past her. The earl stopped at Basil's side and gave him a condescending smile. "I didn't know verbeegs read Stone Giant."

"The written language is properly referred to as Metamorpherie, and not many verbeegs do read it." Basil did not even look up as he corrected the earl. "However, I'm one of the few who do, and quite well. I'll be glad to teach you."

The patronizing grin vanished from Cuthbert's face. "I'm doing quite well on my own, thank you." The earl slipped his hand under the folio's front cover, then grunted with effort as he heaved the granite slab off the table. Basil barely pulled his hand away before the heavy plate slammed down, closing the book. "But we are in a hurry to see Tavis off. Shall we continue?"

Basil frowned at the earl's rudeness, but one glance at Brianna's stern expression squelched any objection he had been preparing to make. The runecaster rose off his knees. "Of course," he said. "You're the host."

"Good."

Cuthbert spun on his heel and resumed his position at the head of the line. He led the party past the remaining folios into yet another library chamber. A huge, glass-topped desk stood in one corner, while a long case filled with rolled parchments occupied the center of the room. Maps of all scales covered the walls like tapestries, showing everything from the entire continent of Faerun to the bottom contours of Lake Cuthbert.

The earl went to the far end of the chamber and pulled a map off a wall, then spread it out on the desk in the corner. The parchment, Brianna saw, portrayed Cuthbert Fief in intricate detail. Near the center of the fief lay Lake Cuthbert, with the castle perched on a craggy island near one bank. The long bridge that connected the citadel to shore was neatly outlined in black dashes to indicate it could be collapsed in an emergency. The hundred hills that surrounded the lake were shown in great detail, with every stream, cliff, terraced slope, well, and spring drawn in a careful, clear hand. The earl had even updated the map, marking each razed village with a tongue of red flame and the date it had been destroyed.

Most importantly, the map showed the mountain range that ringed Cuthbert Fief. Every peak was drawn as it looked from the keep roof, with its name printed alongside and, sometimes, a notation describing what one could see from the summit. The snakelike road that connected the fief to the rest of Hartsvale was shown, and so were all of the treacherous tracks used by hunters, shepherds, and anyone else with business in the high country. Three of these rugged paths crossed the northern range and extended into the Icy Plains beyond, but only a single trail crossed the mountains toward the safety of the south.

"Most impressive, Earl Cuthbert," Brianna said.

"My siege stores may be lacking, but I do know my lands," the earl said. He glanced at Tavis, then back at Brianna. "My queen, given the speed with which the giants surrounded us after failing to capture you in High Meadow, we must assume they have anticipated that you'll send for help."

Cuthbert laid a pudgy finger on the summit of Cuthbert Pass, where the main road crossed into the rest of the kingdom. The drawing there depicted the pass exactly as Brianna remembered: long and winding, with high cliffs flanking both sides and a narrow bottleneck in the center.

"And that means they would also block the only obvious route to safety and help," the earl continued.

"But this route is not so obvious." Brianna pointed to the single trail that ran over the mountains to the southeast. She leaned down to read the name beside it. "Shepherd's Nightmare?"

"That's right," said the earl. "Aside from the road, it's the only path back to Hartsvale. It's not much of a track. The trail disappears into the stream in several places, and at the top it's nothing more than a broken ledge clinging to the side of Wyvern's Eyrie. I doubt the giants know about it, so I suggest Tavis take this route."

The scout set his shoulder satchel and bow aside, then leaned on the table to study the map. "That'll take me too far out of the way," he said. Tavis traced a route running directly south from the castle, over a long, winding glacier that ended in a cup-shaped cirque. "I'll go this way. I can scale that headwall in a day and be at Earl Wendel's by dawn the next morning."

"And you expect to bring an army back the same

way?" Brianna inquired. "Two companies of my guard, plus whatever the northern earls can raise?"

The firbolg studied the map a moment longer, then shook his head. "They're not scouts," he said. "We'd lose more than half of them on the way."

"Then you should go the other way," Brianna recommended. "Unless you already know Shepherd's Nightmare, the extra time will be worth it. When you return, it'll be better to have someone who knows the way leading the army."

"I intend to return ahead of the army," Tavis replied. "It'll take time for them to assemble—"

"Which is all the more reason they'll need an informed guide once they're underway." Brianna reached up and touched the firbolg's rough cheek. "I know you want to be here when the giants attack, but you can't save me by yourself. For that, we need an army."

Avner slipped between Brianna and the firbolg. "Maybe I should go—"

"No!" Brianna and Tavis snapped their refusal as one voice.

The youth was undaunted. "Why not?" he demanded. "I've kept up with Tavis before, and I'm not likely to be much use when a hundred giants pound the gates down."

Earl Cuthbert groaned.

"Avner, I said no." Brianna pushed the boy away before he could get a good look at the map. In spite of her command, Avner was just wild enough to try following Tavis on this perilous mission. "It's too dangerous."

"And being here's not?" Avner scoffed.

"It's safer than defying the queen's command." Tavis gave the boy a stern glare. "Now promise that you'll stay—or must I ask Earl Cuthbert to lock you in his dungeon?"

Avner exhaled sharply. "I promise," he said. "But you're making a mistake. It'd be safer with two of us."

"Not if Tavis is successful," said the earl. He tried to lay a reassuring hand on the boy's shoulder, but Avner sloughed it off and slipped away into the shadows. Cuthbert accepted the boy's surliness with a good-natured shrug, then looked back to the scout. "Would you like to take this map? It's my only copy, but you're welcome to it."

"No." Tavis propped his elbows on the desk and studied the area around Shepherd's Nightmare. "If something happened to me, I wouldn't want this to fall into the giants' hands."

The earl breathed a sigh of relief. "Then there's only one more thing I can do for you," he said. "Do you have everything you need?"

Tavis studied the map for a moment longer, then picked up his shoulder satchel and hickory bow. "I think so. Perhaps even more than I need," he said. "This strikes me as too heavy for a long swim."

The scout unbuckled his sword belt, but the earl caught his hand before he could remove it. "You can keep that, my friend," he said. "You won't have to swim— not tonight."

Brianna frowned. "What do you mean?" she demanded. "We discussed this already. A boat's too likely to be seen."

"He won't need a boat," Cuthbert replied.

The earl stepped over to a long map case in the center of the room and braced his shoulder against the end. A soft rumble reverberated through the chamber. The entire cabinet slid across the floor to reveal a set of mossy stairs leading down into a dark tunnel. The dank odor of lake water began to rise from the passage, and somewhere far below Brianna heard a tiny stream of water trickling through a rocky chute.

"A secret passage?" the queen queried.

The earl nodded. "It runs on a straight course toward Shepherd's Nightmare," he said. "The tunnel would be a little tight for most firbolgs, but Tavis should be small enough to pass."

Tavis scowled. "I don't recall seeing this on the Castle Registry." The registry was an ancient collection of castle plans that Basil had uncovered in the Royal Library. At the verbeeg's request, Brianna had sent an envoy to each of her earls to ask for updates. "You broke the law by failing to report it."

The queen smiled at Tavis's naivete. Although the scout had grown up among humans, he still suffered from the firbolg proclivity to view the law as sacred and inviolable.

"I think we can forgive Cuthbert that oversight," Brianna said. She had never expected her earls to divulge all their secrets, but what each man had revealed told her a great deal about his loyalties. Cuthbert had reported his collapsing bridge and the murderholes that overlooked the waters at the base of his castle walls, and that was more than most earls had done. "However, I *am* disappointed you didn't mention this earlier, Earl. It would have saved me a great deal of worry." Brianna fixed him with a stern look.

Cuthbert shrugged. "This passage has been a family secret since long before you were queen and I was earl," he replied. "I wanted to think matters over before violating an ancestral tradition."

"Then I thank you for making the correct choice," Brianna said, somewhat tartly.

"You should not need to thank him for obeying the law." Tavis buckled his sword belt, then added, "And certainly not when it benefits him as much as his queen. Unless I return with help, the giants will flatten his castle."

A crimson cloud settled over Cuthbert's face. "If saving my castle were my only concern, it would be a simple matter to persuade the giants not to attack."

Tavis's blue eyes grew as cold as the glacier ice they resembled. "If you yield to that temptation, know that I will hunt you down myself."

There was no need for either man to spell out what temptation. Now that it had become obvious that the giants were here for Brianna, they all knew that Earl Cuthbert could save his castle and his family simply by giving the invaders what they wanted. Of course, there would be a terrible battle between his own troops and the Company of the Winter Wolf, but that fight would be far easier to win than the one against the giants.

Tavis continued his threat. "I will make it my business to see your—"

"Tavis, I hardly think that's necessary." Brianna interposed herself between the two men. "Perhaps Earl Cuthbert doesn't have his siege stores in order, but that hardly makes him a traitor."

Tavis switched his gaze to Brianna. "A man who defies your law for no reason—"

"Then it was a poor law," Brianna interrupted. "I know that Earl Cuthbert is a good man. Have you forgotten that he was one of the first to stand with us against my father?"

The scout's eyes softened. "I remember."

"Good," Brianna said, genuinely relieved. Cuthbert clearly feared for his castle and his family, but the queen knew he would never betray her. He always sent his taxes to Castle Hartwick on time, which told her more about the man's trustworthiness than how many dragons he had slain. "Now perhaps Avner and Basil should say their farewells."

The queen turned and saw Avner standing at the edge of the lamp's flickering light, but there was no sign of the runecaster. With a knot of anger forming in her stomach, she called, "Basil!"

The verbeeg's flat feet paddled across the floor as he tried to sneak out of the folio room. A moment later, he appeared at Avner's side, still stooped over because of the low ceiling.

"Yes, Majesty?" He arched his bushy eyebrows in a parody of innocence.

"I told you to leave Earl Cuthbert's books alone."

"But these folios are ancient. They contain the entire history of the giant race!" he objected. "Quite possibly, they might tell us what the Twilight Spirit wants with you."

"They don't," Earl Cuthbert replied. "I have read every volume, and there's no mention of any such spirit."

"Metamorpherie is very subtle," Basil insisted. "You'd miss the reference during a cursory scan."

"Those folios were captured when my ancestors drove the stone giants from this vale!" Cuthbert growled. "I can assure you, I have done more than scan them during the fifty-odd years I have lived in this castle."

"The earl would have remembered something as important as a reference to the Twilight Spirit, I'm certain," Brianna lied. Given Tavis's recent accusations, she thought it would be wiser to smooth their host's rumpled feathers now and arrange later for Basil to examine the volumes. "Tavis is about to leave. I thought you might like to wish him luck."

The verbeeg pulled his satchel off his shoulder and placed it on the floor. "I'll do more than that," he said, opening the leather sack. "I prepared a little something that might help him sneak past the giants."

Basil withdrew a large silver mask from his satchel. It was shaped like a smiling face, with holes where the eyes and mouth should have been. The verbeeg had etched more than a dozen of his magical runes deep into its glistening silver.

"That was a wedding gift from Lady Cuthbert's father!" the earl yelled. "And you've ruined it!"

"I've only made it functional," the verbeeg replied in a proud voice. "Now, it really can disguise someone."

Brianna raised her brow. "How so?"

"Tavis can use it to make himself look like anyone he wishes—even a giant," the runecaster explained. "All he has to do is lay the mask over the face of the person he wants to impersonate—dead or alive—and say the command word."

"*Basil is wise?*" Tavis asked.

The runecaster shook his head and smiled. "*Verbeegs are handsome,*" he said. "The mask will take on the visage of the person it was touching. Then, when you hold it over your own face, you'll take on the same appearance."

"What about size?" asked Avner. "Tavis is hardly big enough to pass for a giant, even if he looks like one. And he sure doesn't have the voice."

Basil pointed to a rune on the cheek, then to one below the lower lip. "These will take care of the size and voice problems." He touched another rune on the mask's temple. "And he'll speak the proper language—you see, I've thought of everything."

"It certainly appears you have." Brianna nodded her head in approval, then turned to Earl Cuthbert. "Perhaps, under the circumstances, you wouldn't mind loaning the mask to Tavis?"

"By all means," the earl grumbled.

Basil handed the mask to the scout. "Good luck, my friend."

"This will make up for a great deal of luck," Tavis said.

"Before you go, there's one thing I should warn you about," the verbeeg said. "The larger the giant you impersonate, the quicker my magic will fail."

"How long will I have?" the scout asked.

"I wish I could say," Basil replied. "For a hill giant, possibly three days. You might last a day as a fog giant. And—may the gods forbid—should you find yourself impersonating something like a storm giant, you'd have only a matter of hours."

"If there's a storm giant out there, none of us has

much longer than that," Tavis replied. He slipped the mask into his satchel. "My thanks to you, Basil—and to you, Earl Cuthbert."

"Wear it in good health." There was only a touch of sarcasm in the earl's voice. Cuthbert took a tallow stick off the map case and lit the wick from Brianna's lamp. "And the strength of Stronmaus to you—you'll need it."

When the earl stepped forward to give the candle to Tavis, he stubbed his foot on Basil's satchel. The sack toppled to the floor with a clack that sounded suspiciously like stone on stone.

"What's this?" the earl screeched. He bent down and rolled the collar of hte satchel back, revealing one of his biotite folios. He looked up at Basil with an utter expression of shock. "Thief!"

"I'm only borrowing it!" the verbeeg retorted, reciting his standard defense in such situations. "You weren't using it, and books are meant—"

"Basil!" Brianna barked.

The verbeeg's mouth snapped shut. He fixed his eyes on the floor. "Yes?" he asked quietly.

"I warned you about this."

"But—"

"There's no excuse!" Brianna yelled. "Since you've shown no inclination to respect our host's property, I have no choice but to have you locked in a secure room."

"Can I at least keep—"

Brianna silenced him with a gesture of her hand, then turned to Cuthbert. "Can you arrange that for me?"

"With pleasure," the earl replied. He handed the candle to Tavis, then stooped down to retrieve his beloved folio, groaning loudly as he struggled to pick it up. "Since he's a member of your company, I'll try not to make it too unpleasant for him."

"Thank you," the queen said. She glanced down at Avner. "The time has come for us to let Tavis go."

The youth nodded and looked up to the scout. "I'm not a child anymore," he said. "You should let me come with you."

The scout shook his head. "I'll be back soon enough."

"That would be more likely with someone to watch your back," the boy grumbled. "But if I've got to stay, I'll try to avoid trouble. At least you won't have to worry about that."

"I didn't think I would." Tavis ruffled the boy's hair, then said, "Take care of the queen for me."

Avner smiled weakly. "Don't I always?"

"Always," Brianna agreed. She gave the lamp to Avner, then waved him and her other two companions toward the door. "If you'll excuse us, I'd like to have a few words with Tavis."

As the trio disappeared into the folio room, Brianna wrapped her arms around Tavis's waist. "Be careful."

The scout did not meet her gaze. "Of course," he said. "I'll be back with help as soon as I can."

Tavis tried to pull away, but Brianna would not release him. "That's not the only reason I want you to come back alive." She looked up at his chiseled face. "You know that."

The firbolg closed his eyes and nodded. "I know," he said. "But it's the only reason that matters—at least until you decide about the alliance with Gilthwit."

"Why?" Brianna demanded. "It doesn't need to be that way. Even if I marry the prince—and that's a big 'if'— Arlien won't stay long. He'll be anxious to return to Gilthwit—"

"After you've produced an heir—and you'd still be his wife," Tavis interrupted. "I'm a firbolg. I can't be a party to such a deception. You've always known that about me."

Brianna felt her mouth open, but she did not have words to push out of it. She felt wounded, as though Tavis had slipped a dagger into her heart, but that simply could not be. He was her firbolg bodyguard, sworn to defend and protect her. He could not hurt her, except by her own command—which, of course, was the situation now. Tavis could not live in deception, and by asking him to try she could only force him away. He could abandon their love, but he could not lie to save it.

"Damn it, you were raised by humans!" Brianna stepped back, but kept her hands on the scout's waist. "Why can't you lie?"

Tavis set the candle aside and took her hands in his. "Because I'm not human," he said. "I'm firbolg."

They were interrupted by a voice from the folio room. "Tavis, wait!" It was Arlien. "I hope you haven't—oh, dear."

Brianna looked toward the door and saw the prince's form silhouetted against the lamp in Avner's hand. She stepped away from Tavis and turned toward the wall, trying to wipe the tears from her eyes.

"I'm s-sorry," Arlien stammered. "I seem to have—ah—interrupted."

"Not at all, Prince," Tavis said. If the firbolg felt any resentment for the intrusion, Brianna did not hear it in his voice. "I was just leaving."

"Then I'm glad I caught you," Arlien replied, limping into the room. "I wanted to present you with a gift."

Although Brianna could feel that her eyes were still swollen from crying, she turned to face the prince. There was no use pretending he had not seen Tavis holding her. Perhaps his father had even forced him to leave his own beloved in order to come and court her.

"You should be resting, Arlien," the queen said. Noting that he was carrying his huge warhammer, she asked, "What's that for? Surely you don't intend to join Tavis?"

The prince shook his head. "I'm afraid I'd only slow the good scout down." He held his warhammer out. "But I want him to take this along. It'll serve him well against the giants."

Tavis clasped his hands on the prince's, but did not take the weapon. "I truly appreciate your offer," he said. "But with any luck, I'll be avoiding our enemies, not fighting them. Besides, you're likely to need that here, and I'd rather you have it at hand to defend Brianna."

At first, Arlien seemed too stunned by the refusal to take the weapon back, but he recovered his wits an instant later and lowered the hammer. "As you wish," he said, forcing a smile. "Rest assured that nothing shall happen to her while I am near."

Tavis lowered his voice, then said, "And I'd also ask you to keep a close eye on Earl Cuthbert. That man is too frightened to be trustworthy."

Brianna started to protest on the earl's behalf, but discovered a lump in her throat too big to speak around.

Arlien nodded grimly. "The same thought had crossed my mind," he said. "Don't worry about him."

"Good."

"And Tavis," the prince added. "Don't worry about me. There's no sense discussing alliances until we know whether Brianna and I come out of this alive."

"Thank you, Prince. That'll make it easier for me to concentrate on the task at hand. But I'm sure we'll do what's best for our kingdoms in the end." Tavis inclined his head to Arlien, then turned and bowed to Brianna. "With your permission, Majesty."

"No, not yet!" Brianna threw her arms around the firbolg's neck and kissed him on the mouth, long and hard.

Prince Arlien politely turned away, fixing his gaze on the map that Earl Cuthbert had left lying on the desk in the corner.

→ 4 ←
The Granite Door

Tavis sat against the tunnel door, whetting his sword and listening to the heavy steps outside. Every muffled boom caused the candle to hiss and sputter ominously, but the scout did not bother to rise and see how much stub remained. He had perched the taper on the edge of the door's counterweight, and the long curtain of wax running down the side told him all he needed to know.

The giants had been out there all night, building war machines or dancing or rutting or whatever. It made little difference to the scout. He did not dare open the door while they were so close. The instant he pulled the counterweight down, the rusty chains would squeal like a raging boar. All he could do was wait—wait and hope the brutes would move off before sunrise.

Dawn could not be far away, for the journey through the secret tunnel had been long and difficult. The passage was so low and cramped that the firbolg had been forced to creep through it nearly doubled over, at times twisting sideways so he could squeeze his broad shoulders through. To make matters worse, a steady trickle of water had seeped down from the lake above, submerging much of the floor beneath an icy black puddle. Nevertheless, the scout had ignored his cold-numbed feet and pressed on steadily over the slick footing, only to hear the giants outside when he finally reached the door. With three-quarters of his candle remaining, he had taken out his whetstone and sat down to hone his weapons.

Now, his dagger and his arrow tips were all freshly

sharpened, he was putting the finishing touches on his sword, and the stomping outside continued unabated. From the way his candle spat and hissed, the wick was all but gone and the flame was sinking into the wax. Tavis tried not to think about how long it took a candle to burn and concentrated on whetting his sword.

The blade was already as sharp as an owl's talon, but the scout found himself scraping the stone along as though honing an unedged sword—and not because he was upset about his foes outside. Tavis knew from long experience it was best to remain patient and calm around giants, and he always did. But he had an aching knot where his heart should have been, and that kind of distress could have only one cause: the queen.

The whetstone shot from beneath his thumb. The scout's hand slid across his sword's sharp edge, opening a deep cut across his palm. Tavis cursed and opened his satchel to retrieve a bandage, grumbling at Brianna for causing him to be so inattentive. Though the firbolg had been raised among humans, he still could not comprehend the way their convoluted minds worked.

Brianna loved Tavis. That was what she claimed, and most of the time she acted like it. Yet she refused to wed him, claiming their union would weaken the kingdom. Then, in the next breath, she expressed her willingness to carry on secretly as though they were husband and wife! The firbolg, of course, had no choice but to refuse. It would be impossible for him to keep such a secret. Besides, if the earls objected to their marriage, he could only imagine how they would react to such a deception. The queen claimed the nobles would accept the arrangement, but the scout could not believe that. Even if he could live a lie, he failed to see how Hartsvale would benefit by asking everyone in the country to do the same.

Now Brianna wanted to marry a man she hardly

knew, a foreign prince, and treat Tavis as her husband! The firbolg could not help questioning her judgment. His understanding of human behavior was limited, but to him such a proposal sounded like a formula for war. Although Arlien had reacted graciously enough when he had stumbled upon them embracing, the prince seemed a man of honor. He would certainly expect his wife to abide by the sacred vows of marriage.

The vows were another matter. Tavis had heard them many times, and they spoke of such things as devotion, fidelity, obedience, a giving of the self. How could Brianna swear those things to the prince of a distant kingdom? By giving herself to Arlien, she was also giving Hartsvale to him. If the earls objected to the queen presenting all that to a citizen of their own country, surely they would object to having it given to a foreigner! Or maybe not. Brianna certainly hadn't seemed to think so, and she was astute about such things.

Tavis ripped a strip off his bandage cloth, then tied the dressing around his palm. Being in love with Brianna was a confusing thing, and it was getting more baffling all the time. The firbolg had endured the past year only by hoping that once she established herself as queen, she would feel secure enough to marry him. But with Arlien's arrival, that hope had grown distant. Now, the scout could look forward only to protecting Brianna while she raised another man's children. He didn't know how he could endure that possibility, but he would find a way. He had to; he had sworn to defend the queen until her death, and firbolgs did as they pledged.

Tavis picked up his whetstone and drew it down his sword in a light, smooth stroke. He would concentrate on his duties and face each day as it came. Maybe Hiatea would look more favorably on him tomorrow, and if not, then perhaps the day after.

The candle flame gave a contemptuous hiss, then finally sank into the wax and pitched Tavis into dank blackness.

* * * * *

Avner knelt before the locked door and examined the keyhole by the light of a flickering candle. The latch was secured by a primitive ward lock, strong but easy enough to pick. The youth put Basil's satchel aside, then reached inside his tunic and withdrew a set of flat metal bars affixed to an iron ring. The tools came in many different sizes, but all were shaped roughly like skeleton keys, with a wide variety of notches and grooves cut into the end tabs. He selected the tool of the proper size and slowly worked it into the keyhole, twisting gently from side to side until he felt it slip past the wards. He gently turned the implement, engaging the bolt.

The lock had barely clicked open before the chamber door flew ajar, jerking the ring of picks from Avner's hand.

"By Karontor!" Basil hissed. The verbeeg dropped to his hands and knees, trying to squeeze his bony shoulders through a portal meant for humans half his size. "I thought you'd never come for me!"

Avner quickly blocked the doorway. "I didn't come *for* you," he corrected. "I came to see you."

"Then see me outside." The runecaster started to crawl forward.

Avner planted both his palms on Basil's crooked nose and pushed, forcing the astonished verbeeg back into his gloomy chamber. "Where do you think you're going?"

"Anywhere," Basil answered. He peered past the boy's shoulder, his baggy eyes wild with desperation. "Anyplace is better than this."

Avner glanced around the room. Although the earl's

men had removed the furniture to make room for the verbeeg, they had been kind enough leave an oil lamp and throw several straw mattresses across a sturdy table to make a bed. There was even a barred window overlooking the inner ward, its shutters thrown wide open despite the cold predawn breeze.

"This isn't so bad, especially considering you'll end up in the dungeon if you try to leave," Avner said. "The castle's crawling with soldiers, and they'd spot someone your size in a minute. It was tough enough to get this back." The youth reached around the corner and retrieved Basil's satchel. "Besides, where do you think you could go? Into the hills with the giants?"

"Perhaps," Basil replied. "Or maybe I could hide in the library."

"That's the first place they'd look," Avner said. He pointed to the makeshift bed beneath the window. "Besides, how long has it been since you had something that comfortable to sleep on?"

"How can a prisoner sleep?" Basil demanded. "While I languish here, life outside is passing me by."

Avner rolled his eyes. "I've spent weeks in pits slimier and darker than this. You haven't been here one night." He took his picks from the lock, then pushed the door closed. "What kind of thief is afraid of jail?"

"One should not be punished for acting in accordance with the principles of one's race," the runecaster replied. "And if you're not here to free me, what do you want? At this hour of the morning, I doubt you've come to pass the time."

"We've got to do something about Arlien." Avner went to sit on the table, dragging Basil's huge satchel with him. "The prince is coming between Tavis and Brianna."

Basil sank to his haunches and sat facing the youth. "What do you mean?"

"Isn't it obvious?" Avner opened the satchel and removed half a dozen apples he had taken from the earl's kitchen. He kept one for himself and tossed the rest to Basil. "The good prince came to marry her."

"I realize that," the runecaster replied. "But I fail to see what we can do about it."

Basil slipped an apple into his mouth. He crushed it with a single chomp and swallowed it, stem, core, and all.

"We'll do whatever it takes to prevent a marriage." Avner bit into his own apple.

Basil raised his bushy eyebrows. "Assassinate the prince?"

Avner sighed in exasperation. "I was hoping we could think of something less drastic. I'm not trying to start a war."

Basil popped another apple into his mouth and gnashed it slowly. "Runes of the heart are hardly my area of expertise," he said. "But I do have a trick or two that might help our cause—perhaps a rune of stammering or foul odors."

"Good!" Avner said. "The prince can't court Brianna if he smells bad—but it'll have to be subtle. We don't want the queen to realize what we're doing."

"Of course not," Basil agreed. He glanced forlornly around the room, studying the gloomy stone walls. "But the rune requires modification, and I can't concentrate here."

"What are you saying?" Avner demanded. "This chamber's not much smaller than your study at Castle Hartwick, and you stay in there for days!"

Basil's eyes lit up. "Yes, but I have my books," he said. "Perhaps, if I had something to occupy my attention, this dreary room would seem more like a proper office."

Avner shook his head. "Not on my life!" he said. "Filching your satchel and a few apples is one thing, but if Earl Cuthbert catches me with his folios, he'll feed us both to the giants!"

Basil's gray eyes grew as hard as the stones of his

cell. "Then I hope you enjoy weddings."

Avner tore a big piece from his apple. He gnawed on this for a time, then said, "Just one, and I take it back as soon as you're done."

"Very well. Even I can read only one book at a time." A treacherous gleam appeared in Basil's eye, then he added, "Of course, the magic of my rune might last longer if I had no fear of growing bored."

"All right," Avner growled. "How often do I have to bring you a new book?"

"We'll set up a signal." Basil thought for a moment, then said, "It'll be best if you can see it from a distance. I'll close my shutters whenever I'm ready."

"Fine." Avner slipped off the table. "I hope I know what I'm getting myself into."

The youth stepped to the window and threw his apple core out into the gray glow of first light.

* * * * *

The stomping had ended some time earlier, pattering into silence after an unexpected crescendo. That had been exactly a thousand breaths ago—Tavis had counted each one, lacking any other way to tell time—and now it was time to go. The scout checked to make sure his sword, quiver, and shoulder satchel were secure, then grabbed the counterweight chain and pulled.

An ear-piercing squeal, almost deafening after the long silence, echoed off the stone walls. The counterweight seemed to stick for a moment, then a loud crack sounded from the threshold as the door broke free. The granite slab began to rise, grudgingly, and a low, grinding growl joined the cacophony of rattling chains. A sliver of gray light appeared on the tunnel floor and slowly spread down the passageway.

Tavis cursed. Although the rays were not bright, he knew what they meant: dawn was coming, and soon. He forced himself to look into the light so his eyes would grow accustomed to it and pulled harder. The door rose another foot.

A gentle tremor shuddered through the tunnel, then another and another: giants searching for the source of the mysterious sounds. More steps joined the first, but none seemed to be growing any louder. That would change quickly enough, Tavis knew. Soon his foes would overcome their initial confusion and track down the source of the clamor.

The scout stopped pulling on the chains and heard the gruff, terse grunts of shouting hill giants. Although the voices were too muffled to understand, they sounded much closer than Tavis would have liked. He gave the chain another long pull, then abruptly stopped. A trio of giants began shouting contradictory commands, confused by the sporadic noise.

Tavis eyed the gap between the door and threshold, finding about three feet of gray light. That was enough space for him to squeeze through, but he feared the granite slab would slide down the instant he released it. The scout pulled again, paused a short time, then gave the chain another tug. The door rose to a height of six feet, and now he could hear the giants clearly.

"Where Gragg hear that sound?"

"Gone 'gain," answered another muffled voice. "But gots to be over there somewhere. Be quiet."

The tunnel stopped shuddering as the giants moved more carefully. The scout could picture them stalking through the predawn light in the typical posture of hunting hill giants: hunched over almost double, tree trunks resting across their stooped shoulders, their dull eyes fixed on the ground with their thick brows screwed into a crumpled parody of concentration. They were hardly as stealthy as fog giants, but they would move with surprising grace for such ungainly beings, their knees bent and their legs flexed. If the need arose, they could spring over the land in great, bounding strides, the impact of each crashing footfall bouncing their terrified quarry off the ground. Tavis did not look forward to becoming their prey, but the prospect of reporting his failure to Brianna was even less appealing.

The scout took a deep breath, then snatched Bear Driller and threw himself into the gray light. The door began to descend with a loud, grating rumble.

The ground failed to appear beneath Tavis. He plummeted headfirst into the gloom and glimpsed the face of a rocky crag slipping past, then the stony dark mass of a hillside emerged before his eyes. He had enough time to cover his head before a wave of stinging numbness coursed through his arms. The scout rolled instantly, and found himself tumbling head-over-heels down a steep bank, ricocheting off boulders and tree trunks and leaving equipment strewn all down the slope. He came to a rest in the bottom of a rocky gulch, dizzy and aching, with the growl of the closing door still rumbling somewhere above.

"Meorf hear sound!" shouted a giant's distant voice.

"Bhurn, too!" answered another. "Come up here, Gragg!"

A series of muffled thuds echoed through the night. Tavis jumped to his feet and collapsed again, too shocked to stand. Both arms stung horribly, but it was his ribs that caused him the most pain. They hurt so much he could not draw air. The firbolg fought the tide of panic rising inside his chest and forced himself to exhale. The ache in his torso began to subside as his lungs expanded again; he had only knocked the wind out of himself. The scout took a few deep breaths, then flexed his elbows, wrists, and fingers. All the joints seemed in good working order, so he had not broken any bones. Tavis rose, relieved to have survived his unexpected fall.

The rumble on the hillside above came to a slow, grinding halt. Tavis looked up and saw the small cliff off which he had inadvertently leaped. The secret passage opened near the center, above a narrow ledge that led across the face to a safe route down. The granite door fit so tightly between two natural crevices that the scout would never have noticed it, save that the rusty counterweight chains had gotten stuck, leaving the granite slab hanging three feet above its threshold.

"Surtr's flame take that earl!" Tavis hissed. He could not leave Cuthbert's secret door open. Even if the hill giants couldn't fit into the narrow passage beyond, they could send a pack of their pet wolves through to wreak havoc. Besides, if they happened to have a shaman, there was no telling what use his magic might make of that tunnel. "If Cuthbert's going to break Brianna's law, at least he could do it well!"

Tavis started up the slope, gathering his satchel and other gear as he climbed.

"Meorf, hear squealing sound?"

"No, stupid," Meorf replied. "Gone 'gain. But let's us look in that ditch over there. That where it was, Bhurn."

The voices of Meorf and Bhurn were coming over the hilltop. The third giant, Gragg, had not spoken, but the scout heard his heavy footsteps pounding along the lakeshore, about thirty paces away at the gulch mouth.

Tavis grabbed his arrows and thrust them back into his quiver, then angled across the hill to retrieve his bow. Once he had his favorite weapon in hand, he would not be so nervous about getting caught on the ledge above. Bear Driller had felled plenty of giants, many far larger than the trio now stalking him.

The pounding of giant steps suddenly faded. The scout looked up to see a pair of stoop-shouldered figures silhouetted on the summit of the hill. They stood almost directly above the secret passage, peering down into the gully toward Tavis.

"Meorf see somethin'?" It was Gragg's voice, rolling up the gulch from the lakeshore.

"No," Meorf replied. "Not Bhurn neither."

Tavis glanced toward the lake, where he saw the last giant silhouetted against the starlit waters. This one was especially rotund, with a shape resembling that of a pear. The scout dropped flat to crawl to his bow.

"How Meorf know what Bhurn see?" Gragg demanded. "Let Bhurn talk!"

"Bhurn don't see nothin'," Meorf insisted. "Right?"

"Right," Bhurn said. "Nothing but little fella." The hill giant pointed a long finger at Tavis.

The scout snatched his bow and leaped to his feet, running away from Cuthbert's tunnel. Trying to reach the passage now would only draw the giants' attention to it and put him in a difficult defensive position. It would be far wiser to lure his pursuers away, then circle back later to close the door.

"Stop, little fella!" Bhurn yelled.

"What fella?" demanded Gragg.

A loud crash sounded on the slope above, then a small boulder bounced past Tavis's head. He dodged away, barely eluding a second, better-aimed stone.

"Stop, stupid fella!" Meorf yelled.

"Where fella?" Gragg was still standing on the lakeshore, peering toward his friends on the hill's summit. "Gragg don't see nothin'!"

Tavis reached the bottom of the slope and started up the other side of the gulch, intentionally kicking stones down the hill to make it easier for Gragg to find him. If the secret passage was to remain hidden, all three giants had to follow him.

"Wait!" yelled Gragg. "Hill giants friends! Not hurt little fella!"

Two more boulders slammed into the ground behind Tavis. The scout paused and looked back across the gulch.

"Why should I stop? Meorf and Bhurn are too stupid to catch me!" he yelled. "And so is Gragg!"

"Meorf don't need smarts to catch little man!"

"Bhurn neither!"

All three giants hefted their clubs and started after Tavis in great, bounding steps. The scout turned and scrambled up the slope. He moved swiftly and in near silence, his feet instinctively seeking out the firm, quiet footing of grass tufts and rocky crags. Now that all three giants were on his trail, he no longer needed to make himself an easy target.

Tavis reached the summit a few moments later, without the necessity of dodging any more boulders. Ahead of him lay the gray crests of dozens of hills, interspersed with shadowy black ravines similar to the one behind him. Out of every third gulch rose the yellow glow of a campfire. The scout did a quick count of the amber lights. Assuming that his three pursuers came from a typical campsite, he estimated that more than a hundred hill giants had encircled Cuthbert Castle.

Tavis turned around to see that Meorf and Bhurn had already crossed the gulch and climbed halfway up the slope. Gragg was still picking his way up the rocky gulch, grumbling bitterly about his difficulties. The scout cursed the giant's stupidity. He had expected the brute to traverse the hillside instead of clambering up the treacherous gully bottom. Slipping around the trio would be much more difficult with one straggling behind.

Tavis went over to a large boulder perched on the summit of the hill. Hoping to slow Meorf and Bhurn enough for Gragg to catch up, the scout pushed the heavy stone down the slope.

"So long, you oafs!"

The scout did not linger to see if his plan worked. He turned and bounded down the other side of the hill, making as much noise as possible. After descending two dozen paces, he stopped and nocked an arrow, then quietly circled back to the summit and hid behind an unruly hedge of juniper bushes.

To his dismay, the scout saw Gragg standing in the gully below, gasping for breath and bracing himself against a tree. Meorf and Bhurn, on the other hand, were standing on the summit less than twenty paces away. Both giants were staring into the next dark gully, their eyes searching in vain for their quarry.

Meorf growled in frustration, then slowly turned around to face Gragg. Tavis aimed his arrow at the giant's throat. If the brute spied the secret tunnel on the opposite ridge, the scout would silence him before he could speak.

Fortunately for Meorf, he was more interested in his rotund fellow than the opposite wall of the canyon. "Stop wastin' time, Gragg!" he ordered. "Stupid little fella gettin' 'way."

"Meorf and Bhurn go on," Gragg said. "Gragg stay here, 'case little fella come back."

"Come back?" Bhurn scoffed. "Gragg lazy. Dekz not like."

"Dekz not here." Gragg looked away from his companions. "Gragg camp boss. Go catch little fella!"

Bhurn kicked a rock down the slope, then turned to descend the other side of the hill. Meorf stayed long enough to snicker as Gragg jumped up to avoid the stone, then bounded after Bhurn.

Gragg watched the summit for a few moments. When no more stones came bouncing down at him, he found a boulder large enough to support his broad posterior and settled in to wait. Tavis slipped out of his hiding place and crept silently down the hill, keeping his arrow pointed at the giant's back. He did not like killing in cold blood, but such things were necessary in war—and the ring of campfires encircling Cuthbert Castle left little doubt that the giants had come to make war.

Tavis was about halfway down when Gragg's roving gaze fell on the open door to Cuthbert's secret passage.

The giant thrust his head forward, then suddenly rose to his feet.

"Hey, Dekz was right!" he boomed. "Them little fellas gots a secret tunnel! Bhurn, Meorf, come—"

Tavis let his arrow fly.

Gragg's command changed to a deafening shriek as the shaft drilled deep into his kidney. The giant stumbled forward, at the same time reaching behind his back to pluck the arrow from his body. His effort did not succeed, for Bear Driller was no ordinary bow. Tavis's mentor had shown him how to double-bend the weapon and reinforce it with dragon bone, so that any arrow fired from it struck with the force of a horse-driven lance. The shaft had passed into Gragg's kidney, fletching and all, and nothing short of healing magic could remove it now.

The scout nocked another arrow and rushed down the slope. Although he would have liked to ask Gragg a few questions, the firbolg's intention was not to interrogate the injured giant. Kidney wounds were far too painful to allow questioning. Tavis was simply looking for a clean shot that would put Gragg out of his misery.

"Gragg, what all this screamin' for?"

Tavis ducked behind a boulder, then glanced up to see Meorf standing on the summit.

"Where that secret tunnel?"

Gragg tried to answer, but all that spilled from his mouth was a long wail of agony. The injured giant spotted Tavis crouching behind the boulder and stumbled away, urgently gesturing at the scout's hiding place.

"Tunnel there?" Meorf asked.

Gragg shook his head, then collapsed into the gulch and began to thrash about, mad with pain. Meorf screwed his brutish face into an expression of utter puzzlement, then suddenly dropped into a crouch. He glanced over his shoulder. "Bhurn come—"

Tavis stuck his head up and loosed an arrow. He had a poor angle, so the shaft failed to pierce the giant's heart and simply buried itself in the rib cage. Meorf raised hand to the wound, then his jaw went slack with surpris as he felt warm blood on his palm. Tavis nocked anothe arrow and stepped from behind his boulder. He neede a clean shot more than cover.

"Little fella hurt Meorf!" the giant bellowed.

Meorf raised his club and launched himself down th slope. Tavis barely had time to pull his bowstring back then his foe was upon him, club raised to strike. Th scout loosed his arrow.

A red dot appeared on Meorf's belly, and his eye went blank. The club flew from his hands and bounce away, then the giant's immense bulk started to fall. Th scout hurled himself aside, barely reaching the safety his boulder before the impact of the dead body shoo the entire slope.

Tavis wasted no time on self-congratulations, fo Bhurn would be coming, and the scout preferred not t give his foe the uphill advantage. He nocked anothe arrow and sprinted toward the summit, his lungs burr ing from the exertion of the battle.

As the scout approached the top, he felt the groun shuddering beneath Bhurn's heavy steps. Even if he di reach the crest first, Tavis realized, there would be n time to put his advantage to good use. When his hea reached eye-level with the top of the ridge, he stoppe and lay on his belly.

The crown of Bhurn's pointed head appeared a instant later. Unlike Meorf, he approached carefully an quietly, peering over the crest to see what all the yellin was about. Tavis jumped up, his arrow aimed directly a the giant's huge eyeball.

Bhurn froze instantly. "Not little fella!" he gasped "Stupid firbolg!"

"I *am* a firbolg," Tavis answered.

"Oh, no!" Bhurn's eyes gleamed silver with recogn tion. "You Tavis Burdun!"

"That's right." Tavis was as famous among giants as he was among humans, though the giants considered him more a dark avenger than a savior. "How did Dekz know about the castle's secret tunnel?"

The emotion drained from the giant's face. "Bhurn not tell." He pinched his eyes shut in fear, then started to raise his club. "Bhurn die honorable."

"If you wish." Tavis loosed his arrow.

Bhurn fell in silence, and the scout retreated down the slope. He finished Gragg with a merciful arrow, then began the long climb to close Earl Cuthbert's secret passage.

⊹ 5 ⊹

Romance Blossoms

The queen stood at the window of her chamber, on the highest floor of the keep, looking across the lake toward the distant wall of granite and ice that Cuthbert said was Shepherd's Nightmare. It was almost dusk, and by now Tavis would be among those treacherous peaks, picking his way across boulder fields and snowbanks. At least that was Brianna's hope, though she had reason to think otherwise.

Shortly after dawn, the queen had spotted a swarm of giants searching the hills near the secret passage exit. Then, later in the day, she had seen them drag three of their fellows to the lakeshore and burn them on a funeral pyre. Clearly, there had been a fight. But Brianna had no way to know whether Tavis had survived. That uncertainty had kept her at her window all day.

A knock sounded at her door. Brianna composed herself, then called, "Enter."

The latch clicked, and the heavy door creaked open. Prince Arlien stepped into the room, still wearing his enchanted armor and borrowed cloak. He paused at the door to take a silver tray from one of Cuthbert's servants.

"That will be all," he said.

The young woman bowed and pulled the door shut. The prince walked into the room and placed the tray on the table.

"I thought you might need some sustenance." Arlien gestured at the tray, which bore a heap of sliced fruit and two steaming mugs of spiced wine. "You've been in here a long time."

Brianna smiled, gathering the strength to be gracious.

Arlien was the last person she wanted to see, but she could hardly afford to offend her only potential ally—not with the giant tribes uniting against Hartsvale.

"That's very considerate," Brianna said. "But at the moment, I'm not hungry. I'm afraid my stomach feels like a butter churn."

A sympathetic frown appeared on Arlien's face. "Worried about your bodyguard?"

At least call him by name, thought Brianna. "I'm afraid so," she said aloud. "Perhaps tonight we should send out a party to see what happened."

The prince came and stood beside Brianna at the window. Instead of looking at the distant mountains, however, he fixed his gaze on the lakeshore, where the hill giants were using tree boles and rope to assemble a fleet of primitive rafts.

"I don't think a spy party would be wise," Arlien said. "After their losses last night, the hill giants will be doubly alert. Anyone you send is more likely to get killed than to return with news of Tavis."

Silently, Brianna cursed Arlien for being so logical.

When the queen did not reply, the prince said, "But if it makes you feel better, perhaps it's worth the chance."

Brianna shook her head. "I can't risk the lives of good men to settle my nerves."

"A wise decision," Arlien agreed. "But you must keep a clear head. Perhaps you should wear the necklace I gave you. Ice diamonds have a soothing effect on the emotions."

"At the moment, I have no wish to be soothed."

"Pardon me for saying so, but your wishes are not of paramount importance." There was a definite edge to Arlien's voice. "I can do the military planning for you, but the people in this castle are your subjects. *You* must provide the leadership."

Brianna glared down at Arlien. "Are you saying I've let them down?"

The prince met her gaze without flinching. "If you spend the day hiding in your chamber, they'll think you are despairing. They will despair, too," he said. "If you let that—"

"I know what will happen, Prince."

"Then you also know you must be cheerful and strong to prevent it," Arlien insisted. He stepped away from Brianna and ran his gaze over the room. "Where is the necklace?"

Instead of responding, Brianna looked out her window, this time studying the soldiers on the walls below. They were stockpiling boulders next to the catapults, hoisting oil barrels onto the ramparts, soaking wooden roofs with lake water, and performing all the other tasks necessary to prepare a castle for battle. Most seemed grimly absorbed in their duties, but every so often a man would cast an uneasy glance up at the queen. When he returned to work, his shoulders were invariably stooped.

Brianna stepped away from her window. "Thank you for having the courage to point out my failure, Prince Arlien," she said. "But at this time, it would be wrong for me to wear your wonderful necklace. After all, you did tell Tavis you wouldn't press me for an alliance until he returned."

"And Tavis told me that we would *all* do what's best for our kingdoms," Arlien reminded her. "But the necklace is a symbol of friendship, not a wedding gift."

"No matter how you intend it, my subjects would view the necklace as a symbol of betrothal."

Arlien inclined his head. "I'm sure you know your subjects better than I do." He went to the table and picked up the steaming mugs, handing one to Brianna. "But even if you don't need Gilthwit's ice diamonds, you do need your strength. You'll find this drink invigorating. It's a specialty of my land."

Brianna accepted the cup. "Thank you," she said. "I could use some fortification before I inspire the troops."

The queen touched her rim to Arlien's, then they both

drank deeply. The beverage tasted of spices and fruit, with just a hint of honey and wine, and it was every bit as invigorating as the prince had promised. As the libation slid down her throat, a warm, exhilarating sense of well-being spread through her body. At the same time, she realized how famished she was, for she had not eaten all day and felt a little light-headed.

Brianna sat at the table and pulled the tray over. "Perhaps I'd better eat something before I go."

Arlien sat across from her. "A wise idea," he said. "As it happens, I wanted to discuss something else with you."

Brianna slipped an apple wedge into her mouth, then took another long swig from her mug. "As long as you're not courting me." She had to stifle an unexpected giggle. "We mustn't break our promise to my bodyguard."

Arlien reached across the table to pat her hand. "Oh, we'd never do that," he said. "As a matter of fact, I bring this up because of something he asked of me."

Brianna slipped a pear half into her mouth, then raised her mug to her lips again. It seemed the more she ate, the thirstier she grew, and the more she drank, the hungrier she became. The queen took a cherry off the plate and popped it into her mouth. "What did my bodyguard ask?"

Arlien looked at the tabletop. "It has to do with Cuthbert," he said in a reluctant tone. "Tavis suggested I keep an eye on him, and, frankly, what I've seen amazes me. The man's either a fool or a traitor."

Brianna stopped short of slipping another apple wedge into her mouth. "I can assure you, he's neither."

"Then perhaps you'd care to tell me why he's positioning the catapults on the ramparts overlooking the lake and putting the ballistae in the gatehouse?"

"I'm sure he has his reasons," Brianna replied. She slipped the apple wedge into her mouth and chewed, annoyed with both Arlien and her bodyguard for so constantly assailing Cuthbert's honor. "Perhaps we should go and ask him."

Arlien was quick to shake his head. "I already have," he growled. "He uttered some drivel about a collapsing bridge and ballistae missiles being more effective in the water."

"What's wrong with that?" Brianna reached for her mug and discovered it was empty, but Arlien quickly pushed his own over to her. "His explanation sounds perfectly reasonable to me."

"Perhaps, if we couldn't see the giants building rafts." Arlien pointed to the window. "But it looks to me like they're too smart to attack across that bridge."

"I don't know if you've spent much time with hill giants, but I have," Brianna replied. "They aren't smart."

"Maybe not, but whoever's commanding them is," Arlien countered. "And he's certainly wise enough to know a competent engineer would trap Cuthbert's bridge."

"I suppose that's true," Brianna replied. She lifted Arlien's mug to her lips, but restrained herself to a few sips. It had occurred to her that her sudden show of thirst might seem unladylike to the prince. "What would you do, Prince, and why?"

Arlien rested his elbows on the table and leaned forward, fixing his brown eyes on hers. Brianna's gaze wandered over the prince's cleft chin, full lips, and patrician nose, and she was surprised to find herself silently thanking the King of Gilthwit for sending a handsome son to court her.

The prince touched his graceful finger to the tabletop and traced a line that roughly paralleled the ramparts facing the hill giants. "I would place the ballistae here, where they command the water approaches," he said. "And I would soak the missile heads in oil, so that we can set them afire. That will do more to stop the giants' rafts than hurling boulders at them."

"And what of the bridge?" Brianna asked. She sipped some more of the prince's libation.

"I would use the catapults to cover it," he said. "If the giants are foolish enough to try that approach, the boulders will keep them in the water after the bridge collapses."

"If that's what you think, that's what we'll do." Brianna drained Arlien's mug, then rose to her feet and started toward the door. "I'll go tell the earl."

"Good," Arlien said. He did not rise. "And you know what else I think, Brianna?"

The queen stopped and turned to look at the prince. He was so handsome—blurry, but handsome. "No, I don't," she said. "How could I know that?"

Arlien smiled, revealing a row of pearly white teeth. "I think you should put on my necklace," he said. "I don't see how there can be any harm in wearing it while we're alone, do you?"

Brianna considered this for a moment, searching for the flaw in the prince's logic. She could sense that there was something wrong in his assertion, but her mind was too clouded—damn wine—to identify what was bothering her. She went over to her trunk and reached inside to open the secret compartment.

* * * * *

The gorge ahead was definitely the entrance to Shepherd's Nightmare, and even from the distant edge of a spruce copse, Tavis could see that the giants had beaten him to it. The small farm at the mouth of the canyon, so carefully detailed on Earl Cuthbert's map, lay in ruins. All three buildings had been pushed off their stone foundations and smashed beyond recognition. The livestock lay scattered across the trampled fields in bloody heaps of fur and bone, and the small stream that flowed out of the valley above now boiled over the remnants of a smashed dam.

This isn't war, Tavis thought. It's mayhem, brutal and vicious.

It was also the end of any hope that the siege against Cuthbert Castle would be quickly relieved. If the giants knew about Shepherd's Nightmare, and it was apparent they did, they would certainly take pains to guard the pass. Tavis would never be able to bring an army back through, at least not without a difficult battle. Such a delay would give the giants plenty of time to storm the castle and capture Brianna.

Tavis slipped out of the pine copse and went forward to investigate the farm more thoroughly. The scout discovered the first human corpses in the pasture. The farmer and his three helpers had made their stand behind the wall, but stacked stones offered little protection from a giant's incredible strength. The men had been knocked various distances across the bloody heath, and now lay twisted and broken beneath droning clouds of flies. Still, as the scout kneeled briefly beside each body, he could tell that all four had died bravely. They had fired every arrow in their quivers, and near each man lay a sword or farm axe he had probably been swinging as he had fallen.

In the soft pasture, Tavis also found the giants' tracks. There were only two sets, both too large for hill giants, with a narrow span and long, graceful toes. The scout thought immediately of stone or fire giants, but ruled out both. Fire giants would have burned the farm, while stone giants took no pleasure in pointless cruelty. The only thing he could say for certain was that the tracks were too small for fog giants or—thankfully—storm and cloud giants.

Tavis took a few minutes to crisscross the pasture, looking for more tracks. He found none. If the raiding party had consisted of more than two giants, they had not approached through this field.

The scout went to the main yard, where he found the

grain stores heaped in a pile and stinking of untold gallons of urine. Next to the stores lay the torso of an old woman, the limbs ripped off as a cruel child might tear the legs off an insect. The evil brutality made the scout think of an ettin, but that made no more sense than fire or stone giants. The tracks in the pasture were too large. More importantly, there had been two sets, and ettins, the most bestial of all giants, never traveled in pairs. The monsters had two ugly heads that could barely get along with each other, much less the two heads of another ettin.

Whoever the killers were, Tavis hoped he would find them somewhere nearby. For the first time in many years, he truly burned with the desire to kill.

The scout went over to the main house, which had been a large structure of mortar and rock. To his relief, no arms or legs protruded from the rubble, and he saw no vermin to suggest that bodies lay buried out of sight.

Near the corner of the house he found a large obsidian flake that seemed strangely out of place among the granite and diorite stones of the building. One side showed the conchoidal fractures typical of the glassy mineral, but a skilled hand had clearly worked the other side into a rounded edge.

Tavis held the flake between both hands. The shard could only have come off a stone giant's club, but he could not believe stone giants would be responsible for this carnage. They were rather cold and distant, but hardly evil.

The scout considered the possibility that another giant had been wielding the club, perhaps having acquired it in trade. But that failed to explain the footprints. The tracks *did* resemble those of stone giants, especially the narrow insteps and long toes. Tavis could see only one reasonable conclusion: stone giants had razed this farm, and they had taken pains to do it brutally. They wanted to anger whoever discovered the carnage, to make him so furious that he became careless.

The murderers had succeeded with part of their plan, at least. Tavis could feel all manner of fiery passions burning in his breast. But the scout would not grow careless. He was too experienced at this sort of thing.

Tavis tossed the flake aside and pulled one of Basil's runearrows from his quiver. Killing hill giants with regular arrows was one thing, but it would be quite another to down a stone giant with a wooden arrow. Their hides were so tough that even Bear Driller lacked the power to slay one of the brutes with a single shaft. For that, he needed magic.

Keeping the arrow ready to nock, Tavis crept around to the back of the farm, to the mouth of Shepherd's Nightmare. The gorge was narrow and wet, with sheer walls of granite and a tangled mass of bog spruce rising from its swampy floor. A single goat trail led up the valley. In the soft mud the firbolg found many pairs of fresh footprints. Most were clearly those of humans, probably women and young adults, but the scout also found two sets of stone giant tracks.

The scout started up the canyon at a run. Maybe Brianna's plan wasn't lost after all. With a little luck, he could slay both stone giants and prevent them from telling any of their fellows about Shepherd's Nightmare. Perhaps he could even save the refugees. Tavis just wished that he understood why the stone giants had taken such pains to annihilate this particular farm.

* * * * *

One of the barrow wheels started to squeal again. Although Avner doubted anyone was awake at this late hour, he turned the cart down a side passage, then grabbed his oil flask and kneeled down to lubricate the axle. It wouldn't do to have someone hear him—not with a biotite folio in his cart, and especially not on the second floor of the keep, where Arlien and several more of the earl's uninvited guests were lodged.

To Avner's grave disappointment, the barrow was working out poorly. The cart had been relatively quiet on the way up to Basil's chamber, but he had been unable to keep the wheels from clunking on the steps as he had descended. It had developed the annoying habit of squealing at the most dangerous points of his journey. Still, the boy did not know what else to do. The folios were so heavy that last night he had been forced to drag the first volume up the stairs in his cloak, a procedure that had resulted in loud and unpredictable bangs. Nor could he ask Basil for magical help. The runecaster had already put off drawing the stink rune until after the third delivery. The youth did not want to give the sly verbeeg an excuse to delay longer.

Having slopped a liberal amount of oil on the axle, Avner put the flask away and started to back into the main corridor. A shrill squeal echoed off the stone walls. The youth cringed, then set the cart down and reached for the oil flask again.

The squeal continued, only this time it sounded more like a woman's chortle. Avner continued to listen, for the way the chuckle erupted from deep in her throat seemed all too familiar. It took the youth only a moment longer to be certain that it was the queen's voice. He stepped around his cart and went to Arlien's door.

Inside the chamber, Brianna stifled her laughter long enough to say, "Fill it again, dear Prince."

"Again?" Avner cried. He threw the door open.

Brianna sat on the bed in rather immodest nightclothes, with one hand looped through the crook of Arlien's arm. Her low-plunging collar framed a necklace of gleaming blue jewels that could be only the ice diamonds Tavis had described to Avner. In her free hand the queen grasped a large mug, which the prince was filling from an earthenware flask.

Arlien's only concession to the hour was that he had

taken the cloak off his enchanted armor, revealing a smooth slit where the breastplate had been jaggedly ripped the day before. Even the prince's terrible wound looked better, with the edges closed to form a long red scar.

Brianna squinted into the doorway, then suddenly jumped up. "Avner? What are you doing here?"

"I've come to ask you the same thing, Majesty." Avner stepped forward and found goosebumps rising on his arms. The chamber was freezing. "Is this the way you repay Tavis's devotion?"

"My relationship with T-Ta—" Brianna stopped, her eyes growing vapid. "My relationship with my bodyguard is not your affair!"

Avner's mouth fell open. "You can't say his name!" The youth cast an accusing look at Arlien. "What have you done to the queen?"

The prince slipped off his bed, smiling patiently. "Done to her? I have no idea what you mean, I'm sure." He took Brianna's arm and looked up into her eyes. "Tavis is only a word. I'm sure the queen could say it if she wished."

"Of course," Brianna replied.

Arlien looked back to Avner, his smile growing less generous. "Now run along to bed, boy, and leave us to discuss the business of our kingdoms."

"I doubt the business you're discussing has anything to do with your kingdoms." Avner stepped forward to glare into Arlien's eyes. As he brushed past Brianna, he noticed that the air seemed to grow even colder. "I know what's going on here."

"Do you?" The prince seemed amused. "Pray tell."

"You're taking advantage of Tavis's absence to—"

"Avner!" Brianna interrupted. "I will not put up with this!"

Arlien raised a hand. "Let him continue, please."

Avner was more than happy to oblige. "Why aren't you out trying to get help, Prince? You're well enough."

The youth jabbed his fingers into the rent in Arlien's armor, and the prince did not even grunt. "You see? But you'd rather stay here to discuss your 'business' than do something brave, like Tavis!"

Arlien's eyes narrowed. "Let me tell you two things, boy," he hissed. "First, if you ever touch my person again, I shall be forced to break your arm. Second, I volunteered to help Tavis however I could, and he asked me to protect Queen Brianna."

"He didn't ask you to seduce her."

Arlien's lips grew white. Avner was tempted to jab the prince's wound again to see if the man had the courage to make good on his threat, but the youth decided he might have need of his arm in the near future.

At last, Arlien regained the power to speak. "Young man, you must have a low opinion of your queen if you think she could be seduced so easily," he said. "She merely came down to look after my wound, and I offered her a warm drink. Now, I am done explaining myself. You may leave."

Avner looked to Brianna. "Are you coming?"

"It's hardly the place of young pages to order their queens about," Arlien growled.

"It is when they're under an enchantment!"

Avner grabbed the ice diamonds hanging from Brianna's throat. A cold, stinging pain shot through his hand, and his arm went numb clear to the elbow. The youth cried out, barely managing to open his stiff fingers and pull his arm back. His hand had gone white with frostbite.

"Avner!" Brianna clutched her chest where his hand had brushed her breast. "What in Hiatea's name are doing?"

"The necklace." Avner had to speak through clenched teeth. "It's enchanted."

"As a matter of fact, it is," Arlien said. "It will freeze the hand of any thief who touches it. And I can't abide thieves!"

The prince shoved Avner out the door with such force that the youth bounced off the far wall of the corridor. Arlien followed close behind and caught the boy on the rebound, then turned to push him toward his own room.

Avner's barrow stood at the end of the corridor, clearly silhouetted against the flickering torchlight in the main hall. Prince Arlien released his grip and marched over to the cart.

"Avner, is this yours?" the prince demanded. He reached into the barrow and tipped the folio up. "And what's this inside? One of Earl Cuthbert's folios?"

Brianna stepped into the hall. "Avner!"

"It's not for me," he began. "I'm just borrowing it for—"

"What you were doing is plain enough!" Arlien snapped.

Brianna locked her arms stiffly at her sides, as if restraining the urge to strike the youth. "You betrayed my trust!" she spat. "You're as bad as Basil!"

"But—"

"Be quiet!" the queen snapped. "You just stand there while I figure out what to do with you."

"If I may, I have a suggestion," said Prince Arlien.

"Please tell me," Brianna said. "I'm too angry to think."

"Return the folio to the library before its absence is noticed," suggested the prince. "Basil has already embarrassed you quite enough with the earl, and Cuthbert's just the type to seize this as an excuse to turn us out."

"Don't you think you're exaggerating?" Brianna asked.

The prince shrugged. "Perhaps, but why take the chance?" he asked. "Even if I'm wrong, admitting that there's a second thief in your party will only lead to more distrust and resentment on Cuthbert's part. Wouldn't it be better to take care of this problem ourselves, and limit our arguments with the earl to matters of strategy?"

Brianna considered this for a moment, then nodded. "You do have a point." She turned to Avner. "Do as the good prince suggests, and put that folio back exactly where you found it."

Arlien scowled as she issued the command. "The boy can't be trusted," he said. "I was thinking we would return the book ourselves."

Brianna shook her head. "You'll wake up the entire keep clanking about in the armor," she said. "Besides, Avner wouldn't dare disobey me again—would you?"

The youth lowered his eyes. "Certainly not, Majesty."

"Good. When you're finished, return to your chamber and wait for me there," she said. "I'll inform you of your punishment in the morning."

Avner bowed to Brianna and started to leave, but Arlien caught his shoulder. "Do as you're told, young man—and don't even think about taking that folio to Basil's room instead," he warned. "I'll be watching."

"At least that'll keep you out of the queen's bedroom," Avner muttered. He tried to jerk free, but the prince's fingers were as powerful as dragon talons.

"What did you say?" Arlien demanded.

The youth looked away and grumbled, "Nothing."

"It would be best if you made that a habit," the prince said. He released Avner's arm, then added, "Think about it."

"I'm already thinking." He was thinking that something seemed very wrong when Brianna could not say Tavis's name, and that, with the future of two kingdoms at stake, the "good prince" might well use a magic necklace to win Brianna's heart. The youth was also thinking that anyone who enchanted the queen of Hartsvale would not hesitate to kill one lowly page, and Avner had no illusions about his ability to protect himself.

If he wanted to see the dawn tomorrow, his only choice was to leave Cuthbert Castle tonight. "You can be sure of that." Avner grabbed the handles of his barrow and started for the keep basement.

✦ 6 ✦
Shepherd's Nightmare

Tavis crested the canyon headwall. Ahead of him la
an undulating meadow of alpine tundra, traversed b
ribs of gray bedrock and partially enclosed by a jagge
wall of peaks. A single granite pinnacle stood for war
from the rest, tipped slightly outward like an ogre'
snaggled fang. It could be only Wyvern's Eyrie.

Near the bottom of the spire, perhaps a hundred fee
off the ground, a lone stone giant was creeping across
narrow rock shelf. From across the emerald meadov
the brute looked like a tiny spider, pulling himself for
ward one limb at a time. Ahead of him, seven smalle
specks, undoubtedly humans, were scurrying aroun
the shoulder of the mountain. It seemed apparent tha
their pursuer would catch them long before they reache
the narrow pass at the end of the ledge.

Tavis snatched a runearrow from his quiver an
started toward the pinnacle at a trot. The firbolg kept
careful watch on the meadow around him, keenly awar
that a second stone giant could be lurking behind any o
the ridges ahead. At the demolished farm the scout ha
found two pairs of giant tracks, and both sets had led u
the canyon into the vale ahead.

As the scout crossed the meadow, Wyvern's Eyrie an
everything on it grew more distinct. He saw that th
ledge was really a series of broken rock lips linke
together by graying logs. The giant's heels hung over th
edge of the narrow shelf, forcing the brute to keep hi
face pressed to the cliff. Tavis could even tell that th
party of humans consisted of four women, two little girl
and a brawny shepherd boy armed with a long pitchforl

The youth kept looking back toward the giant as though aching for a fight he had little hope of winning.

One of the women pointed at Tavis, and the whole procession stopped to look.

"Keep going!" Tavis yelled, continuing to run.

Had there not been a chill wind blowing down from the peaks, the farmers might have heard the firbolg's resonant voice. As it was, however, they stood on the ledge, watching Tavis while the giant crept closer. The scout broke stride long enough to wave them on, but still they waited. When he scrambled up the first of the bedrock ridges traversing the meadow, two of the women pointed to the third crag ahead.

"Be . . . watch . . . giant!"

Tavis could barely hear their shrill voices coming to him on the wind. He waved in acknowledgment, and the farmers turned away to continue their escape. The giant behind them slid across the ledge, coming within three arm-lengths of the shepherd boy. The scout considered stopping to shoot now, but at three hundred paces he was barely inside Bear Driller's range. Given the runearrow's heavy tip and the contrary wind, he had no reasonable chance of making the shot.

Tavis continued forward at his best sprint, angling away from the ambush the farmers had warned him about. He glanced up at the ledge every third step. The giant drew to within two arm-lengths of the boy, and then one. The youth stopped on a log bridge and raised his pitchfork, and that was when Tavis realized accuracy was not as important as he had thought.

"No!" the scout boomed, yelling so hard that his throat went raw. He scrambled up the next rocky bluff. "Keep going!"

The youth glanced down, and the giant made a grab for him. The boy ducked, then thrust his pitchfork at his attacker's huge hand. The wooden tines snapped, and a grim chuckle echoed down from the mountain. The youth slipped back a step, then hurled the useless weapon at his foe. The giant let the stick bounce off his head and slid one foot onto the bridge. The boy turned to flee.

"That's right," Tavis whispered. He nocked his runearrow and drew his bowstring to fire. "Get off the bridge."

The second stone giant rose from behind the ridge ahead and bounded across the meadow, trying to slip between Tavis and his target. The scout kept his gaze trained on Wyvern's Eyrie, silently beseeching the youth to hurry. His entreaties did no good. He found himself looking into a pair of huge black eyes long before the boy reached the end of the bridge.

"It would be better not to do that." The giant's voice was as deep and gravelly as a pit mine. He stooped over, lowering his palm toward Tavis. "Why not give me your toy?"

The scout side-stepped the colossal hand and let his runearrow fly. He saw the shaft sizzle straight toward the bridge, then the giant blocked his view by trying to squash him with a boulderlike fist.

Tavis leaped backward off the bluff, screaming, "Basil is wise!"

If the runearrow exploded, the scout did not hear it. He slammed into a boulder and felt Bear Driller slip from his grasp. His attacker's fist crashed down on the ridge above, sending a deafening crack across the meadow and spraying shards of bedrock in every direction. The giant twisted his fist back and forth, as a man might grind a fly into the table, and did not seem to notice that his quarry had escaped.

Tavis tried to crawl away, only to discover that he had fallen between two boulders and become lodged in place. He reached past his head to grab a handhold. As he dragged himself free, a jagged knob of stone opened a deep gash in his back. The scout swallowed his pain

nd continued to pull, his teeth clenched to keep from
rying out.

The movement drew the stone giant's attention. The
rute's rigid face showed no emotion, but he quickly
ifted his hand and peered at the crater beneath it.

"Missed," he observed in a dispassionate voice.

The giant leaned over the bluff to reach for his prey,
ut could not quite make the stretch. He pulled back and
stooped over behind the ridge.

Tavis leaped to his feet and started toward Bear
Driller. A huge boulder crashed onto the tundra in front
of him. He looked up and saw the giant clambering over
he bluff, a second stone in his hand. The scout feinted a
dash toward his bow. The stone giant's arm came for-
vard, but the brute checked his throw.

"It is written that you are a guileful one," the giant
observed.

"Written?" Tavis echoed. He kept his knees flexed,
eady to dive for his bow the instant the giant made the
mistake of committing to an attack. "Where?"

"In the Chronicles of Stone." The giant's gaze flick-
ered to Bear Driller and back to Tavis, and he wisely
restrained the impulse to make the first move. "Where
lo you think?"

"Then you know who I am?" As he spoke, Tavis
crouched behind the boulder the giant had just thrown
at him. He stretched a hand toward his bow. "I don't see
how you could. There are thousands of firbolgs in the
ce Spires."

"But few runts." The giant stepped on the boulder,
pressing it into the ground. "And only one who serves
he queen of Hartsvale."

"Then you have me at a disadvantage," Tavis said.
Although he could feel his heart pounding, he remained
poised to roll away. "Who are you?"

"I am known as Odion," the giant answered.

"Well, Odion, what now?" Tavis cast a longing glance

toward his beloved bow.

"We will have no more of your tricks." Odion posi
tioned the boulder in his hand over Tavis. "That will only
prolong matters."

The scout sprang forward and smashed an elbow into
the soft spot below Odion's kneecap. The joint popped
and straightened, drawing a deep grunt from above. The
giant dropped his stone, but Tavis had slipped between
the brute's legs and was already darting toward the
bluff.

"Come Tavis! This isn't worthy of you."

Tavis scrambled over the stony ridge without respond
ing. A loud clatter sounded from the other side as Odion
gathered up an armful of throwing boulders.

"Only through the grace of acceptance does one tri
umph over death," admonished the giant. "In every
other aspect your life has been recorded with great
esteem. I pray you, do not sully that account with a
graceless end."

Tavis drew his sword. "You may write that I have no
intention of ending my story here," he called, crouching
behind the bluff. "Let that decision reflect on my annals
as it will."

The scout crept silently forward, hunched over and
staying close to the ridge. After a dozen paces, he
judged it safe to glance at Wyvern's Eyrie. A great star
burst of scorched granite now marred the cliff's silvery
face. Nothing remained of the bridge except the ends of
splintered logs, with Odion's partner dangling from one
of the stubs by a single hand. The stone giant's feet
scraped madly along the cliff, while his free hand
slapped blindly at the ledge above, where the shepherd
youth was dodging back and forth, smashing the brute's
fingers with a large stone. The four women had sent the
young girls ahead and stopped at the next bridge. Two
of them kneeled at each end, working furiously to cut
the heavy logs free.

Tavis heard a loud thump behind him and looked over his shoulder. Odion was leaning over the bluff, staring at a boulder he had just dropped where the scout had been earlier. Realizing the quickest way to defeat the giant would be to give him a false sense of confidence, the firbolg jumped to his feet and zigzagged across the tundra as though terrified.

"This is not worthy of you, Tavis!" A boulder sailed past the scout and thudded into the tundra. "It is your time. Face death as bravely as you faced life!"

Tavis changed directions, narrowly dodging a second stone. He hazarded a glance back and saw Odion bracing for another throw, with three more boulders cradled in his arm. The scout darted to one side and slowed his pace. The next ridge was less than fifty paces away, and he wanted the giant close behind when he reached it.

A frightened cry rang out from Wyvern's Eyrie. Still darting and weaving, the scout looked up to see the giant's free hand close around the shepherd boy. In the same instant, the four women came charging down the trail with a heavy log under their arms. They rammed it into the stone giant's head, and the brute fell away, still holding the shepherd youth in his hand. He disappeared behind the ridge ahead, then a terrible crash shook the meadow.

Odion hurled two more stones. One passed so close to the scout's sword that the steel blade tinkled like a wind chime. Tavis changed directions and heard one more boulder thump down behind him. He glanced back and saw that his pursuer had no more rocks in his arms.

"Surely, now you will concede to the inevitable," Odion called. Despite a pronounced limp, the giant's long strides were quickly closing the distance between him and Tavis. "Even you cannot hope to escape two of us."

Tavis could only guess what his looming foe saw on the other side of the ridge, at the base of Wyvern's

Eyrie. Odion's partner was probably shaking off the effects of his long fall. It would take more than a hundred-foot drop to kill a stone giant.

The scout headed directly for the bluff. Odion caught up in three strides and stooped over to grab his quarry. Tavis threw himself into a forward roll and returned to his feet five paces shy of the ridge. He pumped his legs hard, bounding toward the bluff as swiftly as a stag.

"There is nowhere to go," Odion said. "Accept your fate."

The shadow of the stone giant's hand crept over Tavis. The scout leaped into the air and braced his feet against the side of the bluff, then sprang back toward Odion.

Tavis landed almost exactly where he had intended, requiring only one quick step to place himself beside his foe's leg. He swung his sword hard, then felt a sharp snap as his blade sliced through the delicate tendons behind the giant's knee. Odion bellowed, and his leg buckled. He pitched forward, his huge body folding over the bluff like a corpse over a saddle.

The firbolg grabbed a handful of bloody flesh and pulled himself up Odion's leg. The pain-stricken giant did not react until Tavis started to climb his back, and by then it was too late. When the brute tried to turn over, the scout placed the tip of his sword between two ribs.

"Go ahead and roll," Tavis said. "You'll drive the blade in for me."

Odion wisely returned to his stomach. The firbolg's blade was hardly more than a dirk to him, but a dirk was long enough to puncture a lung. "What is your intention?"

"I hope it isn't to kill you," boomed the second stone giant. "I have not prepared myself to lose a son."

Tavis instantly recognized the sonorous voice. "Gavorial!" The scout pressed the tip of his sword into the back of Odion's neck, then looked up to see a familiar, grimly lined face. "I had thought never to see *you* again."

"Nor I to see you—and both our lives would have been the better for it," Gavorial answered. The stone giant opened his hand to display the shepherd youth he had snatched from the side of Wyvern's Eyrie. The boy was battered and trembling with fear, but he was alive. "Yet here we stand, and now you must surrender—or burden your spirit with the weight of this boy's death."

* * * * *

Avner dived into the moldering grain, burrowing deep and fast. The oats and barley were damp and rank, but he tried not to think about what he smelled. The foul odor would keep anyone from poking around the heap, and that made it an ideal hiding place. He continued digging until he neared the other side, then cleared an eyehole so he could see the wrecked farmhouse and most of the rubble-strewn yard.

The giants had been little more than sticks on the horizon when Avner had stepped out of the spruce copse, but already they were close enough for the youth to see that they were frost giants. They had milky skin and bushy beards that ranged in color from dirty ivory to ice blue, and most were dressed in sleeveless jerkins and kilts made from some long-furred hide. They all carried double-bladed axes large enough to fell a mature spruce in a single swipe, and the leader wore a skullcap with two ivory horns.

When the giants reached the farm boundary, the leader thrust the heel of his hobnailed boot into the rock wall and stepped through the resulting breach. He stopped just inside the main yard, sending the other giants to inspect all corners of the farm. As they spread out, Avner counted fifteen of the milky-skinned brutes. The leader stomped up to the main house and began poking through the ruins, grunting angrily and kicking the stones in disgust.

One of the warriors called to him from the other side of the grain pile. Avner could not understand the words of the icy voice, since the fellow was speaking a racial dialect. This surprised the youth. The tribes of the Ice Spires had long ago embraced Common as their primary language, but he had heard that some giants still used their own tongues as a matter of pride.

When the frost giant leader circled around the pile to answer the warrior's summons, Avner quickly retreated through the grain and opened a new spy hole. He found the two giants squatting beside the limbless torso of an old woman. The leader nodded in approval and slapped the flat of his axe blade down on the corpse. He bared his blue teeth in a cruel smile and rose.

"I didn't think stone giants had the stomach for this work." In contrast to his subordinate, the leader spoke Common.

The warrior snickered an answer, again in tribal dialect. Avner had no idea what the fellow was saying, but he had to bite his lip to keep from crying out in surprise, for he did recognize one word: Gavorial.

Gavorial had served in the Giant Guard, which had once protected the monarchs of Hartsvale. When Brianna had forced her father to abdicate, it had been Gavorial who carried the addled king away, and who had warned Tavis that the giants would not rest until they delivered the queen to the Twilight Spirit. If the stone giant was a part of this, then Brianna was in greater danger than anyone knew.

As Avner watched, the frost giant leader reached into his belt purse and withdrew a rumpled parchment. He unfolded it and stretched it tight, then slowly scanned the surrounding area. After a moment's study, the leader pointed toward the back of the farm, where the mouth of a narrow canyon led to Shepherd's Nightmare.

A cold, sick dread welled up inside Avner. Somehow, the frost giants had learned about the secret pass, and that spelled disaster for Tavis.

When the youth considered what he could do to help his friend, his jaws began to ache as though he were going to retch. He had to cover his mouth and pinch his nostrils shut against the terrible odor of his hiding place, and even then he feared his gagging would draw the frost giants' attention to the grain pile. His best hope of survival lay in staying hidden, but then the giants would be between him and Tavis, precluding any possibility of alerting the scout to his peril. Unfortunately, the boy's other options, such as drawing the giants away or trying to sneak into the canyon first, seemed almost suicidal. Still, the youth had to do something. He could not sit by and let the frost giants tromp up the canyon to kill Tavis.

Avner crawled back through the grain heap, then pulled his sling from inside his tunic and peered into the yard. He saw only two frost giants on this side of the farm. They stood about a hundred paces away, peering into a tangled stand of scrub pine beyond the boundary wall. The youth slipped out of his hiding place and grabbed two rocks. A hundred yards was a long way for his sling to hurl a missile, but he didn't need to be accurate.

Avner fit a stone into the pocket and whirled the cord over his head, then released the rock. The stone arced high into the air, sailing toward the wood, off to one side of the giants. As it passed over their heads, the youth was already placing his second stone in the sling.

The first missile dropped into the forest, bouncing off a tree trunk with a sharp crack. The heads of both giants swiveled toward the sound. Avner hurled his next stone, angling it slightly away from where the warriors were now looking. As the rock reached the top of its arc, he jumped back into the moldering grain.

Avner barely had himself covered before the two giants yelled for their companions. The youth retreated through the pile, amazed to discover that the odor no longer sickened him. Now that he was doing something, he felt better.

By the time Avner reached the other side of the heap, the frost giant leader and all his warriors were tromping off to investigate the pine stand. Avner crawled from his hiding place, then took a deep breath and sprinted for Shepherd's Nightmare.

*　*　*　*　*

Gavorial waited a long time for an answer, and Tavis knew he would continue to wait. Stone giants were a people of infinite patience, given to careful deliberation and long pondering, so it would seem only natural to one that the scout would consider his response carefully. But Tavis had known the instant he heard the ultimatum what his answer would be. Now he was considering ways to reconcile his duty to the queen with his compulsion to save the shepherd youth's life.

The boy himself was the first to break the lengthy silence. "Don't surrender, Tavis." The youth's cracking voice was a fearful contrast to his brave words. "You've done right enough by my mother and my sisters. All I ask is that you kill that one while you can—just like he and his father killed my brothers and father!"

Strictly speaking, the relationship between the two giants did not parallel that of the youth to his father and brothers. Blood ties were not as important to stone giants as philosophical and spiritual heritage. Odion was more an apostle to Gavorial than a true son, but the boy's thirst for vengeance did spark an idea in Tavis's mind.

"Gavorial can still catch your family," said the scout. "They won't be safe until he and I come to an agreement."

"Agreement?" scoffed the youth. "Did you not see what these monsters did to our farm? How can you think he'd honor his word?"

"Because he's a stone giant." Tavis locked gazes with Gavorial, searching in vain for some hint of the stone giant's thoughts. "He won't have it written in the Chronicles of Stone that he broke a pledge."

"Just so," agreed Gavorial. "And I pledge to release the boy and his family if you surrender without harming Odion."

Tavis shook his head. "You know I can't do that, Gavorial," he said. "My duty—"

"It is no longer possible for you to fulfill your duty," the stone giant interrupted. "Even if you elude me, you cannot keep your promise to Brianna. As we speak, fifteen of my cousins from the snow are ascending the canyon."

"Frost giants?" Tavis gasped. He almost allowed the tip of his sword to stray from Odion's ribs.

Gavorial nodded. "We have lured you into a trap," the giant said. "Accept your fate with grace. At least you will save this boy and what remains of his family."

The scout felt his legs go icy and weak, though not because he feared the frost giants. To set their trap, the giants had to have known he was coming—and that meant they had a spy in the castle. Tavis's thoughts leaped immediately to Cuthbert, but he also realized there was another possibility: Arlien. The prince seemed honest enough and brave, and he had even been wounded by a giant, but the mere fact that he was a stranger made him suspect. Perhaps Gavorial could be maneuvered into revealing which of the men had betrayed Brianna.

"I had not thought Cuthbert's loyalties to the old king ran so deep," Tavis said. "Or that Camden would be fool enough to try taking his kingdom back."

"Camden already believes he has recaptured Hartsvale," Gavorial replied. "The old king sits in his grotto from dawn to dusk, wearing a granite crown and sending invisible messengers to phantom earls. He has no part in this."

"Then why is Cuthbert helping you?" Tavis demanded. "To save his castle?"

"I have no knowledge of the earl or his motives," Gavorial said. "Odion and I were called to this place and so we came."

"Called by whom?"

"You know by whom," Gavorial answered. "I warned you what would happen."

"The Twilight Spirit planned this?" Tavis gasped. "He's here?"

"So it is best for you to surrender," Gavorial replied, dodging the question. "You cannot stop us, and now you are too far from Brianna to use your golden arrow."

"That may be true," Tavis said. "But I am no stone giant. For me, the only graceful death is a fighting one."

Gavorial's gaze flicked from Tavis down to Odion, his black eyes betraying his sadness.

"Do not despair, Father," said Odion. "I am ready."

Gavorial nodded and began to close his fingers.

"Wait!" Tavis called. "Your son and the boy can do nothing, and we must fight no matter what becomes of them." He lifted his sword from Odion's back. "Let us spare their lives and resolve this ourselves."

"That'll be no good!" the shepherd youth objected. "As long as there's one giant alive, my sisters are still in danger!"

"I'm sure Odion would pledge to leave them alone and return home," Tavis said. "If that's agreeable to Gavorial."

The stone giant kneeled on the ground, answering with a swiftness uncharacteristic for his race. "It is."

"But this is not necessary, my father!" Odion objected. "I have prepared myself."

"I know, my son, but it is also not necessary that you die," Gavorial said. He opened his hand and allowed the shepherd youth to step onto a bluff. "Tavis is right. The battle has come to him and me. Make the pledge."

Odion remained silent for several long moments, until the scout began to fear the giant would defy his father. Finally, however, Odion said, "I make the pledge. I shall return home as quickly as my wound allows, having nothing more to do with the war against Hartsvale."

Tavis lifted his sword and saluted Gavorial. "Then it is done," he said. "Now it is you and I, old friend."

"I would that it were not so," the giant answered, rising.

Tavis spun. He covered the length of Odion's spine in three long strides and leaped onto the blood-soaked tundra. From behind him came a loud clatter as Gavorial tore handfuls of stone from the bluff. The scout rushed toward the next ridge at a full sprint, trying to cover as much distance as possible before the giant began hurling boulders.

Gavorial had a different strategy in mind. Tavis heard a loud sizzle behind him. His back exploded into stinging pain, and he felt himself being driven forward by a spray of gravel. He pitched into the tundra face first, tiny stones hopping across the meadow all around him.

Tavis rose to his knees. His back was raw and wet, with dozens of stone shards poking him like hot nails. The scout gritted his teeth and twisted around to see Gavorial looming above the bluff. Odion sat nearby, holding his injured knee and showing no interest in the fight. The shepherd youth stood on top of the ridge, watching the battle with terrified eyes.

Gavorial grabbed a boulder and stepped over the bluff.

Groaning in pain, Tavis pushed himself to his feet and resumed running. The scout counted three steps before feinting a dodge to his left. When he heard Gavorial grunt, he angled in the opposite direction. The giant's boulder crashed down a good five paces away, then bounced once and came to rest.

Tavis sprinted straight to the next bluff, tossing his sword onto the summit when he arrived. He felt the ground trembling as Gavorial rushed across the meadow. The scout grabbed a handhold and began to pull, dragging himself up the rocky face in three moves. Behind him, the tundra hissed as Gavorial's tremendous weight smashed it down.

Tavis peered across the top of the crag. His sword lay directly before him, the tip pointing at his nose and the hilt turned so that it lay two feet beyond his grasp. The scout felt a gust of hot breath brush across his back. Guessing what Gavorial would do next, he leaped to the left, reaching for a jagged spine of stone that angled out from the cliff.

Gavorial's open hand slammed into the bluff behind the firbolg. Tavis grabbed the rock spear and swung his legs up hard. He spun over the spike, launching himself toward the bluff's top.

Tavis's feet touched down first, exactly as he had planned, but he had too much speed and tumbled over backward. Gavorial's black eyes appeared in the sky above. The scout did a backward somersault, at the same time reaching for his sword. Gavorial closed his fingers, forming a fist as large as a cloud, and his hand started down. Tavis felt the hilt of his sword and grabbed, pointing the tip up.

The giant's huge fist struck dead on. The pommel clanged against the rocky bluff, driving the blade deep into Gavorial's hand and snapping the steel.

The stone giant bellowed in pain and jerked his hand away, spraying Tavis with hot blood. The scout tossed the useless hilt aside and rolled to his feet. He raced three steps across the bluff and leaped toward his bow. Gavorial sprang onto the bluff behind him, and a loud crash rumbled across the meadow.

Tavis landed and snatched Bear Driller on the run. He ducked behind a stone Odion had hurled at him earlier, then pulled a runearrow from his quiver and nocked it. The firbolg raised his head and saw Gavorial leaping down from the ridge, a huge foot kicking at the boulder.

Tavis did not see the enormous heel strike, or even hear the crash. He simply found himself flying through the air in terrible pain, with Bear Driller sailing in one direction and the runearrow in the other. He landed in a limp heap and bounced across the tundra, tumbling head-over-heels an untold number of times.

When he finally came to rest, the scout did not wait for his head to stop spinning. He jumped up and lurched off in the direction he thought his runearrow had flown, knowing that any move would be safer than waiting for Gavorial to stomp on him. His chest ached where the giant's kick had driven the boulder into him, and his breath came in ragged gasps. The runearrow lay less than five paces ahead. The fletching hung in tatters, but the shaft and head remained intact.

Tavis felt a jolt and thought his knees had buckled, then realized it was only Gavorial's heavy steps shaking the ground. The scout stooped over to grab the runearrow and saw the shadow of a huge foot fall over it. He pulled his hand back, empty, and leaped away. The stone giant's foot came down hard, sending a shudder through the entire meadow.

"Basil is wise!" Tavis yelled.

The scout felt the explosion in the pit of his stomach, a terrible impact that seemed to arise from somewhere deep inside his own being. He found himself hurling through the air amidst a crimson spray laden with smoking flesh and pulverized bone. He did not hear the boom until much later, after the shockwave had slammed him to the ground fifty paces from where it had picked him up. The cool mountain breeze carried the sickening smell of charred meat to his nostrils.

A harsh, anguished moan filled Tavis's ears. At first he thought he might be making the horrid sound, reacting to some injury he had not yet sensed. But the scout had at least a vague awareness of his body, and while he ached all over, he felt no stabbing pains or unexplained numbness. He rose to his knees and looked in Gavorial's direction.

The stone giant was not making the noise, either. He lay propped on his elbows, watching the stumps of his legs pour blood into a smoking crater. His gray skin had turned white, and he held his jaw clenched against the pain, but his black eyes seemed more interested in the process of dying than fearful of it.

The moaning ended in a single cry of despair, and Tavis looked toward the bluff to see Odion's grief-stricken face peering down at his mentor. "My father!"

Gavorial looked up, then motioned to Odion. "Come, my son. The time has come for us to say our farewells."

Dragging his injured leg behind him, Odion clambered over the bluff and slipped down to sit at his father's side. "You have not left me yet." The giant pulled off his tunic and began to rip it into tourniquet strips. "I can drag you back to Stonehome."

Gavorial laid a hand on his son's arm. "How can I continue to walk the warrior's path without legs?" The stone giant began to shiver, and his voice grew weak. "Let me depart proudly the life I have chosen."

Odion's big shoulders fell into a slump. He slipped an arm around Gavorial's neck and cradled his father's head in the crook of his elbow. "It shall be written that you died with pride and grace, my father."

Gavorial managed a weak smile. "Let it also be written that I was felled by the dauntless firbolg Tavis Burdun," he said. "And that we both fought well, in causes as legitimate as they are ancient."

Odion nodded. "I shall inscribe the record myself."

Tavis rose and started forward to say his own farewells, but before he had taken three steps, a deep groan slipped from Gavorial's mouth. The giant's black eyes went gray and vacant, and the purple shadow of death crept down his face.

Odion let Gavorial's head slip from his lap, then stood and looked to the eastern horizon. "I shall see you in Twilight, my father."

The stone giant turned and limped away, leaving Gavorial's body behind as though it were no longer of consequence.

The shepherd boy clambered down the bluff and ran to Tavis, panting heavily from his long sprint. "You won!"

The scout shook his head. "I prevailed," he corrected. "Gavorial was not evil, and in killing him I also lost."

The youth shrugged. "You survived. I'm glad of that."

Tavis nodded. "We can be thankful for that." He looked down at the youth. "What is your name?"

"Eamon Drake at your service." The youth bowed. "And you would be Tavis Burdun, am I right?"

"You are," Tavis answered. He looked toward the ledge on Wyvern's Eyrie, where the boy's mother and sisters still stood, nervously eyeing the injured giant limping toward them. "Can you get back onto the ledge with your family?"

"They have a rope they can lower."

"Good." Tavis pulled one of his regular arrows from his quiver and handed it to the youth. The shaft was only an inch shy of being as tall as the boy. "Take this to Earl Wendel. He'll recognize it by its length and know you speak in my name. Tell him the giants have trapped Queen Brianna in Cuthbert Castle."

The boy's eyes went wide.

"Earl Wendel is to send a rider to summon the Queen's Guard from Castle Hartwick, and he is also to gather as many warriors from his own fief and those of his neighbors as he can," Tavis said. "When the Queen's Guard reaches Wendel Manor, you are to lead the entire army back over this pass. Do you understand?"

Eamon managed to close his gaping mouth, then nodded. "You can trust in me."

Tavis clapped the boy's shoulder. "I know I can."

"Sir, if you don't mind me asking, what are you going to do?" the youth inquired. "You've seen how narrow the canyon is. You'll never get past all those frost giants."

"Don't you worry about that," Tavis said. He pulled Basil's runemask from his satchel and turned toward Gavorial's corpse. "They won't even try to stop me."

❖ 7 ❖

Dangerous Ford

Sitting in the sun, with the smell of pine thick in the air and the sound of water gurgling off the gorge walls, Tavis could have fallen asleep. With a cool breeze wafting down the canyon and a pair of white-winged dippers sweeping low over the stream, it was the kind of day that called out to his firbolg blood, enticing him to rest and enjoy the most valuable of all the treasures the mountains had to offer: an afternoon of blissful, unsullied tranquility.

But even if his duty had permitted such a thing, the scout felt sure the frost giants coming up the canyon would bring the respite to a premature end. From his hiding place behind a boulder he could see fifteen of them filing through the gorge below, their pale, bushy beards and milky skin visible even from a distance of several hundred paces. They were just beyond the crest of a silvery waterfall, preparing to cross the stream at a narrow ford. The first warrior was climbing down to the water alone, while his fellows waited on the trail more than a dozen paces above.

Tavis cursed the giants' caution. The ford was perfect for an ambush, located in one the narrowest places in the canyon and flanked on both sides by high, sheer walls of granite. There was even a large beaver pond less than two hundred paces above the waterfall. If the giants had been foolish enough to cross the stream en masse, the scout could have fired a runearrow into the dam and unleashed a flood that would have washed them all down the gorge.

Tavis did not understand why the frost giants were being so careful today. In a race notorious for its bluster, such caution seemed out of place, almost as though they were expecting trouble. The scout hoped the brutes had not somehow learned of his triumph over Gavorial.

Tavis slid down from his hiding place and retreated up the trail to a small clearing. He sat down next to a pool of still water and took Basil's runemask out of his satchel. It now resembled Gavorial's death mask rather than a smiling human face. The open mouth had tightened into the indifferent grimace of a stone giant, silver lids had descended to cover the gaping eyes, and the magical runes in its surface had rearranged themselves into crow's feet and worry lines.

Tavis set Bear Driller on the ground next to him, then took off his sword belt and placed the mask over his face. A biting chill seeped from the cold silver into his flesh. His skin went numb, though he felt the muscles below being tugged and stretched as the runecaster's magic folded his visage into the deeply lined image of a stone giant. He did not feel as though he were growing to giant size, but he did sense a dull ache in the bones of his skull and face. His jaw dropped and lengthened into a drooping chin, while his nasal septum descended to form an arrow-shaped nose. A pair of deep, permanent furrows etched themselves into his brow, then his bronze hair began to fall out and he saw it floating away on the breeze.

Tavis found the whole process more uncomfortable than painful, thanks in large part to the mask's icy numbness. When the stretching and tugging at last seemed to stop, he leaned over the still pond. The reflection he saw sent a cold chill creeping down his spine, for he felt as though he were looking at a small version of Gavorial's ghost.

A painful lump formed in the scout's throat as his Adam's apple began to swell. He found himself first gasping for air, then unable to draw breath at all. His pulse started to pound in his ears, and he could feel his black eyes bulging from their sockets. A distant ringing echoed in his ears. The canyon started to spin, a black

fog formed at the edges of his vision, and Tavis knew
Basil had made some horrible mistake.

The dark fog grew thicker, until the firbolg could
barely see Gavorial's black eyes staring back out of the
pond. The scout braced his hands on the pool's marshy
bank, fighting against his creeping lethargy. If he fell
unconscious, he would choke on his own Adam's apple,
and then there would be no one to stop the spy from
betraying Brianna.

Tavis's arms trembled, and a terrible thought crossed
his mind. Basil could be the spy! The runecaster himself
had once admitted that verbeeg nobles prided themselves
on treachery, and what if he were a noble? Nothing could
be more perfidious than to earn the queen's confidence,
only to slay her bodyguard and betray her to the giants. It
would make him a legend among his fellows!

The scout fell back onto his haunches and reached up
to tear the mask away. To his horror, he discovered it
melded so completely with his own skin that he could
not grasp the edge. He flailed about blindly and found
his sword belt, then drew his dagger from its scabbard.
He had trouble holding the handle, for he did not seem
able to close his fingers around the hilt. He took it
between his thumb and forefinger like a needle, then
pressed the tip behind his ear.

That was when the scout heard a whistling wind and
felt the air being drawn into his lungs. His Adam's apple
remained painfully swollen, but it no longer prevented
him from breathing. As his foggy vision began to clear,
he rolled his dagger between his fingers. It felt more like
a thorn than a dirk. The weapon had shrunk—or rather,
he had grown larger.

* * * * *

Avner pushed the end of a sturdy tree limb under the
enormous stone, then laid the middle of his makeshift

lever on a fir trunk fulcrum. Holding the setup in place with one foot, he peered around the boulder into the gorge below. He was standing on the canyon rim directly above the beaver dam, just high enough so he could see over the waterfall to where the frost giants were fording the stream. The first two had already waded across and started climbing the steep slope on the other side. The leader and most of the others remained out of sight, hidden behind a bulge in the canyon wall.

Avner sighed in disappointment. He had hoped all the giants would cross the ford at the same time, but they had grown too wary to make such mistakes. The youth had been pushing boulders down on them all morning, and once he had even sent a log jam down the stream, nearly catching them as they waded across a stretch of churning rapids. His exertions were taking a heavy toll on his strength, and he feared this might be the last ambush he had the energy to prepare.

Avner slipped behind his boulder and peered over the top, checking the details of his plan one last time. On the other side of the stone, a steep slope descended twenty paces to the gorge rim. Forty feet below that, no more than ten paces from the canyon wall, lay the beaver dam. If everything went as intended, the rock would smash the stick barricade apart. He had hoped the resulting flood would sweep the entire giant party away, but he would be happy enough if it delayed them for a few minutes.

The youth was about to put his plan into action when he noticed the gray figure of a stone giant slipping out of the trees. The fellow was on the other side of the pond, coming down the canyon toward the frost giants. Avner could not make out the face, but after hearing Gavorial's name at the farm, he knew who he was seeing.

The youth decided to delay his ambush and see what came of the meeting. Besides, if he attacked before Gavorial passed the beaver dam, it would be a simple matter for the stone giant to cross the stream and capture him.

Soon Avner could see the giant well enough to recognize Gavorial's arrow-shaped nose and slender jaw. The youth continued to watch as the giant passed the beaver pond. Instead of descending the steep gully to meet the frost giants, Gavorial climbed into the narrow channel below the dam and crossed the stream. He walked to the edge of the waterfall and braced himself on the gorge wall, then leaned over to peer down at the frost giants below, where a third warrior was crossing the ford.

"Go back!" Gavorial yelled, speaking in Common. The stone giant's rough voice easily overwhelmed the rumbling waterfall. "I have no need of you here!"

"That is not for you to say, Sharpnose!" The frost giant's throaty words were less distinct than Gavorial's, but still understandable. "Julien and Arno bade you wait in the pass. Why have you defied them?"

"I have done battle," Gavorial answered. "And now Tavis Burdun will not cross Shepherd's Nightmare."

"You killed him?"

"All that he owned is mine," the stone giant confirmed.

Gavorial's words struck Avner like a warhammer, filling his breast with a dull, crushing pain. He stumbled back and barely noticed as he tripped over his fulcrum.

"No!" Avner gasped. "Nobody can kill Tavis Burdun— not even Gavorial!"

The youth remained where he was, trying to understand the impossible things he was hearing.

"Tavis was to be ours!" The frost giant's words echoed up from the gorge. "You robbed us!"

"You were too slow," Gavorial replied. "The battle started before you arrived."

"Through no fault of our own, Sharpnose!" the leader growled. "You left a *traell* on the farm. He slowed us."

"A human?" Gavorial's voice sound doubtful. "A single

human stopped so many frost giants?"

"A single human you could not kill," the frost giant countered. "Perhaps because you wanted him to slow us down, so you could present the body of Tavis Burdun to Julien and Arno!"

Noting that this was the second time the giant had referred to Julien and Arno, Avner repeated the names so he would not forget them before he saw Tavis. In spite of Gavorial's words, he could not bring himself to believe the scout was dead.

"There is no corpse," the stone giant called.

"No corpse?" the frost giant stormed. "Why not?"

"The battle was fierce," Gavorial explained. "When it was over, a few drops of Tavis's blood were all that lay on the tundra."

"Hagamil will not believe that, and neither will I!" The frost giant sounded almost happy. "Without a body, how do we know you really killed him?"

"Perhaps this will persuade you."

Avner peered over the boulder and saw Gavorial holding a hickory bow. Though the weapon looked almost tiny compared to the enormous stone giant, the youth instantly recognized it as Tavis's Bear Driller.

A fiery red light blossomed inside Avner's head, then a churning storm of rage and pain boiled up inside him. Tavis was the only father the orphan had ever known.

"Liar!" Avner yelled. "You could never kill Tavis!"

Gavorial twisted around, his mouth hanging agape. The frost giant leader reacted more forcefully, shouting a string of orders in his tribal language. The three warriors that had already crossed the stream glanced up to see where Avner's voice had come from, then resumed climbing at double speed.

"This is for Tavis!" Avner yelled.

The youth scrambled up the slope and pushed down on his lever. The stone tipped forward and hung there. Avner yelled in frustration and threw all his weight onto the limb. The rock broke free with a soft grating, then rumbled down the slope.

* * * * *

Tavis was still wondering why Avner was in the canyon when the boulder came bouncing down the slope. The scout watched the stone sail off the cliff top and arc toward the beaver dam, and then he understood at least one thing: the youth was the *traell* who had been harassing the frost giants—and he was far from finished.

Tavis slipped Bear Driller into Gavorial's mouth—the firbolg found it difficult to think of the enormous gray body as his own—and reached for a handhold on the canyon wall. Avner's boulder smashed into the beaver dam with an ear-splitting crash. Shards of wet, broken stick flew down the canyon as far as the waterfall. Tavis dug his fingers into a small ledge and scraped his feet along the rocky face, searching in vain for knob or shelf on which to step.

A loud, gurgling roar rumbled down the gorge. Tavis looked upstream and saw a frothing wall of water and sticks boiling toward him. The pond was draining fast, ripping the dam apart in great hunks.

Tavis stopped searching for a foothold and pulled with his hands alone. Gavorial's body rose off the ground, but the effort of lifting such an immense bulk was even more exhausting than Basil had warned. The scout's fingers felt like they would rip from his hands, while his shoulders and forearms already burned with fatigue. He continued to drag himself up the cliff, knowing his pain would be worse if he allowed the flood to sweep him over the waterfall.

The scout's chin had barely risen as far as the tiny ledge when the waters caught his feet. Gavorial's massive body slipped sideways. Tavis jerked his legs out of the water and pressed his bent knees against the wall, trembling from the strain of holding the awkward position.

The firbolg peered down. It seemed an immense distance from his head to the churning flood below. The raging waters were continuing to rise, scraping at his toes with sharp sticks torn loose from the dam. A snort of exhaustion shot from Tavis's large nostrils, and his breath began to come in short, panicked spurts. He had to fight his own instincts to keep Bear Driller between his lips, for Gavorial's oxygen-starved body demanded that he open his mouth and start gasping. The scout craned his neck, searching for a more secure position higher on the cliff.

Tavis's eye fell on a broad crevice angling across the face ten feet above. A firbolg could have crawled inside the crack and rested, but not a giant. On the other hand, the fissure would have been well out of a firbolg's reach. Not so for a giant. The scout pulled himself chest height to the ledge, then stretched a hand toward the crevice.

Gavorial's long arm made the reach easily. Tavis slipped his hand into the crack and knotted it into a ball, twisting it sideways to wedge the fist in place. He tugged twice. The rough stone dug deep into the hard stone giant flesh, and the scout knew he would not slip. He braced the soles of his feet on the cliff and leaned back, anchoring himself in a secure tripod position. With his free hand, he took Bear Driller from his mouth and gasped for breath. The muscles of his arms and legs knotted into aching lumps, but he hardly cared. As long he kept his hand wedged in the crevice, he would not fall.

The scout glanced behind him to see three frost giants scrambling toward the ruined beaver dam, their eyes fixed on the rim of the canyon. Tavis followed their gazes and saw the angry youth glaring down at him, no doubt trying to think of some way to dislodge him. The firbolg waved Bear Driller in the boy's direction, hoping Avner might remember Basil's runemask.

The youth spat and yelled something, but Tavis could not hear it over the roaring floodwaters. The boy made no move to escape, and the scout began to fear he intended to give battle.

The three frost giants reached the half-drained beaver pond and crossed its muddy bed in three strides. Moving with calm deliberation, they went to the cliff and boosted one of their number high enough to reach the rim of the gorge. As the warrior slowly pulled himself over the top, Avner took his sling from beneath his cloak and loaded a stone.

"Don't harm the child!" Tavis yelled in Gavorial's booming voice. "That boy is like a son to Queen Brianna! Julien and Arno can make good use of him."

Avner whirled his sling over his head, then whipped it in Tavis's direction. The stone sailed straight at the scout, but he was powerless to dodge or twist away. The rock struck him squarely in the ribs, sending a surprisingly sharp pang through his chest. Tavis groaned, nearly falling into the floodwaters when his aching muscles twitched.

The three frost giants chuckled in delight. Avner grabbed another stone.

"Still want us to catch him alive, Sharpnose?" It was the warrior atop the canyon rim who cackled the question.

"That's what Julien and Arno would want," Tavis answered. Although he had never heard the names before, it seemed apparent that Julien and Arno were leading the assault against Brianna. "I'm sure you'll be well rewarded if you capture him alive—and severely punished if you do not."

This silenced the laughter of the frost giants. The warrior on the canyon rim lay down and dangled an arm over the edge. One of his fellows boosted the other one up to grasp the proffered hand. Avner loosed another stone, striking the brute atop the cliff in the back of the head. The giant yelled in pain, nearly dropping his companion.

"Don't let go, Egarl!" roared the dangling warrior. "Or, by Thrym, I'll cleave your skull!"

"Don't swear oaths you can't keep, Bodvar," advised Egarl. The frost giant glanced over his shoulder. "And you, *traell*! Stone me again and I'll smash you flat as a pond."

The youth yelled something Tavis could not hear, then flung another rock at Egarl. The frost giant cursed and pulled Bodvar up the cliff. Avner slipped his sling into his jerkin and grabbed the tree limb he had used to pry the boulder off the mountain.

"You'd do well to surrender, boy!" Tavis yelled. He glanced down and saw that the beaver pond had finally emptied itself. The floodwaters were subsiding. "No harm will come to you!"

The two frost giants started up the slope. Avner heaved his lever at them. The branch landed far short, then tumbled end-over-end toward its targets. Egarl caught the heavy limb in one hand, then tossed it into the gorge as though it were a stick.

Avner kicked his fulcrum loose. The fir trunk rolled down the hillside toward the frost giants' ankles. Bodvar let the log roll into his hand, then snapped it in two and dropped the pieces at his feet. He continued to climb.

Avner finally turned to flee. As he tried to scramble up the slope, Tavis saw that the youth was exhausted. The boy's legs were barely moving at half speed, and he had to stop every third step to catch his breath.

Tavis climbed down the cliff, then lowered a trembling foot into the subsiding floodwaters. When the current did not threaten to sweep his leg from beneath him, he dropped the rest of the way and started toward the drained beaver pond.

By the time the scout reached the ruined dam, the frost giants had Avner flanked on both sides. The youth feinted toward Egarl, then darted between Bodvar's legs. The giant uttered a cold curse and spun around, snatching Avner up easily.

"Don't harm him!" Tavis yelled. He stepped across the beaver pond's muddy bottom in two quick strides, then went to stand at the third frost giant's side. He raised a hand toward the warrior holding Avner. "Hand him down to me."

A milky hand clasped his arm and pushed it down. "You must think us stupid!" growled the third frost giant. "We caught the *traell*."

"I'll see you get credit," said Tavis. "But I should carry him. I knew the child when I served at Castle Hartwick."

"Liar!" yelled Avner.

Tavis looked up to see the youth's angry eyes glaring down at him. The boy was securely enclosed in Bodvar's fist, with nothing but his head showing over the frost giant's index finger.

"When you were at Castle Hartwick, I lived at Tavis's inn with the other orphans," he said. "The only time I ever saw you was after Tavis chased you off."

The third frost giant narrowed his pale eyes and stared at Tavis in open suspicion. "What kind of trick you playing, Sharpnose?"

The scout silently cursed Avner's irrepressible spirit. So far, Tavis had avoided the necessity of lying, allowing the frost giants to draw their own conclusions from what he said. The boy's sharp tongue threatened to expose his ruse.

Tavis met the frost giant's gaze evenly. "You wouldn't know the *traell*'s value if I hadn't told you who he was," he said. Strictly speaking, Avner was not a *traell*. The name properly applied only to the semicivilized humans who wandered the frozen plains north of the Ice Spires, but frost giants seldom made the distinction. "All I ask is that you let me carry the *traell*."

"No!"

The voice boomed out from the other side of the

gorge, where Tavis saw a frost giant wearing a steel skullcap with ivory horns. The fellow looked large even for his race, with pale yellow eyes and snarling blue lips.

The frost giant started across the pond. "You have Tavis's bow to give to Julien and Arno," he said. "All we have is this miserable *traell*."

"I don't trust you to keep the boy alive, and he'll be no good to Julien and Arno dead," Tavis said. "I'll trade you."

The scout held Bear Driller out to the leader, who was already stepping out of the beaver pond.

"Trade him what?" called Avner. The boy remained gripped securely in Bodvar's fist. "That ol' piece of hickory?"

"That is Bear Driller," said the giant leader. He eyed the bow carefully, but made no move to take it. "I have heard the poets sing its praise often enough to recognize the weapon."

"So?" Avner scoffed. "Just because Gavorial got the bow doesn't mean he got Tavis. I've already caught him in one lie. How do you know he isn't lying about the battle?"

The scout bit his tongue, restraining the urge to tell Avner to shut up. The youth was trying to incite trouble among his captors so he could slip away in the confusion, an art he had apparently cultivated during his years as a street thief. Tavis feared the technique would be the undoing of them both.

The frost giant leader shifted his gaze between Avner and Tavis. "The *traell* does have a point," he said. "Perhaps Tavis dropped his bow while you were chasing him."

"Would he have also dropped his cloak?" Tavis asked, reaching inside his tunic. "And his quiver, his sword belt, and his equipment satchel?"

The scout reached into his large tunic and withdrew each of the items he named, which he had been holding for use after his eventual return to firbolg form. All of the equipment was blood-soaked and tattered from his fight with Gavorial and Odion.

Tavis fixed what he hoped was a stony glare on Avner's shocked face. "Do you still believe Tavis Burdun escaped?"

The youth's eyes swelled to puffy red spheres, and he looked away. Tavis did not enjoy being so cruel, but at least he would no longer have to contend with the youth's sharp tongue.

The frost giant leader lifted his gaze from the blood-soaked gear. "You have convinced me that Tavis is dead, and I think you will convince Hagamil as well," he said. "As for Julien and Arno—who can tell what they will think?"

"Then you'll make the trade?" Tavis asked.

The leader shook his head. "I've no idea why you want the *traell*, but I don't like it, Sharpnose. We'll keep the boy, and you keep your rags," he said. "And don't worry that we'll kill him. Even if Julien and Arno have no use for him, this *traell* has a brave spirit. Hagamil will want to feast him before he dies."

A wave of fatigue rolled through Tavis's body. He slipped his equipment back into his tunic and tucked Bear Driller beneath his belt, trying to find the strength to keep his legs from trembling. He did not know if he had the stamina to continue impersonating Gavorial until he freed Avner, or whether Basil's magic would last until he had the chance. Nor did he know what was happening at Cuthbert Castle, and that ignorance weighed more heavily on him than Gavorial's immense weight.

◈8◈
Traell Country

Tavis groaned. The glacier ahead was a large one, with a high, clifflike snout and a boulder-strewn moraine at least three thousand paces long. Rivers of blue water gushed from several ice caves large enough for a stone giant to stand inside, and the frigid wind hissing off its back had been sopping up the glacial cold for dozens of miles. The first frost giants were already entering a steep chute that ascended to the summit of the terminus, and the scout did not know where he would find the strength to follow them.

After a full day of forcing Gavorial's massive body to keep pace with the frost giants, Tavis was spent to the core. The fatigue seemed as much spiritual as physical. With each step, he felt a cord tugging at that deep place where he stored his courage and fortitude, and his chances of surviving long enough to rescue Avner seemed more remote.

By the time Tavis reached the chute, half the frost giants in line had already started climbing. Still, the trough was narrow, with icy footing that made for slow going, and the scout could see that he had a few minutes before his turn came. Thankful for the chance to rest, he walked a few paces to the valley wall and sat in a dry side ravine. He braced his back against one slope and his feet against the other, then closed his eyes and listened to the wind hiss through the limber pines.

"You stone giants spend too much time thinking and not enough hunting," observed Bodvar, who was standing at the end of the line. "A giant who tires so easily is a poor excuse for a warrior—especially if he's supposed to be the best of his tribe."

Tavis opened one eye and regarded Bodvar stonily. The frost giant was sneering from behind his unruly yellow beard, his pale eyes issuing an unspoken but obvious challenge.

"Tavis Burdun is not an easy firbolg to kill," Tavis said. "Let me rest today, and tomorrow I'll show you who's the poor excuse for a warrior."

The sneer vanished from Bodvar's face. "Thrym stop me! If Julien and Arno had not forbidden challenge fighting, I'd take you up on that offer," he growled. "But I'm sure Hagamil will let me kill you, once all is done."

"By then, it'll be too late to avenge the insult," said Avner, who was tightly gripped in the warrior's fist. Slagfid, the war party's leader, had decided that since Bodvar had captured the *traell*, he would have the honor of carrying the prisoner back to camp. "Gavorial will be long gone. You have to kill him now—if honor means anything to you."

Tavis felt a proud smile creeping across Gavorial's lips. The youth still had not given up hope—far from it; he was taking every opportunity to sow discord among his captors, and trying to avenge the death of a close friend while he was at it.

"What are you smiling at?" demanded Bodvar. "I just might listen to the *traell*."

"And you might get killed," Tavis replied. He knew that any attempt to smooth things over would fail, earning him Bodvar's contempt as well as his animosity. Frost giants respected strength and prowess above all things. "Either way, it makes no difference to me."

The scout closed his eyes and returned to his rest, confident that Bodvar would leave him alone. The warrior would gain nothing by attacking now, for frost giants saw no honor in killing by surprise.

A short time later, Tavis was roused from his nap by a large rock bouncing off his head. "Are you coming,

Sharpnose?" demanded Bodvar's annoyed voice. "Or do you want to spend the night down in this heat?"

The scout rubbed his sore temple and shot a menacing scowl at Bodvar, then braced his hands in the pine needles to push himself to his feet. That was when he noticed a tiny, frightened face peering at him through the boughs of sapling pine.

Tavis blinked twice. The face remained, a small olive-skinned moon with the soft features of an adolescent girl and a halo of black hair. Her flat nose and tiny mouth left no doubt of her race; she was of true *traell* heritage, no doubt from one of the tribes that occasionally crossed the Ice Spires to make a home on the fringes of Hartsvale.

The child's brown, almond-shaped eyes remained moored to Gavorial's grim face, as though she expected the stone giant to reach out and pulp her.

"Well, Sharpnose?" Bodvar insisted.

"Go on," Tavis replied. "I'll be along."

"Can't," the frost giant grumbled. "Slagfid told me to be sure Bear Driller and those rags of yours make it to camp. Hagamil's going to want to see them."

"Okay, I'll come now." The scout pushed himself to his feet.

The girl's eyes widened, but she did not run.

From Gavorial's full height, Tavis saw that the child's hiding place was not nearly as good as it appeared from the ground. He could easily see her crouching behind the sapling, her brown woolen cloak pulled tight around her shoulders. The scout glanced at Bodvar and saw that the frost giant's angle was just as good. If the warrior happened to look in the sapling's direction, he would spot the child.

The scout stepped in front of the girl. "I said I was coming!" he snapped. "You don't have to wait."

Bodvar scowled. "If you say so," he grumbled. "By Thrym's beard, I'd think you'd be in a better humor after killing Tavis Burdun!"

The frost giant started up the chute. Tavis slowly glanced over his shoulder and saw the girl backing away from her hiding place. Their eyes met, then she cried out in alarm and sprinted up the side ravine.

"What's that?" demanded Bodvar.

Tavis returned his gaze to the glacier and saw the frost giant staring down at him. The scout yawned and started forward, dragging his feet to muffle the sound of snapping branches and clattering rocks coming from the ravine behind him.

"Quit your yawning!" Bodvar ordered. "I heard a *traell!*"

The frost giant scrambled out of the chute and brushed past the scout. Egarl, the next warrior in line, was more than twenty paces ahead. He kept his eyes fixed on the ice ramp beneath his feet, too worried about his traction to notice what was happening behind him. Tavis turned around to find Bodvar peering up the side ravine, his free hand cupped to his ear.

"Don't you hear that, Sharpnose?" demanded Bodvar.

Tavis heard it: the soft sobbing of a child in terror. "What should I be listening for?"

"Are stone giants stone deaf?" Bodvar demanded. "The whimpering *traell.*"

Tavis stepped to the frost giant's side and peered up the gully. It was difficult to see much. Both slopes were covered by dense stands of limber pines. The trees had thick, downswept boughs that hung nearly to the ground, providing perfect camouflage for small beasts like *traells* and deer. The small clearings between the trees were full of rocky outcroppings, all the same shade as the child's cloak.

"Are you sure it isn't the wind, Bodvar?" Tavis asked. "I see nothing except trees and rocks."

No sooner had the scout spoken than the girl stepped from behind a boulder, darted up the slope, then vanished between a tangle of pine boughs. The child had already run a surprising distance up the ravine, but Tavis knew that it would not take a frost giant long to catch her.

"I'm sure," Bodvar said. He thrust Avner into Tavis's hand. "Hold this. I'll run that *traell* down."

Tavis accepted the burden, too shocked to reply, and stared blankly down at the youth while Bodvar trundled up the ravine.

"You wanted me, Gavorial," Avner said. "What are you going to do now?"

"Get you out of here," Tavis said. He started down the main valley at a trot.

"Hey, Slagfid!" Avner's voice did not boom like a giant's, but it was loud enough to echo off the canyon wall. "Help! He's stealing me!"

"Quiet! I'm not Gavorial," Tavis hissed. "I'm Tavis."

"Like I'm Queen Brianna!" the boy retorted. "Slagfid, help!"

Tavis stopped and slipped a large finger over Avner's mouth. The youth promptly sunk his teeth into the hard flesh and ripped out a small chunk of gray hide. The scout pinched the boy's head between his thumb and forefinger, holding it steady.

"I'm telling the truth," Tavis said. "I used Basil's mask."

The boy raised his brow and stopped struggling, so Tavis took his bleeding finger away.

"What mask?" The boy's tone was suspicious. "I don't know what you're talking about."

"Of course you do," Tavis replied, glancing toward the glacier. When he saw no warriors pouring out of the chute, he began to hope the frost giants had not heard Avner's cries. He slipped into the woods and started to climb the valley wall. "You remember. We were in Cuthbert's library, and you asked Basil how I could impersonate a giant if I was too small?"

Avner considered this, then a grin of relief spread across his face. Tears of happiness rolled down his cheeks, and he asked, "Aren't you supposed to be in Shepherd's Nightmare?"

"The giants have a spy inside the castle. It was a trap." Tavis was already panting from the climb. "Gavorial and his son were going to block the pass so the frost giants could catch me from behind. If you hadn't delayed Slagfid and his war party, their plan might have worked."

"And you killed both Gavorial and his son?" Avner asked, awed. "Two stone giants?"

Tavis braced himself against a tree and paused to rest. Over in the ravine, he could hear Bodvar crashing through the trees, searching for the *traell* girl.

"I had to kill only Gavorial." He put Avner on the ground. "Odion pledged to return home and have nothing more to do with the war."

"And you believed him?" Avner scoffed. "Now I *know* you're Tavis."

"A stone giant's pledge is sacred," the scout replied. "And speaking of pledges, weren't you supposed to stay in the castle?"

"It's a good thing I didn't," Avner replied. "Bodvar would be carrying *you* into camp."

Tavis pushed off the tree and started up the slope, angling back toward the ravine. "A promise is a promise, Avner," he said. "The last thing you told me—"

"There were circumstances." The youth had to run to keep pace with Tavis's giant strides.

"What circumstances?"

Avner slowed and looked away. "The spy. I know who he is."

Tavis frowned. "Keep moving," he said. "Tell me what you know."

"I saw Brianna with Prince Arlien." The youth hesitated, then added, "Late at night—in his chamber."

A lump formed in the pit of Tavis's stomach. "That

hardly makes him a spy." The firbolg grabbed a tree and used it to pull himself up the slope. "They might have been discussing—"

"Brianna was in her bedclothes—or rather, half out of them," Avner interrupted. "In Arlien's arms."

All the strength went out of Tavis, and he had to stop, head pounding and legs quivering. He doubled over to brace his hands on his knees. "Even if you're sure of what you saw—"

"You think I'd be here if I wasn't?" the youth snapped.

"No," Tavis admitted. His voice sounded rather weak and tinny for a giant, and he wondered if Basil's magic was beginning to wear off. The scout hoped not. He still had business to conclude with Bodvar, and it would be safer if he appeared to be a stone giant. "But the queen must think of Hartsvale."

"Whatever she and Arlien were thinking of, it wasn't Hartsvale," Avner retorted.

Tavis pinched his eyes shut, trying to fight back the image that came unbidden into his mind: an eight-limbed creature of writhing flesh, two backs and two heads, moaning and grunting and smelling of musk . . . The scout didn't have the strength. He slumped to his knees, his entire body trembling, tears of exhaustion welling in his eyes.

Avner was at his side instantly. "What's wrong?"

The scout shook Gavorial's massive gray head. "I'm tired," he said. "Being a stone giant is harder than Basil said."

"You'd better find some strength somewhere," Avner replied. "Because when you hear what I have to say next, you'll want to kill Arlien."

Tavis looked up. "I can't kill a man for the choice a woman makes."

"She didn't make the choice," Avner said. "The prince made it for her."

The scout's jaw clenched tight. "He took her by force?"

Avner shook his head. "By magic," he said. "She was wearing those ice diamonds. I swear they're enchanted. She couldn't even remember your name, and I got my hand frostbitten trying to rip the necklace off."

"Charm magic?" the scout growled. An angry fire began to burn deep within him, renewing his ebbing energies and filling him with a savage, feral strength born of love and fury. "He used charm magic against the queen of Hartsvale?"

Avner nodded.

Bodvar's voice boomed across the slope. "Come out, good little *traell*. Frost giants are nice. Bodvar won't hurt you."

Tavis rose and started up the hill again, still angling toward Bodvar's voice. "You're right about what I want to do to Arlien." The scout spoke as he moved. "But I'm still not sure Arlien is the spy. Was anyone else acting strangely?"

Avner's jaw dropped. "How can you think it was anyone else?"

"Perhaps the prince just wanted to be sure he returned with a queen," Tavis replied. "What he's done is treacherous, but betraying me to the giants would hurt his cause more than it helped. Without the reinforcements Brianna sent me to fetch, the only wedding she'll be attending is in the Twilight Vale."

"Well, no one else was acting like a spy," Avner said.

"What about Cuthbert?"

"The earl wants to see that army more than anyone," the youth answered. "He's scared to death he'll lose his castle."

"That's what worries me," Tavis said. "What better way to save it than strike a bargain with the giants?"

Avner shrugged. "I don't think he's got the guts."

Tavis saw the ravine through the trees. About twenty paces above, it curved sharply toward him and ran across the hillside. From a dozen paces below the bend came Bodvar's brutal voice. "Bodvar sees you, little *traell!*" he called. "You can't hide no more!"

The girl cried out in fear. It sounded as though she had reached the bend.

Tavis handed Bear Driller and the rest of his gear to Avner, then pointed across the slope. "Find someplace to hide," he said. "I'll come as soon as I can."

"What?" the youth nearly screeched the question. "You're not going up there?"

"I can't let Bodvar catch that girl." Tavis heard the frost giant crashing toward the bend. "Not if I can save her."

"What about Brianna?" the youth demanded. "If something happens to you—"

"Nothing will happen," Tavis said. "And if it does, Brianna will be safe. I sent a messenger to Earl Wendel with word of what's happening here."

"I was thinking of Arlien."

Tavis pointed at the runearrows in his quiver. "You know how to use those."

"Against Arlien?" the boy gasped.

Tavis nodded. "If it comes to that."

Avner clutched the equipment to his breast and turned to do as ordered. Tavis resumed his climb, moving as fast as his weary legs would carry him. As he approached the ravine, he saw that above the bend it became something of a gorge, with rocky outcroppings flanking it on each side. He spied the girl standing near the center of the gulch, frozen in fear.

Bodvar's head came around the corner, and his pale eyes went directly to the girl. He stooped over to scoop her up, his long beard swinging like a pendulum over her head. Tavis hurled himself into the ravine. He slammed into the frost giant with a thud, knocking the astonished warrior into the opposite wall.

A sharp crack sounded from the cliff top. Something long and brown sizzled past Tavis's head, then there was a fifteen foot spear standing where Bodvar had been a moment before. The shouts of several angry men echoed down from above. The scout looked up and saw five black-haired humans struggling to pull a small ballista away from the gorge brink.

Bodvar sat upright and stared at the spear lodged in the gully floor. "Sharpnose, you saved my life!" he gasped. "Why'd you do a thing like that?"

Tavis shrugged. "Only Skoraeus knows." As he spoke, the scout kept a sharp eye on the cliffs above. The ambush had caught him unawares, and he wanted no more surprises from the brave little girl and her companions. "You don't deserve it."

Bodvar frowned. "I've smashed my share of *traell* dens," he said, his voice defensive. He stood, then reached down to Tavis. "But reasons don't matter. You did it, and now I owe you a debt."

The scout accepted the proffered hand. "Does that mean you won't be asking Hagamil for a challenge fight?"

"Only if you want—which I truly hope you don't." Bodvar grinned, then said, "I'd be honor-bound to lose."

"That would hardly be amusing," the scout replied. He glanced up and down the ravine, then said, "Let's go, before they attack again."

Bodvar shook his head. "Don't worry, they're back in their holes by now."

"They've done this before?"

Bodvar raised his brow, fixing a suspicious eye on the scout. "You've forgotten what happened when you came to hear Julien and Arno's plan?"

Tavis winced, grinding his teeth together so hard that he tasted powder. "My—uh—my mind's been on other things."

Bodvar fixed the scout with a leery glare, then shook his head. "Stone giants," he grumbled. "You're so lost in your own worlds that you wouldn't notice if Annam returned to this one."

Tavis said nothing.

Bodvar sighed, apparently interpreting the scout's silence as a demand for further information. "The *traells* have been harassing us since Hagamil stomped their village." The frost giant pointed up the slope. "But they escaped into their little mines, and now they keep bothering us. We've already lost three good warriors."

"Three giants?" Such attacks would never drive the giants out, but he was glad to know the *traells* hadn't lost their spirit. "Is that so?"

"'Course it is," Bodvar grumbled. "But don't worry, they won't be back. Let's go get that other *traell* and be on our way."

"*Traell*?" Tavis echoed. He hoped his bewilderment seemed genuine enough.

Bodvar's eyes widened. "The one I gave you!" he rumbled. "You put him someplace safe, didn't you?"

Tavis spread his palms and looked down at his empty hands, trying to appear appropriately sheepish. "I don't have the bow, either."

A blue flush rushed up Bodvar's milky face. "Surtr's fires! You were supposed to hold that stuff!" He grabbed Tavis by the neck and shook him. "Slagfid'll stomp us!"

"It's my fault," Tavis said. "I shouldn't have saved you."

This brought Bodvar's temper back under control. He released Tavis, then started to run his eyes over the ground. "That bow's got to be here somewhere." He looked up at the scout, then asked, "You had the *traell* and bow when you jumped, right?"

Tavis's chest tightened, and a hot flush crept over his body. To answer that question truthfully was to expose himself. But simply refusing to answer, as most firbolgs did in such situations, would only make Bodvar more suspicious.

Bodvar's glare grew more menacing. "You did have

them, didn't you?"

Tavis tried to swallow and found that he could not get past the lump in his throat. He scowled as though thinking, then looked up to meet Bodvar's gaze—the frost giant was about three feet taller than him—and nodded.

Bodvar narrowed his eyes and did not look away.

Runnels of cold sweat began to trickle down the scout's brow. His stomach tied itself into knots, and the exhaustion he had been fighting all day returned with such a vengeance that his knees began to tremble.

Bodvar's lip curled into a contemptuous sneer, then he clapped a hand on the scout's shoulder. "You don't be so scared, Sharpnose," he said. "Even if we don't find 'em, Slagfid's not going to kill us or nothing. Hagamil might, but not Slagfid."

Tavis closed his eyes. "What a relief." The scout's voice cracked as he spoke. He pointed down the ravine and said, "You search in that direction, and I'll look up here. Take your time—Avner's good at hiding."

"Yell if you find anything," Bodvar said.

The frost giant turned around and began his search, overturning boulders and shaking trees so hard that bird nests fell from the boughs. Tavis did the same, though he was careful to keep a watchful eye turned toward the cliff top. In spite of Bodvar's reassurances, he knew that any humans who baited their traps with young girls would not shirk at a few risks.

Tavis glanced behind him and saw that Bodvar was searching very carefully indeed. The frost giant's section of ravine looked as though an avalanche had torn through it, with pines leaning in every direction and a jumbled heap of boulders piled in the center of the gully. The scout silently cursed his companion's thoroughness, then pulled the ballista spear out of the ground and began to poke and prod into crevices and crannies.

About twenty paces up the ravine, the spear pierced something soft. A muffled grunt of pain came from inside the dark nook into which Tavis had thrust the spear. The scout glanced down the gully and did not see Bodvar, though he did hear the crack of a toppling tree around the bend. The firbolg breathed a sigh of relief, but did not withdraw the weapon. Until he could examine the wound, it was best to leave the spear where it was.

The *traell* was not so patient. The weapon jerked once as the victim pulled free of it, then something bright flashed out of the crevice. Tavis had time to realize that the gleam was a steel blade before a battle axe buried itself deep into his big toe.

The scout jumped back, yelling in pain and surprise. The axe pulled free of his foot and rose for another strike. A skinny man with black braids and a gaping hole in his thigh limped out of the cranny. The *traell* swung his weapon again. Tavis jerked his leg away, and the blade sank deep into the blood-soaked ground. The scout brought his foot back and kicked the axe out of the man's grasp.

"Sharpnose?" yelled Bodvar. "What's wrong?"

"Nothing. I have matters well in hand," Tavis could not keep the pain out of his voice, for the axe blow had cut his toe half off. "I'll be fine."

Tavis's attacker stood in front of the crevice, shielding it with his scrawny body and glaring up at the scout. Though the human was trembling with fear, his black eyes showed no emotion but anger and hatred. Behind the man, peering out from the mouth of the nook, stood the girl who had lured Bodvar into the ambush.

"Did you find the *traell*?" Bodvar's heavy steps rumbled through the forest.

"Not Avner," Tavis called. He looked down at the man, then pointed at the cranny and whispered, "Leave your cloak and go!"

The man's expression changed from anger to disbelief, and he seemed too shocked to move. The young girl reacted more quickly, pulling the astonished fellow back into the crevice. She ripped his brown cloak off his back and threw it out, then both humans disappeared into the darkness.

Tavis glanced over his shoulder and saw Bodvar stomping around the bend. The scout used his injured foot to drag the cloak over to the blood-soaked ground, then grabbed the largest stone he could find and raised it over his head.

"Wait!" Bodvar yelled. "Don't kill—"

Tavis hurled the rock down. The effect was perfect. With the axe lying nearby, a corner of the blood-soaked cloak visible, and a crimson stain spreading from beneath the stone, it looked as though the scout had avenged the attack on his toe. He sat down on the stone, then pulled his bleeding foot into his lap and inspected the wound.

The man had clearly known what he was doing. The axe blade had landed in the joint, slicing through the tendons and chipping the toe bone. Until this was healed, Tavis would have a difficult time walking, and running was out of the question. If he wanted to get away from the frost giants now—which seemed wise, given that he had no idea how much longer the magic in Basil's runemask would last—he would have to do it through guile, not speed.

Bodvar pounded up and stopped beside Tavis, then surveyed the bloody scene around the scout's perch. "Didn't you hear me?" demanded the frost giant. "I said—"

"I know what you said," Tavis interrupted.

"Then why'd you kill him?" Bodvar demanded. "Hagamil's been trying to catch one of those *traells* since we got here."

Tavis pointed to his bloody toe.

Bodvar grimaced, but said, "That's nothing."

The frost giant kneeled down and reached into the

neck of his tunic, withdrawing a chain with a large, tear-shaped gem on it. From deep within the jewel's heart scintillated a pale blue light that seemed all too familiar.

Tavis grasped the frost giant's arm. "Bodvar, what's that?"

Bodvar shook his head at the scout's ignorance. "You never seen an ice diamond?"

Tavis wanted to retch, remembering the last ice diamonds he had seen. "Of course," Tavis answered. "But not one so large."

"This thing?" Bodvar scoffed. "This is nothing. You should see Hagamil's. As large as my fist." The giant closed his hand to illustrate.

"They're magic?" the scout asked.

"They never melt, if that's what you mean," Bodvar said. "And you can enchant them, I suppose. But most warriors carry them for other reasons."

The frost giant touched the gem to Tavis's wound. The scout hissed as a bolt of searing cold shot into the gash, then his foot went numb clear to the ankle. The bleeding stopped almost instantly, and he even thought he would be able to walk.

Bodvar slipped the ice diamond back around his neck, then ripped the hem off his patient's robe.

"This will hold you until I can convince Roskilde to heal you," he said, his attention fixed on bandaging Tavis's wound.

"My thanks," Tavis said. He leaned back and braced his hand on the largest stone he could reach. "This is certainly a change from asking for a challenge fight."

"It's little enough after you went and saved my life," Bodvar said. "If it starts to hurt, let me know and I'll touch it with my diamond again."

"What would I have to do to get one of those diamonds?" Tavis asked. "Where do they come from?"

"You could never find one yourself," Bodvar said, knotting the bandage. "Not unless you can follow the

Boreal Lights to the heart of the Endless Ice Sea—and you'd be the first stone giant I've met who can do that."

"Then the diamonds don't come from Gilthwit?"

"Gilthwit?"

Bodvar looked up, his pale eyes as unreadable as ice, and fixed his gaze on Tavis. The scout gripped the stone beneath his hand, fearing that he had betrayed his disguise. He had realized that was a possibility when he had asked the question, but there had been no choice. The answer would tell him who the spy was, and once he identified the spy, he would know how much danger Brianna was in.

At last, Bodvar stood. "How could they come from Gilthwit?" asked the frost giant. "That place is just a legend. Like I said, ice diamonds come from the Endless Ice Sea."

"And no other place?"

" 'Course not. Only the Endless Ice Sea's cold enough to forge 'em," Bodvar answered. "But you don't have to go out there to get one. We can trade for it."

Tavis released his hold on the stone. If ice diamonds came only from the Endless Ice Sea, then the Prince of Gilthwit was a liar—and probably an imposter as well.

The frost giant slipped an arm around Tavis's waist to help him stand. "We'd better be getting back," he said. "Slagfid'll be wondering where we got off to."

"You go ahead—and blame Avner's loss on me," Tavis said, making no move to rise. "I'm going to keep looking."

Bodvar hoisted the scout up. "Don't be stupid. With that foot of yours, you wouldn't last an hour before the *raells* get you," he said. "And now that we don't have the boy, you're the only proof we got that Tavis Burdun is dead."

"But your chief will never take my word!"

A cunning grin crept across Bodvar's lips. "Slagfid wasn't exactly telling you the truth," he said. "The only reason Hagamil wants a body is so he can give it to

131

Julien and Arno and claim that we frost giants kille Tavis Burdun by ourselves. When we show up witho any other proof, he'll be real mad—but he won't hu you. He needs you to tell Julien and Arno what ha pened. They'll be even madder than him tomorrow they don't know for sure that Tavis is dead."

"What's so important about tomorrow?" Tavis asked.

Bodvar glanced down the gulch, then lowered h voice to a whisper. "We're not supposed to tell you, b that's when we're meeting Julien and Arno," he sai "They're gonna have Brianna, and they want to be re sure Tavis Burdun can't come kill her."

⇒ 9 ⇐
Storm Warning

"Do you have everything you need?" Brianna inquired.
We want this weapon ready before the giants attack."

The queen and her retinue had stopped behind a dis-
ssembled ballista that five of Cuthbert's soldiers were
antically reassembling. Next to the weapon lay a stack
f harpoons with pitch-soaked rags swaddled around
eir tips. On a nearby merlon hung a torch, a ribbon of
lack, bitter smoke rising from its head.

"Can I get anything to help?" Brianna asked again.

"It's only a broken skein, Majesty," said the sergeant
f engines.

A rough-featured soldier with purple circles under his
yes and a two-day stubble of beard, the sergeant was
e only man to meet the queen's gaze. The other four
ept their eyes fixed on the ballista. Although they
ffected an attitude of preoccupation, it did not escape
rianna's notice that their hands had fallen idle.

"I reckon we got time to fix it," the sergeant contin-
ed, "providing you let us alone." Without awaiting the
ueen's leave, he turned back to his work.

Brianna felt someone brush past her, then Arlien had
is hand on the man's shoulder. "The queen did not dis-
iss you!" the prince snapped. "Show her the proper
espect!"

Cuthbert stepped forward and pried Arlien's hand off
he sergeant's shoulder, then placed himself between
he two men. "Blane has not slept since the giants
ppeared," the earl said. "I'm certain he intended no dis-
espect."

"That's no excuse," countered Arlien. "When a man is

tired, discipline is more important than ever. In Gilthw[
we—"

"This is not Gilthwit," interjected the earl. "I will n[
have my men bullied about by a stranger."

"Then teach them to honor their queen," the prin[
replied.

Brianna drifted down the rampart, absentminded[
fingering her ice diamonds and leaving the men to the[
quarrel. Arlien was right, of course. The sergeant a[
his men *had* failed to show the respect due a queen, b[
she thought it was probably Cuthbert's place to disc[
pline them instead of the prince's—not that the ea[
would do such a thing. He was soft for an earl, perha[
too soft. Arlien was right about that, too.

Brianna glanced back at the ballista, where the tw[
men were continuing their argument. Behind the[
stood Selwyn, captain of her own Company of the Wint[
Wolf. He was resplendent in his iridescent chain ma[
and purple tabard, looking anywhere but at the two me[
hissing venom at each other. If the disagreement bot[
ered him so much, the queen wondered why he didn[
take one side or the other and put an end to it. Probab[
because he was a sycophant, just as Arlien said. He cut[
dashing enough figure in battle, with a war fever bur[
ing in his eyes and his silver axe flinging gore, but brin[
the man into a castle court, and his courage vanished [
fast as a marmot down a hole.

Brianna suspected she should go back and put an en[
to the quarrel, but feared it would appear she was takin[
sides. That would be as damaging to morale as the arg[
ment itself. She had placed Arlien in charge of the forti[
cations because he seemed so knowledgeable about th[
art of war, and she did not want to do anything to unde[
mine that credibility. However, Selwyn had also reporte[
that most of Cuthbert's soldiers were grumbling abo[
serving a foreign prince, so she could not afford to sa[
anything that might further that impression. The who[

sue of command had become such a muddle that she
ared the confusion would do more than the giants'
oulders to bring down Cuthbert Castle.

Once, not long ago, Brianna would have known how
> solve the problem. But these days it seemed that the
ueen's thoughts swam through a fog, drifting aimlessly
bout her mind with no apparent purpose. And Avner's
isappearance had made matters worse. She could not
elp worrying about the boy, and whenever his name
rossed her mind, whatever she had been thinking van-
hed into the cold whorl where her heart had been.

Arlien said her nerves were causing the confusion,
ut the queen knew better. It was the wine in that
amned libation. Brianna had told him not to put any
1ore spirits in his concoctions, and she was going to
top drinking the stuff entirely—just as soon as she felt
trong enough to do without the extra fortification.

Unable to watch the argument any longer, Brianna
tepped over to an empty embrasure. The hills across
1e lake were bare, all the trees that had once covered
1em now lashed together and floating in the shallows,
vhere more than a hundred giants were piling boulders
nto their primitive rafts. Each craft appeared large
nough to hold four giants, with a simple rudder on the
tern and a single lateen-rigged mast. Although the
atchwork sails were presently furled, the queen knew
hat once they were unfurled, the clumsy vessels would
pproach all too fast. Even if every ballista on the ram-
arts had time to sink two rafts, close to fifty giants
vould still reach the castle. That would be more than
nough to storm the outer curtain. The inner curtain
vould not last long after that, and the attackers would
ear the keep apart within minutes.

Brianna thought Cuthbert Castle's best chance lay in
ioping that a favorable breeze did not rise before her
rmy arrived, but that was a distant prospect at best. On
wo out of the last three days, a stiff wind had risen on

the giants' shore about midmorning, then blown acros
the lake until well into the afternoon. If the same thi
happened tomorrow, the giants would be ready.

Behind her Brianna heard boot heels clicking o
stone. "You mustn't let the men see you staring," sai
Arlien. "It looks as though you're frightened."

"I am frightened," the queen said. She turned arour
and saw that all three of her escorts had come over
join her at the embrasure. "And I doubt that my showir
fear will hurt morale. It seems clear enough the me
have lost their respect for me."

Arlien stepped to her side and took her elbow. "Tl
sergeant's reaction is of no importance," he said. "He
one of Cuthbert's men."

"What do you mean by that?" the earl demanded. H
positioned himself on Brianna's other side and glared
Arlien. "I assure you, my men will fight as valiantly a
Selwyn's."

"They will try," Arlien interrupted. "But you've dam
ened their spirit by displaying your anger with me."

"I have done nothing of the sort!" the earl snapped.
have kept our discussions strictly to myself. If the me
are in poor spirits, it's because of you."

Brianna looked down the rampart and saw that Blan
and his crew still had not returned to work. They wer
watching the argument in open disgust, whisperin
among themselves and shaking their heads at ever
thing Arlien said.

"Quiet!" the queen hissed. "You're both to blame."

Arlien's jaw fell. "Pardon me?" He glared at Brianna
though she were a defiant vassal. "I couldn't have hear
you correctly."

The words sent a chill down Brianna's spine, and sl
felt an inexplicable knot of apprehension in her stomacl
Surprised that the prince's sharp retort caused her suc
anxiety, the queen clenched her jaw and forced herse
to meet his stare. If the possibility of losing Arlien's su

ort caused her such dread, then clearly she had come
o depend on him too much.

"You heard me, Prince." She shifted her gaze to Earl
Cuthbert, relieved to look away from Arlien's angry
eyes. "You will both do me the favor of bringing your
bickering to an end."

Cuthbert's face reddened. "Of course, Majesty." The
earl looked to Arlien and said, "I apologize."

Arlien glanced at Brianna's stern face, then returned
his gaze to Cuthbert. "Apology accepted," the prince
muttered. "I'm sure your men will fight well enough."

"They'll do better than that," Brianna said. "Their
spears will ravage our enemy's fleet so badly that the
giants will turn back before reaching the walls."

Brianna glanced toward Blane and his ballista crew.
The sergeant's only reaction was to roll his eyes and yell
at his men. All five soldiers returned to their task with
weary, resigned expressions.

"What will it take to encourage you men?" Brianna
demanded.

Without waiting for a reply, the queen spun on her
heels and started for the corner tower. She felt tears
welling in her eyes, and she had no wish for her subjects
to see them trickling down her face.

*   *   *   *   *

Basil sat beside his shuttered windows, his eyes
pinched shut against the cramped dinginess of his
prison. Every time he opened them, an unwelcome
image kept returning to his mind, the same image he
always saw in the murky confines of a close space: a
young verbeeg hiding in the cramped tunnel of a long-
abandoned dwarf hole, staring out into the sunlight
while dozens of sooty black legs flashed past the
entrance. Even through the rock, the muffled screams
of his parents, siblings, and cousins came to him, and

also the crackling laughter of the fire giants boasting that any verbeeg who stole their iron would learn to swim in fire. Then a great red eye appeared at the end of the tunnel, and soon after the glowing white tip of a long spear. The hole was too small for Basil to crawl deeper. So he was trapped, and before it was over, he was begging his tormentors to shove the spear through him and be done with it. But of course they had not, and he had hated fire giants ever since—but not as badly as he hated confined places.

Basil's eyes popped open, no longer able to shut the terrible memory from his mind. He stood and flung his shutters open, and they banged against the keep wall with a thunderlike clap, drawing startled shrieks and cries from the ward below. The verbeeg pressed his large face against his window bars and took several long, deep breaths before noticing the nervous soldiers of Selwyn's Company of the Winter Wolf craning their necks to stare up at him.

"I beg your pardon," he called. "I didn't mean to unnerve you."

The men slowly returned to their war preparations, sharpening lances and lighting fires under oil cauldrons. Basil ran his eyes over their number, searching for Avner's familiar face. The shutters had been closed for more than three hours—an interminable length of time for the verbeeg—and still the boy had not come. The young thief was much too wise to volunteer for a job, but Basil was beginning to fear the youth had been pressed into duty.

Perhaps someone would even come for Basil, realizing that a verbeeg's strength could be put to good use in the castle's defenses. If it got him out of this room, the runecaster would even do as they asked, at least for a while. As refreshing as a little physical labor might be, he could not allow it to interfere with his research—not considering what he had discovered, and what it might mean to the queen's chances of winning this battle.

A fanfare of trumpets sounded from the inner curtain's gatehouse, then Brianna came sweeping through the arch with her trio of sycophants in tow. Even from the keep window, Basil could see that her eyes were swollen and red. The runecaster knew the queen well enough to realize that only terrible news could make her cry.

"What's wrong, Milady?" the verbeeg yelled. "Has something happened to Tavis?"

Brianna stopped and looked toward Basil's window, a confused and blank expression on her face.

"To Avner?" Basil gasped. That would explain why the boy had not answered his summons.

The queen's lip began to tremble, then she covered her face and started across the ward at a run.

Basil stumbled back from the window. "Oh, Avner!" he cried.

The verbeeg slumped to the floor, too stunned to think, yet knowing he must. If his research was right, the hill giants were the least of Brianna's problems. There was something foul inside the castle, a scion of an evil as ancient as Toril itself, come to reclaim a treasure lost long before the first human kingdom had arisen in the valley of Hartsvale.

The first thing Basil had to do was be certain of his facts. The folios were instruments of subtle nuance, as full of allegory and myth as of history. It was possible that he had misunderstood a key phrase, or interpreted as reality a parable meant only as symbol. The verbeeg dragged himself across the floor and laid a finger on the mica. The ancient letters came to life, glowing red and yellow and blue, and he read:

So it was that Othea gave birth to Twilight from her own dying shadow, thus imprisoning forever the faithless ones who had poisoned her. And when the winds of life whistled no more inside her breast, Annam's final son crawled at last from her womb. Great was his hunger, for Othea had held him captive a century of centuries and fed him not, and so he chased down a hart and ate it from the antlers to the hooves, and thereafter he called himself Hartkiller.

Now it was that Hartkiller remembered that mighty Annam had conceived him as immortal King of the Giants, and so he went to search out his rightful lands. He came first to the hill giants, and to them he said, "I am Hartkiller, your rightful king, and you shall bow down before me and make me a silver crown to set upon my head."

But the hill giants laughed, for Hartkiller seemed no king to them. Though his voice boomed like thunder and his mighty fist could shatter stone, his eternal fast had made of him the puniest of all Annam's sons, so that he stood barely the height of a firbolg and wore his skin upon a frame more haggard than a verbeeg. So the hill giants would not bow, and they called him Othea's bastard and drove him from their lodge with stones and filth.

Hartkiller went next to the grotto of the fire giants, and to them he said, "I am Hartkiller, your rightful king, and you shall bow down before me and make me a golden crown to set upon my head." But the fire giants said they would not have a king who stood as high as their knees, so they roared their mirth and set a crown of cinders upon his head, and they drove him from their cave with lashing tongues of flame.

Hartkiller climbed last to the windy eyrie of the storm giants, and to them he said, "I am Hartkiller, your rightful king, and you shall bow down before me and make me a crown of diamonds to set upon my head."

The storm giants asked if the hill giants had given him a crown of silver, and Hartkiller said they had driven him from their lodge with stones and filth. The storm giants asked if the fire giants had given him a

crown of gold, and Hartkiller brandished the crown of
cinders they had set upon his head. Then the storm
giants said they would not have an oaf and a runt for a
king, and they blasted him from their mountain with
icy gales of wind.

When he saw that the giants would not have him,
Hartkiller turned his back on the empire of Ostoria
and went into the lands of the humans, and to them he
said, "I am Hartkiller, and if you will have me as your
king, I will drive the giants from this valley and make
your farms safe from their pillage."

And the humans bowed down before Hartkiller. They
made him a crown of steel to set on his head and gave
him a wife to bear his sons, and also warriors to lead
into battle. Hartkiller went first to the hill giants. With
his great axe, he cleaved their chief down the center
and smashed their lodge asunder, and he told them to
flee the hills of his valley and go live in the mountains,
or live not at all.

Next, Hartkiller poured a tarn into the grotto of the
fire giants, and when the flood drove them from their
holes he pierced the heart of their dark khan with a
lance as long as a tree, and he told them to leave the
caves of his valley and go to live among the dwarves of
the south, or live not at all.

Hartkiller went last to the eyrie of the storm giants,
and they offered him crowns of silver and gold and
diamond. Their paramount called him King of
Giants, and said all giants would bow down before
him if he turned his back on the humans. But
Hartkiller would have none of that, for Annam had
made him to be a good and loyal king, and now his
subjects were men.

So the paramount and the king fought. Their fury
boomed over the valley like thunder, spears flashed
across the sky like black lightning, and the land shuddered beneath the might of their blows. For a hundred

days they battled, never eating nor drinking nor sleeping. The ceaseless clanging of their weapons deafened all who heard it, until the Clearwhirl ran red with the blood of their wounds and their cries filled the air like the keening of spirits. Then did they drop their shields and sink to their knees, and they each struck one last blow before falling dead in each other's embrace.

And Hartkiller's son Brun went to the storm giants with all his father's warriors. He said that henceforth humans would live in the valleys and giants would live in the mountains, and they would all abide in peace. But the storm giants had no fear of Brun, and they told him the humans would live as slaves, or live not at all.

Brun returned to his people and commanded them to prepare for a terrible war, and the storm giants summoned the hill giants from the mountains. They summoned the fire giants from the caves, and together they readied their hosts to march against the humans.

But then it was that a mighty keening rose from a hidden vale. So loud was the wailing that the clouds shattered and fell from the sky, and so terrible was it that all the beasts of the north—all the foxes and all the bears, and the wyverns and all the dragons, too—all turned more pale than snow. A cold mist as purple as twilight seeped from the valley, and the armies of the giants fell to coughing and trembling, and every warrior heard in his own ears the hissing voice of a great spirit, and the Twilight Spirit spoke thus:

"Annam gave you a king, a king destined to bring all giants together and remake the lost empire of your fathers. But you would not have Hartkiller for your king. You laughed at him and you set a crown of cinders upon his head, and you sent him into the arms of the humans. In this, you have defied the will of the All Father, and it is fitting that Hartkiller has driven you from your valley and stolen all your lands.

"But your punishment need not be eternal. There is

destined to come a woman of Hartkiller's line who rules your stolen lands. She is your hope, for Annam's blood is strong and it will run thick in her veins. She will bear you a new king, one with the power to undo what you have done and revive the empire of Ostoria. Be patient. Let the humans live in peace, for only through them can you lift the veil of twilight that shrouds the lost glory of your ancestors."

Basil lifted his finger, and the glowing symbols faded. It had taken him only one reading to realize that Brianna was the woman—or should he say, giantess—to which the text referred, and he had certainly discovered nothing to contradict that conclusion. The runecaster found it difficult to believe they would risk her life by storming the castle. They could not be certain the queen would survive the chaos of battle, or that she would not take her own life when the fight went against her.

That meant the hill giants' assault could be only a diversion. They intended to get Brianna out of the castle some other way, while everyone was too busy fighting to notice her disappearance. To do that, they would need help inside the castle, and Basil could guess who that would be.

The verbeeg went to a corner and traced the name Gilthwit in the dust. Below that he rearranged the same eight letters to write the name TWILIGHT. Prince Arlien of TWILIGHT. Basil did not know whether Arlien was one of the actual "faithless ones" who had poisoned Othea so long ago or simply an agent, but he felt sure that the prince had come from the Twilight Vale.

Would eight letters be enough to convince Brianna of Arlien's identity? Basil did not think so. The prince could claim the anagram was a matter of coincidence, and the queen might well give him the benefit of the doubt. The runecaster would need more evidence to establish that Gilthwit and Twilight were one.

Fortunately, Basil knew where to search. Stone giants were scrupulous historians, and the volume preceding the one on his floor was sure to reveal the identity of those who had poisoned Othea. If the runecaster could find some link between the prince's name and the "faithless ones" imprisoned in the Twilight Vale, the link would be irrefutable.

Basil grabbed his satchel and removed a runequill, then crawled to the door and laid his large frame down in front of the latch. The verbeeg propped an elbow on the floor and touched his quill to the lock. A glowing green mark appeared beneath the tip, and he began to trace the delicate rune that would open the door.

*　*　*　*　*

Brianna's legs had gone numb from the calves down, and a cold ache had crept from the chilly floor deep into her knee joints. The queen had no idea how long she had been there, kneeling on the cool floor of Cuthbert's temple, but it had been quite some time. She had placed a burning spear on the altar, and it had long ago burned itself out. All that remained now were warm cinders and the soot-covered head, and still she had discovered no sign of Hiatea. Her mind was too foggy to find the way to her goddess.

But at least the mist was beginning to thin. A couple of times now, Brianna had held a thought for several moments, carefully navigating it from one hazy point to the next. Encouraged by this small progress, she intended to keep kneeling on the cold stone until she found Hiatea.

The temple door creaked open, and a sliver of flickering torchlight crept over the altar. The queen did not rise, or even look over her shoulder.

"Leave me alone," she commanded. "I left orders that I am not to be disturbed."

"But it's getting late," replied Arlien's voice. "You've been in here all afternoon, and most of the evening as well."

The prince started across the room, heels clicking and steel plate jangling. Brianna found it strange that he was still wearing his armor. Earlier in the day, she had noticed that both his wound and his breastplate now seemed completely mended. Still, she knew appearances could be deceiving. Arlien or his armor might well need another day to return to full strength.

The prince stopped at Brianna's side. She kept her eyes focused on the spear and tried to ignore his presence.

"You should be sitting on the bench, Milady," Arlien said. "Kneeling on this cold floor will do your health no good."

Realizing it would take more than a subtle hint to rid herself of the prince, Brianna asked, "Do you not prefer that your subjects humble themselves when they come before you?"

"Of course," Arlien replied. "But—"

"Then how do you think Hiatea will receive my entreaties if I make them from the comfort of a bench?"

"A stone slab is hardly comfortable," Arlien countered. "And I'm sure Hiatea would understand if you made use of it. After all, you're hardly well."

"I'm beginning to feel better," Brianna replied.

Arlien was silent for a moment, then stepped between her and the altar. In his hands he held a flagon and pewter mug. "I'm glad to hear that," he said. "And I'm sure that after you drink your restorative, you'll feel marvelous."

"You may set it on the bench," Brianna said, gesturing behind her. "I'll have it later."

The prince began to pour his concoction into the mug, and a warm, fruity smell pervaded the room. Brianna tasted the spicy libation on the tip of her tongue, her mouth already watering in anticipation of the sweet nectar. A wave of fierce craving rose from deep within her body; not simple thirst, or even gluttony, but a hunger as feral as lust, every bit as powerful and insidious.

"Not now, Arlien." Brianna could not take her eyes off the golden draught flowing into her cup. "I'm trying to pray."

The prince's eyes flashed, and he continued to pour. "It's been too long since you drank—and there's not a drop of wine in it, just as you asked." The prince's voice was as sweet as the libation flowing from his flagon, almost cloying. "And your prayers will go much better once you have restored yourself."

Brianna straightened her stiff legs and lurched to her feet, then took both the mug and the flagon from the prince's hands. "I said later." She put them on the bench and pointed toward the temple door. "Now will you leave me?"

Arlien's lip started to curl, but he managed to keep it from twisting into a full snarl. "Unfortunately, I can't do that," he said. "There's something we must discuss."

"After I'm finished."

"When will that be? Tomorrow, dawn? Noon, perhaps? Or when the giants drag you out of here screaming?" Arlien demanded. "By then, it'll be too late. Duty calls now, Your Highness."

Brianna sighed, then walked over to the window and peered into the dusk light. The temple was high enough in the keep for her to see the purple mountains looming in the distance, but the castle walls mercifully shielded both the lake and the giants from her sight.

"Very well, but I hope this isn't another argument between you and Cuthbert," she said.

"Not a disagreement," he replied. "Rather a precaution."

"And what would that be?"

"Cuthbert is frightened," the prince said. "When he sees the giants coming, he may try to strike a bargain—"

"We have discussed this before," Brianna said, still staring out the window. "And I have taken the safeguards I consider appropriate."

"But your own bodyguard said—"

"I am aware of what he said, but I won't give a foreign prince command of Cuthbert's castle," Brianna replied. She noticed Selwyn walking along the rampart of the inner curtain, stopping to speak with his sentries and check their weapons. "But I *could* turn the castle's defense over to Selwyn, and relieve you both of your responsibilities."

"You *are* feeling better," Arlien commented. He did not sound enthusiastic. "But I'm afraid that Cuthbert is only part of what I came to discuss."

The prince came and stood behind Brianna. She did not turn around. "Go on."

Arlien grunted his irritation. "The truth is, you should leave—tonight. I'll take you out by the secret passage."

Brianna braced her hands on the windowsill. "And why would I do that?"

"Because you must survive," he said. "You owe it to Hartsvale, and this castle can't hold—no matter who's in command."

"Don't you think I know that?" Brianna whirled around. "Why do you think I'm here praying to Hiatea?"

"I don't have the faintest idea," Arlien replied calmly. "As I recall, she's a deity of the giants—the goddess of nature and family, I believe. Hiatea certainly isn't going to help us."

Brianna felt a wave of cold nausea rising from her stomach. The queen looked past the prince to the temple's altar, where the cinders of her offering to the goddess lay cold and ignored.

"Hiatea is my goddess, too." Brianna spoke with more conviction than she felt. "And she also watches over firbolgs and giant-kin as well."

"But she is the daughter of Annam," countered Arlien.

"That makes her a goddess of giants first, all others second."

"Daughters do not always honor their father's wishes," Brianna said. "Hiatea watched over me when Goboka and his ogres kidnapped me."

"But she's not helping you now, is she?" demanded Arlien. "Now she favors the giants."

"You know this?" Brianna demanded. "And so we are destined to loose?"

Arlien stepped closer. "Yes," he said. "It would take a god's intervention to save us now. Even if your body-guard got through—"

"He did. Ta—Tav—" Brianna could almost bring the name to mind. "Tav—"

Arlien raised one brow. "Tavis?"

"Yes, that's right," the queen answered, and the name vanished as quickly as she heard it. "My bodyguard is the finest scout in Hartsvale—in all the Ice Spires. If any-one can get through, he will."

"My point exactly," replied Arlien. "We don't know if anyone *can* get through. And even if he does, he won't return in time. The giants will attack when the wind shifts tomorrow."

"*If* the wind shifts tomorrow."

"Stop fooling yourself!" the prince snapped. "Hiatea has been watching over you on behalf of the giants. Why else do you think she favored such a young girl?"

The queen narrowed her eyes. "How do you know when the goddess came to me?"

Hiatea had granted her favor to the princess of Hartsvale at the age of five—but only Brianna, her father, and Castle Hartwick's high priest knew that.

Arlien seemed lost, then he looked at the floor and admitted, "My spy told me."

"The High Priest!" Brianna gasped, more shocked than angered. "Simon was like an uncle to me!"

Arlien grimaced. "You mustn't go too hard on him," he

said. "He was doing only what was best for both countries."

"I'm certain that's what you told him, but I'm not so foolish," she said sharply. "And now you may leave."

The prince furrowed his dark brow. "Surely you don't intend to stay," he said. "You must see—"

"What I see is a coward." She glared down at Arlien.

The prince's jaw pumped up and down in stunned silence, then finally caught hold of his thoughts. "I'll forgive that unfortunate choice of words. You didn't realize what you were saying. You're still weak and confused from your illness." Arlien went over to the bench and picked up the mug, then returned and handed it to Brianna. "Drink your restorative. I'm sure you'll come to your senses."

"I'm feeling fine—much better, in fact, than I have in days," Brianna replied. She clamped her jaw down against the temptation to drink, then turned and dumped the libation out the window. "And I have no intention of marrying a coward, or of allying Hartsvale with a country that sends one to court me. So, dear prince, it seems you're under no obligation to stay and fight. Feel free to leave any time you wish."

Arlien's face grew as dark as a thunderhead. "You may have misunderstood me, Queen Brianna," he hissed. "When the fighting starts, no one will be closer to your side than me."

"Good," Brianna replied. "I'll see you on the morrow."

Arlien gave her a curt bow, then went to the door and paused there. "I suggest you don't waste all of your newfound vigor praying to Hiatea," he said. "You'll soon have need of your strength. Tomorrow may come sooner than you think."

❖10❖
Cold Camp

A long, uncanny trumpeting trilled over the glacier, at once as shrill as a wyvern's cry and as full as a dragon's roar. Tavis stopped walking and ran his eyes over the milky miles of snow ahead. He saw the dark crags of a few scattered peaks poking through the ice, but otherwise the terrain looked exactly as it was: a vast, barren sheet of snow and ice thick enough to bury entire mountains.

"I didn't call for no rest," growled Slagfid. He shoved Tavis after Bodvar, who was breaking trail through six feet of fresh snow. "Keep going."

Tavis limped forward again, as anxious as Slagfid to maintain a steady pace. The scout judged the magic would fade from his runemask no later than dawn, returning him to firbolg form. Before then, he had to reach the frost giant camp, learn where Hagamil was meeting Julien and Arno, and slip safely away. To complicate matters, he had no idea how much farther he had to travel. Glaciers like this one could swallow entire mountain ranges, spanning distances so huge that even giants could not cross them easily. The war party might not reach camp until after Hagamil had fallen asleep for the night, and Slagfid would hardly be anxious to awaken his chief and report a botched mission.

Despite his mangled toe, Tavis soon caught up to Bodvar and had to slow his pace. Although the snow was barely knee deep, it was heavy and wet, and Bodvar had been breaking trail for most of the journey. The warrior's breath came in wheezes and gasps, and his legs were so weak that he had to catch his balance with each step.

The scout looked back at Slagfid. "Bodvar can barely walk," he said. "The rest of our journey will go faster if someone else breaks trail."

"Bodvar wouldn't be breaking trail if he'd held onto that *traell*, like I told him," Slagfid growled. "But you've got me in trouble, too. *You* can break trail if you want."

Tavis made no move to accept the frost giant's offer. "You've seen my toe. I'd spend more time floundering than breaking trail." He did not add that the effort of impersonating a stone giant had left him nearly as exhausted as Bodvar. The muscles in the scout's legs were quivering like aspen leaves, and his breathing was so heavy he could hardly see through the curtain of white vapor rising from his mouth. "Call Egarl up. He should have come back to look for us."

"That's for me to decide." Slagfid eyed Tavis suspiciously. "I don't see why you're in such a hurry, Sharp-nose. After losing that bow, Hagamil's going to be no happier to see you than Bodvar."

"I'm not frightened of Hagamil," Tavis replied.

"Then you're a fool," Slagfid snorted.

Seeing that the frost giant would not be swayed, the scout limped after Bodvar. Slagfid was right about one thing: Tavis was a fool. Since learning where ice diamonds really came from, the scout had told himself the same thing at least a hundred times. He wanted to gouge out his eyes for not seeing that Arlien was a fake, and to tear off his own ears for failing to hear the ring of falsehood in the man's silky voice. What a chuckle the prince must have had when Tavis warned him to be wary of Cuthbert!

Arlien would probably be with Julien and Arno when they delivered Brianna to the frost giants. If so, the scout would make the prince pay for his treachery.

As he contemplated his vengeance, Tavis's stomach began to burn. He would have no weapons when he

returned to firbolg form. His broken sword still lay back
at Shepherd's Nightmare, and Avner had his bow and
quiver.

Fortunately, unless the youth had undergone an unexpected change of character, Avner wasn't likely to return
to Cuthbert Castle as instructed. He was far more likely
to follow the scout onto the glacier. Assuming he didn't
freeze to death or fall into a hidden crevasse, Tavis
would actually be grateful for the boy's disobedience.

Another eerie trumpet rolled over the ice, reminding
Tavis of the most significant danger to Avner. Plenty of
creatures made their homes on glaciers, many of them
predators. If one of the beasts happened to catch the
youth's scent . . . the scout saw no use in picturing what
would happen.

Ahead of Tavis, Bodvar suddenly pulled up short.
"Praise Thrym!" he puffed. "A rider."

The frost giant was looking toward a nearby nunatak,
one of the craggy stone peaks that occasionally jutted up
through the surface of the glacier. A deep trench encircled the pinnacle, for during the day the spire's dark
rock gathered enough heat from the sun to melt the ice
around it. Like the mountainous nunatak itself, the
hollow was huge, easily the size of a small canyon, and
lumbering out of that icy gorge was the hulking, shaggy
form of a woolly mammoth.

The creature seemed remarkably small, perhaps
because of the young frost giant riding him. The youth's
legs easily straddled the beast's huge back, his feet dangling almost to the ground. The scene reminded Tavis of
a human child riding the family sheepdog.

"Hey, you!" Bodvar waved at the distant youth. "Come
break trail for us!"

Slagfid offered no objection to the request, perhaps
because he sensed Bodvar could not continue much
longer.

The young rider stopped and peered toward the war

party. His mount dug its saber-curved tusks into the ice and gouged a large cake from the glacier.

"Who's that?" the youth called.

"It's Bodvar, with Slagfid and his war party."

The boy's mount wrapped its pendulous trunk around the ice it had gouged free, then flung the block at something behind it that Tavis could not see. A bloodthirsty howl echoed off the snow. The mammoth lurched forward, raising its hairy trunk to voice an angry bugle. The two calls combined to create the eerie trumpeting Tavis had heard before.

Unconcerned by the strange noise, the young giant grabbed his mount's ear and yanked it around, guiding the beast down the glacier to meet the war party. The scout noticed a pair of poles running from the creature's saddle toward the ground behind it, where the rods were lashed to the sides of a narrow, chitinous head with bulbous black eyes and a muzzle full of sharp fangs.

Tavis saw a pair of spiny head-wings flare out from the sides of the ghastly face, and he suddenly understood the mammoth's nervous behavior. The beast behind it was a remorhaz, one of the most vicious and brutal of all glacial predators. The monster's body resembled that of a twenty-foot centipede, with blue segmented sections and two dozen sticklike legs ending in razor-sharp claws. The thing was scuttling along behind the mammoth, hissing madly and flailing at the mammoth's tail with its face tentacles. Only the poles lashed to its head prevented the ravenous creature from hamstringing the mammoth and devouring it on the spot.

Slagfid pushed by Tavis and took Bodvar's place at the head of the line. When the youth arrived, he reached down to scratch the mammoth's woolly ear. "My thanks, Frith."

"Your thanks are nice," said Frith. The boy was young enough that he still had a slender face, with the yellow fuzz of his first beard sprouting on his chin. "A new axe would be better."

Slagfid nodded. "I'll see that Bodvar gives you one." He peered over the mammoth's rump at the hissing remorhaz. "I see you've got yourself a nice little ice worm."

Frith nodded proudly and motioned at the nunatak behind him. "I've been keeping him down there." The youth peered down the war party's line. "You got that Tavis Burdun—alive, I mean? We could throw him to the worm and have us some fun."

"No, Gavorial killed Tavis Burdun," Slagfid reported.

"Too bad," said Frith. "We've got an ogre back at camp, but you know how fast he'll go. Hagamil could use the fun tonight."

Slagfid winced. "He's in a bad mood, is he?"

Frith nodded. "And it'll be worse if I don't get back there." The boy yanked on his mammoth's ear, turning the beast up the glacier. "Don't get too close to my worm. He's hungry."

Slagfid stepped back, allowing the remorhaz to slink into the trail behind the mammoth. With only seven body segments, the creature was not particularly large, but it was definitely hungry. The white stripe down its back had turned bright pink from the heat of its appetite.

Once the ice worm had scuttled past, Slagfid reluctantly started up the trail. With the remorhaz hissing and growling at its tail, the mammoth moved at a brisk pace, plowing through the heavy snow as though it weighed as much as a cloud. Within half an hour, the frost giants were all huffing from the exertion of staying close to the beast. Bodvar and Tavis could not keep pace, even with Slagfid threatening to unleash the remorhaz on them. They soon found themselves being dragged along by a pair of bitterly complaining helpers.

After an excruciating length of time, they came to an uneven ring of nunataks formed by the rim of an ancient volcano. Frith slowed his mammoth and commanded,

"Call."

The beast raised its trunk and let out a long, wavering trumpet. The sound was answered by a tremendous chorus of similar calls from inside the ring. A frost giant sentry appeared on the summit of a nunatak and waved the war party on.

Frith led the way across a narrow isthmus of snow between two nunatak hollows, then the group emerged in the volcano's snow-filled caldera. The frost giants had made camp in the heart of the crater, around a flat area that could only be a frozen lake.

The encampment was one of the coldest and loneliest places the scout had ever visited. The frost giants sat in the frigid moonlight in groups of two or three, conversing in quiet tones or not speaking at all. Most of the children were already asleep, lying in beds of fresh snow or, at most, a small shelter dug into a steep slope. The mammoths were gathered at one end of the lake, near a deep pit they had gouged through the ice. There was no fire or light anywhere.

As Frith guided his mammoth down the slope, several of the giants below pointed toward Slagfid's war party. A gentle murmur started to build. Drowsy children roused themselves from their beds, wiping the sleep from their eyes with handfuls of snow. The entire tribe drifted toward the far end of the caldera, where the mouth of a huge cavern yawned in an ice cliff.

Slagfid's face grew increasingly stormy as the procession crept toward the cavern. Finally, when Frith reached the bottom of the slope, Slagfid clasped a burly hand around Tavis's arm.

"All those giants expect to see Tavis Burdun's body, Sharpnose. They're not going to be happy about taking your word for what happened," the frost giant growled. "So you'd better tell your story well, or Hagamil's liable to feed us both to Frith's worm."

"I'm sure you have a much better idea of what they

want to hear," Tavis said, realizing it would be impossible for him to tell a convincing tale. "Why don't you recount events for me?"

Slagfid's lip twisted into a disdainful sneer. "I imagine you'd like that, wouldn't you?"

The frost giant thrust Tavis's hand away, then turned and stomped off toward the cavern. The scout stood where he was, too preoccupied to follow.

Bodvar clamped a reassuring hand on Tavis's shoulder. "Don't worry. It won't be as tough as he makes out," said the giant. "You're a stone giant. Nobody'll notice if you lie a little—especially about how we lost the *traell* and the bow."

Bodvar started forward, pulling Tavis along. By the time they reached the ice cave, a sharp blue light was glowing from the interior. Frith dismounted and set to work loosing the remorhaz poles from his saddle. Slagfid motioned for Tavis and Bodvar to come inside, then ducked through the entrance.

When the scout followed, he found himself standing inside a vast ice vault. Long, spiraling icicles depended from the arched ceiling, many with jagged ends where the tips had been knocked off by careless passersby. The frost giants stood along the sides of the chamber, around a deep pit hewn into the floor. The listless, hunch-shouldered figure of an ogre sat in the bottom of the hole, his claws reduced to bloody nubs by long hours of clawing at the walls of his icy prison.

At the far end of the room stood the tribal shaman. He was a haggard, one-eyed giant with yellow patterns tattooed on his bald head and the fur of a white mammoth pulled tight around his chest. In his gaunt hand he carried a brilliantly glowing scepter that supplied the only light in the cavern.

Slagfid stopped at the near edge of the ice pit. "Halflook, fetch me Hagamil," he demanded. "Tell him that Slagfid has returned with good tidings!"

Halflook's red-veined gaze darted from Slagfid to Bodvar to Tavis, the muscles of the empty socket working as though it still contained an eyeball. The shaman let his attention rest on the scout and shook his scepter several times, and blue reflections danced wildly across the cavern walls.

"Good tidings, you say," Halflook echoed. His gaze drifted toward the cavern mouth, growing distant and unfocused. "Perhaps better than you know."

Slagfid shifted his weight from one foot to the other. "Enough of your babble," he growled. "Get me Hagamil."

"As you wish."

Halflook's eye rolled back in its socket, then his chin tipped into the air and his tongue rose out his mouth, dancing between his lips like the winged head of a remorhaz.

"I welcome your return, Slagfid." The voice that rumbled from the shaman's mouth was deeper and more gravelly than the one Tavis had heard earlier. "We've all been awaiting you."

When Halflook's head tipped forward again, Tavis was astonished to see a piercing blue eye in each socket. The giant's face suddenly looked much fuller, and his gaunt body seemed stout and robust. Even the tattoos on his bald pate were changing before the scout's eyes, sprouting into long yellow braids.

A pair of comely giantesses wrapped in sleeping robes appeared out of the shadows. They flanked the giant on both sides, casting arrogant glances at the other females in the room.

The giant ignored the women and ordered, "Tell me of your journey, Slagfid."

"Hagamil, I have won much honor for us," said Slagfid.

An approving murmur rustled through the cavern, and Hagamil demanded, "So all went well?"

Slagfid hesitated, his gaze dropping to the ogre in the pit. "In the end, yes," he said. "But Tavis Burdun was not alone. He left a mighty *traell* warrior in the canyon to defend his back trail."

A dubious scowl crept down Hagamil's face. "What warrior?"

"We call him Little Dragon," Slagfid replied.

Tavis was glad Avner was not listening to this. The boy was vain enough without hearing a frost giant call him a mighty warrior.

"While we were in the canyon, his boulders fell like hail on our heads," Slagfid continued. "My warriors could hardly move."

This drew a round of guffaws from the other giants.

"Little Dragon is a fiercer warrior than Tavis Burdun!" Slagfid bellowed. He silenced his fellows with an angry glare. "Tavis Burdun does not cast trees down upon your head, or send crashing floodwaters to sweep you away!"

"And Little Dragon did all this?" demanded Hagamil.

"I tell you, Little Dragon's magic is as powerful as his arm," said Slagfid. "He always strikes by surprise. You never know when he will appear—isn't that so, Bodvar?"

Bodvar gave an emphatic nod. "Compared to Little Dragon, Tavis Burdun is like a calf to a bull mammoth."

Hagamil looked doubtful. "And how many warriors did you lose to this *traell* bull?"

Slagfid straightened his shoulders. "None."

"None?" Hagamil roared. "Why not? Were you afraid to join battle with this fierce pebble-hurler?"

A chorus of nervous laughter rolled through the cavern.

"I was not afraid to catch him!" Slagfid bellowed. He waited for the room to fall quiet, then added, "Or to save Sharpnose from the flood he unleashed."

The frost giant looked to Tavis for confirmation. The scout remained silent. He had no wish to cast doubt on Slagfid's exaggeration, but feared his cracking voice would do more to arouse suspicions than to quell them.

Hagamil gave Tavis a look that suggested he did not

consider Gavorial's salvation a good thing. Before the chieftain could say anything, a loud clatter arose at the cavern entrance.

Tavis looked over his shoulder to see Frith backing into the chamber, followed closely by the hissing remorhaz. The young giant was controlling the beast by means of the two long poles harnessed to the creature's chitinous head, but that did not prevent the ice worm from striking at its handler. So powerful was the creature that the lunge rocked Frith on his heels.

The remorhaz was quick to press its advantage, thrashing wildly as it pushed itself into the cave. Frith slid across the icy floor, grunting and cursing as he tried in vain to get his legs under him. If Slagfid had not laid a hand on the young giant's back, the beast would have pushed him into the pit.

Hagamil's laughter echoed through the chamber. He handed the glowing scepter to one of the giantesses and came forward to inspect the beast. The chieftain was even larger than he had seemed from across the pit. He stood a full head taller than Slagfid, with a barrel chest as big around as a mammoth.

"A spirited worm, as promised." Hagamil laid a hand on one of the poles Frith used to control the ice worm, then a crafty smile creased his lips. He turned to Slagfid and said, "It will be interesting to see how Little Dragon fares against it."

Bodvar's eyes flashed in alarm. He opened his mouth to speak, but Slagfid cut him off with a curt wave of the hand.

"We can't throw Little Dragon into the pit until we've feasted him," Slagfid objected. "He has earned a happy death."

Hagamil glared at the smaller giant, then jerked his hand away from the remorhaz's probing face tentacles. There were red welts where the worm had touched his white skin, but the chieftain showed no sign of pain.

"If Little Dragon is as great as you say, we will feast him after he kills the worm," Hagamil said. "Otherwise, he doesn't deserve such an honor."

Slagfid inclined his head, yielding to the chieftain's logic. "If you wish," he said. "But we should let the ogre fight first. Otherwise, we'll miss half the fun."

Hagamil smiled, then clasped an affable hand on Slagfid's shoulder. "A good idea," he said. "And you can tell me about Tavis Burdun while Sjolf and Snorri fetch a chain and spear for the ogre."

The chieftain motioned to two warriors. They reluctantly turned to leave, grumbling about having to work while Slagfid related his story.

As the pair left, Slagfid said, "The honor of telling that story is not rightfully mine." He grabbed Tavis's arm and pulled him forward. "Sharpnose killed Tavis Burdun."

A dark cloud descended over Hagamil's face. "Is that so?"

Tavis met the chieftain's gaze, but said nothing. Slagfid was hardly being noble. By gallantly sharing the credit, the wily leader was simply trying to make his superior angry enough to forget about Little Dragon. The scout would have been happy to cooperate, had it been possible to do so without lying.

"Well?" Hagamil demanded. "Did you kill him?"

"You may claim that honor for yourself," Tavis responded. "I give it to you as a gift."

Hagamil blinked twice, then shook his head in confusion. "You what?"

"The honor was to belong to your tribe. I return it to you, if you wish to claim it," Tavis said. "It will not be written in the Chronicles of Stone that Gavorial killed Tavis Burdun."

The frost giant considered this with a skeptical frown, then asked, "So you weren't trying to steal it from us?"

Tavis shook his head. "Never," he said. "The battle

started, and I did what was necessary."

A smile started to creep across Hagamil's lips, but it abruptly turned to a snarl. "What do you want for this 'gift'?"

The scout smiled, thinking it might be easier than he had anticipated to learn the location of the rendezvous. "A small boon," he said. "Tell me where you are meeting Julien and Arno."

Hagamil rubbed his chin, then shrugged and gave Tavis a sharp-toothed smile. "Done," he said. "When they send word—"

"They have already sent word," Tavis interrupted. "I want to know where you're meeting them tomorrow."

Hagamil's grin faded. "How'd you find out about that?"

Without waiting for a reply, the chieftain cast an angry glare at Slagfid, who could only shrug and shake his head.

"It's nothing that should be kept secret," Tavis said. "All giants deserve the honor of escorting Brianna to Twilight."

"And that's why you want to be there?" Hagamil demanded.

"I have no intention of claiming that I killed Tavis Burdun, if that's what concerns you."

As he spoke, Tavis silently congratulated himself. Until now, he had only been assuming that the giants intended to take the queen to Twilight. Hagamil had just confirmed his guess.

Sjolf and Snorri returned, carrying a set of rusty shackles, a wooden spear, and a long log with steps carved into it. Giving the ice worm wide berth, they lowered one end of the crude ladder into the pit.

Hagamil watched the first giant start down the log, then looked back to Tavis. "Okay. Give me Tavis's body."

"There is no corpse," Tavis answered.

"What?" Hagamil bellowed. "How can there be no corpse?"

"The battle was fierce, and firbolgs are not so large," the scout replied. "When the fighting was over, all of Tavis Burdun that lay on the tundra were a few drops of blood."

"Sharpnose smashed him," elaborated Bodvar.

Hagamil turned toward the warrior. "If you were close enough to see the fight, why didn't *you* kill Tavis Burdun?"

Bodvar looked away. "I didn't see the fight," he admitted. "Just the proof."

"You have proof?" Hagamil said. "Let me have that, then."

Tavis reached inside his robe and withdrew his empty sword belt and mottled cloak, all that he still possessed of his gear. Hagamil snatched the tiny scraps and held them up to his enormous eye.

"What are these rags?" he demanded.

"Tavis Burdun's sword belt and cloak," Tavis replied.

"This isn't proof!" Hagamil roared.

The frost giant flung the belt and cloak in the general direction of the remorhaz. The beast's head pivoted and lashed out, snatching both items from the air. It swallowed them down in a single gulp, then licked its lips with a glowing red tongue and lunged at Frith one more time.

"Sharpnose had more," whispered Bodvar. "He had that long bow, Bear Driller, and the quiver with the golden arrow."

"*Had?*" Hagamil growled. "What happened to them?"

"I had them before the *traells* ambushed us," Tavis said.

"You were ambushed?" Hagamil demanded, looking at Slagfid.

"Just them." The leader pointed at Tavis and Bodvar. "Sharpnose saved Bodvar's life. That's when he lost the bow and quiver."

Hagamil's face turned as blue as a sapphire. He

whirled on Bodvar and yelled, "Sharpnose lost Bear Driller to save your miserable life?"

The warrior stumbled back, his eyes wide with terror. "I-I-I didn't ask him t-to."

"It—doesn't—matter!" The chieftain was so angry that he could barely sputter the words.

Hagamil's massive hand lashed out and clamped onto Bodvar's ear. For a moment, Tavis thought the angry giant would rip the thing off, but the chieftain's intentions were far more deadly. He flung the elbow of his opposite arm into the side of Bodvar's head, twisting his hips forward to hurl the full force of his weight into the blow.

A tremendous crack echoed through the cavern, as deep as a drumbeat and as sharp as a thunderclap. Bodvar's nostrils and ears began to pour blood, then his limp body slipped from Hagamil's grasp and collapsed in a heap. The warrior's mouth was still gaping open, astonished at the speed with which death had descended upon him.

Hagamil whirled on Tavis next, reaching for his throat. The scout raised his arms inside the chieftain's wrists and knocked the menacing hands away, then drove the heel of his palm into the giant's chin. The blow would have launched any other giant off his feet, but it merely shoved Hagamil's jaw out of socket.

The chieftain did not counterattack. A blank look suddenly replaced his angry mask, then his eyes rolled back in their sockets. The lids fluttered wildly, and one eyeball slowly sank out of sight behind his cheekbone. The yellow hair braids dropped from his head and writhed away like snakes, until they were plucked up and swallowed when they ventured too close to the remorhaz. The frost giant's massive shoulders slumped forward, his milky skin grew pallid and yellow, and Tavis found himself looking at the gaunt, one-eyed form of the shaman.

Halflook raised a bony hand to his dislocated jaw and popped it back into place. After opening and closing his mouth a few times, he fixed his bloodshot eye on Tavis and gave him a snaggletoothed grin.

"It's been a long time since someone struck Hagamil," Halflook said. "Much less knocked him unconscious."

"Yeah, but we can't bait the worm without Hagamil! What do we do now?"

The question came from the pit, where Sjolf and Snorri stood with the haggard ogre stretched between them. Although ogres stood half again as tall as humans, this one seemed as small as he did forlorn. He was about the size of a frost giant's leg, though not nearly so big around, with hunched shoulders and long, gangling arms. His loutish face was as pale as ivory, and his jutting chin trembled so badly that his tusks looked as if they might shake loose. The wooden spear had been thrust into his hand like a cruel joke, and the rusty shackles had been fastened to his ankles like an anchor.

"Is the baiting off?" asked one of the giants—Tavis did not know whether it was Sjolf or Snorri.

Halflook shook his head. "Why would it be?" he demanded. "Doesn't Halflook deserve some fun?"

The giants answered with a hearty chorus of approval. Halflook smiled and took Tavis's arm. He started toward the far end of the chamber, where several seats had been carved into the edge of the pit.

"You also deserve some fun, my friend," he said. "Killing Tavis Burdun could not have been easy."

"The battle was desperate," Tavis replied. "But I have no interest in worm-baiting. If you'll honor Hagamil's agreement and tell me where you're meeting Julien and Arno, I'll be on my way."

Halflook stopped and raised his brow, his single eye twinkling with a knowing light. "Hagamil promised you that?"

"He did," Tavis replied.

The shaman shook his head regretfully. "I can't help you. Hagamil has told me no more than anyone else: We are to break camp tomorrow, and he will lead us to the rendezvous." Halflook worked his bruised jaw back and forth, then added, "And I wouldn't advise you to wait and ask him. He'll be in a foul mood when he returns."

Halflook started forward again, but Tavis did not follow.

The shaman looked back, and a reassuring smile slid across his cracked lips. "Come along, Sharpnose. You've nothing to fear from me, and Hagamil won't be back until morning." His gaze drifted toward the cavern exit and again grew distant and unfocused. "Besides, there's a surprise coming—one you won't want to miss."

Tavis glanced toward the exit and saw nothing except the sable night. Nevertheless, he followed Halflook to one of the seats of honor, quite sure that the shaman would not let him leave now even if he insisted. One of Hagamil's concubines threw a mammoth fur down on Tavis's chair, then held his arm so that he didn't slip as he lowered himself into the icy seat. Even through the thick fur the scout felt the cold creeping into his weary bones. Halflook sat beside his guest, directly on the ice.

In the bottom of the pit, the ogre now stood alone, his neck craned back and his beady, bewildered eyes running over the enormous faces gaping down at him. The last of his two captors was just stepping off the log ladder onto the chamber's main floor. Slagfid and another warrior had taken hold of the remorhaz's harness poles and were holding the writhing beast over the pit. Frith stood next to them, grasping a long halberd, which he would use to slice the harness.

Halflook leaned over to Tavis. "I know stone giants find these things boring, so perhaps we should make a wager," he suggested. "Having something at stake does liven things up."

"What kind of wager?" Tavis asked. He had little interest

in watching the cruel contest and even less in wagering on it, but he knew the shaman had a good reason for proposing a bet.

"Do you think the ogre will injure the remorhaz before he dies?" Halflook asked.

Tavis studied the frightened prisoner for a moment. He bore no love for ogres—they were a brutal, wicked race—but he had learned to respect them. In desperate circumstances, they were especially spirited, and they possessed a certain animal cunning that would prove useful in a battle such as this.

"The ogre won't last long," Tavis decided. "But he'll draw blood."

"Good," replied the shaman. "Then that's our wager."

"And the stakes?" Tavis asked.

"If he fails to draw blood, you tell me how you and Bodvar really lost Bear Driller and Little Dragon," said the shaman.

"How did you know we lost Little Dragon?" Tavis's heart was beginning to pound with cold apprehension. "No one said that."

The shaman smiled. "Is that really what you wish to know if you win?"

"No, of course not." Tavis exhaled slowly, trying to calm himself and keep his face relaxed. "If the ogre draws blood, you'll tell me how to find the rendezvous."

"Why is the rendezvous so important to you?" Halflook asked.

"Why is it so important to you that only frost giants accompany Brianna to Twilight?" the scout countered.

Halflook smiled crookedly. "I had not thought stone giants so covetous of such honors," he said. "But I was speaking truly when I said only Hagamil knows. The best I can do is give you safe passage and one of Bodvar's bulls to ride. Then, perhaps, you could trail us at a safe distance. Our path will not be so hard to follow."

"Perhaps you could heal my toe instead," Tavis suggested. "I'd prefer to walk."

Halflook chuckled at this. "Do you really want me to use frost magic on your stony toe?" he asked. "Or have you never seen how ice can break rocks apart?"

"Perhaps I will accept the mammoth," the scout replied.

"A wise decision."

The shaman looked to the other end of the chamber, where Sjolf and Snorri were pulling the log ladder from the pit. The remorhaz was growling more viciously than ever, while the ogre was dragging his chains across the pit so that he would be in position to attack as soon as the beast fell.

Halflook nodded to Frith. "Release the worm."

The young giant reached out and ran the halberd blade across the worm's harness. After a moment of slicing, the hide strap came apart and the remorhaz slipped into the pit amidst a clatter of legs and chitin.

The ogre lurched forward, his heavy chains clanging against the ice. The remorhaz whirled on him. The brutish prisoner swung his spear like a club, striking the worm's throat with a sharp crack. The creature's sinuous neck crackled and folded around the heft, then the beast's body went slack. For an instant Tavis thought the captive might have won the fight in a single blow. Then, as deep-throated murmurs of disappointment began to echo through the chamber, the ice worm whipped its rear segments forward, slamming its heavy tail into the ogre.

The prisoner sailed across the pit and crashed into an icy wall. The air left his lungs in a loud huff, then the spear dropped from his grasp. He slid down the wall in a limp heap and lay there wheezing, his weapon lying a hand's length beyond his fingertips.

The giants shook the cavern with their cheers. The remorhaz approached cautiously, its neck-wings flapping and its black eyes fixed on the ogre. The worm stopped just out of the captive's reach and stretched its face tentacles toward the spear.

The ogre stopped wheezing and snatched his spear up, slashing the tip at his foe's bulbous eyes. The remorhaz jerked back, then the captive was on his feet and thrusting at the beast's chitinous throat. The ice worm slipped the blow with a well-timed curl of the neck and countered with a lightning-fast head strike.

The ogre blocked with a slap of his weapon's shaft, then dodged behind the worm's head wing. Taking the spear in both hands, he raised the tip high over the white streak on the beast's back.

Even as the spear began its descent, Tavis knew the ogre had made his first mistake. To keep themselves from freezing in the icy wastes, remorhazes generated as much internal heat as red dragons, and their blood was as hot as molten stone. When the spear pierced the worm, a geyser of white fire spewed from the hole. The wooden shaft dissolved into a wisp of smoke.

The astonished ogre bellowed in agony. He raised his hands to his seared face and stumbled away. The ice worm leaped instantly to the attack, trapping the agonized brute beneath its chitinous bulk. The remorhaz curled its head under its bulk to finish its prey, but even then the captive put up a valiant fight. The worm's serpentine body continued to squirm for several moments before it finally raised its bloody maw to bugle its victory cry.

The giants shouted in glee, filling the chamber with such a clamor that several icicles broke off the ceiling and crashed down on their heads. Halflook leaned over to Tavis.

Almost shouting to make himself heard above the din, the giant said, "I believe you owe me an explanation, Sharpnose."

"I think not," Tavis replied.

The scout pointed at the underside of the remorhaz's sinuous neck, where a chitinous scale had been torn away during the battle. A broken ogre tusk protruded from the beast's throat, and a thin red line of steaming blood rimmed the puncture.

"You owe me a mammoth."

Halflook's mouth twisted into half a dozen different kinds of snarls. His red-veined eye remained fixed on the tusk until the remorhaz finished its victory call, then he looked back to Tavis and reluctantly nodded his head.

"So I see," he said.

"If you'll have someone show me how to ride it, I'll be on my way."

Tavis hoisted himself from his seat and climbed onto the main floor. The cold had seeped deep into his joints, so that the effort of standing sent an icy ache through his entire body. He felt more exhausted than ever, and sickened by the spectacle he had been forced to watch.

Halflook also stood, stepping to the scout's side. "Stay a moment longer, I beg you." The shaman's eye turned toward the cavern exit and once again acquired that distant, unfocused look. "The surprise is almost here."

"I've seen enough for one night," the scout replied. "I'm in no mood for surprises."

"Not even this one?"

The shaman pointed toward the exit, where a tall frost giant was stepping into the chamber. Although Tavis had not gotten much of a look at the sentry earlier, this warrior appeared to be about the same size and build.

"You're looking too high." Halflook's bloodshot eye was locked onto Tavis's face as though connected to it. "The surprise is much farther down, near the floor."

Tavis lowered his gaze. For several moments, he saw nothing but the enormous, booted feet of frost giants. Then, as the sentry pushed his way deeper into the cave, the scout glimpsed a small, shivering form among the massive legs: Avner.

✦11✦
Midnight Vigil

A muffled creak came to Basil's ears, or perhaps it was more of a squeal. Fearing his runes of silence had gotten smudged, the verbeeg stopped and looked down at his feet, then cursed himself for not bringing a lamp. The keep corridors were as dark as caves at this hour of night. He could hardly see his boots, much less determine whether the sigils on the insteps were intact, and he still had two squeaky staircases to ascend.

The sound returned, and this time the runecaster heard it more clearly: a sort of muffled, gurgling squeal coming from the corridor on his right. Basil sighed in relief. He had heard similar noises in Castle Hartwick often enough. They always came late at night from behind closed doors, when people seemed to believe darkness would smother their sounds. Foolish humans.

Tightly clutching the folio he had taken from Cuthbert's library, Basil started forward again, running one hand along the wooden ceiling to keep himself from banging his head. He had already skimmed the volume once and knew it told the story of Twilight's creation. There had been no mention of Arlien, but the folio did list all of the giants who had been present. With a few hours of study and contemplation, the verbeeg felt confident he would find the connection between the prince and Twilight.

The ceiling ended at a horizontal corner. The verbeeg ran his hand down the wall to an oaken door, then reached down around his knees to find the latch.

"Noooo!" The cry came from the same corridor as the squealing earlier. The voice sounded like Brianna's.

A muffled thud came next, then the muted growl of an angry man. "Drink!"

Basil rushed back down the hall. Although the floor trembled under the impact of his heavy feet, the runes on his boots allowed him to move across the planks in utter silence. He heard no more sounds from the side corridor. He turned down the narrow passage, squatting down to listen at each door he passed. The verbeeg heard nothing but the rumbling of a few snoring sleepers.

At the end of the corridor, Basil came to a small stairway curving up one of the keep's exterior walls. By the purple midnight blush pouring through the arrow loops, the verbeeg could see that this passageway had been built strictly for humans. It was barely large enough for a single man.

Basil peered up the corridor, trying to gauge whether his hunched shoulders would fit between its walls. In his mind appeared the unwelcome image of a verbeeg youth trapped in a cramped tunnel, and the runecaster felt runnels of hot sweat pouring down his brow. He wondered if he couldn't find another, larger staircase that led to the same place. His shoulders would barely fit into this passage, and the corridor might grow narrower ahead. Besides, he couldn't even be sure Brianna was up there, or that she needed help.

Brianna's voice murmured down the stairwell, "Bastard!"

The word sounded thick and slurred, as though the queen had been drinking. Basil pondered going for help, but rejected the idea. If he embarrassed Brianna by calling the guard when she had only drunk too much wine, the verbeeg felt quite sure the rest of his time at Cuthbert Castle would be spent in the dungeon.

A sharp clatter rattled down the stairwell.

Basil slipped the folio inside his robe, then dropped to his hands and knees. He turned sideways and wormed his way into the narrow stairwell. The step edges dug into his bottom arm, and the walls squeezed his chest so tightly that he could not draw a deep breath. He worked his arms past his head and pulled himself into the gloomy passage.

The walls squeezed his chest more tightly, filling his body with a dull, throbbing ache. His breath came in shallow gasps, whether from panic or inability to expand his lungs he did not know. He squinted up the passage. The purple night glow was too dim to see whether the corridor grew wider above.

Basil reached farther and dragged himself farther up the stairwell. The passage narrowed slightly, and he found himself wedged in place. When he inhaled, his chest filled with crushing agony. The verbeeg pulled harder, twisting his shoulders back and forth, and felt the folio digging into his waist. Then, for no obvious reason, his throat began to close up.

"Nothing's wrong," he gasped. Basil heard his pulse pounding in his ears, and he felt his eyes bulging in their sockets. "I'm panicking, that's all."

Basil's body did not care. It wanted out of the dark corridor, and it wanted out now. The verbeeg found his arms pushing at the wall, trying to force his large mass down the stairway. Through the thin cloth of his trousers, the bottom of the folio snagged on a stone block. He pushed harder, driving the top edge into his stomach.

Only then did it occur to Basil to ask why he had tried to save Brianna. Strictly speaking, he wasn't even one of her subjects, and even if he had been, no verbeeg had ever suffered the compulsion to perform his duty to a liege.

Perhaps it was her library, the runecaster thought. If Brianna perished, the new monarch would name a new librarian, denying Basil access to the thousands of ancient and obscure volumes in the Royal Archives. But what good were all those books if he failed to work himself free?

A loud thump rolled down the stairway, followed by a pained groan. Suddenly it no longer mattered why Basil had crawled into the stairwell. Brianna needed help, and verbeeg or not, the runecaster could no longer turn his back on a friend in need.

"I'm starting to act like a firbolg," Basil grumbled.

The runecaster braced his feet against the walls and dug his fingers deep into a seam between two blocks of stone. He exhaled until he was certain all the air had left his lungs, then he forced himself farther up the stairway. He felt each separate rib grating against the wall, flexing inward and racking his body with pain. An anguished grunt escaped his lips and softly rumbled up the corridor.

Basil redoubled his efforts. His vertebrae and ribs shot sharp pangs of protest through his torso. He ignored them and pushed with every muscle in his body. The verbeeg heard a muted crackle and felt a series of pops run down his spine. He came free and bumped up the stairs. His lungs filled themselves with a sharp gasp, then he spied a sliver of yellow light less than ten steps away. It was dancing beneath a closed door on a small landing above. The runecaster pushed himself to the platform and listened at the door.

From inside came a scratching sound, such as rats make as they gnaw through wood, and the gurgle of flowing liquid.

Basil gently undid the latch, then pulled himself to his feet. He used his toe to push the door open. He could feel the hinges grating against their pins, but the runes painted on his boot kept the portal from making any sound.

Inside lay a modest chamber with a vaulted ceiling and a granite altar at the far end. Standing before this platform, with his back to the door and still wearing his enchanted armor, was Arlien of Gilthwit—or rather, Arlien of Twilight. He had Brianna's feebly struggling form pinned to the altar, with his armored elbow resting

on her sternum and his fingers holding her jaws open
The other hand was pouring the contents of a large si
ver flagon into her mouth.

Brianna seemed lethargic and half asleep, with glaze
eyes and drooping lids. The prince was pouring faste
than she could swallow, so the fruity-smelling concoc
tion dribbled down her cheeks in runnels. One arn
hung limply off the altar. Her other hand waved lan
guidly in the air, the fingers curled into ineffectual claws
Her gown had been torn half off.

"That's better, my dear." Arlien's voice was a mockery
of gentleness. "Drink it all. You'll feel much better."

The runecaster crawled through the door on hi
hands and knees, moving slowly and carefully to avoi
making any noise. Once he was inside the room, where
the vaulted ceiling allowed him to stand upright, he
pulled the folio from his trousers. He considered smash
ing the heavy book over Arlien's head, but could no
bring himself to destroy such a priceless treasure. Basi
leaned the volume beside the door, then calmly walke
to the altar. The prince continued to pour, oblivious t
the angry verbeeg standing behind him.

Basil grabbed the collar of Arlien's backplate an
pulled. The prince did not even budge. Instead, three
buckles popped loose and his backplate swung free.

Basil's jaw dropped open and his bushy eyebrow
came together. He blinked rapidly, squinting and shak
ing his head, absentmindedly allowing his fist to open.

Arlien had a second face.

It was where the prince's right shoulder-blade shoul
have been, hanging upside down with its dull eyes glar
ing at Basil. The face was ugly and brutish, with pal
skin, a pug nose, and a double-chin encrusted with drie
food. The thing's thick lips formed a spiteful sneer.

"Bad plan, Ugly!"

As the head spoke, Arlien spun around, smashing th
flagon into Basil's cheek, then driving an elbow dee

nto his groin. The strength left the runecaster's legs. He dropped to his knees, in too much pain to do anything except gurgle. Arlien grabbed a handful of the verbeeg's thin gray hair and jerked his head up, driving a knee into the runecaster's face.

Basil's nose shattered with a sickening crunch. His head erupted into throbbing pain and his vision fell dark. He tumbled onto his back, blood gushing from both nostrils. A sharp crack reverberated through his skull as it slammed into the floor. Something huge and heavy landed on his chest. He felt fingers—impossibly long fingers—clamping around his throat.

Still blinded by the pain of his broken nose, the verbeeg clutched at the arm above his neck. The thing was so big he could hardly close his hands around it, and it seemed to be growing larger in his grasp. He tried to push the limb away. He may as well have been trying to topple a full-grown spruce. His windpipe grew scratchy and raw. He ached to cough, but that was impossible with the fingers around his throat pinching it shut.

Think, Basil told himself. Only Arlien could be kneeling on his chest. The verbeeg did not understand why the prince weighed so much, and why he seemed to be getting larger. At the moment, that wasn't important. All that mattered was getting that enormous hand off his throat. He could not accomplish that through force alone. To free himself, he had to apply his strength to his opponent's weakness.

Basil considered the structure of the opposable thumb, then knew exactly what to do. He reached across the back of Arlien's hand and grasped the base of the thumb, then pulled straight back, using the heel of his own palm like a lever against his attacker's forearm. The prince's grip came loose, his wrist unable to twist in the direction Basil was bending it. The runecaster's breath returned in a long wheeze.

The verbeeg bridged on his shoulders and thrust his

knee into the middle of Arlien's back. The blow sent the prince pitching over Basil's head. The runecaster rolled away and leaped to his feet. The sudden movement siphoned a wave of pain from his shattered nose, but the runecaster did not care. His vision was clearing, and he could see Brianna's blurry form, trying to prop herself up on the altar.

The verbeeg grabbed the small bench that sat before the platform and spun around. Through his hazy vision, he found himself peering at the murky form of what appeared to be a two-headed giant. The brute stood so tall that he had to stoop over even in the vaulted temple. His twin necks were so short that the pair of heads seemed to sit directly atop his broad chest.

"Hiatea, save us!" the runecaster gasped. The two-headed giant was wearing the same armor Basil had nearly ripped off Arlien's back earlier, save that the enchanted suit was now much larger. "An ettin!"

"Wrong." The silky voice sounded much like Arlien's, save that it was much deeper and more resonant. "*The* ettin."

Basil wasted no time asking what Arlien meant by the correction. He swung the bench at his foe's knee. The seat snapped down the center, sending the two halves clattering across the floor. The ettin's leg did not buckle.

It did not even twitch.

Basil glimpsed an enormous fist descending from on high, then a horrific clap sounded inside his skull. His head snapped sideways, and his feet left the ground. He slammed into a wall. The entire flank of his body erupted into pain, and a loud crack reverberated through the chamber. For one awful instant, Basil thought some part of his body had made the terrible sound. Then he felt a stone crash into his hip and realized the impact of his body had merely knocked a block from the wall.

The verbeeg raised his head and saw that his vision was no longer dim. He could see clearly enough to identify

rince Arlien's cleft chin and patrician nose on the ettin's
econd head. The features were, of course, three times
neir normal size.

The ettin ducked under a low-hanging beam and
ropped to a knee beside Basil. The runecaster pushed
way, scuttling across the floor like a crab. The ettin
eached out to grab him—and the sound of booted feet
ame pounding up the stairway.

"In Stronmaus's name, what's happening up there?" It
as Cuthbert's voice. "Stop it at once, I command it!"

"Help!" Basil yelled. "Hurry, we're in danger!"

The pounding in the stairwell grew louder and faster.

One of the ettin's arm's pulled back, but the other con-
nued to reach for Basil. The brute's enormous body
wisted sideways, as though it were suffering some kind
f seizure.

"Stop it, Arno!" hissed Arlien. "We don't have time."

"We gotta kill him, Julien!" Arno grunted. "If he
ves—"

"Let me worry about that," growled Arlien—or rather,
ulien. One of the hands placed itself over Arno's brutish
ace and shoved the head back over the shoulder, and
ulien said, "You go back where you belong."

As Basil struggled to his feet, both of the ettin's hands
usied themselves pulling the breastplate back into
lace. The giant began to shrink immediately. By the
ime the verbeeg had returned to his wobbly legs, the
ttin was once again the size of a human. Basil grabbed
he stone block that had fallen on him and raised it to
url, but was checked by the sight of a guard rushing
nto the room.

"Don't!" the man ordered. He stepped over to point
is halberd at Basil's throat. "Put it down!"

Five more soldiers streamed through the door and
mmediately rushed to stand at their companion's side.

Basil reluctantly lowered his stone to the height of
is chest, but did not place it on the floor. "I'm not the

dangerouth one here!" The verbeeg's smashed nose gave his voice a heavy nasal accent, while the blow to his head had left him with several broken teeth and a thick tongue. "Ith Julien!"

The guard frowned. "Who?"

"Him!" Basil pointed at the ettin disguised as a human prince. "Prince Arthlien."

"I assure you, I pose no danger to anyone—except those who would harm Queen Brianna." Arlien was glaring at Basil, at the same time tying his armor closed with the remnants of two torn straps. The prince glanced at the altar, where Brianna had pulled herself into a seated position. She was peering around the room with the blurry-eyed look of someone who had drunk too much wine. "Fortunately, she's safe enough at the moment."

"That seems something of an exaggeration," said Cuthbert, stepping into the chamber. The earl wore only his long sleeping gown, but his eyes were alert and sharp. He walked directly to the altar and, making a face at the sweet odor hanging so thickly in the air, took the queen's arm. "Majesty, what happened? Are you well?"

Brianna tried to focus her eyes on the earl, then gave up and looked over his shoulder. "Your queen is tired," she breathed. "Very tired."

Cuthbert winced at the smell of her breath. "So I see." He pulled her tattered dress back up over her shoulders, then asked, "Are you injured? It looks as though you've had a struggle."

Brianna swayed, but shook her head. "Don't worry. The queen's not hurt." She leveled a cross-eyed gaze at Arlien, then said, "She had a little fight."

Cuthbert motioned three of his guards toward the prince, then asked, "With who? Arlien?"

"Of course not!" the imposter snapped. He kept his eyes locked on the queen's as he spoke. "I'm the one who came to her aid—isn't that right, Brianna?"

Cuthbert's eyes flashed in anger. "Prince Arlien,

tonight I will ask the questions! Is that clear?"

"As you wish—tonight."

The earl turned back to Brianna. "Who did you fight with, Majesty?"

"The queen fought with . . . the prince," Brianna answered, thinking hard. Her eyes turned in the imposter's direction, then she asked, "Why would Arlien fight with her? He loves her! Maybe the queen was dreaming."

Cuthbert eyed her tattered dress. "You weren't dreaming."

Brianna scowled. "The queen was dreaming!" she insisted. "Don't you argue!"

The earl rubbed his fingers across his eyes, then turned to the imposter. "What happened here?"

"It wasn't a fight—at least not until Basil arrived," Arlien replied. "When I came to check on Her Majesty, I found her extremely disoriented from her long vigil before the altar. I was trying to convince her to drink a restorative when Basil charged in and attacked. I don't see how he could have thought I was threatening her, but I suppose it is vaguely possible."

Cuthbert looked at the runecaster and scowled. "Well?" he demanded. "What do you have to say?"

Basil pointed his battered chin at the prince. "Thath man ith an impothter—an ettin!"

The earl rolled his eyes. "An ettin?"

"Hith armor keepth him dithguithed," said Basil. "That'th why he never taketh ith off!"

The imposter stepped toward Brianna. "My injury isn't entirely healed. As I've already explained, my armor's magic won't finish the process if I remove it, even temporarily." The prince began to undo the straps he had just tied together. "But if the queen wishes, I shall remove my breastplate and show her what's underneath."

"Waith! Keep away from the queen!" Basil snapped,

remembering how quickly the ettin had appeared the last time Arlien's armor had opened. Still holding the rock in his hands, the verbeeg waved the guards toward the prince. "Be ready. The change will come very fatht!"

The imposter rolled his eyes, then stopped untying his breastplate straps. "I'll wait until you're ready, Basil." The prince glanced at Brianna, who sat wobbling at the edge of the altar, then added, "Providing it is the queen's wish that I ruin my armor's enchantment to defend myself against the charges of a known thief and liar."

Brianna shook her head. "The queen wishes . . . no such thing," she slurred. "She can attest to who you are."

"I don't think you can attest to much of anything at the moment, Majesty," said Cuthbert. "Perhaps we would all sleep better if the prince did show us what's beneath his armor."

"No!" Brianna shouted. She frowned, startled by the vigor of her own voice, then fixed her glassy eyes on the earl. "When the fighting starts . . . tomorrow, we'll need him at his best. I—I forbid him to remove his armor."

The earl raised his brow, but inclined his head. "Then perhaps we should all return to our chambers. We'll sort this out in the morning, when Her Majesty is, ah—" The earl gave Brianna a sideways glance, then finished, "When she's feeling a little more like herself."

"No! Thath'll be too lathe!" Basil blurted. "She could be gone by then!"

"Gone?" Cuthbert demanded. "How could she go any place?"

"Don't you thee?" the runecaster explained. "The printhe ith an impothter. He'th here to kidnap her."

"I can assure you there won't be any kidnappings tonight, my friend," the earl hissed. "Everyone will be locked in his or her own chamber, and even an ettin can't fight past all the guards I intend to post around Queen Brianna tonight."

Arlien's eyes flashed with irritation, but he did not object. "A wise precaution, Earl." He glanced in Basil's direction, then said, "I'd like to make a suggestion myself."

"You can suggest anything you like," Cuthbert replied.

The imposter accepted this with a polite smile. "Thank you," he said. "Given that our verbeeg friend has already escaped a locked chamber, perhaps he should be relocated to a cell in your dungeon."

"I hardly think that's necessary," said Cuthbert.

"Really? How many more of those do you wish to lose?" Arlien pointed toward the entrance.

Cuthbert's eyes followed the imposter's finger toward the door. As soon as they fell on the folio Basil had left leaning against the wall, the earl's face turned scarlet.

A sly smile crossed the imposter's lips. "It occurs to me we might be looking at the purpose behind Basil's accusations," he said. "He hoped to distract us with that ridiculous lie about the ettin so you wouldn't noticed that he had filched one of your ancestral treasures."

"Quite so!" Cuthbert fumed. He tore his eyes away from the folio and bowed to the imposter. "Good prince, you have my thanks for bringing this to my attention, and my apologies for questioning your honor."

Arlien smiled politely. "All is forgotten."

The prince had barely replied before Cuthbert was spinning toward Basil. He motioned to the three soldiers guarding the runecaster. "Take that verbeeg to the dungeon!" he commanded. "Manacle him to the wall, and I swear if he escapes, it'll be a month in the stocks for both of you!"

"But you're making a terrible mithtake!" Basil objected.

"Go!" the earl roared. "And if he shows the slightest hint of resisting, run him through!"

One of the soldiers prodded Basil toward the door. "You'd best be going."

The runecaster reluctantly moved to obey. "Tell me, are the dungeon thellth very large?"

"Yeah, they're real big," snorted the guard. "You'll just about have room to sit up."

❖ 12 ❖
Worm Baiting

With clenched jaw and sweating palms, Tavis watched the sentry herd Avner through the crowded ice cavern. The trip was a slow one, for every frost giant in the chamber insisted on inspecting the prisoner dubbed "Little Dragon." Many even dropped to their hands and knees for a closer look, blocking the youth's path until his puzzled escort shoved them away. Slagfid followed close behind the guard, trying not to look surprised by the boy's unexpected arrival.

To Tavis, the wait seemed forever. A dozen different questions were pounding inside his head, most notably how he was going to get Avner out of the cave before Hagamil returned. The scout was also curious about where the boy had come by the bearskin parka he now wore, and what had happened to Bear Driller. Neither the boy nor his guard were carrying the firbolg's bow or quiver.

But, more than any other answer, the scout wanted to know how Halflook had discerned that the sentry had captured the boy. Did the shaman's mystical sight also allow him to see through Tavis's disguise? That would certainly explain why the giant had insisted that his guest stay until the "surprise" arrived.

At last, the sentry pushed his way past the last curious frost giant and stopped in front of Halflook. Standing between the two giants, Avner seemed incredibly small. The thought of him holding Slagfid's war party at bay seemed as absurd as a mad squirrel holding a bridge against fifteen armored knights.

"Halflook, call Hagamil," ordered the sentry. "Tell him

I caught this *traell* trying to sneak into camp."

"Hagamil's sleeping," the shaman replied. "He already knows about this captive—though he's under the impression that Slagfid bears the honor for capturing him." Halflook's red-veined eye shifted to Slagfid's face.

"That's a lie!" The sentry scowled at Slagfid. "You can see for yourself I'm the one who gots him!"

"But Slagfid had him first," Tavis pointed out, taking a lesson from Avner. If he could start a fight between the two giants, he stood a reasonable chance of snatching the boy and escaping during the confusion. "By rights, the honor belongs to Slagfid."

"That is not for you to decide, Sharpnose!" Halflook's voice had turned deep and gravelly. "You are no chief!"

Tavis turned and saw the shaman's single eyeball rolling back in its socket. Hagamil was returning much earlier than expected.

"Halflook!" the scout shouted. "Our business is not done!"

"Go with Slagfid." The voice was Halflook's, but it sounded rather strained. "He'll show you to one of Bodvar's mammoths."

"I no longer wish a mammoth," Tavis said. "I'll trade the beast for this little *traell*." He gestured at Avner.

A chorus of thunderous laughter echoed off the cavern walls.

"Do not insult us, Sharpnose," warned Slagfid. He glanced into the pit, where the remorhaz was devouring the last of the ogre. "Watching Little Dragon fight the worm is worth at least ten mammoths."

"Is it worth—"

"It doesn't matter what you pay!" To Tavis's astonishment, the speaker was Avner. "I'd rather stay and fight than become a stone giant's slave!"

Tavis scowled down at the youth. Avner couldn't have forgotten his true identity!

"Even if they gave me to you, I wouldn't go." The

boy pointed to the exit. "So you might as well leave, Gavorial."

The scout raised his brow. Avner was trying to tell him something, probably that he had hidden Bear Driller someplace nearby. Unfortunately, Tavis did not see how that helped matters.

Still peering down at Avner, the scout said, "At the moment, what you want is not important. I have better uses for you than feeding ice worms."

"But the *traell* is not your catch," growled Hagamil's voice.

A mass of yellow hair was sprouting on the shaman's head, but the giant still had only a single, red-veined eye. The orb was fluttering up and down in its socket, as though Halflook were fighting to retain control of the body.

"Leave!" the shaman urged. "I doubt Hagamil will honor my promise."

"You heard him!" Avner called. "As far as I'm concerned, the sooner you're gone, the better!"

Tavis shrugged. "It seems I have no choice." He looked down at Avner, hoping to give the youth one last warning. "But I think you'll be surprised at how difficult it is to kill a remorhaz. I'm sure you'll wish you were going home with me instead of dancing across its back with a burning spear in your hand."

An expression of bewilderment flashed across Avner's face, but he quickly replaced it with a disdainful sneer. "The only place I'd rather be is with Tavis." The youth cast a nervous glance toward the pit, then added, "And I'll be joining him soon enough."

Slagfid grabbed Tavis by the wrist. "Let's go," the frost giant urged. "I don't want to miss the fight."

The scout limped after his escort. The effects of Bodvar's ice diamond were wearing off, and his injured toe was starting to pain him.

Outside, a stiff wind had risen. It was whistling

through the gaps between the nunataks, carrying with it
a scouring stream of ice pellets. A ferocious-looking
bank of storm clouds was rolling over the caldera's
northern rim, its leading edge gleaming silver in the
moonlight. It seemed to Tavis that he could actually feel
the temperature dropping.

"It appears there's quite a storm coming our way," the
scout commented.

Slagfid paused long enough to turn his face into the
pelting ice crystals. "Yes, it promises to be a glorious
blizzard!" he shouted. "Thrym favors us!"

The frost giant smiled broadly, then led the way to the
water hole that the mammoths had gouged in the frozen
lake. Although Tavis could hear the ice groaning
beneath the beasts' immense weight, Slagfid did not
show the slightest hesitation as he walked out to them.
The scout decided to wait on shore, suspecting that if
the ice broke, the cold would affect him far more than
the frost giant.

Slagfid waded into the herd, looking remarkably similar to a human shepherd pushing his way through a
flock of goats. The frost giant stooped over and began
grabbing ears. He tipped each beast's head back so that
he could inspect the left tusk, no doubt looking for an
ownership mark etched into the ivory. The mammoths
trumpeted their protest and occasionally tried to push
him away, but the creatures were no match for the
giant's strength. He simply stood his ground and
grabbed each animal's trunk, pinching it shut until the
beast stopped struggling.

The frost giant had sorted through about half the
herd when the creatures began flapping their ears and
changing positions, aligning themselves shoulder-to-
shoulder with their heads pointed into the wind. They
raised their trunks and let out an intimidating wail,
slashing their long tusks through the air and pawing at
the ice.

The vibrations caused a large slab of ice to break free, dropping three mammoths and Slagfid into the frigid lake. The plunge didn't bother any of them. The beasts simply wrapped their trunks around the legs of the closest herd members, then hoisted themselves up with one or two clumsy leaps. No water dripped out of their matted fur, for it had turned to ice the instant the animals had left the lake. Slagfid followed the mammoths' example, save that he used his hands instead of a prehensile trunk.

The frost giant peered in the same direction as the mammoths. "What's wrong over there?" he demanded, knocking ice chunks off his body. "Do you see anything?"

Tavis glanced in the direction the giant indicated. "Yes: snow, ice, and shadows."

The scout did not add that one of the shadows looked to be about the size of a *traell*. The fellow was lying behind a jagged ridge of ice, with a long bow that could only be Bear Driller on the ground in front of him. Apparently, Avner had recruited some help at the bottom of the glacier. That was why he had been so confident.

Slagfid peered at the shore a moment longer, then shrugged. "Probably bears. Little vermin like that scares mammoths as bad as dragons." He turned to face the herd again, then shook his head and swore, "By the Endless Ice Sea! Now I've got to start over!"

* * * * *

Avner dangled upside down at the end of a greasy rope. A pair of rusty shackles bound his ankles, and in his hands he clutched a blade-tipped spear. The remorhaz danced on the ice almost thirty feet below.

At the top end of Avner's rope, Hagamil and Halflook were carrying on a bizarre quarrel. The argument would have been comical had the youth's life not depended on the outcome.

"The body belongs to me until morning!" said Halflook. "If you want to set Little Dragon against the worm, you can wait."

"By morning, we'll be on our way." Hagamil's gravelly voice rasped from the same mouth out of which Halflook's had just come. "It's a long way to Split Mountain."

"Split Mountain?" snarled Halflook. "We should have left yesterday!"

As the pair argued, Avner slipped his spear between his knees. He took his lockpicking tools out of his belt pouch, then laboriously raised his body up until he could grab his shackle chains. Once the giants dropped him, he would need his mobility—at least if he intended to survive until Tavis returned.

"Hey, what's Little Dragon doing?" called one of the frost giant spectators. "Is he tryin' to cheat?"

"Yeah! Ain't he smart?" answered another. "Just like Slagfid said!"

Hagamil and Halflook glanced briefly at their captive, but made no move to prevent him from unlocking his shackles. Apparently, it was okay to cheat at frost giant games. Under different circumstances, Avner might have enjoyed the company of his captors.

"I would've left the day before yesterday," Hagamil said, continuing the argument. When he spoke, his second eye hung half-descended into the socket. "But we had to wait 'til Slagfid killed Tavis Burdun. So now we've gotta do this thing with Little Dragon tonight."

The first shackle came loose with a pop. Avner twined his arm around the rope, then slipped the pick into the second lock.

"Fine," Halflook said. "Then I get to watch the match."

Avner twisted the pick, and the lock popped open. His feet swung free, leaving the shackles in place and him dangling above the remorhaz by a single arm.

"Hey, Little Dragon done it!" called one of the spectators. "He got loose!"

Avner slipped his lockpick back into his belt pouch, then grabbed the spear from between his knees.

Halflook peered down and frowned, then Hagamil's voice declared, "We're doing it now!"

The giant—which one, Avner was not quite sure—let the rope slip between his fingers, lowering the youth into the pit like a spider on a thread. The remorhaz reared its chitinous head, ready to strike the instant its prey came into range.

Avner tucked his spear beneath his arm, then began whipping his legs to and fro until he was swinging like a pendulum. The ice worm rocked back and forth in time with the motion. A growing murmur buzzed through the cold chamber as the giants debated the purpose and effectiveness of Little Dragon's maneuver.

When his captor had lowered him to within a spear's length of the remorhaz, the youth released the rope at the far end of his arc. His momentum catapulted him far past the ice worm's tail. He hit the ice close to twenty paces away from the beast, then lost his footing and skidded across the floor. He did not stop sliding until he bounced off a wall.

Much to the giants' delight, the youth instantly leaped to his feet and came up facing the remorhaz. His shackles clanged to the floor on the opposite side of the pit. The ice worm, which had been turning toward the youth, whirled around and scurried toward the noise, hissing and sputtering.

Avner gripped his spear and crept after the beast in silence, hoping to sneak up on the blind spot behind the creature's head. The youth kept a careful watch on the ice worm's legs, alert for any movement that suggested it was whirling toward him. Despite their sticklike appearance, the remorhaz's legs were surprisingly large, with bulbous joints as big around as a human knee.

The ice worm stopped beside the shackles and ran a face tentacle over the cold steel. Avner was puzzled to see little wisps of vapor rising from the ice beneath the metal. He did not understand what was causing the steam, but it seemed clear enough that he would be wise to avoid the tentacles.

After a time, the remorhaz tossed the irons aside with a contemptuous flick of its head, apparently satisfied that the lifeless steel would cause it no harm. The beast carefully turned around, searching for its prey.

Avner slipped to the side, taking care to stay in the worm's blind spot, and deftly glided toward the shackles. The maneuver elicited a round of thunderous chuckles from the giants above.

When the ice worm did not find its quarry in the expected place, it vented a gurgling roar and spun around in a whirling blue flash. Avner thrust the tip of his spear into the floor and pushed off, launching himself toward the shackles in a crazy, slip-sliding sprint. The remorhaz hissed in glee and came scratching after him, its many claws gouging long furrows in the ice.

Avner snatched the irons on the move. Allowing himself to glide across the bumpy floor for a moment, he turned and hurled his spear at the remorhaz. The ice worm ducked, though it hardly needed to, and the shaft sailed harmlessly past its head. The youth resumed his sprint, his fingers tearing madly at the rope attached to the heavy chain. He managed to undo the knot quickly, for it had been tied by giant fingers and was quite loose. Behind him he heard the remorhaz's claws warily clattering on the ice.

"Hey, what are you afraid of!" Avner called. He reached the wall and stopped, then turned around to see the ice worm slowly stalking toward him. He beat the shackles against the ice, yelling, "Come and get me. Hear that dinner bell?"

The remorhaz charged. Avner waited until the worm was moving so fast that it could not possibly stop, then pushed off the wall and ran straight toward the beast. The remorhaz raised its head to strike. The youth dropped to his hip and hit the ice sliding, whirling the shackles like a morningstar. He passed beneath the beast's belly before it could attack, whipping the irons into the creature's legs. He heard the satisfying crunch of crackling chitin and felt two limbs fracture.

The remorhaz roared and sprang sideways, trying to leap away from its tormentor. Avner grabbed one of its bulbous knees and held tight, and when the beast landed, the youth was still beneath it. He slipped one of the open shackles around the worm's leg, closing the cuff above the creature's round ankle.

The remorhaz thrust its head under its belly, jaws snapping and face tendrils flaying. The youth managed to whirl away from the beast's needle-toothed maw, but its tentacles thrashed him several times. Scorching pains shot through his face and arms, and red welts rose wherever the tendrils touched. Avner continued to roll, jerking the worm's shackled leg after him.

The remorhaz roared in pain and dropped to its side, slashing Avner with the legs along its other flank. The youth turned his head away from the slicing claws and blindly thrust an arm out, clamping onto one of the flailing legs. He tugged the limb toward him and clasped the second shackle above the ankle.

When the youth heard the lock click shut, he slipped between two slashing legs and scrambled away, leaving a trail of blood on the ice. He snatched up his spear and retreated to the nearest corner. Only then did he turn to inspect his work.

The remorhaz had righted itself, but the beast was far from the agile terror it had been earlier. On one side of its body, two of the legs Avner had hit with the irons hung limp and useless, so that the beast was creeping toward him with a severe list. More importantly, the two shackled legs bent inward at awkward angles, further reducing the worm's mobility.

The youth did not make the mistake of thinking he had won the battle. With its serpentine neck and darting head, the remorhaz could still snatch Avner off the ice in the blink of an eye. And he was not foolish enough to believe that he had the strength to drive his little spear through the beast's hard carapace.

As the creature hobbled toward him, Avner used the tip of his spear to chip a small hollow in the ice. During the few moments it took him to complete the task, he dripped enough blood on the floor to stain the whole area red. When he finished, he braced the butt of his weapon in the cup he had created and angled the tip toward the approaching remorhaz.

"Maybe this will hold you off," he whispered, "at least until Tavis gets back."

* * * * *

After several minutes of searching, Slagfid finally grabbed one of the beasts by the ear and started toward the shore. The rest of the herd seemed to forget about the danger they had sensed earlier and followed close behind, an eerie, mournful wail pouring from their upraised trunks.

Tavis pointed at the herd and asked, "What's all this?"

"Good-byes," the frost giant explained. "They think he's being led to butcher."

Tavis winced. "You slaughter their kin in front of them?"

Slagfid shook his head. "Of course not. But they see our clothes and smell the cook fires." The frost giant led the mammoth over to Tavis. "Doesn't take 'em long to figure it out."

"And they don't try to flee?"

"Some do." A cruel smile crossed Slagfid's mouth. "But when we catch 'em, *that's* when the herd sees a slaughter. We butcher the one that ran and its mother, calf, and siblings. After that, we usually don't lose another one for twenty years."

"Mammoths must be intelligent."

"Smarter than hill giants, anyway," Slagfid allowed. "And they remember faces a lot longer."

The frost giant pulled on the mammoth's ear, forcing it to present its flank to Tavis. The creature's back came up only to the waist of Gavorial's body, with a thick covering of coarse fur that would offer at least minimal padding.

The frost giant pressed the tip of his boot into the back of the beast's knee. "Down, Graytusk." Once the mammoth had kneeled before Tavis, Slagfid said, "Just climb on and grab an ear. He'll turn the way you pull, and tug 'em both when you want to stop."

Tavis swung a leg over Graytusk's back. The sensation reminded the firbolg of the few times he had climbed onto a horse's back. It felt like he should be carrying his mount, not the other way around.

"How do I make him go?"

"When I take my foot off his leg, he'll stand up and start moving," Slagfid explained. He grinned shrewdly, then added, "At least for a little while."

Tavis scowled. "What do you mean?"

The frost giant chuckled. "I shouldn't tell you this," he said. "But you tried to get me the honor for catching Little Dragon, so I figure I owe you something."

"What?"

"Mammoths aren't strong enough to haul grownups— it's all they can do to carry a young giant," Slagfid explained. "You'll ride this fellow to death before you're off the glacier."

With that, the frost giant took his foot off Graytusk's knee and stepped away. The mammoth pushed himself up, spewing a long snort from his hairy trunk and rocking so violently that Tavis nearly fell off. The beast instantly ambled forward with a lurching, uneven gait. The scout yanked on both ears, bringing the beast to a swift halt, and leaned over to speak with Slagfid.

"That's why Hagamil kept the shaman's promise!"

Slagfid nodded. "And that's why Halflook made it in the first place," the giant chortled. "You really don't think the frost giants are going to share . . ."

Slagfid's jaw fell open and he let his sentence trail off. He pinched his eyes closed, then opened them again and stared at Tavis with a bewildered expression. "Sharpnose, what's happening to you?"

A cold numbness fell over the scout's face, and his skin suddenly seemed as stiff and rigid as steel. His facial muscles began to twitch and snap. A loud, metallic ping echoed through his nasal cavities, then Basil's runemask popped off and struck Slagfid squarely on the forehead. Tavis's face erupted into searing pain. The bones of his jaw began to shrink, causing his teeth to grind against each other like stones. His entire head throbbed in agony.

"You're not Sharpnose!" Slagfid gasped.

Tavis raised his foot and drove the heel into the frost giant's midsection, then grabbed Graytusk's ear and jerked the mammoth around. The beast broke into a shaky, bone-jarring trot. The scout's throat started to shrink and he found himself choking on his own Adam's apple, which was reducing its size only half as fast as the air passage around it. He guided his mount toward the place he had last seen the *traell*'s shadow, praying the fellow had not moved.

Slagfid's voice commanded, "Graytusk, stand!"

The mammoth halted instantly. Tavis pitched forward, and only his secure grip on the beast's ears prevented him from flying off. He craned his neck around to see Slagfid's looming face just a few paces behind him. A distant ringing echoed in the scout's ears, and black wisps of fog formed at the edges of his vision. He felt Gray-tusk's back broadening beneath his legs, and he realized he was shrinking fast.

"You're no stone giant," Slagfid growled. "You're just a scrawny little firbolg!"

The frost giant lowered a hand to pluck Tavis off the mammoth's back. The scout pushed himself out of the way, then slid down Graytusk's flank and dropped onto the snow. He crawled under the beast's belly and scrambled to his feet on the other side, dizzy and still choking.

Slagfid shoved the mammoth out of his way. "You're Tavis Burdun!"

Tavis stumbled forward. The black fog closed in, reducing his vision to a narrow tunnel. He tried to cry out for his bow, but could not choke the words out of his constricted throat. The ice trembled and crunched as Slagfid kneeled behind him.

"Catching you alive will bring me more honor than Hagamil!"

Tavis felt the giant's fingers close around him, and his vision went dark. A scream of fury erupted deep inside the firbolg. It rose as high as the choking lump in his throat and remained there, simmering. The scout grabbed one of Slagfid's fingers and pushed against the joint, determined to break the digit before he fell unconscious.

Tavis never had the chance. An arrow sizzled past several feet over his head, then sank into Slagfid's eye with a mucky hiss. A pained bellow boomed over the ice, and the giant's hand opened, spilling Tavis onto the ground.

Somewhere ahead, an old man's voice yelled, "Basiliz wives!"

Tavis staggered toward the voice as fast as his growing dizziness allowed. Behind him, Slagfid scrambled to his feet, roaring, and stomped off toward the cavern.

"Basiliz wives!" the voice repeated, this time more urgently.

It occurred to the scout that his savior was attempting to activate one of Basil's runearrows, but the fellow had such a *traell* accent that his words were hardly comprehensible. Tavis tried to give the command, but still could not speak. He dropped to his knees. He heard several humans rush up to him, then felt their hands grasping his arms.

"What wrong, Dafis?" asked an old man's voice. "Hurt bad?"

The scout shook his head. He could still hear Slagfid's steps pounding toward the ice cavern, but the giant's bellows had changed to an alarm cry. Tavis could do nothing to silence him, at least not until he changed back to a firbolg. The few moments the transformation required seemed to pass at an interminable pace. Once the frost giant alerted his fellows to the presence of Tavis Burdun, the *traells* would not have much time to escape—and the scout would have even less time to rescue Avner.

When the scout's throat finally cleared and his vision returned to normal, he saw that his rescuers were the same dark-haired *traells* that had lured Bodvar into the ambush. Neither the young girl nor the man Tavis had inadvertently wounded were present, but he recognized the child's features in the face of the old man and one other warrior.

The scout quickly turned toward the ice cavern and saw that Slagfid had already disappeared inside. Tavis did not speak the runearrow's command word. Even if his voice would carry that far, it was already too late to stop the giant from sounding the alarm. It would be far wiser to reserve the magic until later, when he could see what results the explosion might bring.

"Here, Dafis." The old man thrust the scout's quiver and bow into his hands. "My name Olchak. Afner say give these to you."

"Thank you," the scout replied. "I'm grateful for your help against the giant."

"Frost giants!" Olchak spat into the snow. "Dey should stay in Ice Plains, where dey belong!"

"Perhaps we can send them back," Tavis said, looking toward the ice cave. "Will you help me, Olchak?"

"Dat why we came," the old man replied. "What you want?"

Tavis checked the supply of arrows remaining in his quiver—three runearrows, several dozen normal arrows, and, of course, the golden shaft reserved for Brianna. He started toward Graytusk, speaking as he moved.

"See if you can find some frost giant rope." The scout was still limping, for the transformation had done nothing to mend his wounded toe. "And if you can, take it to the cave entrance. Here's what I want you to do."

* * * * *

The remorhaz struck at Avner yet again. The youth angled his spear toward the worm's descending head. As it had many times before, the beast stopped short of impaling itself. But this time, it twined a face tentacle around the shaft and yanked.

Avner held firm, rising off the ice as the beast tried to jerk the spear from his hands. The youth circled the end of his weapon over the tentacle, then flicked the tip down. The steel head severed the tendril. The worm bellowed in pain and, madly shaking its head, retreated.

The frost giants roared their approval.

Avner flicked the tendril away and started forward to press his advantage. Then he remembered Tavis's ambiguous warning about the beast's back and decided to wait. The youth retreated to his bloody corner and braced the butt of his weapon in its cup.

A disappointed murmur rustled through the cavern. Avner did not care. He was fighting for his life, not the amusement of the frost giants.

The remorhaz flapped its head, spraying droplets of sizzling blood across the ice. The beast cautiously advanced again. It had just closed to striking range when Slagfid's voice rumbled over the pit like thunder.

"Help!" His voice was so pained that it was barely intelligible. "My eye!"

The crowd on the pit rim slowly parted, then Slagfid's head came into view. The giant held one hand cupped over his eye, with the dark fletching of one of Tavis's runearrows protruding between his fingers. A stream of blood was flowing down his cheek and pouring off his jaw in a bright red cascade.

"What happened?" demanded Hagamil.

Slagfid's only reply was an incoherent wail.

Avner did not have time to watch what happened next, for the remorhaz was approaching again. This time, the worm scuttled toward him sideways. It held its head low to the ground, while, twenty feet away, its tail twitched high the air.

The youth saw at once that the beast had at last hit upon a strategy to defeat him. If he lowered the spear to defend against the head, the remorhaz would lash out with its tail and batter him senseless in a single blow. If he kept his weapon high, the worm would grab him by the ankles.

There was only one thing left to do.

Avner hurled his spear at the remorhaz's eye. The worm jerked its mouth up and snatched the weapon out of the air. The beast snapped the shaft in two with a single chomp, but the maneuver bought the youth enough time to dart out of the corner.

The creature whirled around and hobbled after him, still crippled by its shackles and broken legs. The youth stopped in the center of the pit, where he would have plenty of room to keep dodging. Eventually, he knew, the remorhaz would wear him down, but his deftness was the only weapon Avner had left.

* * * * *

The second time Tavis stepped through the cavern mouth, the ice cave felt immeasurably vast. The icicles that had appeared to hang so low to a stone giant now looked as high as stars, and the far wall seemed a distant blue horizon.

The air reverberated with the booming voices of astonished giants, dozens at once yelling at Slagfid, calling him a fool and shouting questions. The warrior was in too much pain to provide the explanations they demanded. He seemed unable to do anything except bellow in agony and keep his hands clutched over his eye. As a result, the entire tribe's attention remained fixed on him.

Keeping a careful eye on the throng, Tavis sneaked through the cave's mouth and angled toward the log ladder lying near the pit. As the scout moved, he felt the cold hand of panic beginning to squeeze his heart. The clamor in the cavern prevented him from hearing anything in the pit, but he found it ominous that the spectators had lost interest in the remorhaz.

Tavis had nearly reached the log when Hagamil's voice blustered above the rest. "Quiet!"

The cavern instantly fell so silent that Tavis could hear the soft clatter of the remorhaz's many legs in the pit below. The worm sounded slow and languid, and the scout could also detect the sporadic clanking of a chain, as though the beast were dragging shackles across the ice. In his mind, the scout envisioned the creature hauling Avner's limp body into a corner.

On the far side of the pit, Hagamil grasped Slagfid by the shoulders. "Be quiet, you!" he yelled. "Tell me what happened, then I'll fetch Halflook to take care of your eye."

This offer seemed to help Slagfid get a hold on himself. The frost giant quieted, then gasped, "Tavis Burdun shot me!"

"That can't be!" Hagamil roared, shaking the injured warrior. "Sharpnose said he killed Tavis Burdun!"

Tavis reached the ladder and crouched down at the end. He braced his shoulder against the log, ready to push it forward the instant the giants made enough noise to cover the sound.

"That wasn't Sharpnose here," Slagfid tried to explain. "It was Tavis Burdun, pretending to be Sharpnose."

This drew an incredulous murmur from the giants.

Hagamil promptly silenced them with a single, roving glare. "How could a little firbolg pretend to be a stone giant?"

Slagfid did not answer immediately, and the clattering of remorhaz legs fell silent. The scout's heart felt as if it would burst.

After a moment, Slagfid said, "He was wearing a mask."

A chorus of thunderous laughter shook the cavern. Tavis shoved the log forward until the end hung over the edge. The far side of the pit floor came into view, where a spear lay broken and discarded. A trail of blood ran from one corner toward the center of the arena, and that was all the scout could see. The hand around his heart clamped tighter, filling his entire being with a sick, cold ache.

Tavis couldn't leave, not until he saw the body. With the thunderous guffaws of the giants still shaking the cavern, he lay beside the log and crept forward, pulling Bear Driller along with him.

"Quiet!" Hagamil thundered. The laughter died away, and the chieftain asked, "A mask, Slagfid?"

"It was silver," the warrior said meekly. "It fell off Sharpnose's face, and then he changed into Tavis Burdun."

"And he shot you in the eye?"

"No. There was about a hundred *traells* waiting for him. One of them did it, and it hurts pretty bad," Slagfid whimpered. "Now I've told all I know. Call Halflook, like you promised."

"Call Halflook?" the chieftain roared. "After you let Tavis Burdun escape—for the second time?"

The scout glanced over the log and saw Hagamil jerk Slagfid's hand away from the wounded giant's face.

"You don't deserve no shaman!" the chieftain growled.

With that, Hagamil pinched the runearrow between his thumb and finger, then plucked it from the warrior's eye. Although the shaft was little more than a sliver to a frost giant, Hagamil's careless extraction resulted in the removal of more than the splinter. Slagfid howled in pain, slapping one palm over his emptied socket and grasping after Hagamil's hand with the other. Wincing at the chieftain's cruelty, Tavis lowered his head and dragged himself to the edge of the pit.

What the scout saw nearly made him howl more loudly than Slagfid—though in joy, not pain. Avner and the remorhaz stood in the center of the pit, warily circling each other. The battle had obviously been a difficult one for the boy, at least if his bloodied back and chattering teeth were any indication. But the youth had given better than he had received. Blood was streaming down the remorhaz's face from an amputated tentacle, it was listing badly toward several mangled legs, and it was holding one segment of its body higher than the rest to keep its manacled legs off the ice.

Wondering how Avner had ever shackled the beast, Tavis nocked an arrow and stood, already pulling his bowstring back. He loosed the shaft the instant his feet were steady. The missile did not pierce so much as shatter the ice worm's chitinous head, and the beast collapsed to the floor in a clattering heap.

Avner spun around and looked up at Tavis, silently

mouthing, "It's about time!"

The youth wasn't the only who noticed the remorhaz's death. At the sound of its clattering demise, Hagamil and several other giants looked into the pit, their faces betraying their disappointment at missing the climax of the worm-baiting. When they saw Tavis's arrow lying near the lifeless beast, their expressions quickly changed to bewilderment. The chieftain was the quickest to realize what had happened and lifted his gaze to the rim of the pit.

"There's Tavis Burdun!" Hagamil gestured at the scout with the gruesome orb at the end of the runearrow. "After him!"

"Basil is wise!" Tavis yelled.

The runearrow exploded in Hagamil's grasp, hurling the chieftain—now missing one hand—and all the giants behind him into the wall. The impact dislodged a dozen huge icicles, which dropped from the ceiling like spears and lodged themselves amidst the confused tangle.

Avner started toward the scout's corner in a slipping, sliding sprint. Tavis placed a foot in one of the log's enormous steps and gave it a shove, at the same time pulling a regular arrow from his quiver. As the youth climbed the ladder, the scout nocked his shaft and started toward the exit.

Clutching the bloody stump at the end of his wrist, Hagamil rose and moved to cut the escapees off. Tavis fired, and the arrow lodged itself deep in the giant's midriff. Although the impact hardly slowed the frost giant, his face paled to a sickly shade of ivory. He looked down at the dark fletching in horror.

"Another step and I'll say the words!" Tavis warned.

Hagamil stopped, two of his enormous paces from the exit. Several more warriors extracted themselves from the groaning pile behind the chieftain and came to stand at his side, but he motioned for them to go no farther. The scout drew a real runearrow from his quiver, but did not nock it.

"If you let us go, that arrow in your stomach won't explode," Tavis said, choosing his words carefully and keeping a sharp eye on Hagamil. "But the instant anyone so much as steps toward the exit, you die."

The threat caused several giants to raise a thoughtful brow.

"And if I go, so does Halflook," Hagamil was quick to add. "You don't want to be without your shaman, do you?"

The giants frowned and stepped back, giving Tavis and Avner a clear path. The two slipped along the wall, taking care to stay well out of Hagamil's reach, and backed through the exit into the windy night. The scout glanced down the slope to make certain Graytusk was where he had left the beast, then nocked his third-to-last runearrow.

Avner whispered, "I hope you noticed that isn't a runearrow in Hagamil's gut."

"I can't afford to waste any," the scout explained.

From inside the cavern echoed a nervous groan, followed by Hagamil's angry voice, "It's out. Get them!"

"Now, Olchak!" Tavis yelled, praying the old man and his fellows had gotten into position in time. "They're coming!"

Olchak and two assistants leaped from their hiding places beside the cavern, tugging on one end of a thick rope. As they pulled, a heavy line rose out of the snow at the cave's mouth, coming taut at a height of about six feet. The *traells* quickly knotted their rope around an ice crag, then sprinted toward Graytusk.

Tavis pulled his bowstring back, aiming his runearrow at the ice far above the cavern mouth. He had to hold the tension for only a moment before the first frost giant came running out of the cave. The brute's ankle caught on the line and snapped it like twine, but that did not save him from tripping and crashing face-first into the snow. The second giant fell over him, and the scout released his shaft as the third warrior appeared in the entrance. The runearrow struck perhaps a hundred feet above their heads, burying itself deep into the icy cliff.

"Basil is wise!" Avner yelled gleefully.

A deafening crack rang out across the caldera, then a mountain of ice crashed down on the fallen giants. They did not even have time to scream before they vanished beneath the roaring avalanche.

"That should keep Hagamil penned until morning," Tavis said, yelling to make himself heard above the din. He took Avner by the arm and limped toward Graytusk. "Let's hope there isn't another exit."

"Yeah," said Avner. "Then it'd be a lot easier for them to beat us to Split Mountain."

"Split Mountain?" Tavis asked. "Why would we go there?"

Avner shrugged. "I don't know." A mischievous grin crept across the youth's lips. "But the *traells* heard you say you wanted to go to some meeting the frost giants are having. That's where it's supposed to be."

➤ 13 ➤
Blizzard

The gray snow clouds streamed across the ominous white sky like battle standards, which, to Tavis, they were. The storm had hung back all day long, licking at Graytusk's wooly heels as he ambled across glacier and valley, his sauntering gait lapping up miles as briskly as the strides of a galloping horse. For a while, the scout had thought the beast would stay ahead of the blizzard. But now, with the sky darkening toward dusk and hoarfrost swirling in the wind, he saw that his forecast had been little more than a forlorn hope. The clouds were pouring over the mountains with a speed that warned of the storm's power, and already the mammoth's fur was covered with those tiny snow stars that meant the blizzard would be as cold as it was ferocious.

Tavis ran his gaze around the broad cirque into which they were descending. The basin was shaped like a human jaw, with dozens of jagged spires surrounding a flat, mottled vale of pale meadows and swarthy stands of spruce. To the scout's dismay, low-hanging clouds with long skirts of swirling snow already capped most of the peaks. Any of those pinnacles could be Split Mountain and he would never see it.

Tavis glanced over his shoulder, where Avner and Olchak rode. Both the boy and old man sat sideways, for their legs were too short to straddle the mammoth's broad back. They held themselves in place by clutching a makeshift harness that Avner had rigged from a frost giant rope.

"Are you sure this is the valley, Olchak?" the scout asked.

The old man looked around the cirque. By the vacant look in his eye, Tavis could tell the *traell* did not recognize the place.

"A shortcut doesn't do much good if we don't know where it comes out," the scout grumbled.

"You say 'take Split Mountain fast!' " Olchak replied. "Olchak do that. Mountain here somewhere—if not this valley, next one."

"It'd better be this one," Tavis muttered. "By the time we reach the floor, we won't be able to see Graytusk's trunk, much less Split Mountain."

"What if we don't find it?" asked Avner. The youth turned toward Tavis, the hood of his borrowed bearskin parka pulled far forward to shelter his face from the cold. Despite the boy's precautions, his nose and cheeks had turned pallid white. "I mean, what if we don't find Split Mountain tonight?"

Tavis fixed an icy glare on the youth, then drew a heavy fur muffler from his satchel. "Tie this over your face, Avner." He tossed the scarf at the boy. "You're already frostbitten."

Without saying another word, the scout turned around to guide Graytusk into the basin. The task was largely unnecessary. The mammoth knew his own limitations and was traversing the slope at a shallow angle, taking care to pick solid footing and keep his immense weight squarely over his legs. The beast's only fault lay in his habit of brushing against the goblet pines that flecked the hillside, forcing his passengers to keep ducking or risk being swept off their mount by a face full of stiff boughs. Tavis did his best to guide the mammoth away from the trees, but the creature seemed to grow only more stubborn as the storm worsened.

By the time they reached the bottom of the hill, a gauzy veil of snow had fallen over the valley. The thickets of weeping spruce ahead seemed no more than drooping silhouettes. The lush meadows of alpine grass

ecame patches of unblemished white against a streaky
ackground of blue-tinted pearl. Even the craggy peaks
vere hidden behind an impenetrable curtain of white.
avis knew he and his companions would be hard-
ressed to reach any of the pinnacles, much less the cor-
ect one.

Graytusk seemed to know exactly where he was
oing. The beast ambled onto the basin floor and
rashed into the nearest spruce thicket. Tavis pressed
imself tightly against the mammoth's skull to keep
rom being swept off and hauled back on both ears.
raytusk merely flapped his head, nearly throwing the
cout off, and broke into a small meadow. He raised his
runk and gave an ear-piercing trumpet, then stepped
cross a gurgling stream in a single stride.

"Wait!" Olchak called. "That Dragon Rock! Stop!"

Tavis could not comply. Their mount had taken charge
f the journey and was continuing toward the next copse
t a determined lope. The scout knew little about mam-
noth habits and could not say what had triggered Gray-
usk's excitement. Perhaps the beast smelled something
ood to eat, or was simply anxious to find a sheltered
lace before the full force of the blizzard hit. Whatever
he reason, he would not stop.

Graytusk crashed into the next copse with a lowered
ead, snapping branches as thick as Tavis's wrist. The
cout pressed himself close to the beast's neck and
tretched a hand back toward Avner.

"Give me your rope," Tavis ordered. "You can hold
nto the mammoth's fur."

Avner struggled with the knot, dodging spruce
oughs as he untied the makeshift harness. Finally, he
reed the coarse line and passed it to Tavis, who used a
lip-knot to fashion a running noose. When the mam-
noth emerged from the trees, the scout sat upright. As
efore, Graytusk raised his hairy trunk to bugle.

The scout tossed the noose. The loop passed over the

upturned trunk and slipped down toward Graytusk's mouth. Tavis pulled the slip-knot tight, pinching the nasal passages shut. A coarse snarl rumbled up from the mammoth's chest and blasted out his open jaw. He began to huff through his mouth, filling the air with the cloying smell of half-digested grass.

Graytusk lumbered to a stop, tossing his head wildly about in a vain effort to toss the noose. The scout held the line taut, one hand wrapped in the rope and the other entwined in the mammoth's long hair. With each tug, the beast only tightened the slipknot more. He began to spin in circles, trying to reach the cord with his tusks and contorting his neck into all manner of positions.

Tavis passed the rope to Avner. "Hold that tight."

Graytusk tossed his head again, almost flinging the youth off his back.

"I'll trryyyy!" Avner yelled.

The scout stretched forward and grabbed both ears, then steadily pulled back. Graytusk slowly seemed to understand what was required and stopped struggling.

"Should I give him some slack?" Avner asked.

Tavis nodded. He continued to pull back on Graytusk's ears, but stayed ready to grab the rope, half expecting the mammoth to resume its struggle the minute the pressure was released.

Graytusk was smarter than that. He flipped the tip of his trunk back and ran his sensitive nostrils over the line, then stood fast.

Tavis looked back at Olchak. "What's this about Dragon Rock?"

"Back there!" The old man pointed toward the copse behind them. He began to lower himself down Graytusk's flank, using thick tangles of hair as handholds. "Come, I show you."

Olchak's legs sank to midcalf in dry, powdery snow. Tavis cringed, remembering that the alpine grass had

een visible from the top of the ridge. By the time they
ound Split Mountain and recovered Brianna, the likeli-
ood of avalanches would make it too dangerous to
limb any steep slope. The only safe escape route would
e down the valley, which was a grim prospect. The frost
iants would certainly realize the same thing.

Olchak waded through the deepening snow, following
ue mammoth's footprints into the spruce copse. Tavis
ulled on one of Graytusk's ears, trying to swing the
east around to follow. The mammoth stubbornly turned
is head in the other direction and would not budge.
he scout grabbed the trunk rope and gave a cautionary
rk, then tugged the ear again. This time, the creature
eluctantly allowed his head to be dragged around, spit-
ng a series of angry bugles from his hairy nose.

By the time Tavis got their mount turned around and
oving, Olchak had disappeared into the copse. The
cout released Graytusk's ears and took the trunk rope
om Avner. The mammoth resentfully plodded forward,
ragging his feet through the snow and casting yearnful
lances over his shoulder. They did not catch Olchak
ntil they reached the stream where he had first called
r a halt. The old man was standing on the bank, peer-
ig into the blizzard with both hands cupped around his
yes. Although the current kept the main channel open,
in sheets of silvery ice were rapidly forming along the
dges of the gurgling waters.

Tavis stopped Graytusk beside Olchak. In the meadow
cross the stream, the scout could barely make out the
impy silhouette of a rocky outcropping. The snow was
lling too hard for him to determine its shape.

"Is that Dragon Rock?" the scout asked. "Will it help
s find Split Mountain?"

Olchak nodded. Before he could speak, Graytusk
icked his head, casually running a tusk through the old
raell and tossing him into the air. The old man came
own in the deep snow across the stream, too surprised

to cry out. The mammoth gave a satisfied snort, then twisted around to glare at Tavis with a heavy-lidded eye.

Olchak raised both hands to his abdomen and screamed. Even from across the stream, Tavis could see a dark stain creeping from beneath the old man.

"By Stronmaus's angry fist!" Tavis pulled Graytusk's trunk rope until the noose bit deep into the mammoth's nose. He passed the line to Avner. "Keep that taut. If he so much as flinches—"

"I'll pull as hard as I can," the youth finished. He wrapped the line around both wrists and braced his feet against Graytusk's enormous shoulder blades. "But don't expect me to win a tug-of-war with a mammoth."

"It shouldn't come to that," Tavis said. "His nose seems pretty sensitive."

The scout lowered himself to the ground, holding onto Graytusk's ear so he would swing with the head if the mammoth tried to gore him. The beast allowed Tavis to climb down without attacking, then watched with a single, enigmatic eye as the firbolg limped out of tusk range.

The scout went to the stream and waded into the icy water. Normally, he would have tried to cross without soaking his boots, since wet feet would freeze quickly in these plummeting temperatures. Unfortunately, he lacked the time to look for a dry ford, and his injured toe made it impossible to dance across the snow-capped boulders jutting up from the brook.

As the scout climbed out of the stream, Olchak clamped his jaw shut and fixed a bewildered gaze on Tavis's face. The scout kneeled at the *traell*'s side and opened the flap of the old man's blood-soaked parka. The hole underneath was as big as around as a human wrist, and ran all the way through the abdomen. The firbolg needed to look only a moment to know he would not save Olchak. He could pack punctures and sew gashes, but rejoining severed intestines and pierced spleens were tasks far beyond his meager talents.

"How look?" asked Olchak. "Not bad, Olchak think. It not feel that bad."

Tavis looked up to find the old man staring at him. Olchak's face was full of trust and hope. Not for the first time in his life, the scout wished lying came to him as easily as to humans. He closed the *traell*'s parka.

Olchak's black eyes flashed in alarm. "What you doing?" he demanded. "Fix wound!"

Tavis shook his head. "There's nothing I can do for you, my friend," he said. "I'm sorry, but you're going to die."

The color drained from Olchak's face. "No," he said. "Hole not hurt that bad."

"You're still shocked. The pain will come in a little while," Tavis answered. "I'm sorry."

Olchak looked away. Deciding it would be best to allow the old man a few moments to consider his fate, the scout stood and gazed toward the craggy outcropping the *traell* had called Dragon Rock. A whistling wind was blowing down from the ridge they had descended earlier, whipping the snow into an opaque white curtain. Tavis could not see the faintest hint of the crag's silhouette, or even of the first spruce copse through which they had passed. Trying to look across the meadow was like trying to stare through the inside of his own eyelids, save that he saw a white blur instead of a dark one.

Behind Tavis, Avner's voice rang out above the whistling wind. "Whoa! Stop!" the boy yelled. "Stand—"

The sentence ended with a splash.

Tavis whirled around. Through the blowing snow he saw Graytusk's hazy back lying parallel to the stream. Avner was in the churning current, clinging to the trunk rope to keep himself from being swept downstream. The mammoth rolled to his knees, dragging the youth onto the icy shore.

"Hold that line!" Tavis yelled, leaping into the stream.

"Don't let go!"

"Who c-c-can let g-go?" Avner chattered. "My hands are f-f-frozen sssstiff!"

The scout splashed across the stream in three quick strides, arriving at the shore as Graytusk began to rise. He leaped over Avner's half-frozen form, then dodged past a tusk and grabbed the rope close to the slip knot. The mammoth stood, lifting the firbolg into the air. Tavis braced his feet against the side of the beast's head and cinched the noose down so tightly that blood oozed up through the long fur. The creature huffed in pain and tried to shake the scout off, but only tightened the knot.

After struggling a few more moments, Graytusk abruptly began to tremble. With a great sigh of resignation, the mammoth sank to his knees, then curled the tip of his trunk back to gently pat Tavis on the head. After that, the beast remained motionless, save for his body's uncontrollable quivering.

"I th-think he's g-g-given up," Avner said. The youth was standing a pace behind Tavis, still holding the end of the rope.

The scout looked into Graytusk's dark eye. When the mammoth lowered his gaze and looked away, Tavis stepped into the snow. He tied the slip knot in place and stepped away.

The mammoth continued to tremble and look at the ground.

"That's right," Tavis said. "If you want that knot loosened, you have to wait for me."

When Graytusk did not move, the scout felt secure in attending to Avner. After being dumped in the stream, the youth's clothes were thoroughly soaked. More importantly, his skin felt as cold as ice, and he was shivering uncontrollably.

Tavis pulled the end of the rope from Avner's frozen hands and let it fall to the ground. He stripped the boy's icy clothes off and replaced them with his own cloak.

The bitter wind instantly bit through the scout's tunic and breeches, but he ignored the stinging pain. Firbolgs could endure frigid temperatures with little more than discomfort, but wet humans froze to death with distressing frequency.

Once he had Avner swaddled in his cloak, the firbolg carried the youth over to Graytusk's leeward side and nestled him in the woolly hollow between the mammoth's front leg and chest. Tavis was concerned about leaving the boy there alone, but he suspected he had finally won the war of wills with the beast, and Avner needed the warmth.

"I'll go and find a good place to start a fire," the scout said. "You stay close to Graytusk until I get back."

"Wh-what about B-Brianna?" the youth asked. "If we-we m-m-miss the r-rendezvous, we'll n-n-never f-find her."

"You'll have to stay behind," Tavis said. He didn't like the thought of leaving the youth half-frozen in a blizzard, but he had no choice. His duty to the queen demanded that he continue to search for Split Mountain, no matter what the cost to himself or others. "I'll leave you with plenty of wood. Once you're warm, you know enough to take care of yourself."

"No!" Avner shouted. "I'm g-going w-with you."

Tavis shook his head. "You could freeze."

"I'll f-follow anyway," the youth warned. "I will."

Tavis sighed, knowing he would not win this argument. Later, after the cold wore down the boy's willpower, he would try again. "You can come," the scout said. "But the instant you start to feel sleepy—"

"I'll l-let you know," Avner promised. "You j-just worry about f-finding Split M-Mountain."

Tavis crossed the stream again—his feet were already beginning to grow numb from the cold—and struggled through the blizzard to Olchak's side. The old man was covered head to foot beneath a fleecy white mound. As the scout brushed the snow away, he saw that the *traell*'s eyes had glassed over.

"Olchak, I need to ask you something."

The old man grasped Tavis's arm and pulled the scout's ear close to his quivering lips. "Now it hurt."

Tavis nodded. "I'm sorry," he said. "But I need to know about the Dragon Rock."

"Take Olchak home, Tavis," Olchak pleaded. "*Traells* got good shaman there."

Tavis shook his head. "I can't," he said. "Even if you lived that long—which you wouldn't—my duty is to the queen. I must find Split Mountain. Does Dragon Rock point toward it?"

"What good is queen to me?" asked the old man. "Take Olchak home before he die."

"You're going to die anyway," Tavis answered. "Tell me about Dragon Rock."

"Later." The old man looked away and closed his eyes. "After shaman heals me."

Tavis cursed Olchak for a coward, but slipped his arms under the old man and gently picked him up. He waded back across the stream, then removed the *traell*'s furry parka and folded it around Avner's shoulders.

"You're going to have to hold Olchak against your chest." As he spoke, the scout hoisted Avner onto Graytusk's trembling back. "Are you strong enough to do that?"

"I th-think ssso," Avner answered.

Tavis passed Olchak up to the youth. Avner pulled the old man close and closed the parka around them both. The scout cautiously slipped between the mammoth's tusks and loosened the trunk noose, then climbed up the beast's head. Graytusk's body stopped quivering, but he kept his eyes averted and made no objection to the scout's unusual method of mounting.

Once Tavis was securely seated, he gave the trunk rope a tug and Graytusk rose. With his eyes nearly pinched shut against the stinging barrage of snow, the scout guided their mount across the stream. The storm was blowing so ferociously that the firbolg could barely see the tip of the mammoth's long trunk, and everything else—the sky, the ground, the horizon—was a white haze.

Tavis pointed the mammoth more or less in the direction Olchak had been looking before he was gored, and not long after a stony outcropping emerged from the white murk ahead. The bluff was only a little higher than the mammoth's back. The scout circled the crag and soon understood why the *traell* had called it Dragon Rock. In the front was a long, serpentine protrusion similar to a dragon's neck.

Tavis glanced over his shoulder. Olchak's eyes were half-closed and unfocused. It seemed doubtful that the old man was even aware of where he was, but the scout saw no harm in asking for his help one more time.

"Olchak, we've reached the Dragon Rock," Tavis said. "Does the head point toward Split Mountain?"

The old man raised his eyelids. "What—what will you sacrifice for queen, Tavis Burdun?" he gasped. "My life . . . your life . . . boy's life, too?"

The scout did not need to ask to know what Olchak meant. Avner looked nearly as bad as the old man. The youth was shivering so hard that it appeared he would shake both himself and the *traell* off Graytusk's back, and his lips had turned an alarming shade of blue. The boy desperately needed a fire and hot food, and soon.

Tavis shifted his gaze back to Olchak. "Does the head point toward Split Mountain?"

"Olchak . . . not die for queen," the old man replied. "Duty, it mean nothing . . . to dead."

"Y-You're d-dying anyway," Avner chattered. "T-Tavis c-can't save you. At least l-let him s-save the w-woman he loves."

"Love?" Olchak scoffed. "Olchak die . . . for someone

else's love? Hah!"

"Love has nothing to do with why I'm here," Tavis said. "Even if I save Brianna, I can't marry her."

"What?" Avner screeched. "But I t-told you! Arlien used m-magic!"

"Perhaps, but his magic didn't steal her away," the scout answered. "She's always belonged to Hartsvale. That means she can never be my wife."

"That's n-nonsense!"

"It is also the queen's decree, and so I have buried my feelings for her," Tavis said. "Saving her from the giants is strictly a matter of duty—yours as well as mine, Olchak."

As the firbolg shifted his gaze back to the *traell*'s face, he saw that his appeal had been wasted. Tavis could see vapor condensing from the old man's breath, but Olchak's eyes had fallen closed. The scout doubted they would ever reopen.

Tavis turned Graytusk parallel to the dragon's head, then took the lodestone from his satchel and suspended it by the steel chain running through its center. As it always did, the arrow-shaped rock promptly swung around to point northward, which was only a shallow angle from the direction they were currently facing. By maintaining the same relationship between the arrow's tip and their direction of travel, the scout could be certain they were going the way the dragon's head pointed.

As it turned out, Tavis hardly needed the lodestone. Graytusk proved an uncanny navigator, marching through the storm straight in the direction the scout had originally pointed him. Every so often, the mammoth would pause to wave his trunk in the air and let out a brief trumpet that his passengers could barely hear over the howling wind. Then the beast would continue on, his course never varying from the one indicated by Tavis's lodestone.

The storm continued to worsen, the wind threatening

to tear the scout and his companions from their mount's back. The snow grew so deep that Graytusk had to plow through it, sending great plumes of the powdery stuff arcing high into the air. Tavis could no longer feel his feet, which meant they had become little more than ice blocks, and now and then he even caught himself shivering.

Avner had fallen into a lethargic slump. One hand was clutching Olchak's unconscious body to his chest and the other was frozen into the mammoth's long fur. The boy's skin was beginning to take on the same blue tint as his lips, and he was staring into the blizzard as though he saw something more than white nothingness ahead.

After a while, it seemed to Tavis that they were no longer even moving—then, with a start, he realized they weren't. Graytusk had stopped. The scout could not say whether they were in the center of a meadow, the bottom of a ravine, or even at the base of a mountain. Dusk was coming, and he could barely see the mammoth's hairy trunk probing through the snow. The firbolg raised his lodestone. When he saw that they were still traveling in the right direction, he tugged on the trunk rope.

"Let's go, Graytusk," he growled.

The mammoth pulled his nose out of the snow and flung a snootful of brown mud at the scout. When the foul-smelling muck spattered him, Tavis was surprised to discover that it felt vaguely warm. He scraped some of the stuff off his face and saw tiny bits of half-digested twigs and grass. Manure.

Mammoth manure.

During the long journey from the glacier, the scout had certainly seen enough of Graytusk's droppings to recognize the stuff. Of course, it was possible that a wild herd had drifted south from the Icy Plains and crossed the Ice Spires into this valley, but the firbolg could think of a more likely explanation: The frost giants had escaped from their ice cave and beat him into the valley.

Tavis put his lodestone away and took Bear Driller off his back, then swung his quiver around to where he could grab his arrows easily. He had only two runearrows left, one for Julien and one for Arno. The scout let the trunk rope fall slack, then slipped the end under his thigh.

"We're g-getting c-close now, Avner," Tavis said, shouting to make himself heard above the roaring wind. He was not happy to hear himself stammering. When a firbolg stammered, the weather was truly cold. "B-Be alert."

"Arrmphg augh?" The boy's speech was so slurred the scout could not understand it.

Tavis glanced over his shoulder. The storm was growing dark now, but enough light remained to see that Avner's pupils were almost as large as their irises. The youth's breath came in quick, shallow gasps, and the scout knew the boy was the verge of falling unconscious.

"S-Stay with me," Tavis said. Although he was speaking in a normal voice, even he couldn't hear himself over the raging wind. "It can't be much f-farther."

Tavis turned and used the tip of his bow to tap Graytusk on the head. The mammoth rooted around under the snow for a moment longer, then turned slightly north and resumed his trek. Whenever the beast stopped to stick his nose under the snow, the scout tugged on the trunk rope until the mammoth hurled some more dung at him. The manure grew steadily warmer, and Tavis guessed they couldn't be more than thirty minutes behind the main herd.

It was during one of those stops that Tavis caught a whiff of something more interesting than mammoth dung: the acrid smoke of burning spruce. The wind was swirling and howling from a hundred different directions, but the scout suspected that the smell came from someplace ahead. More importantly, he felt certain that he knew who had made the fire. Frost giants had little need for campfires, but Julien and Arno might, and Brianna certainly would.

A confident smile cracked across Tavis's frozen face. Although the storm's swirling winds would make it impossible to locate the fire by smell alone, smoke was not so different than anything else he had ever pursued. In the short run, it might dart here and there, laying a crazy path that only the gods could decipher. But over a longer distance, it would travel in a straight line, a line that a good tracker could calculate not by examining each individual sign, but by finding the underlying pattern.

The scout allowed Graytusk to guide them for a while longer, counting off the seconds before he caught the odor of smoke once more, and then the interval until he smelled it again. He repeated this process over and over, and the period between whiffs steadily grew shorter. At the same time, Tavis used his lodestone to determine that they were traveling almost due north. When the mammoth finally veered westward, still following the scent of his herd mates, the interval between smoke whiffs began to increase.

Tavis steered Graytusk northward again. The mammoth tried to jerk his head back westward, but a quick tug on the trunk rope returned the beast to good behavior. They continued north and soon entered a spruce copse. Here, the blizzard did not seem so bad. The trees acted as a windbreak, reducing the storm's howl to a mere whistle. The thick boughs provided a dark contrast to the white haze, and trapped much of the blowing snow in their long needles. Even in the darkening dusk light, the scout could see the silhouettes of trees more than thirty paces ahead.

Tavis continued northward until the copse started to thin and, in the openings between the trees, he could see the raging white wall of the storm. The scout stopped

Graytusk beside a particularly large spruce, then used Bear Driller to scrape the snow off the branches as high up as he could reach. Next, he dismounted into waist-deep snow and forced the beast to kneel. He crawled into the cavelike den beneath the conifer's dense boughs, where he tied the mammoth's trunk line to the bole.

With the snow piled five feet high around the base of the tree and a canopy of dense boughs above, the weeping spruce offered a convenient shelter from the wind. There was even a ready supply of firewood, for dead branches ringed the lowest part of the trunk. Tavis crawled back outside and pulled Avner's stuporous form off the mammoth's back. Olchak's frozen corpse slid into the snow beside the beast. The scout left it there and took the boy into the den.

Tavis pulled some dried moss tinder from his satchel, then warmed his stiff fingers under his armpits until they were nimble enough to hold his flint and steel. He struck a few sparks into the tinder and created a flame. This he fed with twigs and sticks. When he had a small fire, he broke several branches off the tree and added them.

The campfire increased the likelihood of a frost giant stumbling across Avner, but only slightly. Hagamil's warriors would likely attribute any smoke they smelled to Julien and Arno. Besides, the scout had little to lose. If Hagamil's tribe found the youth again, they would probably kill him—but the boy would certainly die without a fire.

Within a few minutes, the glow of orange flames lit the cave, and the air started to grow warm. The scout worked his way around the tree trunk, snapping off dried branches and stacking them near the fire. When he had removed all the limbs he could reach, he propped Avner's lethargic form against the bole. The boy's skin still had a blue tint, and his pupils remained far too large, ut at least his breathing seemed regular.

Tavis shook the boy's shoulders. "Avner! P-Pay at-t-ention!" There it was again, a firbolg stuttering.

The youth's glassy eyes wandered toward the scout's ace, but remained unfocused. "Tlaaaavis?" His speech vas so slurred that the scout could hardly understand it. Did we ressssscue Bleeeeanna?"

"You've g-got to feed the f-fire," Tavis said. He pointed o the branches he had piled near the campfire. "I've left ou s-some wood. C-Can you do that?"

Avner's eyes wandered to the pile. "Wood." He nodded.

"It's imp-p-portant. If you forget, you'll d-die."

The youth leaned forward and slipped his frozen fingers under a branch, then carefully balanced the stick as ae moved it. He did not seem to notice the flames licking his hand as he dropped the limb into the fire.

"Good," Tavis said. "I can't s-stay, Avner. I'm s-s-sorry."

The youth nodded. "Queen."

Tavis clasped Avner's shoulder, relieved to see that he seemed to be recovering his wits. "That's right," he said. 'I'm p-proud of you, Avner."

"T-Tell me late—later." The boy reached for another stick.

Wondering if that would be possible, Tavis turned to go. He felt something wet roll down his cheek, and the ear made it as far as his jawline before freezing solid. The little den was warming up nicely.

Outside, the scout trudged through the snow to another spruce and cut two dozen long boughs off the ree. He cleared the snow off a fallen log, then sat down o fashion a pair of makeshift snowshoes. He bent the flexible limbs under his boot soles and threaded the ends through the lacing eyelets. It was delicate work for stiff fingers, and the scout had to stop several times to warm his frozen hands in his armpits. Certainly, he could have finished more quickly inside Avner's cozy

den, but then his feet would have thawed. He did no
want that. He could walk miles on frozen feet, but afte
they started to warm, the excruciating pain would make
it impossible to take more than a few steps.

Once he had threaded the boughs through the eye
lets, the scout secured them in place by slipping the
ends under the leather laces. He cinched his boots down
on the icy lumps that had been his feet and started walk
ing. The makeshift snowshoes were far from ideal, bu
they served to keep him from sinking past his knees in
the deep powder.

When he reached the edge of the copse, a stinging
blinding wall of snow once more assailed Tavis. He
pulled the lodestone from his satchel and waited for it to
swing northward, then stepped into the blizzard
Although it was impossible to see any hint of sky
through the raging storm, the dim gray light suggested
that the hour was slipping past twilight. Once night fell
the basin would change from howling white to roaring
black. The firbolg would no longer be able to see the
lodestone in his hand. If he was going to find the camp
fire he smelled, he had to do it before dark.

Within ten steps of leaving the copse, the scout
found himself panting for breath. He kept stumbling
and his shivering grew worse. A knot of fear formed in
Tavis's stomach, for he knew what the signs meant
People grew fatigued and clumsy before they froze to
death. The safe thing would be to return to the fire with
Avner, but he could not warm himself without also
thawing his feet, and then he'd still be lying beneath
the spruce when the frost giants carried Brianna into
the Twilight Vale.

The scout continued forward, thrusting Bear Driller
into the snow like a staff. He soon found himself raising
his arm each time he planted the tip of his bow and sud
denly realized he was traveling uphill. With all of his ref
erence points lost in a white blur and four feet of snow

concealing the terrain, he had not perceived it at first, but he was climbing a slope.

The discovery did little to make Tavis feel better. Confusion was also a symptom of freezing, and the firbolg felt nothing if not obtuse. More importantly, so much fresh snow made avalanches a real possibility on any steep grade—and judging by the height he had to raise his knees, the slope beneath him was anything but gentle. At least the fluffy snow would take longer to suffocate him if he got swept away and buried.

Tavis tried not to think about how long he might survive beneath tons of snow—one scout had lasted more than a week before a patrol noticed his boot—and continued to climb.

Sometime after his legs began to tremble and his lungs to ache, the scout smelled burning spruce—not the fleeting, acrid whiffs he had been sniffing up until now, but a steady, mordant stream of smoke. It was rolling down the hill, straight into his face, and now he could smell something else, as well: burned meat. Tavis continued his climb, forcing himself to maintain the same soft tread.

Sometime later, the sound of the wind faded to a steady whistle and the scout found himself ascending a steep, narrow gorge flanked by cliffs of blond granite. The chute could have been a couloir high on the side of Split Mountain, or merely a gully cutting through a low hill; with the light fading to black and a torrent of swirling snow choking the passage, Tavis had no way to tell. But he did know two things: the passage was the ideal place for an avalanche, and the smell of roasting meat hung in the wind so thickly that his mouth had begun to water.

Tavis put his lodestone away, then stepped over to a cliff and found two secure handholds. He stomped on the snow several times, ready to transfer his weight to his arms if he dislodged the white mass. When it did not slide, he decided the chute was stable enough to climb and lowered himself back into the gully. He continued up the gulch a long time, stopping every twenty steps to repeat the test, until the last vestiges of light seeped from the storm. The odor of roasted meat—he thought it might be pork—was stronger than ever, and the scout felt warmer just smelling it. He blindly continued up the chute, sweeping Bear Driller back and forth to keep the walls located.

After a time, the scout heard voices—not words, just voices—mingled with the whistling of the wind. Then he saw a flickering orange light gleaming off the walls ahead, and what looked like the crest of the chute. Tavis stopped. He slipped his frozen hands into his armpits and concentrated on breathing in a slow, steady rhythm. Now that he knew where Julien and Arno had made their camp, the firbolg could picture the terrain above. They were probably camped in the shelter of a dry overflow gulch, at the bottom end of an alpine lake. He was climbing up what would be a waterfall when spring meltwater swelled the pond and sent it pouring over its shores. When he attacked, there would be little maneuvering room for his foes. He would kill them both simply and quickly. The most dangerous part of the rescue would be retreating down this avalanche gully with Brianna.

When Tavis's cold fingers finally felt limber enough to draw a bowstring, he fumbled in his quiver until he found his last two runearrows. He put one shaft between his teeth and the other in his hand, then climbed to the top of the chute. He stopped behind the crest and knelt in the snow.

About thirty paces ahead, the flickering yellow light of a bonfire cut axelike through the blizzard, illuminating the entire width of the gully. On one side of the gulch sat a figure no larger than a hill giant, his back braced against the wall and a haunch of scorched meat in each and. The scout could see only the profile of the giant's face, but that was enough to determine that the fellow was a pale-skinned brute with a pug nose and a greasy double chin. The fine ermine cloak over his broad shoulders seemed a strange contrast to his slovenly visage.

In front of the giant, the bonfire's flames licked at a pit holding the remains of a good-sized animal. Much of the creature was gone, so it took Tavis a moment to identify it—and when he did, he wished he had not. Knowing that his mouth had watered at the smell of roasting human sent a shiver down his spine.

On the other side of the bonfire, just at the edge of the bonfire's light, sat Hagamil's large form. One of the frost giant's wrists ended in a bloody bandage, while his face looked as haggard and weary as the scout felt. The chieftain was gnawing hungrily on a human arm.

Tavis saw no sign of a third giant, Prince Arlien, or Brianna. He felt certain that the giants would not have roasted the queen after all they had gone through to capture her, but that knowledge did not prevent a terrible, cold ache from sinking into his bones. He spent a moment trying to eavesdrop on their conversation, but heard nothing more than a series of deep-throated murmurs. He slipped over the crest of the chute and crept forward, swimming through the snow more than crawling through it. As he moved, the scout kept a watchful eye on Hagamil, who was the most likely of the giants to notice him.

A short distance later, Tavis found he could understand the giants' words. He stopped and stuck the runearrows in the snow beside him, then slipped his hands into his armpits and listened.

". . . came as fast as we could, Arno." It was Hagamil, sounding both apologetic and exhausted.

"But you haven't got Tavis Burdun!" Arno shook one of his meat haunches—it was a human thigh—at the frost giant. "We said bring him here!"

"Your plan didn't work," Hagamil countered. "I already told you what happened."

"It would have worked if you weren't such an idiot, Hagamil." It was a third voice, deeper and smoother than either the frost giant's or Arno's. Something about it sounded vaguely familiar, but the whistling wind made it difficult for Tavis to say what. He concentrated his efforts on locating the face that went with the voice. "Even a hill giant wouldn't mistake a firbolg for a stone giant. Not even a fomorian would make such an error."

Hagamil narrowed his eyes and fixed them on Arno. "He had some sort of magic mask," the frost giant said, his tone as cold as the snow. "I tried to tell you that, Julien."

Tavis peered closer at the giant sitting by the fire. When the brute raised a haunch of meat and stuck it somewhere on the other side of Arno's face, the scout realized where the extra voice was coming from. Arno had a second head. He was an ettin!

Tavis scowled, perplexed by this discovery. All the ettins he had seen were as stupid as they were cruel, hardly capable of speech. Yet, this one was conversing intelligently with not only itself, but Hagamil as well. Even more surprising, the chieftain acted as though he were the inferior. That made no sense. No giant would take orders from an ettin.

"I know what you told me!" Julien hissed at Hagamil. "I also know what your failure means. Tavis Burdun has sworn to kill Brianna rather than let us have her. As long as he's alive, we can't take her to Twilight."

As Julien spoke, Tavis realized why his voice sounded so familiar. It was a deeper, louder version of Prince Arlien's! The ettin had been inside Cuthbert Castle all along, no doubt disguised by some magic similar to the runemask the scout himself had used to impersonate Gavorial.

"Why can't we take her to Twilight?" Hagamil

demanded. He nibbled at the arm in his hand, then added, "Tavis'll never catch us in this blizzard. All we have to do is take her through Split Mountain, and we'll be in the vale before the storm clears."

The ettin's far hand threw its haunch at the frost giant. "Stupid frost giant!" Arno growled. "Do you see Brianna here?"

Hagamil ran his eyes over the campsite. "But you said you'd have her tonight."

"What we have is a verbeeg problem," Julien replied. "The runecaster's made it impractical to slip her out quietly."

The cold ache in Tavis's bones began to fade. The "verbeeg problem" had to be Basil. The runecaster had seen through the ettin's disguise.

"But we got another way to get her," Arno added.

"How?" the frost giant asked.

"That's what we're up here to explain!" growled Arno. "You come down to the castle and attack."

Hagamil frowned. "But Tavis—"

"You *will* have him by then," Julien interrupted.

The frost giant's face flushed to a pale shade of blue. "We'll find him," he promised. "But even then, battles are confusing. Brianna could be killed."

"Not with her faithful prince there to protect her," snickered Julien. "Besides, that fool Cuthbert's a coward. Once the fighting starts, he'll be quick enough to hand her over—especially after I whisper the idea in his ear."

Hagamil looked doubtful, but asked, "When do you want us?"

"Soon," Arno replied.

Hagamil nodded. "We'll leave in the morning." He chewed the last of the meat off the greasy bone in his hand and tossed it aside, then gestured at the cooking fire. "I'll have that other arm, if you please."

The ettin took the spit off the bonfire and ripped the

second arm off the corpse. He tossed the limb to the frost giant, then his two heads began eating the rest of the charred flesh directly off the stick.

The scout nocked his first runearrow and aimed at Arno's neck, but held his fire. Normally, he could hit such a large target easily at this distance, but his fingers remained stiff from the cold. More importantly, the winds in the gully were gusty, and the shot would be tricky enough with Basil's heavy runearrow.

Tavis lowered his aim to the ettin's shoulder. "Arno!"

"Huh? Who that?"

Arno scowled and turned toward the voice, exposing more than enough of his broad chest to give the scout a good shot. Tavis loosed his arrow, then heard a dull clank as it pierced the armor beneath the ettin's cloak.

"Basil is wise!" he called.

The blast hurled the ettin against the gulch wall. Arno's head slammed into the stone with a crack that Tavis heard even over the explosion. The brute's churlish eyes went vacant with death. The scout felt the gully quiver as untold tons of snow shifted beneath his feet.

Hagamil leapt up, fumbling at his belt axe with his one good hand. "Tavis Burdun!" he yelled.

"That's right." Tavis grabbed his second runearrow. So far, everything was proceeding according to plan—except that Brianna was not here with him. She was back at Cuthbert Castle: safe, and likely to stay that way if he could kill Hagamil. "I thought I'd make myself easy for you to find."

The scout nocked the shaft and swung the tip toward the frost giant, who wisely retreated out of the firelight with a single long step. Then, as Tavis drew his bowstring back to fire, the ettin groaned. He pushed himself away from the wall, Arno's lifeless face dangling over the gaping hole in his chest.

Tavis cursed and swung his last runearrow around to finish the job the first had left undone. Julien turned his head toward the firbolg, revealing a much larger version of Prince Arlien's handsome face. The scout aimed at the thick neck beneath the imposter's cleft chin.

The ettin dived away, yelling, "Basil—"

Tavis loosed his arrow.

"—is wise," Julien finished.

White light flashed three paces in front of Tavis, then he felt himself flying backward. His whole body exploded into searing, agonizing pain and Bear Driller disintegrated in his hands. The scout fell a long way, the sonorous growl of an avalanche rumbling somewhere beneath him, and he bounced off a rocky slope. He had hit somewhere behind the snowslide, he realized, and he wondered if that was good or bad.

Tavis slammed into the ground again. This time, he went ricocheting down the icy chute, bouncing from one jagged rock to another, opening long gashes all over his body. The scout caught the avalanche. He slipped into the powdery snow like a bird into the air, and the world went still.

❖14❖
Waiting Game

For the second morning in a row, Brianna peered out her window, over the bustling ramparts and across the sparkling lake, to find the hill giants standing beside their rafts and a favorable wind blowing across the blue waters. They had oaken shields strapped to their forearms and knobby tree trunks resting across their shoulders. Strangely enough, the sight didn't alarm her. Maybe she was just too groggy, or maybe she had more confidence in the castle defenses than she realized, but the queen was not frightened this morning.

Brianna resented being so calm when she didn't understand the reason for her composure. She felt like a goose being fattened for slaughter, too content and stupid to realize what was happening.

There came a knock at the door. "Enter," Brianna called. She pulled her dressing gown more tightly around her throat, but continued to peer out the window.

The hinges squealed. "How are you feeling this morning, Majesty?" asked Cuthbert. "Better, I hope."

"I am," Brianna answered absently. It was something about the hill giants, she realized. They were the reason she felt so calm. "I still can't remember what happened in the temple the other night, if that's what you're wondering."

"Actually, that's the least of my worries." Cuthbert started across the room. "With Basil in the dungeon and Arlien out looking for our reinforcements, I doubt we'll have any more trouble."

Brianna hardly heard him. Her attention remained fixed on the giants.

"I can't stop watching them, either," Cuthbert said, joining her. "Do you think they'll attack today?"

Brianna shook her head. "No, not today."

The queen finally realized why she wasn't afraid. Even from across the lake, she could see heads tipping back as the giants yawned, or bodies swaying from side to side as they shifted their weight back and forth. They were bored. Brianna knew enough about battle to realize that any number of emotions might run through a warrior's heart in the moments before combat, but lethargy wasn't one of them.

"You can tell your men to get some rest," Brianna said. "They're putting on a show for us."

"A show? Why don't they just attack?" Cuthbert's voice sounded as brittle as ice. "All this waiting . . . it's very wearing on the men, I can tell you that."

For the first time since the earl had entered the room, Brianna glanced down at him and saw the dark bags under his eyes. He was already dressed for battle, with his breastplate, vambraces, and greaves cinched down tightly. He carried his helmet under one arm, and his heavy axe was leaning against the doorjamb.

"I don't mind the wait," Brianna said. "Our reinforcements should be arriving within two days. The longer the wait, the better—don't you think, Earl?"

"Yes, of course," Cuthbert replied, his face reddening. "I don't mean to imply I'm anxious to lose my castle. But the waiting makes no sense. I hope the hill giants don't know more than we do."

"That's certainly possible," Brianna allowed. "We have no idea whether T-Ta—, er . . . whether my bodyguard actually reached Wendel Manor. They would know if he failed."

Cuthbert nodded. "That's what worries me. They're acting too confident, like they know everything we might do." He fell silent, then shook his head. "Maybe I shouldn't have let Arlien go, after all. But on the chance that he *is* a spy, I thought it'd be better to have him outside the castle. Even if he returns, I don't think I'll let—"

"I miss him."

Cuthbert furrowed his brow. "Milady?"

Brianna did not answer immediately. The words had slipped from her lips before she realized she had uttered them, and she was trying to figure out why. The queen wasn't aware of any longing for Arlien, or of any other feeling except the vague suspicion that it was wiser not to be alone with the prince.

"Majesty, did you say you *missed* Prince Arlien?"

"I believe I did." She said it quietly, as though admitting something rather distasteful.

The earl scowled. "Does that mean you want me to admit him into the castle if he returns?"

Brianna tried to consider the question, but when she pondered the possibility that Arlien might be a spy, her thoughts began to wander in a hundred different directions. She found herself lost in her clouded minded.

"Milady?" Cuthbert asked. "Should I—"

"Do what you think is best, Earl!" Brianna was surprised at the tone of her voice, for she had not intended the reply to be a sharp one. "Now, please excuse me. I don't think I'm feeling well, after all."

* * * * *

The avalanche had hit the spruce copse with the power of Stronmaus. The edge of the stand had been reduced to an impassable tangle of snapped and splintered trees packed in a powdery wall of snow. Avner had walked Graytusk the length of the barrier several times, looking for a way to cross. The combination of soft snow and tangled logs made it impossible for the mammoth to climb. They would have to find another way out onto the avalanche.

Avner stretched forward and tugged his mount's ear,

intending to go around the wall. Graytusk had other ideas. The mammoth pulled his ear from the youth's hand, then walked up to the wall and dug his tusks into the snow. He twisted his head about for a short time and wrapped his long trunk around a broken spruce. With a loud snort, the beast slowly backed away, filling the copse with sharp bangs and cracks as he tore a hole in the snowy barrier. Avner cringed at the loud sounds, fearing the frost giants might hear it, but allowed his mount to finish the job. If Hagamil's warriors were still within earshot, the damage was already done.

Graytusk repeated the procedure a dozen more times before the painful radiance of sunlight on snow came pouring through the breach. Avner and his mount both turned their heads aside, allowing their eyes to adjust to the brilliance. The boy took the opportunity to rub the bony dome atop the mammoth's head. Even that gentle contact sent waves of searing pain hissing up the youth's arm. Last night's blizzard had left his hand, as well as his face and other extremities, badly frostbitten. When Tavis's fire had warmed him enough for the circulation to return, the pain had been so bad that he had nearly left his shelter and crawled back into the storm.

Avner pulled his aching hand away. "Good job, Graytusk," he said. "I hope you figure out the rest of my plan that easily."

The mammoth snorted impatiently, then turned and climbed into the gorgelike breach. On the slope above Avner could see a huge triangle of rocky outcroppings and grass exposed by last night's avalanche. The apex was located directly beneath a narrow chute cutting through a high cliff of blond granite.

The youth knew Tavis had started the avalanche. He had heard the muffled booms of two exploding rune-arrows. The entire copse had begun to tremble, then there had been a tremendous crashing and banging as tons of snow slammed into the spruce stand. Avner had gone outside to see what was happening, but a scouring torrent of snow had driven him back into his den. Now, with the sun hanging in a cloudless blue sky and the temperature hovering a little below freezing, he found it difficult to remember how terrible last night's blizzard had been.

Once they reached the other side of the gorge Graytusk had opened, the mammoth had little trouble climbing onto the avalanche fan. The snow here was well packed. Five frost giants had spent the early part of the morning trampling it down, haphazardly thrusting long spears into the snow in an attempt to locate Tavis's buried body. Finally, as the sun climbed toward its zenith, they had given up and left, complaining bitterly about all the time they had wasted when they were supposed to be on their way to catch Brianna.

Because Avner had been watching them the entire time, he knew that a random search was unlikely to uncover the scout. Nor could he hope to make a methodic search of the avalanche. It was too large and too deep for him to succeed, especially considering the condition of his feet and hands. If the youth intended to find Tavis, he would need a better method.

That was where Graytusk's sensitive nose would prove useful.

Avner guided the mammoth toward the center of the avalanche fan, more or less directly beneath the chute. Tavis had taught him that it was important to work quickly when searching for people buried in snow, since most victims suffocated within an hour of being buried. Thankfully, that applied more to wet, heavy snow than this fluffy stuff. A firbolg could probably last longer in this powder—exactly how much longer, the youth could not say—and there were things a victim could do to help himself, like crossing his arms in front of his face. Avner remembered Tavis drilling that into him time after time, saying it would double or even triple the amount of time before the air ran out. So, if he assumed the scout would last twice as long in light snow as the heavy wet stuff, that would be two hours, and tripling that for knowing what to do would give him six hours.

By the youth's best guess, Tavis had now been buried for twelve hours.

Avner shoved the thought aside. The boy intended to keep looking until he found his friend, and it wouldn't matter if a week had passed. The youth turned his mount toward the chute. The frost giants had been in enough of a hurry that they hadn't wasted time searching near the top of the avalanche, which was the least likely place for a victim to be buried.

Nevertheless, after watching the warriors search all morning, Avner had come to the conclusion that the top of the fan was the best place to start looking. If Tavis had been swept into the tangled mess at the copse's edge, his body would hardly be worth finding, and the giants had already explored all the obvious accumulation zones in the middle part of the avalanche.

Besides, Avner thought it most likely that Tavis lay buried high up the slope. In last night's blizzard, visibility on the open hillside would have been a mere foot or two, rendering a bow and arrows useless. But the scout would have been able to see much farther in the shelter of the gully, so he had almost certainly been in the chute when he fired the arrows. And if he had been at the top of the avalanche when it started, it seemed likely that he lay near the top now.

Graytusk left the trampled snow that the giants had already searched and waded into the deep powder higher up the slope. Avner stopped the beast here. From his satchel the youth withdrew one of the thistle roots Tavis had given him to eat earlier. He tossed it into the snow a few feet in front of the mammoth's trunk.

The root sank out of sight. Graytusk plunged his nose into the snow and sniffed the root out, then slipped the morsel into his mouth. Avner dropped a rock he had collected in the spruce copse. Again, the mammoth dipped his nose into the snow and sniffed around. The youth pulled himself to the top of his mount's head and watched the beast's face intently. He had no idea what Graytusk would do if he caught a whiff of Tavis, but Avner felt certain the mammoth would react in some way.

After several moments of not finding the root, Graytusk pulled his trunk from the avalanche and sprayed his passenger with snow.

"Sorry, but you've got to work for your treats," Avner said.

The youth guided his mount up the slope, stopping every dozen paces or so to repeat the process. He soon learned to vary the order and number of thistle roots he tossed into the snow, since Graytusk would not sniff around if he thought Avner had dropped a rock.

They were about twenty paces from the top when the mammoth's ears swung forward. A series of muffled squeals rose from the beast's submerged trunk, then Graytusk followed his probing nose across the avalanche. A short distance later, he stopped and lowered his tusks into the snow, angrily swinging his head from side-to-side.

Avner grabbed both woolly ears. "No, Graytusk!" The boy's heart was beating like a drum. "Gently."

The youth allowed Graytusk to lower his head again, but did not release the beast's ears. The mammoth dug more carefully, and within a few minutes he had excavated a hollow ten feet deep. The beast stopped digging, then snorted and tilted his head to gore something beneath the snow.

Avner yanked on the trunk rope, forcing Graytusk to raise his head. The youth peered around his mount's ear. In the bottom of the hole, he saw a scrap of frozen tunic showing through a patch of icy red snow. His heart started to pound so hard he thought it would burst.

Keeping the trunk rope taut, Avner climbed down his mount's woolly flank. He dropped the rest of the thistle roots in the snow. "You've done your part, Graytusk," he said. "Good boy."

The mammoth cast a suspicious glance into the hole, then diffidently looked away and began to eat the delicacies. Avner tied the trunk rope around his waist—whatever happened, he did not want Graytusk to leave—and waded toward the scrap of tunic. Even this far beneath the surface of the avalanche, the snow remained so fluffy that he sank to his hips with each step.

The youth stopped and knelt in the blood-soaked snow. He placed a hand on the tunic. Under the frozen cloth, he felt a shoulder blade.

"Tavis!"

No response.

Avner dug through the crimson snow and located Tavis's head. The scout lay facedown, curled into a fetal position, with his arms crossed in front of his face and his knees tucked to his elbows. The resulting air pocket looked quite large, but the heat of the firbolg's breath had lined much of it with a glassy layer of ice, sealing the cavity like a tomb.

Avner yelled, "Can you hear me?"

Again, no response.

The youth reached into the hole and laid his fingers over Tavis's nose and mouth. With his hand still stinging from his frostbite, he could not feel much, but the scout's skin did seem to feel a little warmer than the snow. Avner withdrew his arm and saw tiny beads of water on his fingers. It could only be condensation from the scout's breath.

Avner's stomach somersaulted.

Working frantically, the youth cleared the snow away so he could inspect Tavis's injuries. A weblike tangle of jagged, ugly gashes covered the scout's back and limbs, while a fiery blast had scorched the front of his body from his head to his knees. Both arms and one leg had nasty-looking lumps that might indicate cracked bones, but there were no unusual bends or kinks to suggest a severe break. A large, egg-shaped lump had risen on the side of his head.

Satisfied that Tavis would suffer no further injury by being moved, Avner went back to Graytusk. The youth turned the mammoth so that the beast was standing on the scout's downhill side, then forced him to kneel. The creature sank so deeply that he almost disappeared in the snow.

Avner dragged his patient to the mammoth and mounted, pulling the heavy firbolg up in front of him. Graytusk stood without command. As the beast started to turn away, Avner caught a glimpse of familiar brown leather lying in the bottom of the hole.

"Not so fast, Graytusk!"

The youth stretched over Tavis's inert form to grab his mount's ears and stop the beast. He cut four short lengths of line off Graytusk's trunk rope and tied the scout's limbs into the mammoth's shaggy fur. Avner turned the creature back toward the hole. Still holding the trunk rope, he slipped down Graytusk's flank, then waded over to the familiar brown leather. He brushed the snow away and pulled Tavis's quiver from where it had lain half-buried. The case still contained thirteen arrows, twelve of wood and one of gold.

✦15✦
Lake Monster

Before each embrasure swarmed a band of soldiers, standing on their toes and shoving each other aside to see what was coming down the lake. Brianna did not even try to push through the throng. She stepped over to a merlon and put her height to good use by peering over the top. The queen saw a small flotilla of hill giant rafts angling past the far corner of Cuthbert Castle's outer curtain. By the tiny, toylike appearance of the crude vessels, she estimated their distance to be five hundred yards, just beyond catapult range.

At first, Brianna did not understand where the giants were going. Then, a little beyond the raft flotilla, she spied the arrow-shaped wake of something swimming toward the castle. At the tip of the rippling triangle appeared to be a tangled mass of brown lake weeds, about half as large as the hill giant rafts. It was coming straight toward the castle at a steady rate. The queen watched for several moments, until she thought she could make out the form of a needlelike snout, the crown of a pear-shaped head, and the broad oval of a back. The rest of the creature's body remained submerged.

From a short distance down the rampart resounded the clack of a catapult spoon slamming its crossbar. The dark blotch of a small boulder arced over the lake and seemed to hang in the sky forever, then finally splashed down short of the creature.

The beast's slender snout rose out of the water, dancing like a snake about to strike. An uncanny trill trumpeted across the lake, at once as shrill as a wyvern's cry and as full as a dragon's roar.

239

"They've got the lake monster on their side!" cried a warrior.

"Cover your ears!" yelled another. "His voice kills!"

A murmur of fear filled the air, and soldiers began cupping their hands over their ears. Other men, wise enough to realize they'd already be dead if the beast's voice was fatal, assailed anyone who would listen with frightening anecdotes about the lake monster, many of them undoubtedly made up on the spot.

Above it all rang the voice of Blane, Sergeant of the Engines. "Crank her down again, boys! By the time you're ready, that monster'll be close enough to hit!"

A second catapult crew arrived, wheeling their weapon along the back of the rampart, and tried to push their way to an embrasure near Brianna. The queen stepped over to help, pulling panicked soldiers away from the wall.

"Stand aside!" she commanded. "Give these men room to work!"

The crowd's attention remained on the lake monster, the men moving aside only when she shoved them away. She shook her head in dismay, knowing such confusion boded ill for the coming battle.

"Return to your posts!" she yelled. "This could be why the giants have been waiting!"

A few soldiers scowled and slipped off to another embrasure, but most simply ignored their queen. Brianna restrained the impulse to start hurling men over the wall and contented herself with keeping the area clear for the catapult crew. Although it had been nearly three days since the incident in the temple, her thoughts remained cloudy enough that she did not trust herself to chastise the troops. When Selwyn and Cuthbert arrived, they could restore order, and she would make it clear that she expected better discipline than this.

Blane's catapult clacked again. Brianna stepped over to a merlon and watched the boulder splash down along-

ide the monster. It took several moments for the first
ing of waves to ripple over the beast's back.

"Don't worry boys," counseled Blane. "There's plenty
f time to sink that thing. Just pull your spoon down and
ad up."

The beast let out another bugle. The tips of two white
angs broke the surface below its upraised snout. This
ent another wave of hysterical speculation along the
amparts, and the confusion grew even worse as some
nen tried to retreat while others pressed forward to get
better look.

Selwyn and Cuthbert finally arrived, shoving through
he crowd to join the queen at her merlon. They stood
ide by side, holding their helmets beneath their arms
nd craning their necks to peer through the embrasure
Brianna had cleared for the catapult crew.

"Stronmaus save us!" gasped the earl. "Karontor's
ent one of his warped beasts to aid our enemies!"

"What is that thing?" asked Selwyn, his tone more
curious than frightened.

"No creature of Hiatea's, I fear," answered Brianna. A
air of short antennae appeared behind the beast's mas-
ive head and began fluttering. "Its too hideous to be a
hing of nature."

"How can we fight something like that? We have no
wizards!" gasped Cuthbert. "What are we going to do?"

Brianna grabbed the earl's shoulder and pulled him
way from the embrasure. She wheeled him around to
ace her. "First, you're going to get hold of yourself!" she
snapped. "Then you're going to restore order to this
nob. If the giants attack now, this castle won't last five
ninutes."

"Quite right, Majesty," agreed Selwyn. He turned and
started down the rampart, yelling, "To your posts!
Return to your stations at once!"

At first, the captain had little more luck than Brianna
had. That changed when he started cuffing disobedient

soldiers, even going so far as to shove one stubborn slacker off the ramparts. The queen winced, but made no move to reprove Selwyn.

Cuthbert watched the display in gape-mouthed horror. "You're going to allow that, Milady?"

"We may not have much time before the battle begins, Earl Cuthbert," she said. "I suggest you restore order in the best way you know how, or the men will suffer worse than that."

The earl paled, but nodded and set his helmet on his head. Brianna returned her attention to the lake. The creature was angling away from the rafts, and the queen could see that its fluttering antennae rose from a small bald spot on its neck. Since the wind was no longer to the benefit of the hill giants, they were frantically pulling down their sails and using their clubs to paddle after the monster.

Brianna heard Blane's catapult resonate again, then saw a boulder, a little larger than the first two, arc over the lake. This time, the stone struck a glancing blow off the monster's rear quarters. The beast whistled in pain. It plunged its head into the water and dived. A skinny tail with a bushy end and two round feet followed a fat, hairy posterior beneath the surface.

"Hiatea forgive me!" Brianna gasped. "It's a mammoth!"

No sooner had the queen grasped this than she also realized the beast had a rider. Mammoths don't have antennae, so the fluttering tendrils had to be waving arms.

Brianna turned to the catapult crew beside her. "Don't aim at the monster," she commanded. "It's a mammoth, and it's trying to reach us. Sink the hill giant rafts instead."

The old man in charge of the engine looked doubtful. "That's not what Blane's orders—"

Brianna stretched across the catapult and grabbed the

man by the collar, then dragged him over the spoon to her side. The fellow went limp in her grasp, too astonished by the queen's unexpected strength to react.

"I am your queen!" she growled. "You'll do what I command, or suffer the punishment for treason. Is that clear?"

"Y-Yes, Majesty."

Brianna put the man on the ground. "Good," she said. "Aim carefully."

The queen stepped to the next embrasure, where Selwyn's efforts to restore order had already brought some results. The area was empty, save for two soldiers setting up a crossbow so large that it rested on a wooden tripod. She pointed at the taller of the two men.

"You, run down to Sergeant Blane and tell him to leave the lake monster alone," she said. "He's to sink the rafts only."

"Yes, Majesty," the tall soldier said. "The rafts only."

The man started to leave, but Brianna caught his shoulder.

"And in case the sergeant has any thoughts about second-guessing me, inform him that I've seen a rider's arms waving from the beast's back," Brianna said. She remembered how disrespectful Blane had been during their first meeting. "I'll hold him responsible if any harm comes to that rider."

The mammoth was still too distant to tell who was riding the beast, but the queen knew of only one person imprudent enough to dare such a thing. She intended to give him a stern lecture once she got him back into the castle.

The soldier waited a moment to see if Brianna wished to add anything else, then bowed and rushed down the rampart. The queen turned her attention to the fellow's shorter partner.

"You, go and find a long rope to lower over the wall," she commanded. "And tell the sentries to send word if more hill giants launch their rafts. I don't know what's happening out there, but we'd better be on our alert."

"Yes, Majesty." The soldier bowed, then ran toward the corner tower.

Brianna looked onto the lake again and saw that the mammoth had surfaced. It was now swimming parallel to the castle ramparts, reluctant to approach any closer. The queen could barely make out the figure of the tiny rider stretching forward to tug on its ear. To her astonishment, he seemed to be leaning over someone draped across the beast's neck.

The four giants on the first raft hurled a volley of stones at the beast. The rocks all fell short, but not by much, and the mammoth dived again.

Both catapults fired. Two boulders arced away from the castle, splashing down on each side of the giants' raft.

"We've got the range now," said the commander of the catapult next to Brianna. "Crank her down."

The queen glanced over and saw two soldiers laboriously working the tension levers to bring the spoon down. She went to the closest man and took his place.

"You help your partner." She pointed to the other side of the catapult. "I'll work this side."

The two soldiers looked doubtful, but they had seen the queen reprimand their commander and knew better than to disobey. Brianna pushed her lever down as though there were no tension at all on it. The mouths of both soldiers fell open and they looked at each other in surprise.

"I *am* a Hartwick, you know."

Although the queen had always been too ladylike to make a point of exhibiting her power, like all of her kingly ancestors, she was blessed with supernatural strength. She worked the lever so fast that, even together, the two soldiers could do no more than hold the skein's tension while she ratcheted her pole back. It took less than a minute to lock the catapult arm in firing position.

The burly loader placed a medium-sized boulder into the spoon, and the commander peered through the embrasure. The old man told his crew to turn the catapult a little to the right, then pulled the release cord. The spoon slammed into the crossbar. Brianna heard the boulder splash into the lake, but by then she was already levering the spoon back down. Like most siege engines, catapults were poorly suited to firing at moving objects, and the queen knew it would take many attempts to hit their target.

They had to repeat the process six more times, loading slightly heavier boulders into the spoon for each shot, before Brianna heard the bang of a stone crashing through timber. Several hill giants bellowed in alarm and began to slap the water with flailing arms.

The old man looked back, beaming at the queen with a gap-toothed grin. "You're a fine artilleryman, Majesty," he said. "Even Blane's crew fired only twice."

As he spoke, a chorus of deep-throated grunts rumbled across the lake, then Brianna heard a number of boulders splash into the water near the castle wall. The hill giants were returning fire.

"How's the mammoth doing?" Brianna asked, levering the spoon down again.

"No more than fifty paces out," said the old man. "We sank the first raft, but there are two others close behind. It'll be a close thing."

As Brianna finished levering the spoon down, the short soldier she had sent for a rope returned with a large coil slung over his shoulder. The queen waited until the loader had locked the arm into place, then stepped away from the catapult.

"Keep firing," she said. "I'm afraid I must attend to some other things."

The queen took the rope and went to an open embrasure. The mammoth was so close now that she could see its frightened eyes peering up from the surface of the lake. As she had surmised earlier, it was young Avner sitting on the beast's neck, one hand buried deep in the creature's long hair and the other holding his fellow rider's head above water. To Brianna's astonishment, she recognized the rugged face of this second passenger as that of her firbolg bodyguard. She could not even begin to guess how the boy had come by his unconscious body, but she suspected that the scout's return meant he had failed to summon reinforcements.

There were half a dozen hill giant rafts behind the mammoth, at distances varying between thirty and a hundred paces. Fortunately, the clumsy vessels made awkward platforms for stone hurling, and only the giants on the two nearest craft stood any chance of hitting their targets.

"Avner, rope!" Brianna called.

The queen passed several loops to one hand, then used the other to throw the rope. The coils unfurled perfectly, spinning out to fall just short of the mammoth's trunk.

The hill giants hurled another volley of boulders at the beast. The stones splashed down in a tight circle, swamping Avner's mount beneath a mantle of white spume. A shrill, ear-piercing screech echoed off the castle wall. When the froth spattered back into the lake, one side of the mammoth's rear quarters had slipped beneath the water. His speed had slowed considerably.

The catapults slammed another pair of boulders into the air. Both stones, now the heaviest the engines could launch, came down on the same raft. The vessel disintegrated in a wet, crunching roar, leaving three battered hill giants in the bloodied water. The brutes slapped at the splinters of their raft, desperately trying to grab something buoyant enough to keep their heavy bodies from sinking.

The mammoth gave a joyful trumpet and continued

swimming. Avner grabbed the end of Brianna's rope and tied it around the chest of Brianna's bodyguard. The queen was glad to see that the boy had thought to place the knot between the scout's shoulder blades, so that he would be dragged backwards, with his head still above water, when she pulled him to the castle.

"Haul away!" the youth yelled.

"You come, too," Brianna called. "I can bring you both up."

"It'll be faster one at a time." As the youth spoke, he was dragging himself over the mammoth's head. "Besides, I've got to do something."

Brianna pulled. Even the hill giants on the farthest rafts redoubled their boulder-casting, hurling a constant storm of rocks that fell far short of the mammoth. The four warriors on the closest vessel gave up throwing in favor of paddling and rapidly began to gain on Avner's injured mount.

Brianna continued to pull, at the same time casting anxious glances down the ramparts in both directions. Selwyn and Cuthbert had restored enough order so that soldiers armed with heavy crossbows now stood in most embrasures. The spoon on Blane's catapult was cranked about halfway down. The engine close to her was not even that close to firing. She looked back at the lake and saw Avner treading water beside the mammoth's head, tugging at a rope tied to the beast's trunk.

"Damn it, Avner!" she hissed. "The next time I tell you to grab the rope, do it!"

The giants on the closest raft stopped paddling and laid their clubs aside to reach for boulders. The first warrior launched his stone just as Brianna's bodyguard reached the base of the castle wall. The rock arced not toward Avner or the mammoth, but at the unconscious firbolg at the end of the queen's rope. The missile splashed into the water less than two paces from its target, sending a plume of water so high that droplets hit the queen's face.

"Fire on those giants!" Brianna yelled.

The cords of several heavy crossbows popped simultaneously, sending javelin-sized bolts sizzling down at the raft. One of the giants bellowed in pain and dropped to the deck, clutching his thigh. Two more reached for boulders, while the third grabbed two shields and positioned himself in front of his companions.

Brianna started pulling her bodyguard up the wall. She saw Avner slip the rope off the mammoth's snout, then push on the side of the beast's head to direct it toward the open lake.

"Avner, come on!"

The boy looked up and nodded, then swam away. The mammoth bugled its good riddance and dived.

The giants on the raft hurled their boulders. The stones hit on each side of her bodyguard and shattered against the castle wall. Brianna pulled harder, yanking the rope up so fast that it grew hot in her hands. The hill giants turned to reach for more rocks.

The bow of the raft suddenly rose, pitching both giants into the lake, then the mammoth's head appeared beneath the logs. The beast drove one corner of the vessel high into the air and flipped it aside with an angry snort. Though the craft did not capsize, the two passengers slipped off its deck into the churning waters. The mammoth let out a blood-curdling bugle and paused long enough to gore a giant before turning toward the far end of the lake and diving out of sight.

"That's quite a mammoth you've got there, Avner!" As she called to the youth, Brianna was hauling her bodyguard into the embrasure. "Do you know where we can get a dozen for the royal stables?"

"The same place I got that one!" The youth was treading water at the base of the wall. "From the frost giants— and they should be here any time!"

The youth's comment sent a concerned murmur

rustling down the wall. Brianna lowered her bodyguard onto the rampart at her feet. He was in bad shape: burned, cut, battered, and blistered from frostbite, not to mention half drowned. A pang of remorse shot through her breast, though she could not say why. She had seen many of her soldiers injured more severely than this, and while she was concerned for them, she had never felt anything like guilt because of their injuries.

As Brianna struggled to untie the wet rope around the scout's torso, Cuthbert scurried over to her. The earl's eye went straight to the scout's face.

"Is that your . . . ?" He let the question trail off, his jowls trembling. "It is! Tavis! Have all the gods deserted us?"

Brianna gave up on the knot and pulled the earl's dagger from its sheathe. "What are you talking about, Cuthbert?"

"The hill giants are attacking!" he cried. "That's what I came to tell you. They just launched their entire fleet."

Brianna looked up. "That *is* interesting."

A hill giant boulder crashed off the castle wall and was immediately answered by both catapults. The queen returned her attention to her bodyguard and cut the rope just above the knot. "Avner's reported that the frost giants are coming, too."

"Then we're doomed," Cuthbert uttered. "If Tavis is here, no reinforcements will be coming."

"We don't know that, Earl." Brianna turned back to the embrasure. "And even if it's true, haven't I spoken to you about demoralizing the men?"

Cuthbert mumbled an apology, then stooped over to pull the unconscious scout away from the embrasure. Out on the lake Brianna saw that the catapults had claimed another raft. The remaining hill giants had given up the chase and were slowly paddling toward the other side of the castle, presumably to join their fellows in the main attack. Brianna dropped the rope to Avner.

The youth tied a loop into the end and slipped his foot into the eyelet, then allowed himself to be hoisted up.

Brianna grabbed the youth's wet arm and pulled him over the embrasure. "What's all this about frost giants?" she demanded. The boy looked almost as bad as her bodyguard, with his face and hands blistered and dark from the effects of frostbite. "And where have you been?"

The youth gestured toward the castle gate, sweeping his hand across the hills beyond the bridge. "The frost giants are hiding behind those ridges. That's why we had to swim instead of using the gate." Avner looked down at the scout's unconscious form, then added, "As for where I've been, that should be obvious. The real question is, what are you going to do about Tavis?"

Brianna regarded the battered firbolg at her feet. "What do you mean?"

"Heal him!" Avner demanded. "You *are* a priestess—or have you forgotten?"

Brianna's insides turned cold and queasy. "I remember," she said. "But I haven't been feeling well. I-I can't do it."

The boy's mouth gaped open. "Then it's true!" he cried. "You *don't* love him!"

"Love him?" Brianna echoed. The haze was starting to gather in her mind again. "Love my bodyguard?"

"Is that all Tavis is to you?" Avner retorted. "Someone to save you from ogres, or to fight stone giants and spy on frost giants while you make love to Prince Arlien?"

Cuthbert interposed himself between Brianna and the youth. "See here, young man! You *will* show the queen the proper respect, or you can share a dungeon cell with your thieving verbeeg friend!"

"The dungeon?" Avner gasped. "You put Basil down there?"

"The earl had no choice." The queen swept Cuthbert aside and scowled at the youth, then found herself struggling to keep hold of her slippery thoughts. "And what I do . . . or don't do . . . with Prince Arlien—that should not concern you, young man. But your imagination . . . your imagination seems to have gotten out of hand." Brianna was trying to sound indignant, but found the task difficult, her thoughts flitting off in all directions.

"So you don't love the prince?" Avner asked.

"What did I . . . didn't I just say that?"

"Prove it," the youth demanded. "Heal Tavis."

Cuthbert was at Avner's side again, taking him by the arm. "Can't you hear, boy?" he demanded. "The queen said she hasn't been feeling well."

Avner jerked away from the earl and stepped forward until he stood almost on Brianna's feet. "She looks well enough to me. Besides, the queen I remember would've crawled off her deathbed to heal Tavis Burdun." The youth glared up at her as he spoke. "But maybe *that* was my imagination, too."

The youth's accusatory tone should have angered Brianna, but it did not. Instead, the queen found herself filled with emotions she did not understand, her stomach churning with guilt and her heart aching with shame. She did not understand why, but the feelings were so intense that she almost could not hide them.

"Get me some water," Brianna said. "I'll try."

Avner rushed down the rampart. The queen went over and kneeled at her bodyguard's side. During the past year, Brianna's goddess had blessed her with many new healing powers, but the firbolg was such a mess that even if she could call on them, he would still be far from whole. The burns, which had begun to ooze and peel, were the most grotesque of his many injuries, but the queen worried more about the tremendous lump she found on his skull. The head injury was undoubtedly the cause of his unconsciousness, and also the most likely to prove fatal. She would try mending it first.

Avner returned and set a sloshing bucket at the

scout's side. Brianna unclasped her silver necklace, from which hung the flaming spear symbol of her goddess. She placed this talisman inside the bucket, then turned her eyes toward the sky.

"Valorous Hiatea, bless this water with your magic, so that it may purify this warrior's spirit and make him worthy of your healing magic."

A gentle gurgle arose as the water began to bubble and churn, spewing a cloud of white vapor into the air.

"You can still heal him," Avner said.

"Blessing the water is not the same as healing the patient," countered Brianna. "It merely shows that Hiatea looks favorably on my entreaty, not that I will succeed."

The queen took her talisman from the bucket, then dumped the steaming contents over her patient's injuries. Dark bubbles frothed up from his many wounds, covering his singed body with a thick, brown-streaked foam that would cleanse his spirit of wicked thoughts and emotions.

While Brianna waited for the blessed water to do its work, alarmed cries and yells began to ring out from ramparts at the front of the castle. The clamor was followed by the resounding clatter of a dozen firing catapults.

"That would be the frost giants coming into view," said Brianna.

Cuthbert nodded, looking as though he might faint. "Selwyn is commanding the gatehouse," he said. "He'll keep us informed."

A loud bang reverberated through the castle as the first of the giant's boulders crashed into the wall. It struck with such force that Brianna felt the rampart shudder under her feet. Another stone hit, then another and another, until a steady, drumlike cadence filled the air. The rhythm was punctuated every now and then by the clack of a catapult returning fire.

Brianna glanced toward the front wall. "I hope your

masons have kept the curtain in good repair, Earl."

"I hope so, too," he said.

The queen cringed at the apprehensive reply and turned to her patient. The water had stopped frothing. Brianna held her talisman against the lump on her bodyguard's head, but before she could cast the spell, a runner came rushing down the rampart. He stopped before Brianna and bowed.

"Captain Selwyn begs to report that Prince Arlien has returned," the soldier panted.

"Arlien?" Brianna gasped. Her hands grew sweaty so that the talisman slipped from her grasp, and the fog inside her head grew as dense as a snow cloud. Her thoughts raced blindly through the gray murk, and she asked, "The prince . . . Arlien has returned?"

The messenger nodded. "He should be inside the castle within minutes," the man reported. "He's crossing the bridge now."

"With the queen's army?" Cuthbert's voice was full of hope.

"No, Milord, not with him," the messenger replied, his voice mirroring the earl's optimism. "But he was shouting something. We couldn't hear it over the battle din."

"It must be news of our reinforcements!" Cuthbert faced Brianna, his arms raised as though he might embrace her. "Majesty, your army must be right behind the prince!"

"Only if they're chasing him," Avner scoffed. "Tell Selwyn to keep the gate closed."

The glee drained from Cuthbert's face. He grabbed the boy and spun him around, demanding, "What are you saying?"

"Arlien's a spy." The boy pulled free. "He told the giants about Shepherd's Nightmare and almost got Tavis killed."

"I don't believe that . . . it can't be true," Brianna said. The words seemed to flow out of her haze-filled mind straight into her mouth. "It could have been anyone . . . What proof do you have that Arlien has . . . that the prince is a . . ."

The queen let the question trail off, unable to utter the suggestion that Arlien had betrayed her.

"What proof do I have that Arlien's a traitor?" the youth asked. "How about your ice diamonds? He's been using them to charm you. That's why you're defending him."

Cuthbert turned to Brianna. "Are you wearing the necklace now, Milady?"

Brianna opened the collar of her cloak and displayed her bare throat. She said nothing.

Cuthbert looked back to Avner. "It appears you're wrong about the ice diamonds. Do you have any other proof?" he demanded. "And be certain of yourself. The prince may be risking his life to bring us word of the queen's army. Knowing what he has to say could save my castle—and your life."

Avner pointed at the unconscious scout. "Do you need more proof than that?"

"You saw Arlien do this?" the earl demanded.

Avner remained silent for a moment, then looked Cuthbert squarely in eye. "That's right."

The earl looked doubtful. "Tell me, what weapon did Arlien use?" Cuthbert pointed at the scout's seared flesh. "I don't recall the prince hurling fireballs about."

Avner's eyes widened. "It was his hammer!" the boy said, too quickly. "He shot a tongue of flame—"

The earl raised his hand. "Young man, I've been listening to liars for decades," he said. "And you're just good enough that I can't trust a thing you say."

Avner's mouth fell open.

Cuthbert turned to Brianna. "What do you think, Majesty?" he asked. "This boy isn't the first liar to accuse Arlien of being an imposter. Shall we take their word for it, or should I let the good prince in?"

A nebulous, absurd fear seized Brianna. A whispering voice deep in her heart wanted to say *no, leave him out with the giants,* but the words vanished as soon as they entered her cloudy mind, and she heard herself say, "Do as you think best, Earl."

Cuthbert bowed. "Then I shall." He glanced at Avner. "Rest assured that I'll keep a careful watch on the prince."

The boy rolled his eyes. "A lot of good that'll do."

"It will do more good than your lies."

With that, the earl motioned to his messenger and scurried toward the gate tower. Avner gestured at the unconscious firbolg.

"Hurry up," he said. "If Cuthbert's going to let the prince in, we don't have much time. Heal him!"

Brianna returned her talisman to her bodyguard's injured head, then tried to remember the mystical syllables of her healing spell. Nothing came to her except swirls of gray miasma. She pinched her eyes shut, trying to summon the incantation through sheer willpower.

"Well?" Avner asked. "What are you waiting for?"

"The words," Brianna hissed.

"What words?" the boy demanded. "You never had to wait before!"

The queen opened her eyes. "You're not helping."

"Neither are you," Avner retorted.

The youth fell silent, leaving nothing but the rumble of boulders and the snapping of catapults to disturb Brianna's concentration. She tried to ignore the war sounds, but each crash loosened her tenuous hold on her own mind. And even when she did succeed in drawing a thought out of the mist, it was the leering image of Prince Arlien, or the sneering face of a frost giant.

"Hiatea, I beg you!" Brianna whispered. "Send me the incantation!"

Nothing came. She waited the space of ten crashing boulders, then twenty, then listened to the catapults clatter in reply. A chorus of cheers echoed from the gatehouse, and Brianna assumed a giant had fallen. The queen could not remember how the spell began—could not remember the first syllable, not even the first sound.

Brianna looked at Avner and shook her head. "I'm sorry," she said. "I told you I wasn't feeling well."

"That's not the reason," the youth replied. "It's Arlien. You're thinking about him, and that's why you can't save Tavis."

Brianna felt her face flush, then saw Avner's eyes grow wide and angry. "The prince *is* on my mind," she admitted. "But not the way you think. I'm not in . . . I don't care for . . . "

Brianna could not bring herself to deny that she loved Arlien. It wasn't that she did—to the contrary, she feared him—but she couldn't say the words.

"You're not what? Not in love with him?" Avner demanded. "You know me better than that. I'm no fool."

"Avner, I'm trying, but all the noise—it's so hard to concentrate." Brianna scooped the scout up. "We'll take him to my chamber, where it's quiet."

"That won't do any good!" Avner screamed. There were tears in the boy's eyes. "You can't heal anymore!" The youth turned and ran toward the corner tower.

"Avner, wait!" Brianna yelled. "Where are you going?"

"To find someone who can help Tavis!" Avner yelled. "You can't!"

The boy's angry words demolished what little strength remained in Brianna's anguished heart. A loud, croaking sob erupted from her throat, then tears began to cascade down her face like rain. She was crying not because of Avner's anger. Like most youths his age, he was prone to emotional outbursts. Nor was she crying for her injured bodyguard, although deep inside, a voice seemed to be saying she should.

The queen was crying for something even more dear, for something that had been part of her since her childhood, something that she had lost after taking refuge in Cuthbert Castle. Avner was right: There was a time when she would have—could have—healed her bodyguard, no matter how sick she was herself. If she could not cast the spell now, it had little to do with her illness. The queen had lost touch with her goddess.

Brianna had to heal the scout—not for his sake, and not for Avner's, but for her own. She had to find her way back to Hiatea. To do that, she would need to shut the battle sounds out of her mind and think. She would need to calm herself. She would need to wear her ice diamonds.

← 16 →

The Storming of the Castle

A volley of boulders slammed into the castle's windward wall. The cobblestones bucked beneath Avner's feet, hurling him into the air. In the pit of his stomach he felt the shock wave of a boom so loud he did not even hear it. His ears merely started to ring, then he crashed into one of the gate towers that guarded the entrance to the inner ward. He slid to the ground in an aching, breathless heap and found himself looking across the front bailey to the outer gate.

Earl Cuthbert and several of his men lay in the shadowy passage beneath the archway, struggling to stand after the salvo had knocked them off their feet. A few feet beyond them, an armored figure in burnished battle plate kneeled on the threshold of the gate's open mandoor, his greaves and vambraces flashing like mirrors as he pushed himself to his feet. Although he wore his visor down, the curved horns rising from the temples of his helm left no doubts about the warrior's identity.

Prince Arlien had returned.

Avner rolled to his knees and found himself staring at the castle's windward wall. The ramparts were littered with rubble: shattered merlons, demolished ballistae, flailing wounded, motionless corpses. In one place, where a loose torch had fallen into a pool of spilled oil, a group of terrified soldiers were throwing buckets of water at a creeping tide of fire. The massive curtain had cracked in several places, and the youth saw blue lake water glinting through three of the fissures.

Avner cursed, knowing that the giants would breach the walls all too soon. He glanced back at the rampart where he had left Tavis and Brianna less than a minute earlier. The queen was nowhere in sight. She was probably descending the stairs in the corner tower and would soon be carrying the scout across the front bailey toward the inner gate. If Arlien saw them, all would be lost. The prince would need merely to delay them until the giants breached the outer curtain—a few minutes from now, at best—then the queen would be captured and Tavis killed.

Avner forced his aching body to rise, then rushed around the corner toward the inner gate. He had to move fast if he was going to win the time he needed to find Basil. The youth did not know what would happen after the verbeeg was free, but if anyone could restore Brianna to her senses, it would be the runecaster.

At the other end of the dark archway, the iron portcullis hung less than six feet from the ground. The main gates were already closed fast, though the mandoor at the bottom remained open. Avner slipped through the portal. On the other side he found two sentries in the White Wolf tabards of Selwyn's company.

"I have an order from the queen!" he lied. The youth saw no use in trying to explain that Prince Arlien was a spy. Even if the guards believed him, which was doubtful, there would be too many questions. He gestured at the shorter of the two guards and commanded, "Tell Prince Arlien to await her majesty on the windward wall of the outer curtain. The queen will join him shortly. She has a special plan to turn the giants back!"

The guards looked at each other doubtfully. "Turn the giants back?" scoffed the short one. He was a squat man with a curly red beard. "Now I know she's lost her mind!"

"Shall I tell her you said so?" Avner demanded.

The guard ignored the youth and looked to his tall fellow. "What do you think?"

"He *is* the queen's favorite page," answered the soldier. He fixed a suspicious glare on the youth, then added, "But I thought you'd run off—"

"I've returned!" Avner snapped. "And my next message is for Captain Selwyn. Shall I tell him you two elected not to obey a direct order from the queen?"

The guard's eyes widened, but he shook his head and looked to his shorter companion. "You'd better do as he says."

Avner waited for the messenger to depart, then turned to the tall guard. "Where's the dungeon?" he asked. "I'm to fetch Basil before I see Selwyn. The queen needs his magic to save us."

"It'll take more than a few runes," the soldier replied.

Despite his pessimistic reply, the man pointed to the tower near the center of the inner curtain. Avner sprinted away. As he crossed the inner ward, another boulder volley struck the castle's windward wall. The foundations of the inner curtain absorbed much of the impact, but the youth still felt the cobblestones tremble beneath his feet.

At the tower, Avner found another sentry standing in the doorway. This one wore a leather hauberk emblazoned with Cuthbert's crossed shepherd's staves. To the youth's surprise, the guard made no move to bar the door.

"You're the last of the women and children, I hope." The soldier motioned Avner into the tower.

The youth shrugged. "I don't know."

The guard scowled and muttered a curse, then said, "Well, the tunnel's in the second sub-basement, hidden behind a swinging shelf." He pointed down a damp, spiraling stairway a few steps inside the doorway. "Be sure to pull it closed behind you."

"I'll be sure," Avner promised.

Although the passage was well lit by torches, the youth forced himself to descend at a walk. The stairs were as ancient as they were moldy, littered with jagged bits of mortar knocked from the walls and ceiling by the boulders' barrages. Avner had just reached the first landing when another volley hit the outer curtain, causing the entire corridor to jump and showering him with hunks of crumbling mortar. A loud crash sounded inside the chamber beside him, then the vinegary smell of sour wine filled the corridor.

Avner continued his descent. The assault changed into a steady barrage that left the walls trembling and the air rumbling. The youth stopped at the second subbasement, then opened the door into a chamber thick with the smell of moldering cereal. A single flickering torch hung in a sconce on the far wall, and by its light he saw that the room contained hundreds of grain sacks. Most of the corners had been chewed open by rats.

The youth weaved his way to the rear of the room, where he found the swinging shelf that the guard had described. It hung partially ajar, revealing the entrance to a narrow, rough-hewn tunnel that ran roughly toward the main keep.

One look into the cramped passage was enough for Avner to know Basil would never enter it. They would have to fight their way past the soldier at the top of the stairs, which would certainly prove more bruising for him than the youth and the verbeeg. Avner pushed the shelf to the wall and made certain that he heard the latch click.

The youth returned to the stairwell and continued his descent. The dungeon, he knew from bitter experience, would be in the lowest, dankest chamber of the tower foundations. Although the passage here was unlit, he did not bother to retrieve a torch. After a lifetime of thievery, he was accustomed to moving swiftly through the dark.

Avner descended past one more basement, this one smelling of pine pitch, then the stairwell gave way to a flat, curving corridor. At the end of the hall hung a partially open door, with the dim light of a candle flickering on the other side of the threshold. The youth heard a guard running a whetstone over the blade of a weapon.

Whatever Basil had done to land himself in the dungeon, it must have angered Cuthbert greatly. Once a prisoner was safely chained to the wall and his door barred, few earls would have bothered to keep guards posted in the antechamber—especially during a giant attack.

Avner retreated up the stairs and fitted a chunk of loose mortar into the pocket of his sling. He ran back down the stairs, stomping his feet and whirling his weapon.

"Who's there?" The guard appeared in the doorway, holding a tallow candle in one hand and a battle axe in the other.

Avner whipped his sling at the guard's bare head. The mortar struck with an echoing crack, and the soldier's eyes rolled back in their sockets. His knees buckled, and he collapsed in the doorway. The candle landed on the damp floor and sputtered out, plunging the corridor into darkness as black as obsidian.

Avner felt his way along the dank wall until he reached the doorway, where he paused long enough to find the sentry. He didn't mind knocking an occasional guard unconscious, but he had yet to kill one. After making certain that the man was still breathing, he stepped over the fellow into the dungeon's antechamber. "Basil? Where are you?"

"Avner? You're alive?" The runecaster's voice was muffled by a heavy door. "Or—or did I finally die?"

"Relax," Avner replied, following the words through the musty darkness. "We're both alive."

"Oh, good!" Basil's voice was growing increasingly squeaky. "By the light, that's good!"

Near the center of the room, Avner reached an oaken door fastened by a simple crossbar. As soon as he lifted the beam off its hooks, the door flew open and knocked him across the chamber. A thump resounded through the darkness as some part of Basil's large body flopped out of the cell.

"Get me out of here!" The runecaster's chains chinked sharply as he jerked them taut. "Get me out now!"

"Those chains are mortared into the tower foundation. Even a verbeeg can't pull them loose." Avner reached for his lockpicks. "Just calm down, and I'll get you loose."

"Calm down?" the verbeeg shrieked, still rattling his chains. "I've been stuffed in that hole at least a month! What took you so long?"

"It can't have been a month," Avner said, growing more concerned. He had expected the verbeeg's nerves to be worn, but Basil seemed as though he had lost his reason. "I've been gone only four days."

"Liar!" Basil yelled. "Don't try that—"

"Basil, you're no good to me like this," Avner said evenly.

"Good to you?" the verbeeg yelled. "I'm the one who's been locked up in the dark—"

"We don't have time for this," Avner warned. "If you don't pull yourself together and shut up, I swear I'm going to leave you down here."

Basil fell instantly silent.

Avner heard the verbeeg take several deep breaths.

"Avner?"

"Yes?"

"I'm feeling much better now," he said. "You don't have to leave me down here."

"That's good, Basil." Avner stepped to the verbeeg's side and located his manacled wrists. "Now hold still. Picking locks in the dark is difficult enough."

The verbeeg remained as still as stone.

"Basil, we've got a big problem." Avner spoke as he worked. "Tavis is hurt, and Brianna's lost her healing powers. I think it has something to do with Prince Arlien."

"Of course it does," Basil answered.

"Then you know what's happening?" The wrist manacles came open, and Avner worked his way down to the verbeeg's ankles. "Can you do something about it?"

"If you can get me my runebrush and a chalice," the verbeeg replied. "Reversing the love spell is easy enough. But getting rid of Arlien—that's going to be a challenge."

Avner found the runecaster's shackles and set to work opening them. "It is?" he asked. "How come?"

"Because he's the ettin."

"An ettin?" Avner gasped. For a moment, he couldn't understand how this was possible. Then he remembered how effective Basil's runemask had been in transforming Tavis into a stone giant. "In disguise?"

"His enchanted armor," Basil confirmed. "That's why he never takes it off."

Avner popped the lock open. "We can still get rid of him if you really can cure Brianna," the youth said. "After she's back to normal, all she has to do is heal Tavis. I'll bet he's killed plenty of ettins."

Basil grabbed Avner by the shoulder. "You don't understand," he whispered. "Arlien isn't just any ettin."

"What are you talking about?"

"His name—rather, their names—were in the last folio I took from Cuthbert's library: Arno and Julien. Together, Arlien."

"So what?"

"That book tells of Twilight's creation—thousands of years ago," Basil said. "Arno and Julien are mentioned in it. They aren't an ettin, they're *the* ettin—the first one."

* * * * *

Sweet wintergreen.

Tavis smelled wintergreen. It was a familiar fragrance, and one he could not imagine sensing in the depths of

264

an avalanche. He would not be able to smell anything, except perhaps his own singed body, and then only until he suffocated. So he could not imagine why his nose was full of that most pleasant of all odors.

"Brianna?" He barely croaked her name, and the effort sent stinging waves of pain through his charred face. "Brianna?"

And there was a pounding, not in his head, but somewhere outside. Rocks crashing against rocks. And men yelling, twanging ballista skeins, banging catapults.

"Where . . . am . . . I?" Tavis opened his eyes. Lances of bright light shot through his head. His face felt cracked and leathery, his throat so parched that he could have emptied a horse trough. But still he smelled the wintergreen. The queen's perfume. "Brianna?"

"Merciful Hiatea!" A blurry face surrounded by a golden halo appeared over Tavis's head. Someone sat on the bed beside him. "How are you feeling?"

"Everything hurts," Tavis groaned. "How'd I get here? Avner?"

The queen nodded.

"Then he must be all right." Tavis pushed himself into a seated position, then nearly blacked out from the throbbing in his head.

The rumble of collapsing stonework echoed through the window. Brianna cast a nervous glance toward the sound.

"What's happening?" Tavis asked.

"The giants are attacking," the queen said. Then, as an afterthought, she added, "I assume you didn't get through to Earl Wendel."

"I sent a message," Tavis answered. His vision was beginning to clear. There were two purple blotches where the queen's eyes were supposed to be, and he could see the scintillating blue lights of a necklace hanging around her throat. Ice diamonds. Avner had told him they were enchanted. "The army isn't here?"

"You were supposed to *bring* it," Brianna scolded.

"The giants ambushed me in Shepherd's Nightmare. They had a spy in the castle," Tavis explained. "It seemed more urgent to warn you about the traitor."

Brianna raised her brow. "A spy," she said. "I've heard that before."

"It's Prince Arlien," the scout reported. "Has he returned? I injured him, but I don't know if I stopped him."

"Arlien?" Brianna gasped. Her voice sounded at once bewildered and frightened. "How can . . . you can't be sure!"

"I saw him speaking with the frost giant chieftain," Tavis replied. "Now you must tell me—has he returned to the castle?"

Brianna looked away, and in a distant voice she said, "You must . . . be mistaken."

Tavis squinted at her, trying to clear his vision. He could not see well enough to judge her expression, but he guessed her eyes would seem vacant or glassy. Her voice certainly sounded unsure and stilted, almost as though the words were spilling from her mouth on their own.

"I'm not mistaken." The scout waved his hand over his singed body. "Arlien's the one who did this to me."

Brianna rose. "You . . . why are you lying?"

"Listen to yourself, Brianna." Although he had to speak loudly to make himself heard over the battle din outside, Tavis kept his voice calm and reasonable. "I'm a firbolg—you'd hear it if I were lying."

The queen backed away, trembling and staring at the floor, shaking her head and mumbling to herself.

"It's Arlien. His magic is confusing you." The scout motioned for her to come over to him. "I can help you."

"N-No. I need no . . . I don't need your help." Brianna turned toward the door. "I have to go."

"To where? Arlien?"

As he spoke, Tavis swung his legs around and stood.
He took three steps, then he realized he was trying to
run on mushy lumps of flesh. He glanced down and saw
black, swollen masses of toes and insteps where his feet
should have been. Two searing waves of agony shot up
his legs.

"Forgive my rudeness, Majesty."

Tavis threw himself forward, clasping Brianna's shoulder with one hand and grabbing the ice diamonds with
the other. His fingers instantly blanched to a pallid,
frozen white, and searing coldness shot up his arm. The
scout did not care. He forced himself to clench the gems
more tightly, then yanked the necklace off the queen's
throat.

Brianna whirled around, pulling free of Tavis's grasp.
The mushy-footed scout fell to the floor.

"How dare you!" the queen hissed. Her violet eyes
had gone almost black with anger. "What are you doing
with my ice diamonds?"

"They're enchanted," Tavis explained. He continued
to hold the necklace, and the coldness became an icy,
stinging numbness. The feeling was similar to the one
he had experienced when Bodvar had deadened the
pain in his injured toe, save that it was a dozen times
more chilling. "Say my name."

Brianna looked confused. "Your name?" she asked.
The anger was fading from her eyes, but any sparkle of
wit had yet to creep back into them. "Whatever for?"

"You loved me once," Tavis said. "Try to remember."

"Loved *you?*" she scoffed. "You're my bodyguard!
Now I know where Avner gets his crazy ideas."

It did not matter to Tavis that Brianna's forgetfulness
had been caused by Arlien's magic; her words made him
feel tired and weak and defeated. If she could not
remember the emotions they had shared, then she
remained under Arlien's spell.

The scout shook his head. "It's just as well that you've

forgotten," he said. "Love between us could never be."

"Now you're coming to your senses." Brianna pointed at her ice diamonds. "So you *will* return my jewelry."

She reached for the necklace, but Tavis pulled it away. Even if the diamonds were not the source of the queen's enchantment, the fact that she was wearing them now suggested that the necklace supplemented Arlien's hold on her mind. The queen was hardly the type of woman to wear such gaudy jewelry into battle.

"I'm sorry, I can't return your necklace," Tavis said. The hand holding the ice diamonds had gone so numb that he doubted he could release his hold if he wanted to. "That would be a violation of my duty to you."

"I'm your queen!" Brianna spat. "I name your duty!"

"When your mind is clear, yes," he replied. "But not when your thoughts are chained by a spy's magic."

A dull flash appeared somewhere deep behind Brianna's eyes, then the anger slowly faded from her face. She gaped at Tavis with an expression that seemed as lost as it did suspicious. The scout locked gazes with her. They stared at each other for a long time, until a set of heavy footsteps came pounding up the corridor. Someone rapped on the door, and the queen looked away from Tavis.

"Enter," she called.

The door swung open. In the corridor outside stood a squat soldier with a curly red beard. His tabard was so besmirched by soot that Tavis could barely make out the White Wolf badge of his company.

"Majesty! What are you doing here?" In his excitement, the soldier forgot to bow. "The frost giants have frozen the channel, and even now they're coming across with a battering ram. The main gate will fall soon. Now is the time for your special plan—"

"Special plan?" Brianna interrupted. "What special plan?"

"The plan that Avner said—" The soldier stopped as

soon as he spoke the youth's name. He closed his eyes
in exasperation, then shook his head violently. "Damn
that boy! Why would he lie about such a thing?"

"Tell us what he said," Tavis commanded.

The soldier glanced down at the scout, but if he was
surprised to see the queen's bodyguard sitting helpless
on the floor, his face did not show it. "The swine told us
that Queen Brianna had a special plan to turn the giants
back," the man explained. "He sent me to Prince
Arlien—"

"Then Arlien's here?" Tavis demanded. He braced his
hands on a chair seat and pulled himself to his feet.
"Arlien is in the castle?"

The man nodded. "He's with Earl Cuthbert, on the
windward wall—at least until it collapses," he confirmed.
"That's where Avner said to send . . . "

The soldier let his sentence trail off, for Brianna's face
had gone pale. She was slowly backing across the room,
her gaze fixed on the empty air.

"Milady?" Tavis asked. He started to stumble toward
her, but stopped when her expression changed to one of
fear. "What is it?"

Brianna shook her head, freeing herself of whatever it
was that had gripped her mind. "It's the prince," she
admitted. "There's something about him."

Tavis nodded. "There is indeed," he said. "But I'll protect you. That's my duty."

The queen blinked several times, then ran a doubtful
gaze over Tavis's battered body. "You're hardly in condition to perform that duty—or any other."

"But I can—if you'll lend me your ice diamonds,"
Tavis said, tightly gripping the necklace. "They'll numb
my pain."

"But they were a gift—"

"From a man you fear," Tavis said. When Brianna
frowned and started to object, the scout quickly interrupted. "Don't deny it. I can see in your eyes that he

frightens you. How can you value any gift of his?"

A confused expression came over Brianna's face. She looked away and forced herself to shake her head. "I suppose I shouldn't," she said. "You may borrow the diamonds."

"Thank you, Majesty," Tavis sighed. "Now we can defeat the prince."

The scout sat in a chair and rubbed the cold stones over his anguished feet. As the icy numbness began to replace the searing agony in his feet, he motioned the red-bearded soldier over.

"I want you to take a message to Captain Selwyn."

* * * * *

Basil painted the last line of his rune, then raised the silver chalice to admire his work. "A true work of art, if I say so myself," he said. "My thanks for providing such excellent material, Avner."

The youth gave a casual shrug. "I used to find stuff like that all the time."

They were in the small chamber where Basil had originally been confined. Avner sat in the windowsill, keeping an eye on the battle outside. Although he could not see over the inner curtain, the youth could tell by the number of refugees streaming through the inner gate that the giants had broken through the outer curtain.

"I don't understand why you needed a cup," Avner said, continuing to watch the inner gate. "What are you going to do, crush the ice diamonds and make Brianna drink them?"

"Oh, dear me, no!" the verbeeg replied. "Where'd you get an idea like that?"

"You said you were going to reverse the love magic," Avner said. "And the magic's in her necklace."

Basil shook his head. "That's what you're supposed to think."

"*Supposed* to think?" Avner asked. "Says who?"

"Says the Twilight Spirit," Basil explained. "His real name is Lanaxis, by the way."

A deafening boom sounded in the front bailey, then Avner saw the head of a frost giant's axe rise briefly above the inner curtain.

"What are you talking about, Basil?" the youth demanded. "Who's this Lanaxis?"

"I wish I had the proper folio—but I'm sure the earl has returned it to his library by now," Basil said. "I'd read it to you. You might find it quite interesting."

"I'll settle for the short version."

Basil nodded. "I thought you might." The verbeeg cast an annoyed glance toward the battle outside, then raised his voice like an orator speaking over the din of a storm. "It seems that many millennia ago, before the first human kingdoms arose, this part of the world was ruled by an empire of giants known as Ostoria. The kings of this realm were the firstborn of each race of giants, immortal sons born directly of Annam the All Father and Othea the Mother Queen.

"Unfortunately for these kings, a marital dispute between their parents resulted in the creation of the Endless Ice Sea, which promptly began to swallow their lands. Needless to say, this upset the giant kings, so they decided to destroy the glacier. But their mother, Othea, heard about the plan and forbade her sons from carrying it out.

"So Lanaxis, the first titan, and Julien and Arno, the first ettin, poisoned her. Unfortunately, they inadvertently poisoned most of their brothers as well."

"Most?" Avner asked. Somewhere outside, a chorus of screams announced the destruction of a catapult crew.

"All except one, and he's of no consequence to us," Basil clarified. "What is of import is this: before Othea died, she sentenced Lanaxis and the ettin to live in the twilight of her shadow for as long as they wished to

271

remain immortal—and so they have."

"That's where the Twilight Vale is," Avner surmised.

Basil nodded. "But now, the ettin has sacrificed his immortality to kidnap Brianna."

Avner frowned. "What about Tavis?" he demanded. "Doesn't he know about the golden arrow—?"

"The ettin knows," Basil interrupted. "That's why he isolated us in this remote castle, where only a great scout stood any chance of summoning help. Then, once Tavis was out of the way, the ettin made his attempt." The verbeeg smiled very proudly at this point. "I stopped him."

"Good for you," Avner said. At another time, he might have asked Basil to elaborate. "I still don't see what that has to do with the ice diamonds."

"You've never played *Wyverns and Wyrms*, have you, my boy?" Before Avner could answer, the runecaster continued, "You see, to win, you must guess the opponent's plans. So a good player, knowing that the other player will try to figure out his plans, always plants false clues."

"And that's what Arlien did to us."

"Exactly," Basil said. "Lanaxis has had a very long time to learn the game of *Wyverns and Wyrms*—thousands and thousands of years. The ice diamonds were a decoy. The necklace seems to have a certain deadening effect on Brianna's emotions, but the real magic is in the potion that Arlien's been feeding her. We were lucky to find him out when we did."

Avner nodded. "Fine," he said. "But I still don't get what they want with Brianna. Giving up your immortality is an awfully high price to pay for a woman—even a queen."

"But not for someone who can bear a king that will restore your lost empire," Basil said.

"The giants think Brianna can do that?" Avner gasped. He was still watching the inner gate.

Basil nodded. "And they may be right. You see, when Othea died, she was still carrying Annam's last unborn son. . . . "

Avner did not hear the rest of the explanation, for his attention had been captured by a pair of armored figures climbing through the mandoor of the inner gate. One of them was wearing a distinctive horned helm.

"We're out of time," the youth reported. "Arlien's coming, and Cuthbert's with him!"

As the youth spoke, an extremely long wooden arrow raced away from the keep, apparently fired from a window one floor below. The shaft hissed across the ward in the blink of an eye, then bounced off Arlien's magical armor without causing any harm.

"Tavis is awake!" Avner yelled.

Basil rose to his knees and stuck his massive head into the window, nearly crushing the youth against the sill. Another wooden arrow hissed away from the keep, but the prince and everyone around him were already scrambling for cover. The shaft missed its target cleanly and lodged itself in the gate.

"But Brianna couldn't possibly heal him until her mind is clear!" Basil objected. "He can't be in any condition to fight!"

"As long as he can crawl, Tavis can fight," Avner replied. "I just don't know if he can win."

A third arrow arced across the ward, this time glancing off one of Arlien's pauldrons. The prince watched the shaft clatter to the cobblestones, then rushed through the entrance to the nearest gate tower and disappeared from sight. Through the tower, Prince Arlien would have access to the ramparts of the inner curtain and, eventually, to the keep itself.

Earl Cuthbert reacted more slowly, simply bracing himself against the wall of the gate tower and staring toward the keep as if he couldn't quite comprehend what was happening. When no more arrows came arcing across the ward, he finally seemed to recover from his shock. He waved a dozen soldiers over and tried to follow Arlien into the gate tower, but the door did not open. The earl spun around, leading his small company across the ward toward the dungeon tower.

"Basil, there's a secret tunnel in that tower." Avner pointed toward the earl's destination. "I think it leads to the keep. Arlien and Cuthbert will trap Tavis between them!"

Basil furrowed his brow. "We can't know what Cuthbert intends, but I suppose we must assume the worst." The verbeeg pulled his massive head back into the chamber, then thrust the silver chalice into Avner's hand. "Take this to Arlien's room. Somewhere, you'll find a vial or flagon filled with a magic potion. Pour that into this goblet and have Brianna drink it. Then tell her to await Tavis in the temple."

"And what are you going to do?" Avner asked.

"Catch Tavis and send him to the temple, of course."

* * * * *

Tavis rushed across the narrow drawbridge toward a small tower on the rear wall of the inner curtain. Each breath brought with it the sickening stench of battle: the coppery fetor of spilled blood, the acrid reek of flaming oil, the charred rankness of burning flesh. The scout seemed to stumble every third step, for he felt as though he were walking on someone else's mangled feet. Although he was wearing Brianna's ice diamonds around his neck, the cold stones merely replaced his agony with icy numbness. They did nothing to heal the firbolg.

Tavis worried that the necklace's enchantment would leave him as befuddled as Brianna, but he suspected the spell worked its magic gradually so as not to be noticed. So far, he seemed to be right, for he hadn't noticed any ill effects. Besides, the scout had little choice except to wear the jewelry. Without the relief of the frigid gems, his battered body simply would not function well enough for battle.

The scout reached the far end of the bridge and stepped into the fortified tower. He traveled down a short corridor lined by murder holes, then opened a heavy oaken door into the tower's main room. In the center of the chamber stood two of Selwyn's Winter Wolves, busily reloading their tripod-mounted crossbows.

A hill giant thrust his enormous fingers through one of the arrow loops that overlooked the castle's rear bailey. The entire tower trembled as the brute hammered at the exterior wall. One of the Winter Wolves locked his bowstring into place, then slipped a long iron quarrel into his weapon's firing groove. He dragged the heavy crossbow forward and fired through the arrow loop containing the giant's hand. The brute bellowed, then the pounding stopped and the enormous fingers vanished from sight.

Tavis slipped his bow, taken from the keep armory, over his shoulder. He replaced it with a shield and battle axe that he borrowed from one of the Winter Wolves. Having watched his arrows bounce harmlessly off Arlien's armor, the scout now realized the only way to stop the prince was in close-quarters combat.

Fortunately, that would be easy to arrange. The single avenue into the keep was across the drawbridge that Tavis had just crossed. The one path to the bridge was through this bridge tower, and the only route into the tower was along the top of the inner curtain. The scout intended to meet Arlien as far down the ramparts as possible, then fight him every step of the way.

Tavis left the tower and limped along the rear wall toward one of the great corner towers of the inner curtain. The battle din grew more distinct than it had been in the keep, with boulder after boulder pounding the walls, ballista skeins crackling like lightning, and the dirge of dying warriors echoing over the ward.

The scout hardly noticed the clamor. His attention was locked on the inner curtain's western rampart, where he expected to see Arlien at any moment. Picking out the prince's armored form would not be easy. A pall of black smoke covered much of the rampart's length, and the rubble of shattered merlons choked the few visible sections of wall. Bleeding and dazed men were everywhere, lying half-buried under debris, wandering aimlessly along the walkways, sitting in pools of oil that had not yet caught fire.

As Tavis approached the corner tower, he caught a glimpse of Selwyn. The captain was about halfway down the rampart, sprinting alongside a dozen of his Winter Wolves. With tabards singed, helmets missing, and breastplates torn half off, they all looked terribly battered. That did not stop them from hefting their axes and charging into the smoke with a chilling battle howl. The scout caught a glimpse of the red-bearded soldier he had sent to warn Selwyn about Arlien's identity, then the entire group vanished from sight.

Tavis rushed through the corner tower, which was a larger version of the bridge tower, and threw open the door leading to the western rampart. In the smoke ahead, he heard the harsh clang of steel on steel. Selwyn's voice cried out in pain.

Tavis limped toward the howl as fast as he could. The scout had lurched forward no more than five steps when he spied the captain and two soldiers backing out of the smoke. All three Winter Wolves were soaked with blood. Arlien followed close behind, his armor and weapons smeared with crimson—none of it from his own wounds. The prince fixed his gaze on Selwyn, then shrieked wildly and charged. The three Winter Wolves spread across the rampart, lifting their own weapons to meet the attack.

Arlien tore into them like a whirlwind, crushing the

outside man's breastplate with a hammer strike so powerful that it flung his disjointed body into a merlon. The prince took the second Winter Wolf on the back swing. The blow easily overpowered the fellow's guard and smashed his head in the same stroke.

Selwyn countered with a vicious strike to the midsection, but the battle axe merely chimed off Arlien's enchanted armor. The prince smashed the heft of his hammer into the captain's head. The steel helmet split in two, Selwyn collapsed at the prince's feet, and the battle was done in the time it had taken Tavis to travel four steps.

Arlien kicked Selwyn's body aside, then looked down the rampart toward the firbolg. "Tavis Burdun," he said. "I thought it would take more than an avalanche to kill you."

"It will." Tavis hefted his battle axe. "Much more."

◆ 17 ◆
Bitter Wine

From the keep roof, the battle seemed a thing as murky and frenzied as the queen's whirling thoughts. To the east, fifty men stood on the ramparts of the inner curtain, hurling boulders and flaming oil down on a long file of cone-shaped helmets, all Brianna could see of the frost giants fighting toward the castle's rear bailey. To the west, dozens of hill giant rafts were burning out on the lake, pouring so much smoke through the battered remnants of the outer curtain that the outer ward had disappeared beneath an unfathomable sea of gray fume.

The queen hardly had a better view of the ramparts themselves. Pools of burning oil were steadily creeping down the walkways and dribbling into the inner ward, filling the air with clouds of dark, greasy smoke that permitted only intermittent views of the debris-choked ramparts. When Brianna did catch a glimpse of the walls, she saw corpses and wounded lying everywhere, trapped beneath the rubble of shattered merlons or strewn among the splinters of smashed ballistae.

The queen's shoulders slumped under a guilty weight. She ached to send the keep guard down to help the men on the walls, but she knew that would accomplish nothing. The battle was already lost, and committing her last reserves would make the giants' final victory only easier. It would be better to wait here and make the enemy attack the keep's formidable defenses. The small company would never hold, of course, but more giants would fall. Brianna owed her soldiers that much.

A short distance from the rear corner tower, two plumes of smoke temporarily drifted apart, revealing Arlien's armored form striding along the ramparts. Several paces in front him stood Brianna's battered bodyguard. The firbolg still wore her ice diamonds, but he was now armed with a shield and battle axe. A cold queasiness filled the queen's stomach, and she found her hand drifting toward her bare throat.

Brianna heard someone approaching from the center of the roof, then Avner cried, "What's Tavis doing down there? He's in no condition to fight!"

The hole in the smoke closed as quickly as it had opened, once again concealing the two warriors. Brianna turned her attention to Avner. The boy was holding a silver chalice and the flagon from which Prince Arlien had poured his concoctions.

"What are you doing with that?" she demanded.

"You have to drink this." Avner filled the chalice, then raised it toward her. "It'll make you feel better."

The familiar odor of fruit and spice pervaded the queen's nostrils. Her stomach began to churn, and she felt an irrational sense of dread building within her breast. Brianna raised her hands to ward off the proffered cup.

"Take it away," she said. "It clouds my head."

"Not this time, it won't." The boy turned the chalice around, displaying a painted rune. "Basil said the prince has been using a love potion on you. Drinking out of this cup will reverse the effects."

Brianna narrowed her eyes. "Basil's in the dungeon."

"Basil *was* in the dungeon," Avner corrected. "But right now, he's trying to catch Tavis so you can heal him."

"Avner, I've tried," Brianna said. "I can't."

"Drink this, and you can," the youth countered. "Trust me."

Brianna made no move to take the goblet. "Trust you?" she scoffed. "Aren't you the same boy I caught stealing Cuthbert's folios? And who sneaked off rather than face his punishment?"

Avner continued to hold the goblet. "You're not drinking this for me, or even for Tavis," he said. "You're drinking it for Hiatea."

"For Hiatea?" Brianna asked.

"It'll clear your mind." Avner took her arm with his free hand, then slipped the chalice into her grasp. "So you can find her again. You'll remember your spells."

Brianna bit her lip, glaring down at the youth. "Avner, if this is some kind of trick—"

"It isn't."

Brianna raised the cup and nearly gagged on the cloying smell. Wondering how she could have once thought that the stuff tasted good, the queen tipped her head back and let the syrup run down her throat. The libation scalded like overheated milk, settling into her stomach with all the appeal of a greasy pudding. She suddenly felt flushed, her head spinning and feverish. The queen tossed the empty chalice aside and braced herself on Avner's shoulder.

"By the Huntress, that was awful!" she croaked. "I hope that's a good sign."

"What's your bodyguard's name?" the youth demanded.

Brianna scowled. "Are you going to start . . . ?" Suddenly, the name came to her, burning through the haze inside her head like the bright, searing sun. "Tavis! His name is Tavis Burdun!"

"How do you feel about him?" the boy pressed.

"I love him!" She gasped. A chain of familiar feelings rushed over the queen, sweeping the muddling fog of Arlien's potion from her mind. She remembered all that Tavis was to her: loyal comrade and fearless protector, her only trusted confidant, the man with whom she ached to share her bed. "Hiatea help me! What have I done?"

* * * * *

Tavis's arms ached from the strain of keeping his heavy shield raised and his battle axe cocked. The thickening smoke filled his throat with a bitter, acrid burning that made it increasingly difficult to breathe. Nevertheless, the scout stood fast. Combats between opponents of skill were won more often by wit than strength, and the advantage seldom went to he who committed first.

Finally, when the smoke had grown so dense that Arlien's armored form was beginning to take on a wraithlike appearance, the prince circled toward Tavis's flank. The scout pivoted back toward the tower, simultaneously keeping his chest toward his enemy and his body between his foe and the path to Brianna.

Arlien stopped behind a crippled ballista, then suddenly thrust a foot into the stock. The kick landed with a giant's incredible power, swinging the entire weapon around so that the windlass arced straight toward Tavis's knees. The prince charged in the same instant, his hammer flashing toward the firbolg's head.

The scout dropped to a crouch, lowering his shield to protect his knee. Arlien's hammer sailed past above his head, then the windlass slammed home. Although Tavis had braced himself for the impact, the blow nearly knocked him off his feet. He launched himself upward, transferring the momentum into his own attack as he swung his battle axe at the prince's unarmored armpit.

Arlien's hammer flashed down to block. Tavis's weapon clanged against the shaft and stopped dead, a mere finger's breadth from its target. The firbolg tried to pull back for another blow, but the prince's free hand shot out and grabbed his weapon arm. The scout swung his other arm low, driving the edge of his shield into his foe's armored knee.

The steel joint buckled—slightly.

Arlien jerked Tavis up and swung his hammer. Tavis twisted sideways, at the same time bringing his shield around to protect his head. The prince's blow landed with a resounding boom, denting the steel shield and driving the firbolg's clenched fist into his own cheek.

Tavis countered instantly, leveling his shield and driving the bottom point into the seam between the prince's chinpiece and gorget. Arlien's head snapped back. A strangled gurgle echoed from behind his visor, and he staggered back. When the scout cocked his arm to repeat the strike, the prince flung him away. He flew through the air as though he were a sprite instead of a firbolg.

Tavis felt his heart beat seven times before he finally crashed into a merlon. He dropped to the rampart beside the groaning remains of one of Cuthbert's soldiers, then instantly rolled to his knees. Anticipating his foe's next attack, he raised his shield and set it at a steep angle. The scout did not even see Arlien's hammer when it struck. He simply heard an ear-rending crack and felt his shield arm go limp.

The enchanted hammer started to circle back over Tavis's head, but the scout was already swinging at it. He felt a sharp jolt as the shaft of his battle axe struck the magic weapon and sent it sailing over the inner ward.

The scout breathed a sigh of relief, knowing it would have been impossible to dodge the thing many more times. He tried to move his numb arm and discovered that it would not respond. He pushed his battered shield off the useless limb, then grasped his battle axe and stood.

Tavis saw Arlien standing at the edge of the rampart, one arm stretched over the inner ward in the direction his hammer had flown. In the thick smoke, the scout could not see the weapon, but he suspected it would be floating back to the prince's hand.

The rampart shuddered as some part of the inner curtain gave way under the constant barrage of hill giant boulders. For the first time since joining combat with Arlien, Tavis grew cognizant of the battle around him, and he realized he was the only one of Brianna's men still standing along this section of wall. Everyone else was dead, wounded, or gone.

The scout turned and scrambled toward the corner tower. It was time to seek a more defensible position.

* * * * *

Basil rushed out of the bridge tower as rapidly as his flat feet would carry him. He expected the trembling rampart to crumble beneath him at any moment. When the runecaster reached the corner tower, he pulled the oaken door open and squeezed through the cramped corridor at a dead run. In the main chamber, he found close to a dozen soldiers—Cuthbert's and Brianna's—furiously cranking their crossbow strings back.

The verbeeg went to the nearest one and jerked the weapon from the warrior's hands. "Perhaps you wouldn't mind if I borrowed this," he said, pulling the string over the trigger with his bare hands. He took a javelin-sized quarrel from the man's quiver and slipped it into the firing groove. "I shall only need it a moment. I'm sure the angle will be much better here than it was in the bridge tower."

Before the astonished soldier could reply, the verbeeg rushed to an arrow loop and peered into the rear bailey. He saw a throng of frost giants directly below. Most were beating the flats of their huge axe blades against the inner curtain, but a single giant, a one-eyed fellow with dozens of yellow tattoos on his bald head, was using the dismembered trunk of a mammoth to spray a powerful stream of water into the crevices his companions were opening in the wall.

The runecaster needed no introductions to know the bald giant was a shaman, nor any explanations to realize why he was spraying water into the cracks. When water freezes, it expands, and if it happens to be inside a stone, the stone crumbles.

Basil aimed the crossbow at the shaman's bald head and pulled the trigger. The bolt hissed away, planting itself deep in the target's temple. A dark trickle appeared beneath the wound. The frost giant collapsed without even crying out.

The verbeeg stepped away from the arrow loop. "That'll buy us a few more minutes." He returned the crossbow to the man from whom he had taken it, then asked, "Now, can anyone tell me where Tavis has gotten to?"

"I'm right here," called the scout. He came limping into the room from the far corridor, one arm hanging useless at his side and looking more like a tattered beggar than the queen's bodyguard. If the scout was surprised to see the runecaster, he was too weary to show it. He went directly to the soldiers in the center of the room. "You men, turn your weapons around."

The men raised their brows. "But the frost giants—"

"Are not nearly as dangerous as Arlien, who'll be coming in that door at any moment." The scout pointed down the corridor through which he had just come. "We'll set an ambush here."

"It won't do any good," said Basil, crossing to the scout. "Arlien's armor was made by the Twilight Spirit himself. I doubt very much that you can kill him while he's wearing it, and certainly not in your current condition."

"I've got to try," Tavis said.

"Then try after you've been healed," Basil said. "I ainted a rune for the queen. By now, she should be free f her affliction."

Tavis raised his brow. "She can cast spells?"

"Isn't that what I said?" Basil grabbed the scout's good rm and dragged him toward the door. "She'll be waiting or you in the temple."

Tavis shook his head. "It's no good," he said. "Arlien's ight behind me."

Basil took a runebrush from inside his tunic. "You an't stop Arlien, but I can slow him down." The verbeeg ontinued to pull the scout along. "Leave him to me."

Tavis did not resist. "Are you sure about this?"

"No," Basil admitted. "But it's the best chance we ave."

A tremendous crash echoed from the corridor by vhich Tavis had entered, and Basil heard a heavy plank rack. At most, the door would last two more blows.

"You men, go upstairs!" Tavis motioned the soldiers oward the stairway.

Basil wrapped his arm around the scout and half-carried him down the corridor. Once they were outside, he verbeeg kicked the door shut and slashed his rune-rush across the oaken panels. Although he had not lipped the bristles in any sort of paint, a glowing green ine appeared beneath the tip. He traced a total of three squiggly lines, creating what looked like a pair of waves bisected by a crooked lance, then took the scout to the middle of the rampart.

"Go on." Basil shoved the scout toward the bridge tower, then kneeled on the walkway. "I'll see you in the keep."

The entire rampart was still reverberating from the blows of the frost giants.

"Don't tarry," Tavis warned, following the rune-caster's instructions. "Arlien's as efficient a killer as he is ruthless."

"He's certainly had long enough to learn the art," Basil replied, clearing the dirt away from a small section of stone.

A loud thump reverberated from the door Basil had sealed. "By the titan!" came Arlien's muffled voice. "I'll feed your heart to one of my ettins, Tavis Burdun!"

The threat was followed by the pounding of the prince's hammer against the other side of the door. Instead of splitting, the oaken planks merely bowed and flexed back into their original position. Basil smiled and touched his brush to the walkway.

The runecaster found his task more difficult than anticipated. The rampart shuddered constantly, making it impossible to draw a straight line. He found it necessary to retrace each stroke several times, and even then the rune had the thick, squiggly appearance of an amateur. It would hardly be one of his most powerful spells, but with a little luck, it would delay the ettin long enough for Brianna to heal Tavis.

A tremendous clatter arose from the corner tower. Basil looked up and saw the door he had sealed disintegrating beneath the impact of Arlien's hammer. Judging that he had time for one last stroke, the verbeeg laid his brush on its side and began to drag it lightly over the rune. Wherever the stem touched, the glowing symbol vanished from sight.

Before Basil had finished, an ominous rumble reverberated from deep within the curtain. The entire rampart began to shudder violently. A long series of pops and crackles echoed up from the sides of the wall, followed by the clatter of falling stone. The verbeeg jumped up, leaving his final stroke half finished. If the wall was collapsing, it was because of the frost giants' hammering, not his rune.

The door to the corner tower crashed down, and Arlien stepped out onto the rampart. His visor instantly tipped toward the half-concealed rune at Basil's feet.

"No!" Arlien yelled, apparently mistaking the verbeeg's sigil for the cause of the collapse. The prince
hurled his hammer and rushed forward.

Basil spun away and threw himself down. He heard
the hammer whoop by over his head, then saw the walkway crumbling. He heard Arlien scream, but the ear-
splitting roar of the wall's collapse quickly drowned out
the prince's angry cry. A boiling cloud of dust billowed
up beneath him, filling his mouth with the bitter taste of
rock and mortar.

* * * * *

Brianna kneeled before the altar. Somewhere outside,
the frost giants were already pounding at the keep's
thick foundations, but the queen did not notice the floor
trembling beneath her knees, or hear the mighty booms
reverberating through the stone walls. She knew only
the burning spear before her. She saw only its dancing
light, smelled only its sweet smoke, harkened only the
crackle of its orange flame. She had returned to Hiatea,
and now she felt only the heat of her goddess's power,
coursing like fire through her veins.

"Your Majesty?" The voice came from a long way off,
but it was a familiar one—and a welcome one. "Milady?"

Brianna returned instantly to the battle-torn world of
Cuthbert Castle. "Tavis!" She leaped to her feet and
spun around, repeating his name just to prove she could:
"Tavis Burdun!"

"It's good to see you're feeling better, Milady."

Tavis was propped between two Winter Wolves.
Apparently they had more or less carried him into the
temple, for both men had one arm around his waist and
were panting heavily. Despite their fatigue, they had also
dragged their heavy crossbows and quivers up the
stairs. Clearly, they did not think any place in the keep
was safe—at least not for long.

Tavis looked awful. One dislocated shoulder sagged from its socket at an impossible angle, while the glaze in his eyes suggested he might collapse from sheer exhaustion at any moment. He had fresh cuts across old ones, bruises atop lumps, and burn blisters rising from scorched flesh. His feet looked even more hideous than the rest of him, with black, swollen flesh bulging over his boot ankles.

Brianna went straight over to him. She wrapped him in her arms and kissed him squarely on his cracked lips, ignoring the raised eyebrows of his two escorts.

Tavis pulled away.

"Please, Milady!" the scout said. He cocked an ear toward the battle clamor roaring through the window. "We must hurry. The frost giants will break through at any moment. And I doubt we've seen the last of Prince Arlien."

A cold, frightening ache filled Brianna's chest—and not because the scout had mentioned Arlien. She remembered what had happened that awful night he had come to her in this temple, at least until he had overpowered her and poured his vile potion down her throat, and the next time she saw the prince it would be he who regretted the meeting. What scared the queen now was Tavis, or more accurately, the aloofness she sensed in his voice.

Brianna stepped back. "I don't care about the giants or Arlien," she said. "If I've lost you, I'd rather they take me."

Tavis frowned, considering. Finally, he said, "You haven't lost me. I'm still your bodyguard."

Brianna shook her head. "You're much more than that to me—and to the kingdom," she said. "I owe you an apology."

The scout shook his head. "What happened with Arlien wasn't your fault," he said. "The magic—"

"I'm talking about what happened *before* I drank the

otion," Brianna said. "I was wrong to insist that we keep our love secret."

"No, you were right," Tavis said. "We have to think of Hartsvale."

"I *am* thinking of Hartsvale," Brianna said. "If I'm afraid to act on my true feelings, then I'm not strong enough to rule this kingdom or any other. There will always be someone like Prince Arlien, shrewd enough and unscrupulous enough to pry at the seam between appearances and reality."

The keep shuddered under some terrific blow, like a man about to fall unconscious. A booming clatter echoed up the stairway. The floor joists creaked plaintively, and an entire corner of the room suddenly sank.

Avner stepped away from the altar, where he had been waiting, and came to Brianna's side. "Maybe we should do this somewhere else."

The queen shook her head. "No. My spells will be more powerful here."

"Then let's get to the healing." The boy eyed the sagging corner, then grabbed Tavis's wrist and started forward. "I'm kind of in a hurry to get out of here."

Tavis raised an eyebrow. "And go where?"

"The secret tunnels," the youth said. "There are more beneath this castle than Cuthbert has admitted. Basil and I saw him running for one in the dungeon tower. I think it—"

"You're getting ahead of us, Avner," Brianna interrupted, following the boy to the front of the room. "Before we worry about our escape, we have to mend Tavis."

Brianna slipped the bow and quiver off Tavis's dislocated shoulder, noting that the golden arrow still remained in its special pocket. Next, as Avner tugged the boots off the firbolg's swollen feet, she removed his cloak and what remained of the singed clothes underneath. Finally, she unclasped the necklace of ice diamonds hanging around his neck and pitched them through the window into the maelstrom outside.

"I don't ever want to see an ice diamond again." Brianna gently pushed the scout onto his back. "I'm sure Hiatea's magic will work much better without them near."

Brianna and Avner had already made all the necessary preparations. She picked up the bucket they had placed beside the altar earlier, then poured the contents over the firbolg's body. His spirit had been cleansed earlier in the day, so the water frothed and bubbled for only a moment before she was ready to begin the actual healing.

A fierce bang resounded in the stairwell outside the room, followed by the rattle of stones tumbling down steps. The youngest Winter Wolf stuck his head out the door to see what was happening. When he turned back to Brianna, there were beads of sweat on his upper lip.

"Milady, we'd better go."

"Not now," Brianna said. She was dusting Tavis's feet with powdered brimstone.

"But the giants have knocked a hole—"

"Quiet!"

As Brianna laid her goddess's amulet on Tavis's ankle, the scout looked over at the two soldiers. "Keep the giants away from the stairs. We'll need them to get out of here," he ordered. "Use the hole as an arrow loop."

"As you command, Milord," said the second Winter Wolf, older than his companion. "We'll wait for you on the stairs."

With that, the two soldiers clambered out of the room.

Brianna smiled at Tavis, then said, "This is going to hurt."

The scout winced, but nodded.

Brianna uttered the mystic syllables to her spell. The flames on her amulet began to dance and glow, first red, then orange and yellow. When they turned white, the brimstone powder ignited in a single brilliant flash. A golden fire danced over the scout's feet, filling the air with wisps of black smoke. A long hiss of pain slipped from Tavis's clenched teeth, but his frost-blackened flesh returned to its normal color and the swelling subsided. When Hiatea's healing fires finally died, the firbolg's feet looked more or less normal. The skin was still slightly gray and there was a little puffiness around the toes, but it looked as though he would be able to run.

The clack of firing crossbows echoed up the stairwell. A giant's scream rolled through the temple window, then the veteran began yelling, "Reload, reload, reload!"

Brianna sprinkled more brimstone powder on the scout's scorched flesh, covering him with a fine yellow coating from his ankles to his chin. She cast her next healing spell. As it had before, the powder ignited in a white flash, spreading yellow fire over Tavis's body. The scout let out a long groan. When the golden flames died away, he looked as though he had suffered a bad sunburn, but the blisters and ugly patches of scorched hide had vanished.

A crash reverberated up of the stairwell, and the young soldier cried out. The floor joists crackled and groaned, dropping the corner of the room another two feet, and a long crack shot across the temple ceiling.

"I think we're out of time." Avner's gaze was fixed on the widening gap over their heads.

"I have one more spell to cast." Brianna motioned the boy toward Tavis's head, then grabbed the arm of the scout's dislocated shoulder. "Hold him steady."

Avner kneeled beside the bench and wrapped his arms around Tavis's collar.

The scout looked up at Brianna. "This is really going to hurt, isn't it?"

Brianna smiled reassuringly. "What makes you say

that?"

As she spoke, the queen gave a sharp tug on the scout's arm. The shoulder slipped back into its socket with a sickening pop, and the scout yelled in pain. Brianna laid her amulet over the joint, but did not sprinkle any brimstone powder on it.

The queen uttered her incantation. Hiatea's spear turned white, and its golden flames danced over the firbolg's skin. The magical fire continued to flicker for several moments, its mending heat sinking deep into Tavis's flesh to strengthen the weakened tendons and muscles. When the flames finally died away, Brianna took her amulet off the firbolg's shoulder, leaving a spear-shaped brand where it had lain.

"Now can we go?" Avner demanded.

A thunderous boom shook the keep, and pieces of rock began to drop through the crack in the ceiling. The two soldiers in the stairwell remained ominously silent.

"I think we'd better." Tavis rose and slipped his cloak over his shoulders, then swung his arm in a circle to test its mobility. He smiled and grabbed his bow and quiver, saying, "My thanks, Majesty. I'll go first."

Stopping only to pick up her satchel of spell components, the queen followed Avner and Tavis out of the temple. They found the stairway half blocked by rubble. It sagged toward a large hole in the wall. There was no sign of what had happened to the older soldier, but the young one lay dead at the edge of the breach, one arm stretched into the void. Through the gap came a few wisps of acrid black smoke and the steady din of the giants pounding at the keep foundations. When Brianna looked out the hole, she could see two frost giants and several hill giants clambering over the rubble of the inner curtain.

Tavis started down the stairs, staying close to the interior wall. Avner followed close behind, with Brianna bringing up the rear. They were about halfway to the breach when the ivory-colored hand of a frost giant appeared in the hole, feeling around for a hand grip.

Tavis stopped and looked back at Brianna. "Let me have your hand-axe," he whispered.

The queen slipped the silver-plated weapon off her belt and passed it over Avner's head. As the scout descended the stairs, she took Hiatea's amulet between her fingers, hoping she would not need to cast another healing spell soon.

The giant turned his hand sideways and wrapped his fingers over the edge of the gap. The jagged stub of a wrist came through the hole and pressed against the other side of the breach. A thin layer of red, delicate hide had already formed over the bone, with a series of crooked seams where a shaman had stitched the skin closed.

"Hagamil!" Tavis hissed.

The scout reached the breach and swung Brianna's axe at the good hand. The blade bit deeply into the joint of the middle finger. The blow elicited a thunderous bellow of pain, but the giant did not lose his grip. He swung his other arm across, smashing the stub of his wrist against Tavis's flank. The firbolg bounced off the wall and fell on the stairs.

The giant's head rose into view. The brute had piercing blue eyes, with a full face, long yellow hair, and a thick beard. To Brianna's astonishment, the end of an iron crossbow bolt protruded from one of his temples. There was no blood or any sign of an entrance wound. The dart was simply there, as though it were a part of his head.

As the scout scrambled to his feet, the frost giant squinted at him through the shattered wall. "Tavis Burdun!" he growled. Hagamil looked past the scout to Brianna, then turned to yell over his shoulder, "Hey, Julien! Here they are! Both of 'em!"

Tavis moved forward to attack again, but Hagamil quickly brought the stub of his wrist around. The scout stopped a few feet short of the giant's reach.

A muffled crash rumbled up from somewhere lower down in the keep. The staircase trembled, then a series of hairline cracks appeared in the steps between Brianna and her bodyguard.

"Tavis, maybe Brianna ought to handle this," said Avner, stepping back toward the queen. "You're about to go down the fast way!"

As the youth spoke, Brianna extended her arm, pointing the tip of her spear amulet at the iron bolt protruding from the giant's temple. Tavis looked down at the cracks widening beneath his feet, then turned and rushed up the stairs toward the queen.

Brianna spoke her incantation. Yelling in alarm, Hagamil turned to leap off the tower. He was too late. A bolt of lightning sizzled from the queen's talisman straight to the iron quarrel in his temple. It struck with a thunderous crackle, then the giant fell out of sight, leaving only a puff of pink-tinged smoke where his head had been a moment before.

Brianna felt Tavis grab her arm and pull her up the stairs. She looked down and saw the step in front of her falling away. The lower half of the stairway was tumbling into the inner ward.

"Come on," Tavis said. "That was Arlien that Hagamil called to. He'll be coming any minute. We've got to get ready."

"Ready?" Brianna asked, her stomach knotting with apprehension at the thought of facing the prince again. "Then you have a plan?"

"It's a little rough, but I think it'll work," he said, starting up the stairway. "I'll explain it to you as soon as we find a good place to make a stand."

Brianna turned to follow, nearly falling as the step beneath her lower foot cracked loose. It dropped more than three stories into the rubble below.

"A *good* place to make a stand?" she gasped. "Where do you think we're going to find that in all this havoc?"

The answer came from the temple door, where Avner stood looking toward the front of the chamber. "It may have to be right here," he said. "We seem to be surrounded."

⭖18⭖
Secret Passages

Before following Avner into the temple, Tavis glanced past Brianna, down the crumbling staircase. In the outer ward far below he saw Arlien clambering toward the base of the keep. The scout saw no sign of Basil in the rubble of the inner curtain and did not know what had become of the runecaster. Nevertheless, it seemed clear that the verbeeg's last spell had been an effective one, for the prince's armor was battered and gouged, with sizable gaps showing in many seams. It also seemed just as clear that any damage Arlien had suffered would not prevent him from pursuing the queen. He had tossed his helmet aside and was staring up at his quarry with a dark, acid gaze.

"Tavis, are you coming?" Avner was calling from inside the temple. "I really think this is something you should handle."

The scout turned and stepped through the doorway. He saw the top of the altar lying on the floor and a procession of Cuthbert's men climbing out of the dais. Four warriors already stood near the front of the room, casting nervous glances at the crumbling ceiling above their heads. All of the men were fully armored, with loaded crossbows in their hands, full quivers hanging across their shoulders, and hefty axes attached to their belts. Judging by the amount of space they had left between themselves and the altar, they expected at least eight more men to follow. The scout could already see the helmet of the next one rising into sight.

Tavis pulled Avner back, passing both him and the hand-axe to Brianna. He nocked an arrow in his bow and pointed it at the warrior climbing out of the altar.

"I'd advise you not to come any farther, soldier," the scout said. "I may not be holding Bear Driller, but at this range, even this bow has enough power to bore a hole through your steel hat."

The man stopped and turned toward the scout, eyes wide with astonishment. The four soldiers already in the room gripped their crossbows more tightly, but wisely refrained from raising their weapons. The scout could have killed any two of them before the first one aimed his quarrel.

"Tavis, what *are* you doing?" gasped Brianna.

"I overheard the ettin—Arlien—say that he'd spare Cuthbert and his family in exchange for betraying you," explained the scout. "Apparently he accepted."

"How dare you insinuate such a thing!" shouted the earl's muffled voice. The soldier in the altar retreated down the stairs, then Cuthbert clanged into view, his visor pushed up to reveal a face red with fury. "I assure you, once we're done with the giants, I'll defend my name on the field of honor!"

"Defend your name wherever you like," Tavis said, his arrow now trained on the earl. "It won't change what I heard at Split Mountain."

"Or what I saw in this castle," Avner added.

The keep shook under a fresh wave of frost giant assaults, shaking a few more steps loose from the shattered stairway below. Brianna and Avner shoved into the temple behind the scout, pushing him farther into the room.

"And exactly what did you see, Avner?" Brianna demanded.

"Arlien and Cuthbert coming through the inner gate together, and they didn't look too mad at each other," the youth explained. "Tavis fired on the prince from the keep, so they split up. Arlien came down the ramparts, and the earl came through his secret passage. Now here we are, trapped in the middle."

"I came through the passage because the prince barred the gate tower door. That's when I knew for certain that he was a spy," Cuthbert replied. "I assure you, he never would have escaped my men if Tavis's arrows hadn't come as such a surprise."

The earl climbed out of the altar, then glanced at the temple's sagging corner and motioned at the four men already in the room. "You four go back down and wait for us."

None of the warriors moved, and one said, "It appears you may need us here, Earl."

"Nonsense. This is just a misunderstanding," Cuthbert said. "Besides, as a noble, I live at the queen's pleasure. Even if she allowed an impudent firbolg to kill me, you would not interfere."

"As you order, Milord," grunted the warrior.

The soldier and his three companions clanked toward the altar.

"Well said, Earl," Brianna commented. "But Tavis is hardly an impudent—"

The queen was interrupted when the walls around the temple's sagging corner fell away, leaving a large section of floor hanging free over the ward. Although Tavis could not see what was happening at the base of the building, he did spy several frost giants staring up toward the temple staircase as though watching Arlien climb. If the collapsing wall had caused the prince any trouble, the scout saw no sign of it in their faces.

Tavis turned to Cuthbert. "Tell your men to clear the passage," he ordered. "And if you try to lead us into a trap—"

"I won't. I assure you." The earl pointed to the arrow in Tavis's bow. "You can hold that on my back. If anything happens, I'll be the first to die."

"Sounds good to me," said Avner.

Without awaiting permission, the youth went to the

altar and climbed in after the last warrior. Brianna started to follow, but Tavis restrained her with a hand.

"Cuthbert first, then me, then you." The scout motioned the earl into the altar. "And I won't hesitate—"

"I'm sure you won't," the earl replied. "But please don't insult me further by dwelling on the matter."

Cuthbert climbed over the lip of the altar and clanged down the steps. Tavis slipped into the narrow stairway somewhat more silently, bowing his shoulders inward so they would fit between the dusty walls. He kept his arrow pointed at the earl, who had kindly illuminated himself by taking a burning torch from one of his men.

The earl clanged down the murky corridor, following several paces behind Avner and his own warriors. Tavis waited until Brianna was behind him, then stooped beneath the tunnel's low ceiling and followed at a distance of four paces. In the cramped confines, the acrid torch fumes were as thick as the oil smoke billowing over the ramparts.

From the back of the line, Brianna asked, "Exactly where are you taking us, Earl?"

"To the secret passage in my map room. My wife and daughters are waiting there," Cuthbert replied, speaking over his shoulder. There was a catch in his voice. "I'm afraid Cuthbert Castle has fallen. I'd like you to escort my family to safety."

"What about the hill giants?" Avner demanded, his voice echoing back up the corridor. "Don't you have any other secret tunnels out of here?"

"One other, but it opens beyond the near shore— where the frost giants came from," the earl replied.

"What about boats?" the youth asked. "You must have boats."

"I do," the earl replied. "In fact, Prince Arlien had the temerity to suggest I could save my castle by allowing him to take Brianna out on one of them."

"How would that have saved you?" the queen asked.

"Once the giants saw you leaving, the prince assured me they would have abandoned their attack," the earl replied. "I would have cuffed him, had one of Tavis's arrows not bounced off his armor at that very moment."

"How convenient for you," Tavis remarked dryly.

"Yes, quite," the earl replied, apparently missing the sarcasm in the scout's voice. "I'm sure he would have killed me on the spot. But, returning to Avner's concerns about eluding the giants, it really is best to use the map room passage. You see, before he died, the captain of my Keep Guard spied the queen's army coming down from the Shepherd's Nightmare. You may have to fight past a few hill giant sentries when you leave the passage, but at least help will be close at hand."

"Earl, you keeping say 'you,'" Brianna observed.

"This is my ancestral castle, Majesty." Cuthbert stopped and ran his hand over a rough-hewn wall. "Now that it has fallen, I have no desire to leave alive."

Brianna nodded. "I understand," she said. "But the responsibility does not lie on your shoulders. I brought all this on Cuthbert Castle. If I leave, then so must you."

The earl shook his head. "Not so, my queen." He wiped a tear from his eye. "You *are* Hartsvale. If you perish, the rest of the kingdom follows. It has been my duty to defend you, and it is my regret that I have done so poorly."

Tavis felt Brianna touch his shoulder. "You can lower your arrow," she said. "I think we can trust Cuthbert."

"We can't be certain," the scout countered. "Arlien's tongue was slicker than the earl's."

Brianna reached around him and pushed the arrow down. "If Cuthbert were going to betray me, don't you think he would have done it before the giants demolished his castle?"

The scout frowned, unable to think of any reason even the most treacherous traitor would have waited so long. He took his arrow off his bowstring and returned it to his quiver.

"My apologies, Earl," Tavis said. "The queen has often said I must learn to make allowances for human nature. If you wish to avenge my slight on the field of honor—"

"That won't be necessary, Tavis," Brianna interrupted. "After Arlien's duplicity, you're right to be cautious. And speaking of the prince, why don't you tell us about this plan you have for dealing with him?"

* * * * *

At last, Basil saw sunlight filtering through the rubble above, and he sniffed the caustic smoke of burning oil. Wine had never smelled so sweet—even to him. The runecaster pulled another block out of the wreckage overhead and tossed it toward the other end of the cramped chamber.

The verbeeg was trapped in a storage room buried in the curtain foundation. By the pale illumination seeping down from above, he could see a small door near where he had been tossing the stones. As battered and weak as he was after his fall with the collapsing ramparts, it might have been easier to crawl out through that portal. But the runecaster could not bring himself to do it. The passage beyond was musty, as black as pitch, and small. He'd rather face the giants than risk lodging himself in the depths of that gloomy tunnel.

Basil removed another block of jagged ceiling, then backed away as a cascade of shattered stones and splintered timbers poured into the chamber. When it stopped, a pillar of brilliant white light was shining down through the swirling dust. The verbeeg crawled atop the rubble and stuck his head up through the hole, pinching his eyes shut against the sky's effulgence.

The castle had fallen surprisingly quiet. He could still hear the fires crackling on the ramparts, the wounded screaming for help or just plain screaming, and the growl of murmuring giants somewhere close. But there was no more crashing. The castle had succumbed to the attack.

Basil raised his eyelids and blinked against the brightness. He managed to hold them open until his vision adjusted to the light. His head was sticking up a little higher than ground level, and he found himself looking across mounds of rubble in the direction of the keep. The frost giants had hammered away one entire corner of the structure. Several of the brutes were watching a small, armored figure, Arlien, climb into a room hanging exposed on the fourth story. If any defenders remained inside the structure, they were no longer firing their weapons.

Out of the corner of his eye Basil caught a flash of blue twinkling in the rubble. He looked toward the sparkle and, a short distance away, saw a pale zaffer light glinting from beneath the shadow of a stone block. The verbeeg glanced in all directions. When he did not see any giants looking toward him, he pulled himself out of his hole, then crawled forward on his belly until he could reach under the rock. He felt the cold bite of an ice diamond.

Even as the stone began to numb his hand, the verbeeg felt a sick feeling welling up inside him. The last time he had seen Tavis, the scout had been wearing the necklace. Basil tugged gently on the ice diamond. It slipped from beneath the rock easily, bringing along a string of many more of the frigid gems. The verbeeg quickly examined the silver chain's clasp and saw that it had been unhooked, not torn off. The necklace had been deliberately removed, probably because Brianna feared it would interfere with her healing spells. And if there had been time for the queen to heal the scout, it did not seem unreasonable to hope that she and her party were well on their way out of Cuthbert Castle by now.

Basil exhaled in relief. "A lucky find for me, I guess."

The pain-numbing properties of the enchanted gems were certain to make an interesting study. The verbeeg wrapped the necklace twice around his wrist and clasped it in place, then considered his next move.

The keep's shattered corner stood less than thirty paces ahead, a yawning enticement to visit the libraries below. To accept the invitation, all Basil would have to do was dodge a dozen frost giants and duck down the stairs before they smashed him into a pulp. Of course, then he would be alone in the keep with Arlien. . . .

The verbeeg sighed. As valuable as the folios were, they were not worth dying for. He reluctantly turned away and, casting one last look over his shoulder, crawled toward the lake.

* * * * *

The muffled creak of grating hinges squealed from a distant door. The cluttered map room instantly fell silent, and Tavis heard the slap-drag of someone limping through the library.

"Basil!" Avner hissed.

"It isn't Basil," Tavis replied. On their way down, they had encountered a keep guard who reported seeing both Arlien and the verbeeg engulfed by the collapse of the inner curtain.

"If the prince survived, why not Basil?"

"Maybe he did, but that's not him," Tavis answered. "He'd never make it down here, not with the keep surrounded by frost giants."

They were all silent for a moment, then Cuthbert said, "I'll bar the folio room door." The earl's eyes were red and swollen, for he had sent his family into the secret passage only a few minutes earlier. "That should buy you time to prepare."

"Hartsvale shall miss you, Cuthbert." Brianna stooped down to kiss him on his ruddy cheek. "If I survive, you'll be remembered always as the Loyal Earl."

Cuthbert managed a weak smile. He pulled his visor down and left the room, battle axe in hand.

The queen turned to Tavis. "Shall we ready ourselves?"

Avner cast a yearnful glance toward the sliding map case, which stood pushed open above the secret passage. "We could still call the earl's men back."

Tavis shook his head. "Their weapons won't pierce Arlien's armor. They'd just be in the way, and their presence might alert the prince to our plan," he said. "It's better to let them drive the giants away from the exit."

The youth gulped, then turned to clear the maps and shelves out of a cabinet near the chamber entrance. Brianna closed and barred the door, while Tavis made sure that every sconce in the chamber held a lit torch. When the battle against Arlien began, the last thing he wanted was for the room to suddenly fall dark. When they had finished their preparations, Avner climbed into the case he had cleared. Since it had no doors, he was clearly visible, but if all went according to plan, the prince would not be looking in his direction. Tavis pulled the sliding map case halfway back over the secret passage and summoned the queen to his side.

"I hope you're a good actress," the scout said.

Brianna smiled confidently. "I think you'll be surprised."

A muted boom sounded from the folio room, followed by Cuthbert's battle cry and the clang of his axe striking Arlien's armor. In the next instant, the earl's steel-sheathed body crashed through the map room door and fell to the floor in a bloody, jangling heap. His breastplate had been cleft down the center, and his sternum was split apart.

Tavis leaned against the map case. It slid open with a harsh, grating sound.

"Down you go, Majesty!" The scout pushed Brianna into the stairwell, keeping himself half turned toward he doorway.

Arlien stepped into the room and booted Cuthbert's
lifeless body aside. Although the armored corpse probably weighed as much as a small bear, the kick sent it
tumbling halfway down the wall. Tavis slipped an arm
around Brianna's neck, then drew his dagger and
pressed the tip to her throat. "Don't come any farther,"
the scout warned. "You know what I'm sworn to do."

"You won't kill her." Arlien's voice had a hoarse,
throaty sound. "You're in love with her."

The prince stepped forward, more or less dragging
one of his legs. Apparently, he had not escaped the rampart collapse completely without injury.

Tavis lightly drew the dagger across Brianna's throat,
opening a shallow cut. She cried out in a groggy voice,
and the scout turned her toward Arlien to display the
gash.

"I'm a firbolg," he said. "I'll do my duty."

Arlien stopped four steps into the room. The prince
asked, "Why don't we let the queen decide?" He
stretched a hand toward Brianna. "Come to me, my
dear."

The queen's body stiffened ever so slightly, and she
tossed her head, as if trying to clear it. "Arlien?" she
gasped. "What are you doing here?"

The prince gestured her forward. "I've come for you."
His voice had a sharp edge. "Come here."

Brianna tried to pull away, but Tavis would not release
her. He backed into the secret tunnel, starting down the
stairs. As he tried to pull the queen after him, she shot
one hand up through the crook of his arm and drove her
other elbow into his ribs. The scout dropped backward
and descended the stairs in a controlled tumble, grunting and slapping the stone steps to make the fall sound
as convincing as possible.

At the top of the stairs, Brianna walked slowly forward.
"Arlien, I thought . . . " She let the thought trail off,

allowing Tavis time to reach the bottom of the stairwell and regain his feet. "I thought you had abandoned me."

"Never, my dear," said the prince. "Now come to me."

Brianna moved forward, stepping out of Tavis's sight. The scout pulled his bow off his shoulder and the golden arrow from his quiver, then bounded up the stairs. He trained his golden arrow on the center of the queen's back.

"Majesty, no!" he yelled.

Brianna slowly turned, then Arlien's hand flashed up and pulled her back. The prince stepped forward, placing his body between her and the golden shaft, and cocked his warhammer to throw. Tavis raised his aim, pointing his arrow over his foe's shoulder at the queen's head.

"She's taller than you," the scout warned. "I'll kill her."

Arlien did not throw his weapon. Behind him, Brianna reached for her hand-axe, and Avner slipped from his hiding place.

"What do you want?" asked Arlien.

"I want you to tell Lanaxis that he can't have Brianna—even if she is the first queen of Hartkiller's line." Avner had told Tavis and Brianna about Basil's discoveries. "And I want her back."

Brianna freed her axe, then held it poised to strike. Avner reached for a torch.

Arlien's eyes narrowed. A cunning smile crossed his lips, and he said, "If you know her ancestry, then you also know our blood runs strong in her veins. I can only imagine how your earls will feel when they learn—"

As Avner slipped his torch from the sconce, the prince suddenly fell silent and cocked an ear.

"Now, Brianna!" Tavis yelled.

The queen brought her hand-axe down, not attacking the prince but slicing the buckles off his breastplate. With her free hand, she grabbed his collar and pulled, ripping the armor off.

"By the titan, what are you doing?" The prince whirled on Brianna, more confused than angry.

Tavis drew his bowstring taut, training his arrow on the center of the prince's back. In the same instant, Avner stepped forward, bringing his torch down on Arlien's weapon hand.

The prince roared in pain and dropped his hammer. His hand instinctively jerked away, then snapped back into the youth's face just as reflexively. The impact launched the boy across the room, his nose flattened and a spray of teeth flying from his mouth.

"Avner!" Brianna cried.

The boy crashed into a map cabinet and crumpled to the floor. The burning torch slipped from his limp hand, rolling across the cold stones to the base of a cabinet filled with vellum maps. Tavis loosed his golden arrow and rushed up the stairs, and Brianna swung her axe at the prince's neck. But even as their weapons flashed through the air, Arlien was exploding to his true size, dropping his helmet and leg armor as a molting locust sheds its exoskeleton.

When Brianna's axe struck, the prince had grown so tall that the blade hit his weapon arm instead of his neck. And by the time Tavis's arrow arrived, Arlien's shoulders were pressed against the ceiling. The shaft sank not into his back, but deep into his thigh.

The prince did not even feel the missile strike, for Basil's rune magic prevented the shaft from causing any pain. The arrow paled to the color of ivory. A glassy yellow cast spread outward from the wound, turning the flesh of the entire leg as flaxen and glossy as gold. The knee buckled, and Arlien crashed to the floor. He landed on his side, his body so huge that it completely hid Brianna from the scout's sight.

The flaxen death magic lost its vigor as it crept past the ettin's hip, so that by the time it was spreading up Arlien's back, his flesh was no longer turning yellow and lustrous. His skin merely paled to a dull, jaundiced color, his ribs continuing to rise and fall as the astonished prince gasped for breath.

Tavis cursed himself for not anticipating the explosive change in size, then pulled another arrow from his quiver. As he nocked the shaft, the ettin rolled toward him and the scout found himself looking up into Julien's swarthy face. Arno's brutish head, desiccated and lifeless, lay flopped over the festering sore where the rune-arrow had detonated during the blizzard.

Tavis quickly loosed his arrow. The shaft disappeared into the knotted muscles of the ettin's massive neck, and Julien roared. The scout glimpsed a great hand arcing toward him from the ceiling, then his entire body went numb as the enormous fist smashed into his chest, shattering bones from his clavicle to his lowest ribs. He bounced off the sliding map case and dropped into the secret passage, listening to his own bones crunch and grind as he bounced down the stairs.

By the time he reached the bottom, the agony was beginning to set in. Every breath sent stabbing pains shooting through his chest and abdomen, while the anguish in his left shoulder was so fierce that he knew even attempting to move the arm would prove futile. He rolled to his knees, but grew dizzy and nearly fainted when he tried to stand.

Tavis smelled smoke. He looked up the staircase and saw dark fumes curling down the passage. That was when he thought of Avner. The youth's torch had not rolled far after being dropped. If the map cabinets were on fire, it would not be long before the boy burned as well. The scout dragged himself up a stair, then saw Julien dropping to his belly at the top of the passage.

Tavis grabbed his bow and quiver and lay on his back, his feet pointing up the stairs. The ettin thrust a torch into the passage, but Brianna suddenly leaped into view, swinging her hand-axe at his temple. Julien glimpsed the attack at the last instant and turned away. A loud crack echoed through the chamber as the blade scraped along his huge skull.

Blood sprayed in all directions, but Tavis guessed that Julien had suffered only a superficial scalp wound—messy, but hardly fatal. Using his good arm, the scout hooked his bow over his toes, then nocked an arrow.

Julien looked at Brianna. "Stay away!" he growled, shoving her back. "You can't save him now."

The ettin thrust his long arm back into the passage, trying to reach Tavis with the torch in his hand. The scout fired, and his wooden arrow sank deep into his attacker's forearm. The flaming brand dropped harmlessly on the stairs.

Julien withdrew his hand and plucked the shaft from his forearm like an annoying splinter. Tavis nocked another arrow, grunting from the sharp pains the movement sent shooting through his chest. The scout saw a billowing cloud of smoke behind the ettin, and he heard the queen coughing.

"Brianna!" he yelled. "Avner—don't let him burn!"

Julien peered down the stairs. "I'll trade you," he said. "The boy's life for yours."

"So you can take Brianna to the titan?" Tavis aimed his arrow at Julien's brown eye. "Not even for Avner!"

The ettin quickly placed a shielding hand between the shaft and his face. Plumes of smoke swirled between his huge fingers.

"My offer is better than you think. Lanaxis doesn't need Brianna forever," Julien said. "He'll allow her to return to Hartsvale after she delivers the child I got on her."

The bowstring nearly slipped from Tavis's fingers. "What?"

The ettin lowered his hand. "It's true," Julien said. "One child. That's all we want. Is that so much to ask?"

Tavis did not know what to think. If the ettin had

fathered a child by Brianna, the king of giants would be born whether they escaped or not. Would Ostoria then be fated to rise again, and what would that mean for Hartsvale? A vision of the human roasting over the ettin's campfire flashed through the scout's mind, and he knew he would have to kill Brianna's child, or even the queen herself, before he allowed such a thing.

From somewhere behind Julien, Brianna screamed, "You fathered nothing on me!"

The prince's discarded warhammer flashed into view, slamming into the side of the ettin's skull. A tremendous crack resounded down the stairs. Julien's brown eyes glassed over, but the brute did not fall.

"Liar!" Tavis yelled.

The scout drew his arrow back until he heard the little bow crack in protest, then released the string. The shaft flashed away, and the last Tavis saw of it was when the dark fletching disappeared into the ettin's eyeball.

A shocked gurgle rose from Julien's throat. His hands started to rise toward his head, then dropped to the floor as his entire body fell limp. His huge torso collapsed over the stairwell, plunging it into darkness and driving a pillar of choking smoke down the narrow passageway.

Tavis tossed his bow aside. He struggled to his feet and staggered up the dark stairs as quickly as his battered body would allow. When he reached the top, he threw his good shoulder into the ettin's lifeless chest and tried to push the huge corpse away. He gulped down a lungful of smoke seeping into the passageway and started to cough. The attack racked his shattered body with such pain that he nearly tumbled back down the stairs.

Tavis knelt on a step until the fit passed, then held his breath and redoubled his efforts. An agonized groan burst from his lips. A sliver of hazy yellow light appeared between the ettin's body and the edge of the portal. Clouds of silvery smoke boiled into the passage. The scout pushed his aching body into the narrow gap until he could brace his feet against a stairwell wall and shove the corpse completely out of the way.

Tavis heard Brianna coughing and gasping. He climbed into the map room and saw the queen coming toward him out of the smoke. She held Avner's limp body cradled in her arms.

"Is he—"

"He'll need some healing, but he'll survive," the queen said.

She slipped past Tavis and descended the steps, holding the youth against her chest like an infant. The scout grabbed a torch and followed her. The smoke thinned as they neared the bottom of the stairwell, and they both stopped coughing. The bodyguard and his queen continued down the dank passageway for several minutes, until the water seeping down from Cuthbert Lake started to lap at their feet and the fire behind them seemed a harmless and distant thing.

Brianna stopped and faced Tavis. She was cradling Avner in one arm, as mothers sometimes hold their babies. "About what Julien claimed," she said. "I hope you aren't gullible enough to believe everything you hear."

"Of course not. I may be a firbolg, but I'm not naive." Tavis placed his good arm around Brianna's shoulders and drew her close. "But I do believe *you*. I always have."

Epilogue

Brianna stepped into the cool mountain breeze and inhaled deeply, filling her lungs with the crisp smell of pine. To her side, at the bottom of the cliff onto which the secret passage opened, lay the two hill giants that Cuthbert's guards had slain when they had opened the passage. Though there had been more waiting in the ravine below, her army had indeed been close by. Earl Wendel had been the first to hear the sounds of battle, and had personally led the charge to drive the outnumbered brutes into the lake.

"Majesty!" Wendel was clanking across the ledge in full armor. He was a burly, middle-aged man with a full beard and a warm twinkle in his eye. A lanky young farm boy followed close behind him. "Thank Stronmaus! Thank Hiatea! You look—well, you look healthy enough!"

Brianna glanced down at her soiled and tattered frock, then answered, "I am, due in no small part to your quick response. My thanks for answering my summons."

The earl's eyes darted toward the lake, where the smoke from Cuthbert Castle still poured across the water.

"I'm only sorry we failed to arrive sooner," Wendel replied. He shook his head sadly, then turned sideways and gestured to the youth behind him. "Your Majesty, I'd like to present Eamon Drake. This lad ran across half of Northern Hartsvale to fetch us."

Eamon bowed, and Brianna smiled at him. "I'm sure we can find a place among the palace squires for you, if you're interested."

"Of course, Majesty," the boy replied. He peered around Brianna into the passage's dark mouth, a concerned look on his face. "But what happened to Tavis?"

Brianna glanced back at the secret door. "Tavis?"

"I'm right behind you," the scout answered.

He emerged from the passage, sopped to the hip and hunched over his battered ribs. Behind him came two of Cuthbert's soldiers, bearing Avner's unconscious form. They had volunteered to carry the boy when they returned to check on their queen's progress.

Tavis stopped behind Brianna and nodded to Eamon. "I see you made it through, Mister Drake. You did well."

"Yes, he did." As Wendel spoke, his eyes remained fixed on Avner. "But what of this boy? That's young Avner, isn't it?"

"He'll be fine, but we need to lay him someplace safe," Brianna said. "And I'd also like to find a good vantage point to see the castle."

Wendel nodded. "There's a watching post atop this hill." The earl turned to lead the way down the ledge. "We can lay him in a tent and have a look. But I think you'll be impressed. We've set up along every shore. When those filthy bastard giants—"

"I'd watch my tongue if I were you," Tavis interrupted. "There's a giant among us—"

Brianna whirled around, holding her finger to her lips. "I'm sure we can find a better time to explain that, my dear!"

Wendel stepped off the ledge and raised a questioning eyebrow. "My dear?"

Brianna slipped her hand through Tavis's elbow. "Yes," she said. "I'm going to need a strong husband at my side—especially if this business with the giants breaks into all-out war."

Wendel accepted this news with a noncommittal grunt, then turned up the hill. "If it's a war they want, I'd say they're off to a bad start," he said. "Like I was saying, when our enemies try to swim ashore, they'll find themselves at the sharp end of a horse lance. They'll let us place them in chains—or die."

They crested the summit, and Brianna saw Lake Cuthbert spread out below, a great sapphire carpet stained by the mountain of smoking rubble that had once been Cuthbert Castle. Although there were dozens of hill giants clinging to the flotsam of their smashed rafts, none appeared to be swimming toward shore—probably because, as Wendel had claimed, the entire body of water was surrounded by mounted warriors from Wendel Manor and a dozen other fiefs.

"The longer they wait, the worse it'll be for them. We'll be bringing in catapults tomorrow," reported Wendel. "But look, here comes the first of the filthy—er, our enemies—now!"

The earl pointed toward a small boat creeping across the lake. The lone rower was definitely too large to be human, but far too small to be hill giant. The figure stood and began waving his arm back and forth, and on his wrist Brianna saw the telltale sparkle of her ice diamond necklace.

"That's no giant," Tavis observed.

The queen shook her head. "No, it can be only Basil," she growled. "And we're not letting him ashore until he throws those ice diamonds into the lake."